THE SOUL OF BEIJING

THE SOUL OF BEIJING

TOM PELLMAN

A Camphor Press book

Published by Camphor Press Ltd

83 Ducie Street, Manchester, M1 2JQ
United Kingdom

www.camphorpress.com

ISBN   978-1-78869-213-7 (paperback)
            978-1-78869-214-4 (hardcover)

Set in 11 pt Libertinus

Contents

WINTER

1

New Year

You always hear New Year before you see it. Panzi scanned the horizon from the third-floor window, following the noise of firecrackers chattering somewhere below. The sky was a bright-blue dome, uncharacteristic of late-January Beijing. The light show — the bright, glittering pyrotechnics would begin in a few hours, after nightfall. For now, there were only sounds — the seething firecrackers, the deep artillery booms, the shrieking whistles.

"Look! Over there!" a boy's voice called from the alley below.

Panzi poked his head out the window and saw two figures race past. The boys — they couldn't have been more than eight years old — rounded the corner and stopped when they reached an old man unfurling a giant red wheel of firecrackers. The narrow red band snaked past the noodle shop, the hair salon, the convenience store. Three women laden with shopping bags minced past it, toward the alley's opening to the main street. The boys danced in place as they watched the man squat next to it and click his lighter.

When the eruption began, the boys flinched and ducked back around the corner to safety, cupping their ears. Once the terrible noise finally stopped, they reappeared, dashing into the acrid smoke, kicking at the tufts of exploded red paper left behind. Panzi envied them most at that moment — boys unafraid of the smell of sulfur. Boys with happy memories of New Year.

"What are you doing!" yelled Panzi's mother. "Close the window!"

Panzi turned and saw her standing in the kitchen doorway, wiping flour on her apron. "And go get Grandpa. It's time to eat," she said, turning back.

But Panzi lingered. He watched the man in the alley reach into his trash bag and present both boys with pink wands.

"Is this one very loud?" one of them asked.

"Hardly any sound at all. Now straighten your arm."

Panzi watched as the boys stood side by side, arms straight up, like ancient statues, until the wicks caught with two sharp fizzles. *Whoosh! Whoosh!* Two white fireballs shot straight up, leaving behind twin trails of smoke. The boys were too thrilled and nervous to move their arms and point elsewhere — the one on the left had his eyes closed. Panzi couldn't remember the last time he'd seen such unbridled joy. After the last flare had been launched, both boys stood with their batons fixed in the air, both fearing and hoping they held one last burst. There was the briefest moment of reverence, of stillness over what had just happened. Then they started sword fighting with the empty cardboard tubes.

"Panzi!" yelled his mother again.

"Okay!" he called back, sliding the window closed.

Grandpa was sitting at his desk with a binder of old coins when Panzi knocked. The old man looked up at the door's creak and blinked like a mole at the light and noise.

"Grandpa, time to eat," Panzi said softly.

"So early? We're supposed to wait until midnight."

"Midnight!" yelled Panzi's mother somewhere behind him. "Who's going to stay up until midnight?" She set down a bowl of pork dumplings on the table and disappeared again.

"We should be eating stir-fry first," Grandpa insisted. "We're supposed to eat dumplings later!"

"Grandpa, look." Panzi gestured to the table. "They're already made. Let's have some now and save some for midnight."

The old man turned back to his coins, the way he ended most conversations. Panzi fought an impulse to stand there and try to reason with him, but he knew Grandpa would sulk by himself for twenty minutes, and then it'd be over. These little outbursts were becoming more common. Worse were the memory lapses. Panzi still hadn't told his mother about the episode three days prior, when he'd returned home to a pot boiling over on the stove — water dripping down the cabinets and forming puddles on the floor. After he'd rushed to turn off the gas, Panzi found Grandpa in bed, napping.

Panzi returned to the living room and arranged the

bowls stacked on the table and tore open a bag of sun-flower seeds, dumping its contents into a shallow basket. On television, three presenters in shiny clothes were repeating the word "brilliant" over each other. Brilliant songs, brilliant skits, a brilliant Year of the Dragon. The stage behind them did not look brilliant; harsh lights beat down on an empty swath of dull-red carpet. It looked shabbier, almost retro, compared to the flashing, graphics-heavy productions of recent years. Mother said this year's Spring Festival Gala was toned-down by design because CCTV's spending had come under criticism by the president himself.

Panzi and his mother took their places beside each other on the sofa. Grandpa, too, soon emerged from the dark bedroom and smoked meekly next to the rosewood dresser. Television laughter, slurps of vinegar, explosions outside, cracks of seed shells. A powerful, dull calm settled over the three of them as the program spooled onward. Panzi watched the slapstick and singing without interest; his mind was elsewhere. In an hour, he would leave home to meet Xiao Song. She'd mentioned something about watching fireworks, a plan that already made him nervous, but that was the extent of what he knew. *She* may not even have known what she had planned. It was Xiao Song, after all.

He couldn't get her singing out of his head. Two days of explosions, his mother's scolding, the squawking television — none of it was loud enough to dislodge the memory of Xiao Song standing in the karaoke room, belting out the Faye Wong standard "I'm Willing."

Two nights ago, Panzi hid at the far end of the couch, avoiding the microphone and nodding along vaguely to a classmate reeling off the minutiae of his ten-year life plan. Panzi's old high school classmates often gathered for meals and karaoke during the holidays, when many of them were back in Beijing on break from university. Not that he usually joined them.

Two more years of undergrad study, this classmate was saying, then two years of graduate school, hopefully in Britain, then maybe he'd come back to Beijing — maybe join a bank as an equities analyst, which paid decently well so long as you knew how to build financial models. Anyway, he should be able to put a down payment on an apartment by the time he was twenty-eight or so. Married by thirty, certainly. Panzi nodded once more, exhausted for him.

The future equities analyst paused, waiting for Panzi to launch into the details of his own life plan. Where was he going to university now? (Wasn't). When was he planning on getting married? (Wasn't). When did he plan on going abroad? (Wasn't). Panzi took a swig of beer and sighed; what had he expected coming to gatherings like this?

"Who is that singing?" Panzi asked, just to change the subject. He pointed his bottle at the girl singing "I'm Willing," a heavy figure in a white floral dress and shoulder-length dyed-blonde hair.

"You don't recognize her, do you? That's Song Mozhi, from primary school. Dumb Cat! Remember? Look how fat she's gotten!"

Panzi squinted but still couldn't recognize her. Xiao Song did not hold the microphone with dainty fingertips like their other female classmates; she throttled it in her left hand, the way she did the bottle of beer in her right. Her voice was brassy and frank, as if flaunting the notes she missed. Panzi watched her from across the room until she finished and sat again, her platinum hair turning blue in the shifting light.

"So, where are you studying?" the equities analyst asked.

"I'm not."

He looked away, embarrassed. They always did.

"So...."

"I'm working for my family's business. Real estate," Panzi said.

The classmate perked back up at this. He wanted to know about the properties Panzi's mother bought and sold. They talked idly about housing prices in different Beijing neighborhoods, areas poised for growth. Panzi kept an eye on Xiao Song, still marveling at the discovery. He watched her clink bottles with two brush-cuts from chemistry. She tossed her head back and laughed, not graceful or ladylike at all, but like someone hungry to be alive. Did no one else in the room notice it?

The equities analyst stopped talking and gave Panzi a knowing glance. "Xiao Song!" he called across the room with a grin. "Come here!"

"No, no. Don't. C'mon," Panzi hissed. But it was already too late; Xiao Song was on her way over. The equities analyst stood and whispered something to her that Panzi couldn't hear. Xiao Song nearly sat down in Panzi's lap.

"Hi," he said.

She looked at him for a beat and smiled. "I like your ears. I can almost see the light through them."

Panzi blushed. Of all his dislikable features — his too-short teeth, his broad forehead, his narrow-set eyes — he was most self-conscious about his ears. "Bat wings," his mother called them.

When he didn't respond to her, Xiao Song seemed to start over. "You haven't sung anything all night," she said.

"My voice isn't very good," he muttered. "Yours is nice, though. I liked 'I'm Willing.'"

"You just have to practice is all. Did you know in Japan there are these private booths where people go by themselves to practice karaoke? You walk around at night and see young girls standing in these glass booths alone, weeping and belting out love ballads."

Japan? Panzi couldn't think of anything to say. Up close, he could see the dark roots of Xiao Song's natural hair beginning to show beneath the gold. She wasn't conventionally beautiful, that was obvious. There was nothing pale and willowy about her; no large eyes; no perfectly oval face. Still, Panzi found himself engaged, nervous.

"I backpacked there for a while," she went on. "I just got back."

"So, what do you do now?"

Xiao Song took a manly swig of beer. "Do you mind if we don't have this conversation?"

"What?"

"I mean, is it okay if we don't talk about our lives?"

Panzi tapped his fingers on his knee.

"Anyway, are you happy, whatever you're doing?" she asked.

Xiao Song was turned completely toward him, offering her undivided attention. Her dress was low-cut, and Panzi had to concentrate on keeping my eyes away from the dark shadow between her breasts. She gazed straight into his eyes — uncomfortably close; and Panzi stared back for moment, to show he wasn't intimidated.

Because, in truth, he wasn't intimidated. Panzi felt an odd impulse to speak from the heart, to confide in this strange girl he hadn't seen since primary school. Panzi blinked. Then he lied.

"Everything's fine. You've changed a lot," he said quickly. "You were so shy when we were in school together. I remember you crawling on the ground by yourself, pretending to be a cat. Now look at you. You're such an extrovert now."

"Number Five," her lips mumbled.

"What?"

"Oh!" she exclaimed, as if surprised he'd heard her. "Nothing. I was just ... well, you're a Number Five, an Observer. When I meet people, I like guessing which personality type they are. Well, not so much guessing but determining which one they are. But you're easy. You're a Number Five."

Panzi asked her what that meant. Xiao Song turned her shoulders, settling deeper into the couch.

"Well, like right then, when I asked you how you were doing, and you just brushed me off. That's something Observers do. Let's see." She began counting on her fingers.

"You're reserved and secretive. You prefer to watch people from the margins rather than engage directly. You think learning and exploring are more important than goals and achievements. You feel most comfortable staying unattached. You enjoy feeling different from others but don't like drawing attention to it. Oversensitive. Vulnerable."

She paused for a moment, nose wrinkled in concentration. "Oh! When you're overwhelmed, you fixate on tiny details and observations, to ground you. You can easily get caught up in the lonely world of ideas...."

Xiao Song went on, though Panzi wasn't sure for how long. He felt the room — its music and lights and chatter — melt away until only her string of syllables remained. The rhythm and cadence of her voice washed over him in waves, like a voice from inside his own head, like singing.

How long had Xiao Song been talking? Suddenly, she was standing to leave. Panzi lifted his eyes to meet hers but couldn't speak. He heard her say goodbye. Panzi's brain fired a final, desperate signal to his mouth.

"Can I see you again?" he said. She smiled at him.

"Oh, one final thing," she added. "Number Fives are easily prone to being influenced by others, especially dominant type personalities. You should be careful."

* * *

Grandpa wouldn't touch the dumplings until midnight, but he cracked sunflower seeds between his teeth, sprinkling the wet husks on top of his cigarette butts in the ashtray. Panzi watched him out of the corner of his eye, and when he sensed Grandpa's mood had softened, he suggested they go outside to do the thing he knew was weighing on the old man's mind. Panzi's mother helped Grandpa into his padded coat and ski hat while Panzi fetched the paper bag from the hallway closet.

Grandpa's coat smelled like cigarette smoke and bird shit. Old Li, as his dwindling number of friends called him, kept a dozen pigeons in chicken-wire cages on the roof. He never gave them names, the birds, only numbers, which he meticulously recorded in a yellow notebook. On the days he and Panzi's mother got along, she liked to tease Old Li that he was becoming part pigeon himself. "Look at those bird feathers!" she'd say, pointing at the gray tufts of hair coming out of his ears. On those good days, watching them banter back and forth, Panzi sometimes allowed himself a fragile, secret daydream — *this is what it was like when Dad was still alive.*

Out in the alley, Panzi made a modest clearing, swiping the bits of red paper away with his foot. The three of them squatted as the neighborhood explosions sounded in all directions.

Old Li held the lighter's flame up to the pile of crumpled joss paper. Each hundred-million-yuan note had the God of Wealth's face printed on the front, next to the words "Heaven's Bank." The printing was smeared and off-center — cheap paper made to be burned. Two wide ribbons licked the edges of the pile. Flames raced through the delicate architecture, consuming it.

Qinyan hugged herself for warmth. She tolerated this ritual, just as she did Old Li's demand, every April, for the family to make the inconvenient, day-long trip to the large collection of Li family graves way out in Beijing's suburbs for Tomb Sweeping Day. But that didn't mean she liked it. Qinyan wasn't against tradition per se, just as long as it had a point. Why honor her dead husband like this every year when he had abandoned them? What was the point of dredging all this up every year?

Panzi watched the weightless flakes of ash swirl up and away, trying to recall details of his father but thinking mostly of Xiao Song. He forced himself to imagine the serious, bespectacled man reading at his desk. Father seemed enormous, towering over the stack of books, his cigarette smoldering on the desk. Or that one summer, at the beachside seafood restaurant, when Father gulped down an entire mug of beer in a single swallow. Panzi hated how childish all these children's memories were — Dad as superhero. He wanted a conversation with his father here and now, now that he was twenty years old, wanted to ask him the obvious questions, but mostly wanted to map the islands of his unhappiness.

You're asking questions that have no answers. That's what Panzi's mother told him one of the only times she'd allowed him to ask. Grandpa, too, had little to offer him on the subject, even years ago, when he was still lucid. It was easier for Old Li to commune with his son in death than it had been in life.

Would Grandpa even be here for New Year next year? The year after that?

Panzi watched Grandpa stir the small mound of ashes with a stick and felt truly stricken for the first time, imagining him gone. The embers glowed a final time, and then a gust of wind rushed past their legs.

* * *

The night sky was already glowing red when Panzi met Xiao Song and they set off on their bicycles. Turning west into the wide, empty mouth of Di'anmen East Avenue, the high-rise apartments and office buildings clinging to the East Second Ring Road shone dimly in the haze. The street's six lanes were eerily devoid of traffic, a luxury Xiao Song savored by weaving across them, ahead of Panzi. His own rusted Forever bike groaned to keep up.

They stopped at a connecting alley, where a group of middle-aged men were about to set off a box of explosives the size of a beer crate. Panzi and Xiao Song stood over their bikes, blowing into their cupped hands for warmth. The alley, a familiar one to Panzi, looked uncanny without its usual controlled chaos. No old women dragging their vegetable strollers, no overloaded three-wheel bikes, no dogs pissing on hubcaps or car alarms sounding. There was such little movement to the scene — only a solemn row of men in down coats moving their arms — that the blasts that followed seemed miraculous.

"Where are we going, anyway?" Panzi yelled above the din.

"You'll see. But you have to ride faster. It's already eleven thirty."

They turned north into the quickening headwind. Bits of red paper swished past them on either side. They crossed the frozen Liangma River, where the willow tree branches along its banks were dancing. Panzi watched as a gust carried one limb out onto the ice, nearly reaching one of the small, dark fishing holes. Finally, Xiao Song pulled over to the curb. They dismounted and walked their bikes along the sidewalk until they found a shadow to lock their bikes under.

"Isn't this, like, a private club?" Panzi asked, once he saw the skyscraper she was leading him toward.

"You'll see," Xiao Song smiled.

A security guard standing inside the building shouted at them: "What's your business here?" His coat sleeves hung to his fingertips, which were pink from the cold. He couldn't have been more than fifteen years old. Xiao Song's yellow head emerged from her coat's hood before she replied.

"Twenty-fifth floor. Capital Mansions Club."

The boy-guard squinted. "What membership number?"

"Two-two-four. You don't recognize me? With this hair?"

Panzi studied the boy, trying but ultimately failing to gauge what he might be thinking. The guard turned his eyes toward the revolving door and cocked his head — a practiced move — to indicate they were allowed to proceed inside.

Xiao Song led him into the elevator and pressed the button for the twenty-fourth floor instead. The elevator opened on to the dark lobby of an abandoned office. They used flashlights on their cell phones to make their way down a hallway. A bicycle lock, snipped in half, dangled from a glass door she pulled open.

"What is this place?"

Xiao Song was walking ahead of him and didn't turn around. They filed by rows of empty desks, broken chairs, tangles of black wire. Someone had fingered a name in the heavy dust. Panzi followed Xiao Song to the far wall, where two wooden planks faced a low window. The glass was frosted with dust and grime, but the view outside was clear enough — the white river, the dark, huddled embassy district, and the faint silhouettes of the central business district farther south.

Panzi was about to ask Xiao Song again how on earth she'd found out about this place, when he saw her climb out the window. He yelped a warning, but her figure — a puffy black coat over a ruffled, blood-red dress and black boots — was already halfway outside. Panzi followed her; what else could he do?

The unseen window ledge outside was a ten-meter-wide slab along the south face of the tower. Light from inside the Capital Mansions Club, one floor above them, angled down, grazing the edge of the platform. Panzi could hear the wind whistling along the gray tile, near the building's corner to his left, but the air around him was still. They slid their backs down the wall and sat on the cold concrete, not far from the window they'd climbed out of. He was terrified.

"I don't think we should...."

"A friend of mine brought me here once," she said. "I always imagined what the fireworks would look like from up here."

He grabbed her hand. "Are you okay?" she asked, laughing.

"I don't really like heights."

"C'mon! We're not going back inside. Look at this!"

Panzi wanted to enjoy himself, wanted Xiao Song to see him enjoying himself, but the wind was too loud, the explosions too close. He could see ash and debris fluttering down, covering the river below. He hadn't really noticed the smell of sulfur on their bike ride; he'd been too excited and nervous. But up here it seemed to surround him, filling his nostrils, which didn't make any sense given how high up they were.

"I'll wait for you inside," he said weakly. "I really don't —"

Xiao Song gripped his hand and he didn't finish the sentence.

"You really don't like heights," she said. "I know. It's okay. We don't have to stay up here too long. I just wanted to show you this."

"I was going to say that I don't really like fireworks. Or New Year."

Xiao Song laughed, though not cruelly. She laughed as if delighted by something she'd never heard before: some people don't like New Year.

"My dad killed himself close to New Year!"

Panzi had meant it as an explanation, but the mortifying words just leapt from his mouth all at once. He stared straight ahead, heart in throat, straining to keep Xiao Song from the corner of his eye.

"Oh," she said finally. "Did he ... uh...." She looked over the edge.

"It was years ago," Panzi said quickly, though he knew the damage was done. "I was four."

Xiao Song wrapped her arm around him. Maybe it was out of pity; he didn't care. The wind seemed to die down; the panic seemed to ebb. It must have just turned midnight, because the horizon was now a seething boil of red, white, and green. Out on the frozen river, someone was setting off a fresh box. The fiery salvos climbed twenty stories or so, still well underfoot, before their momentum stopped and they hung weightless for moment and then burst.

"What about your family?" Panzi said finally. "You don't need to be with them for New Year?"

"No, don't just change the subject. Tell me about your dad."

Panzi swallowed. "Uh, I was young. I don't remember him all that well. He ... he was unhappy for a long time."

"I'm really sorry."

"Well, it was years ago," he repeated.

"But the feelings are still there," she said.

"What feelings?"

"What do you mean 'What feelings?' You were sad, weren't you? You were in pain, right? Talk to me about it." He realized Xiao Song still had her arm around him.

"In pain? No, not really."

Xiao Song rolled her eyes.

"Right, you tell me out of nowhere that your dad killed himself and then don't want to talk about it. Makes a lot of sense."

"Why are you yelling at me?"

He felt Xiao Song's arm slip back to her side. She turned her shoulders toward him. "Listen, you can't just cut yourself off like that. It's okay if you feel pain. You're lucky if you can feel pain. Not everyone can."

"But I'm not in pain."

She looked away into the glittering night. Panzi saw her chapped lips mutter something, but the words were lost to the roar. It seemed like she said, "Number Five."

2

Tall, Rich, Handsome

As David awoke to the weakest of gray light sifting
through the curtains, his brain registered a pain
perfect in its wholeness. He pinched his eyes shut again,
but he was conscious now, this was certain. A dull body
ache began to break down, bit by bit, into its component parts. That was unmistakably his swollen ankle
attached to his right foot with the shoe still on. There,
his sandpaper tongue. Tar-layered lungs pleading for
shallow breaths. David kept his eyes closed — closed, at
all costs — groping along the wooden floorboards like a
blind man until he found his cell phone, which was out
of power. The inside of his mouth was raw. This reality
did not suit David; he fell back asleep.

An hour later, he blinked awake to discover he was
not in his own bedroom, indeed not in any bedroom.
From his present angle, a large open-plan living room

and kitchen spread out before him. The room was all gray, beige, light blue — lifestyle magazine colors. David recognized where he was just as Cindy entered the kitchen from the hallway in a seafoam bathrobe.

"Hey," called David in a hoarse whisper.

"You're up."

She walked away from him, toward the kitchen counter, busying herself with something David couldn't see. He asked her what time it was, and after she told him, he called her over to sit with him. Cindy remained on a gray, overstuffed chair, a safe distance from David, one hand holding a coffee mug, the other pulling the neck of her robe closed. Her hair was pulled back from her smooth, unmade face. Her eyebrows were two faint shadows.

"Last night," David began. "I drank too much."

"What are you doing here?"

"I ... I missed you," he said. David tried propping his head up a bit higher but stopped.

"What are you doing here?" Cindy repeated in the same even tone. "I. Told. You. Not. To. Come. Back." She spoke English in slow, child-like phrases when she was annoyed with him. The implication seemed to be that *he* was the one who couldn't understand English.

"I. Know. It's. Not. Okay." He closed his eyes. "Do you have aspirin?"

Cindy returned to the kitchen. She was naturally beautiful, even in her frumpy bathrobe — clear skin, large eyes, and jet-black hair parted down the middle from a slight widow's peak. She was, what, thirty-eight already? And still looked fantastic. Maybe only the first glimmers of crow's feet if you caught her at the wrong angle. On the soundstage of *Outstanding Talents*, David sometimes watched her pace between the cameras from his high-backed plush red chair next to the other two judges. The set swarmed with skinny, makeup-caked girls — performers, actresses, backstage staff. Cindy marshaled everyone in her signature red baseball cap and jeans, and easily outshone them all.

"No, you're not resting. You have to leave. Now."

"Five minutes," David croaked. He shifted his weight on the couch and little fireflies swirled in the room. He needed to elicit some sympathy, but the truth was he had no recollection of how he'd ended up here.

"I missed you," he ventured, "that's why I called you late last night."

Cindy snorted. "Called? What do you mean *called*? You buzzed from the lobby at four a.m., yelling about how you'd broken your leg."

David shut his eyes again. Too loud. "Well, yeah, I needed your help. You're sure you don't have any aspirin?"

"What if he had been here?"

"He just visited, didn't he? He wasn't going to be here."

All David wanted was a drink of water but knew he couldn't ask for it. He remembered the wig, a rainbow-colored afro, produced by Phil and Trish for the birthday boy. They were still at the teppanyaki restaurant then, rousing the surrounding tables to applause and whistles when they stretched it on his skull. It smelled like petrochemicals. The taste of warm, sweaty soju rose in David's throat, and he swallowed dryly to keep it down.

When he opened his eyes, Cindy was in the kitchen again. He tried a new line of argument.

"But it was my birthday! And I missed you."

David swung his legs down from the couch, and as he planted both feet on the ground, knives of hot pain shot up his right leg. He yelled, more shocked than in pain. He touched two fingers to his ankle, and Cindy made her way back over to the living room. David rocked backward on the couch, swearing, tears pooling in the corners of his eyes.

"David, it's over," Cindy said evenly. "I'm going to take a shower, and you'd better be gone when I get out."

"C'mon! Jesus! At least help me look for my wallet."

He rolled to one side of the couch as Cindy overturned a few couch cushions and found nothing. David threw his head back and closed his eyes again.

A flight of stairs. There were at least two trips down them to the bathroom, where he blurrily passed the tall, bored hostesses with dangling earrings. A sloppy crash of beer glasses. There was Phil next to him, leaning in close and shouting about off-season baseball trades. He remembered raising his voice to the waitress for another bottle of soju and then swigging directly from the porcelain lip. An image of a girl dressed as a sexy vampire walked by, but she didn't seem to belong in the restaurant. A blast of hot air from the entrance of a shopping mall. Were they at a club on the east side? David pinched the bridge of his nose. This was hopeless.

"Listen, I'll go," he said finally. "But I need to borrow some money; I can't find my wallet. I'll pay you back next month, when the new season starts, all right? We'll go out for dinner."

"No," she said firmly. "It's over, David." Cindy located her purse and handed over a single one-hundred-yuan note, an amount that seemed ominous.

"I need you *out*. Of my life." Cindy broke eye contact with him. "Look, we already screen tested a new foreign host, okay? Two weeks ago. I wasn't going to tell you like this."

A faint buzzing started in David's ears. He closed his eyes once more, as if that might help him stop hearing. He needed a goddamn drink of water. "What are you talking about? Who?"

"David, what does it matter?"

"No, I want to know." Who was this new fucking foreign host? This seemed vitally important.

"A girl, another American."

"What about Jessica?"

"She'll still be there."

"So, you're going to have two foreign girls as hosts? That's ridiculous."

"David, look at yourself. You had to know something like this was coming."

"Fuck this," David said. He jammed the bill in his front pocket and rocked forward, hissing between clenched teeth. Cindy watched him hobble toward the elevator from the open front door. He pressed the button and stood leaning against the wall like an injured flamingo.

"You're angry. I get it. I'll call you when —" He stopped himself. "I'll call you."

"Goodbye," Cindy said as the elevator doors closed.

Cindy's apartment complex had high walls and stands of planted bamboo to block out the sounds of the city, but as soon as David stepped outside, car horns and jackhammering arrived in stereo. Of course. His scalp throbbed. David limped to the sidewalk, and the sour smell of coal settled on the back of his tongue alongside the dregs of the previous night. He held a bent arm into the wind until he finally managed to hail a cab and go home.

* * *

It was already afternoon by the time David set off on his bicycle from Sanlitun Soho. He'd managed to wrap his ankle with a pilling salmon-colored bandage that unraveled and spilled from his sock as he pedaled. Bitter gusts of wind blew in his face at every turn. It was as if the day had been designed as punishment for the previous night.

And where the hell was his assistant? She wouldn't answer her phone. Dealing with the aftermath of a lost wallet — bankcards and keys and gym cards — that was all PA work. He'd paid her everything he'd owed her, hadn't he? But no, here he was, on this rusted heap with flat tires, on his way to stand in line at the bank. What kind of country won't let you cancel a bankcard over the phone anyway? David's chest heaved with cold air and pollution as the hangover weariness began to settle on his shoulders. He'd have to find a new PA soon.

Twenty minutes later, David sat on a steel bench inside the Bank of China, staring at his phone to kill the time. There were eleven people — eleven ancient, shuffling peasants — with eleven paper tickets, in front of him, and each time one was called a little cascading

24

jingle sounded. Television screens advertised bankcards, gold bars, and commemorative coin sets. All of the bank tellers were attractive women in their twenties with perfect posture.

In his head, David rehearsed what he would need to communicate in Chinese when his number was called: "Close account," "stolen bank card," "confirm balance."

His ticket was called, and David approached, pulling the office chair opposite a thick glass wall from the teller with her palm cocked in a sort of half-salute to the approaching customer. As he began stating his business, the microphone — a metallic snake charmed to attention — began to squeal with feedback, and David recoiled.

"So, you lost your card last night," the teller repeated sweetly. She wore a neat dark business suit with a silk handkerchief tied around her neck. Did she recognize him from TV, he wondered?

"It was a debit card."

"Can I see your passport?"

David handed over the booklet, and the teller flipped through a few stamped pages, just out of curiosity.

"American," he smiled.

She punched a few keys, covered the end of her metallic snake, and yelled — jarring and guttural — to her manager hovering behind one of her colleagues.

"This foreigner lost his debit card!"

David's head started to pound again as the girl stood and went off in search of a manager to tell her what to do.

Another jingle sounded and a middle-aged man with a flattop approached the window adjacent to David's, carrying a canvas duffel bag. He casually unzipped it and began stuffing ten-thousand-yuan bundles, at least twenty of them, through the slot in the counter. Two hundred thousand yuan. David hadn't seen that much money since his role in *The Art of Peace*.

"You did not receive your debit card at this branch office," pronounced the teller when she returned on the other side of the glass.

"That is true," David said carefully. "But I need to cancel my card immediately to make sure there are no problems. This is the closest branch office to my house."

"Well, we can help you apply for a new account and debit card," she said brightly.

"I don't think you understand. I need to cancel my old debit card immediately. It was stolen last night, and I don't want other people to use it."

"Maybe it's easier for you to open a new account. Then we can transfer all the money from your old account to your new account."

"So, you won't close my old account?"

"That's right."

This didn't make a lot of sense to David, but he didn't really care. That was China for you. A million empty, dormant bank accounts — clogging computer systems, generating paper statements every month — and nobody cared. Easier to start something new than fix a problem.

The teller slid a number of carbon paper forms through the opening. David scanned them and got to work, scribbling with a blue ballpoint tethered to the counter with a string. He was on the second form when he looked up and asked the teller for the remaining balance to be transferred to the new account.

She tapped three keys and said, "Your account has two hundred and thirty point six four renminbi."

David stared hard at the girl through the glass. The amount was less than fifty dollars. "Say that again?"

"Two hundred and thirty point six four renminbi."

She began to write the figures on a scrap piece of paper, thinking the foreigner couldn't understand what she'd said. David set the pen down on the counter.

"There is a big problem," David said carefully. "My account should have much more money than that." Why this extreme calm in his voice, he wondered? His eyes must have been boring holes into the girl; she looked nervous and yelled again for the manager. The manager wore the same suit with a different color handkerchief.

"And how much money should be in your account?" the manager asked.

"About twenty-five thousand renminbi."

At least there had been twenty-five thousand when he checked a month ago. There was no way he could have spent that much in a month. No, his wallet was stolen.

"You're sure it wasn't a credit card you lost?" the manager said.

"Not lost. Stolen."

David thought he saw the manager's eyebrow rise.

"For someone else to use your debit card, they need your PIN," she said.

David looked down at his half-finished paperwork, and waves of consequences crashed down on him. He needed to pay rent in two weeks. His agent had been pestering him for back pay for the last three months. The cleaning lady. What kind of visa would he have to stay on if Cindy were serious about firing him from *Outstanding Talents*?

"I don't *know* how they got my PIN, okay?" he said in

rapid-fire Mandarin. "All I know is someone stole my card and used it!" *Take a breath.* "You can check to see —"

The metallic snake hissed at him again, and he had to pull back.

"You can check to see where it was used last night."

"Sorry, we don't have that information here," chirped the original teller.

"Just check the activity from last night!"

"Sir, we don't have that."

"You're a fucking bank!" David yelled. Both sets of eyes widened with shock hearing a foreigner swear. "How can you not have the account activity from last night? It's your job!" David took a breath, trying one last time to steady himself.

"Tell me what I need to do to be reimbursed for that money. Do I have to call a service phone number? Do I have to explain it to another bank manager? If you look at the records, you can —"

"Sir, we don't have those records."

"Just tell me what I need to do to be re—"

The microphone shrieked at him a final time, and David shot to his feet and started pounding on the glass with his open palm.

"Tell me what I fucking need to do!" he was yelling in English now. "Why can't you fucking help me?" All other sounds in the room had stopped. Both the teller and her manager pushed their chairs backward, away from the glass, like in a prison visit gone horribly wrong.

A man's voice from the waiting area barked something at David that he didn't catch. David limped a few steps toward the entrance before remembering that his passport was on the other side of the glass.

"I'm sorry. I'm sorry," he muttered in even Chinese again. "Please give me my passport and I'll leave."

The thirty people in the room were staring at him, the foreigner gone berserk. David snatched the booklet and hobbled out of the entrance, more deflated than angry now. Outside, fumbling with his rusted bicycle lock, David tried to muster another eruption of rage and frustration, but nothing came. He stared far in the distance down Chaoyangmenwai Avenue, the smog rubbing out the buildings' features. As he pedaled away, he noticed the end of his bandage dragging along the road. He pulled over to the shoulder and tucked the blackened tip back inside his sock.

* * *

All long-term expats hated Beijing to one degree or another, but only some were enlightened about that hate. The pollution, the traffic, the censorship — it was a hard, messy, crude place to live, one that eventually weeded out the part-timers, the carpetbaggers. Those who thrived in Beijing were, like the city itself, unfinished. Beijing was a mirror that held their own great contradictions: chaos and order, potential and failure, hope and cynicism. And the glass warped over time until the city's hardships became its charms, and it no longer made sense to talk about loving or hating parts of it — the extremes came full circle. To the enlightened expat, hating Beijing meant loving it.

Did he even still believe that? That was the question that occurred to David that evening as he lay in bed, his laptop rising and falling on his chest with each breath. He had one new email, from his mother, with the subject line "Happy Birthday!!" He ignored it and instead opened a folder titled "Dispatches" in his email inbox and began reading at random as night gathered outside the window.

* * *

David had first brushed up against China back in St. Louis — two semesters of language study at Wash U — and moved to Beijing after graduation as a way of doubling down. The city he arrived in six years ago was bright and pulsing, clamoring for him. He carried around pocket notebooks and filled them with unfamiliar characters, observations from the streets, slang from the subway. His Mandarin, whetted on waitresses and cab drivers, became fluent but stayed narrow. He had the same conversation over and over. Loiter near a street-side chess game long enough for someone to ask you where you're from. Ask a granny on the bus what she thinks of the president. When a friend told David about a small-budget film seeking foreign actors for a daylong shoot, he volunteered immediately. It was just another China experience. He showed up for the next one too. And the one after that.

It was in his third year in Beijing — just after he had finished working on *The Art of Peace* and *The Valley of the Heart* and he'd landed the co-hosting role on *Outstanding Talents* — when David thought he might stay, build a life in Beijing. Why not? He'd moved into his designer two-bedroom in Sanlitun Soho that year, the one whose rent now felt monstrous. He entertained

A-list Chinese actresses there with bottles of good red wine and fresh strawberries.

David was hardly "David" at all that year. He mostly went by "Gao Fushuai," his Chinese stage name, which meant "tall, rich, handsome." It was such a common Chinese expression that his name usually got a laugh from those who heard it for the first time. But it wasn't funny to David. That year, when he shaved in the mornings, he saw Gao Fushuai in the mirror — a strong jawline, piercing blue eyes, glossy ringlets of his trademark long hair. There was a rumor that director Zhang Yimou was interested in Gao Fushuai for a supporting role in an upcoming film on the Opium Wars, at least according to David's agent. Sometimes as he fell asleep, David had a crystalline vision of himself in the near future — standing in a three-piece navy suit on New Year's Eve, making a toast in Chinese in front of a dozen of the city's young elite. Tall, rich, and handsome.

Never mind that *Outstanding Talents* was an inane, cartoonish talent show on local television; David was destined for bigger things. The show was a stepping-stone and, his first year there, he treated it like one, a cavalier attitude that always got a rise out of the producer. David's first year on set, Cindy had already been named one of China's "One Hundred Influential Women in Media." She tugged at the bill of her red baseball cap and yelled at him to stop being so *canren*, so cruel, to the nervous performers on stage. David tried to explain that Gao Fushuai should be the cruel judge of the show; every talent show needed one of those. But in the end, Cindy never blinked; Gao Fushuai was supposed to encourage people's dreams, not tear holes in them.

David didn't understand this strain of forced optimism in such an otherwise sober, intelligent woman until he spent his first night with Cindy. Dreams were a sensitive topic with her. For as accomplished and attractive as Cindy was, she wasn't happy. That first night together, he and Cindy laid on her clean bedroom floor, wrapped in the comforter, where they had a better view of the silvery moon, which helped distract her from the gathering guilt of what they'd just done.

Cindy's face looked impossibly soft in the moonlight as they chatted idly about his hometown in America. How much better it must be than Beijing, she sighed. Before he could respond, Cindy began complaining to him — a cascade of worries and frustrations David never would have expected. The air was poisoned here; the food was full of chemicals and metals. The schools, the hospitals, even the television station — they were all corrupt. Soon, Cindy was huddled close to his shoulder, whispering about her barren marriage, her husband in Hong Kong, turning forty.

"A desert," Cindy replied, when David had asked her what she really wanted. "With no trees, no buildings, no people. I just want to sit in a chair and watch the desert in peace."

David had wanted to argue with her a little, maybe cheer her up, tell her that she was great at her job and thrived on the stress and upheaval. She needed all that to thrive! But how fragile she looked in that moment. Nearly forty years old, and Cindy looked more like a child.

And he had listened to her, been there for her, for years! And now she was taking him off the show?

David snapped the spacebar of his laptop to wake up the darkened screen. Cindy was frustrated, sure, and he was the easy target. Still, how could she just spring all this on him? The bitch! She hadn't answered her phone all day.

When David finally opened the birthday email from his mother, he saw that it included one of those vaguely Christian parables she liked to forward him from time to time, presented in a typeface that was supposed to look like handwriting. It was about a nun arriving in India for a future life of mission work. The nun arrived outside the New Delhi airport, the tale began, with two suitcases bulging with clothes, medicine, toys, and books for the needy and for herself. She was immediately besieged by beggars, the crippled, and naked children.

Overwhelmed by the raw need, the nun was compelled to give a few things away at the gate. But the wave of people did not break until she emptied her bags completely, right there in the airport. Then she handed the empty suitcases to the first pair of hands that grabbed for them. Her pockets were pulled inside out. This was how she walked through the terminal door to begin her new life in India. *Sometimes, the only choice is to start over completely*, the message concluded. Subtle, Mom.

Even if he had nothing in Beijing, had no reason to stay, David couldn't imagine life elsewhere. He couldn't face going home to America, not like this. No, he didn't *want* to go back; he had unfinished business in China! Only Beijing could get his blood boiling, could make him feel alive. Every Christmas, when David returned to suburban St. Louis, he found the landscape too still. It was *nice* being back home, it was *easy*. A ham sandwich.

Football on TV. David's parents insisted it wasn't too late for him to apply to law school, that he'd had an *amazing* experience over there in *Bay-zhing*, as they called it. But they couldn't understand that it was more than just work; David needed to be *here*, where everything was happening. He hated it too much to leave.

David slammed his laptop lid shut again and jumped to his feet with a surge of determination, forgetting his tender ankle. Tears of pain filled his eyes, but when the throbbing had subsided, he found himself still crying. His newfound resolve vanished as quickly as it had arrived, and he began weeping in earnest, head bowed, bracing himself against a door jamb with the palm that still tingled from its encounter with the Bank of China glass. The precise number had burrowed its way deep into David's ear: 230.64 yuan.

He surveyed his all-white living room — white modern sofa with white pillows, white coffee table centered on a white carpet, white walls, a white lamp. David wasn't particularly attached to any of it, but standing there, misty and overcome with the sudden terrible certainty that he would have to leave, move into some place cheaper, it all looked beautiful.

He would start over again too — new job, new friends, new healthy routines — a new focused life. It was time to get serious now that he was in his thirties. He would get enlightened again, fall back in love with China and the Chinese language. Travel again! He would start saving money.

All the crying and vowing seemed to help, and David decided he deserved a drink to celebrate. He hobbled toward the kitchen for the bottle of Lagavulin he kept in the kitchen cupboard. He poured a finger, drank it, and then another before realizing his ears were still buzzing from the morning. From where he stood in the kitchen doorway, he could see the one shockingly non-white thing in his apartment, a large color photograph that dominated the far wall.

In it, a middle-aged man is squatting under a scholar tree. He grins in a way you immediately recognize in the mentally ill. His left hand holds a meal bowl filled with dirt; his right hand is ready to claw out another handful. His face is streaked, clothes filthy tatters of rough, tweedy fiber — maybe a potato or rice sack. His outfit is matched by an incongruously neat bowl hair-cut. His remaining teeth flash at the camera — a wide grin — though you can tell he hasn't been told to smile. Bits of dry, loose dirt spill from either side of his mouth. Behind him, a woman walking her Pekinese lap dog has stopped to gawk. You can imagine her conferring with the security guard next to her, pointing out something obvious like, "He must be crazy."

The piece was called *Chi Tu*, which means "Eat Dirt," and was shot by a well-known Beijing photographer. It was six square feet and, at nearly ten thousand dollars, the most expensive object David had ever purchased. David set down his whisky glass, walked to the center of the living room and took a photograph of the photograph. He would sell it, David thought without remorse. He would move out of Sanlitun Soho. He would find a new job. He would turn his pockets inside out, eat dirt, whatever you wanted to call it. This was the start of a new decade.

3

The Soul of Beijing

THE Soul of Beijing had four pillars, that much was clear. Sun Zhenhua and two colleagues at the Beijing City Planning Commission stood around his desk taking turns picking up the chopped, single-page official notice from the Party Secretary's office. The "Soul of Beijing" directive, as it were, had been issued that morning. It exhorted Party members to "live according to the Soul of Beijing" and "build a city brimming with the Soul of Beijing," but it offered little by way of concrete instruction. Further implementation guidelines would be arriving shortly, the directive read. As soon as the City Planning Commission wrote them.

Zhenhua sat the conference room table, pencil poised, as his two superiors wandered back and forth in front of the room's only window.

"Innovative. Green. Lawful. Harmonious," repeated

Vice Director Dong for the third time. The paper drooped forward in his spotted hands, nearly touching his belly. "Look at the *order* of the pillars." He repeated the four words. "Innovation is first. So, the Soul of Beijing must be innovative first and foremost."

"Well, what about harmony?" mused Vice Director Zhao. "You can't be innovative without the foundation of social harmony, can you? Think about it."

Zhenhua remained silent, waiting for the vice directors to bore themselves into agreement so he might get down to work. The men were mirror images — all baggy shirtsleeves and paunch. The vice directors, now in their fifties — too old for promotion, too young for retirement — had, at some indistinct point in the past, converged, physically. They dressed alike and went to the toilet at the same time. They arrived at meetings in tandem. After six months working in City Planning's office, Zhenhua still occasionally confused them.

Vice Director Dong looked at his watch and puffed his cheeks. They had been in the room for forty-five minutes. "Well, that should be enough to get you started, Zhenhua," he said. "Director Li will want our outline by tomorrow."

He glanced a final time at the paper before placing it back on the table. Zhenhua gave a curt affirmation and the two vice directors walked away toward the building's lobby together for congratulatory cigarettes.

Zhenhua returned to his desk, slipped off his dress shoes, and rubbed his feet together. Cold air seeped in from the thin window his desk was pushed against. Even from City Planning's office on the twentieth story, the view from his window still strained for a glimpse of the West Second Ring Road. The gleaming, modern National Oceanic Administration office towered just to the south. The National Development and Reform Commission loomed to the north, next to the Children's Hospital. For all the clout that City Planning wielded in Beijing — tearing down old structures, overseeing real estate development, setting building regulations — its office was old, an ugly 1990s-era white-tile octagon, a stunted, old-growth trunk in a forest of sprawling national agency saplings.

Zhenhua sighed at his reflection in the window. The office could be worse, he thought. Six months ago, when he was still a researcher at the Dongcheng District Planning Commission, Zhenhua worked in a grimy concrete shell that was adjacent to a large Muslim restaurant that discharged plumes of barbecue smoke every day starting at noon. There, for nearly five years, Zhenhua shared a wooden desk with another low-level researcher on the third floor. When he left the office every evening, his clothes reeked of smoke. Everyone in the office complained about it, but his boss always laughed it off. Sure, as the head of Dongcheng Planning he could have had the restaurant demolished years ago. But the lamb kebabs were too damn good.

"Zhenhua! Hurry up! We're leaving!"

Zhenhua looked up from the Soul of Beijing directive on his desk and saw Yang Hong, one of the other City Planning researchers, standing next to his desk.

"I've got to work on this," Zhenhua began.

"You're not going to eat? We're taking a car. Hurry up! Ma Jun's already waiting." Yang Hong rearranged the items on Zhenhua's desk as he talked. He reminded

Zhenhua of a large hen — fidgety, motherly, clucking. Zhenhua was the youngest cadre in the office. If the two senior City Planning researchers wanted to ride around, uncomfortably or otherwise, in one of department's Audis to lunch, Zhenhua was powerless to stay no.

"I...."

"C'mon. We'll be back soon."

Thirty minutes later, Zhenhua sat in the middle back seat of City Planning's black Audi — pinned between Yang Hong and Ma Jun. It was already past one o'clock, and the car hadn't moved in five minutes. Car horns blasted on all sides. Up ahead along the North Second Ring Road, both lanes of traffic were backed up behind two cars parked side by side in the middle of the highway with hazard lights flashing — a fender bender.

"Don't forget Old Zhao," Ma Jun was saying, on Zhenhua's right. "He's already been at the Party secretary level in Zhangjiakou. He'll be one of the three promoted, that's what I heard."

"No, no," Yang Hong shook his head. "Zhao got his hands too dirty out in Hebei already. *That's* why they brought him back to Beijing in the first place!"

What was he doing out here, still a traffic-choked hour's drive from the office? Zhenhua sighed.

"Zhenhua, you know Old Zhao from your days at Dongcheng District, right? What is he like?"

"It's hard to say," Zhenhua muttered, staring ahead through the windshield, willing the cars forward. "We'll just have to wait until October to see."

October. That was why people like Yang Hong and Ma Jun spent hours going out to lunch every day; there was hardly any work to do. The entire Beijing City government had been distracted for months. In October, four of the city's downtown districts would be merged into two — swallowing the careers of hundreds of Party officials. The political air was charged, and the uncertainty created all sorts of novel possibilities for those with something to offer. And for those without any real power to leverage — the Ma Juns and Yang Hongs of the system — they consoled themselves with endless gossip and speculation. Who would stay? Who would go? Where were the new nodes of power?

Who cares? That was Zhenhua's question. None of the great political machinations were within his control. If Ma Jun, Yang Hong, and the others spent even a fraction as much of their time honing skills and useful contacts as they did eating three-hour lunches and gossiping among themselves, maybe they.... Zhenhua took a breath.

It would be all right, he thought. At least today he had some real work to do; the Soul of Beijing directive was the first real policy document City Planning had seen in months.

As the Audi crawled past the scene of the accident, the talking stopped, and everyone craned their necks to see the extent of the damage. Nothing looked wrong with either the cars or their drivers, who were sitting side by side on the concrete median, each on his cell phone.

"Fuck!" breathed the driver. The wait had not been worth it.

* * *

All careers in officialdom need their patron saint, and Zhenhua had stumbled upon his two years ago in Chen

Yihui, one of the city's eight vice mayors. Zhenhua was still whiling away in the Dongcheng lamb smoke when his boss asked him to do a favor: write up a five-hundred-character essay based on a speech Vice Mayor Chen had recently given. It became the first of a dozen articles in total, published for internal government reports under the vice mayor's name. Zhenhua's essays were all the same, more or less — elegant repackagings of buzzwords sent over by Chen's office. Zhenhua's writing was good, everyone agreed. And after some time, Vice Mayor Chen's office made contact to arrange a lunch for the two to meet.

It was the only time Zhenhua had ever met Vice Mayor Chen face-to-face — a perfunctory Taiwanese meal that never moved past pleasantries. Chen's head was massive and lion-shaped, Zhenhua remembered, and the vice mayor was distracted by a phone call for most of the hour. Zhenhua left the lunch doubting the man had looked at him at all.

Zhenhua went back to writing, and Chen's name kept appearing in print. The relationship was never formalized. There was no feedback, no schedule, no remuneration. Occasionally Chen's secretary sent back a curt "thank you" or "received" when Zhenhua sent over a new draft.

But everything changed after The Call. Zhenhua was studying a blueprint for a courtyard renovation when his boss at Dongcheng District called him into his office and handed over a still-warm black receiver.

"Comrade Sun," Vice Mayor Chen's voice boomed on the other end. "Keep working diligently every day. The people of Beijing are counting on you! I told Director

Li at City Planning to expect you this afternoon to start filling out paperwork."

Zhenhua wasn't sure if he could speak, but he heard his voice murmuring the appropriate number of thank-yous. He handed the receiver back to his boss, who was grinning at him. They both knew that for someone Zhenhua's age, a promotion to City Planning meant his career was being fast-tracked.

* * *

By the time Zhenhua finally returned to his desk at the white octagon, it was already mid-afternoon. The vice directors had already left for the day. Someone from admin was counting tax receipts and adding totals on a calculator. Zhenhua's lunch colleagues disappeared, and a semblance of peace began to materialize, mercifully. He shook the mouse of his computer and his screen came to life, just as Director Li emerged from his office wearing his coat and marched toward him.

"Zhenhua, where have you been?" his boss demanded. Director Li stood with his feet apart and spoke in a voice loud enough so that everyone in the shared room might hear clearly.

"Did you want my feedback on the Soul of Beijing report before the meeting tomorrow morning? Perhaps the draft is already finished, which is why you were out of the office all afternoon?"

Li was a round, alert forty-eight-year-old who had made his contempt of Zhenhua known immediately. He was wary of Zhenhua's ties to Vice Mayor Chen and had kept him at arm's length since day one.

"Yes, Director Li," Zhenhua replied meekly. He glanced at Li's eyes, which were gleaming, hateful. The man was clearly enjoying this. "I will be sure to have a full draft ready for discussion tomorrow morning."

"City Planning is different than District Planning," the lecture went on. Li assumed a stern, fatherly tone. "You've been with us for only six months. You're probably still trying to get your bearings. But you must always remember that Beijing is a big place and we are only small cadres. You must work harder to impress people at this level."

"There's still a lot to learn," Zhenhua murmured. When in doubt, always play the diligent student.

"Remember why gold is so expensive — because it is scarce," Director Li summarized, cryptically. This didn't appear to require a reply, so Zhenhua offered none. Li lingered a moment longer at Zhenhua's desk, eyes scanning for something else to criticize. Finding nothing, he turned and headed toward the elevator, finished for the day.

Zhenhua glanced down at the Soul of Beijing directive on his desk again and sighed, knowing how the next twenty-four hours would play out. Whatever draft he produced would be invariably torn apart and criticized by Director Li in the morning, but he would be in more trouble if he arrived empty-handed. The only thing to do was to write a draft full of vagaries tonight and listen to Director Li expound on it the following morning. Then revise again. The Soul of Beijing was whatever your boss said it was.

* * *

Zhenhua returned home that night just before midnight and walked directly into the kitchen to boil water for tea. He stood gazing out of the fifteenth-story window, nibbling from the plates of cold braised pork belly and stir-fried greens on the counter — leftovers of the dinner he'd missed. Even after living in this new apartment for six months, it still felt odd to look out and see the grounds of the Central Party School, his alma mater, spread out before him across the street. The walking paths woven through the central grounds looked utterly still in the moonlight. Brown veins of ivy crawled sideways across the brick-and-limestone face of the main teaching building guarding the entrance, a faded five-point star barely visible from its original red.

These were the kinds of cold, tranquil nights on which Zhenhua used to walk those paths, composing poems and letters to Rui. Every week as a student, Zhenhua found a few quiet nights to walk alone, circling again and again beneath the pines and magnolia trees, until the grounds offered their inspiration. He'd often stop at the huddled graveyard to jot down a few characters. The cemetery was walled and locked at night, but you could still see the white rounded tips of a few dozen stone steles peeking out, marking the remains of foreign missionaries from hundreds of years ago. It was too dark to make out any of the inscriptions, but Zhenhua had studied them in the daylight and once even tried to translate bits of the Latin to impress Rui.

How many florid love letters had he composed on nights like tonight? How many times had he invoked the magnolia trees, the moonlight, the eternity of the cemetery? Zhenhua had known Rui only three months before he left Jiangsu for the Party School in Beijing and their courtship in letters began in earnest. Because she had studied literature during their undergraduate days, Zhenhua took the task seriously. A part of him knew, even then, that he was in love with the idealized, poetic form of Rui — the slender fingers and porcelain skin from the photograph he kept in his dorm room desk. Once, he asked her over the phone, point-blank, whether or not she thought his poetry was any good.

The line went silent. "Well, your penmanship isn't bad," she'd said finally. When their laughter subsided, Zhenhua wanted nothing more than to leap through the phone line and kiss her for the first time.

Even toward the end of his four years studying in Beijing, when cell phones and the internet put Zhenhua and Rui in daily contact, they continued with the letters. Written words held a level of intimacy and clarity neither could find in any other form. Often when they talked on the phone, Zhenhua kept a notepad on hand to scratch down ideas he might spend more time with by the graveyard.

When Zhenhua's classmates found out about Rui and the love letters, they teased him; but he didn't care, so long as Rui kept writing him back — her slanted characters in blue ink — telling him about some dream she'd had or that she felt like chopping off all her hair. It was in a letter that she had once written: "Would you think I'm strange if I say I always feel closest to you when I read your writing? Maybe that's because it's only when you're writing to me that I'm sure anyone in the world is truly thinking about me."

After five years of married life, a more solid and

pragmatic form of love emerged — a cold-pork-belly love. Its language was not the written word but the rhythm of days — the ritual of supper, the kiss before bed. Zhenhua and Rui grew closer because there was nowhere else to grow. Millions of small, shared moments piled up, since forgotten, flooding whatever boundaries remained between them like submerged walls of a sunken town.

Rui was ambivalent about politics and Beijing. The dry, sprawling capital felt inhuman compared to the lush village in Jiangsu Province she called home. Everything about the city was blunt: its over-salted food, its vast intersections and hulking buildings, its growling local dialect. Beijing was said to be China's center of history, culture, and the arts, but there was nothing delicate or refined about the place. In the spring, when dust storms turned the sky the color of rust, Rui liked to stare out from her living room at the vanished city and rebuild it into something more lyrical.

Only once, less than a year ago, had Rui tried talking Zhenhua into leaving Beijing and returning to their native Jiangsu. Her uncle had ties to Yangzhou University and, without telling her husband, she had discreetly asked around about teaching jobs for them both. Zhenhua was still working at Dongcheng Planning then and had, for months, been returning home late in a kind of numb stupor. Still, he was a proud man; Zhenhua never complained about work until Rui's father and their daughter Yuqing went to bed. No sense in bringing politics to the dinner table.

But in the dark bedroom, head buried in the crook of her hip, Zhenhua seemed fragile in a way Rui had never seen before. She stroked his neck and thinning hair, listening to him. It was jarring to hear him voice his doubts, since his confidence, his self-assurance, had been the thing that always made her feel safe. Zhenhua used to talk about work as if it were a diversion, a series of puzzles. All success in politics boils down to the same simple formula, he liked to boast: align yourself with the most able leader, find out what he cares about, support him in your work, and stay loyal.

Rui admired Zhenhua because he had no family background in politics, no support network outside of Jiangsu, no influential college classmates. He was upright. He complained about other officials taking dark shortcuts. Behind every power play, every deception, every corrupt act was one thing, Zhenhua liked to say: weakness. And he was strong; he didn't need any of that.

But the office politics, the thankless ghostwriting, the lamb smoke were all wearing him down, she could tell. Maybe his golden formula was wrong, Zhenhua conceded to Rui in the dark. Maybe it was missing a variable. Rui always said the right things. Don't give up. Your work is bound to be recognized soon. You are doing everything right. She worried about him though, about them both.

When Yangzhou University called her back wanting to arrange a meeting, Rui knew she finally had to tell her husband about it. She gently moved Zhenhua's head back to the headboard and propped herself on one elbow. She took a deep breath and began talking. It was dark in the room so she couldn't see Zhenhua's face as she sketched out a new life for them both.

"Think of it," she whispered. "We would live on a beautiful campus, with trees and space to fly kites with

Yuqing. With your time at the Party School, the local government would search you out to help with all sorts of new building projects. We could take trips in the summer when school is out — visit France and London. And you would have more time to write, Zhenhua. Think of it."

"The life of an academic...," Zhenhua said, his voice trailing off into the darkness. He imagined himself as a university professor — standing at a wooden lectern before a class of forty students, reciting aloud from a textbook. Grading homework. Chalk dust.

"Everything that matters is happening in Beijing, not in the South," he said. "I have a chance to do something here, in this city. This is the capital, Rui. We are at the very center."

Rui waited a beat in the quiet room. "I just," she trailed off. "You know I have faith in you, and I will follow you anywhere. But why do we need to be at the center so badly? It takes so much from people to stay fixed in the center. Your heart is different than most of these other officials."

"You don't understand politics," Zhenhua snapped. He was sitting now, back rigid against the headboard. "There are good cadres and bad cadres. What would happen if all the good cadres left to go off flying kites?"

"I'm saying that there are other ways to help the country. Education. You could help teach the next generation," Rui countered.

"The next generation!" he whisper-shouted. "What about us, Rui? Are we already gray-haired?"

She didn't respond. Her husband hardly ever raised his voice beyond a calm, clear baritone, so when he did, it swept the room of further argument. Zhenhua would get The Call less than a week after their quarrel over Yangzhou University that night, and, when he did, Rui was ecstatic for her husband, just as she'd promised to be.

* * *

The sound of boiling water reached Zhenhua's ears and he switched off the electric kettle. The apartment was quiet and dark, a tranquility that he respected by padding around the wooden floors in his dress socks. He watched Rui for signs of life as he undressed next to the open wardrobe door. She breathed heavily with the covers pulled to her chin, the only way she could fall asleep.

Zhenhua checked on his daughter and father-in-law next, cracking the bedroom door as a sliver of light from the hall cut across Yuqing's pillow. The apartment had three bedrooms, but Grandpa and Yuqing preferred sharing, each taking a twin bed with identical floral bedsheets on opposite walls. Zhenhua couldn't see the old man's face clearly in the darkness but he heard his steady snoring, head buried deep in the pillow and facing the wall. His bottles of medicine were arranged on the nightstand like chess pieces. Zhenhua paused a moment at the doorway, savoring the first feeling of absolute peace. He closed the bedroom door, easing the tongue into the latch with a practiced silence.

The Soul of Beijing report would need another two hours of attention before he could realize the promise of his own warm bed. He sat at the desk in his living room, a cup of tea steaming into the lamplight. The surface was covered with his daughter's calligraphy homework, which he started to shuffle into a pile.

Page after page of thin rice paper was covered with the same character, repeated twelve times per page along the grid lines: *yong*, which means "forever." Since ancient times, students were forced to practice writing it over and over, pages and pages, because its shape contained every stroke one needed to learn to write properly. If you could write "forever" properly, you could write anything. A simple formula.

He pushed the calligraphy papers to the edge of the desk and got out the most recent draft of the white paper he needed to edit. The four pillar values emblazoned on the cover page stared back at him: Innovative, Green, Lawful, Harmonious. He glanced at the clock on the desk and took a sip of tea, first blowing the leaves to the far side of the cup. Out the window, across the street, the windows of the dormitory buildings were all dark. His eyes wandered back over to the corner of the desk, to the stack of papers repeating the same word: Forever, Forever, Forever....

4

The Red Gate

WHEN Xiao Song moved into the apartment where Panzi was staying two weeks after New Year, she brought only a pink backpack. She emptied its contents at the foot of her bed: a toothbrush, some dresses, a zip-up clutch of makeup, three pairs of high heels, a few paperbacks, and a plastic folder with the words "Insomnia Methods" written in dark-blue ink. It was a matter of convenience, she said; he had an extra bedroom and she was spending more time on the south side of town anyway. Xiao Song's moving in caught Panzi off guard, not because they'd only just met or because he hadn't been consulted — this was Xiao Song, after all. He was surprised, watching her smooth the bedsheets, because it resembled something like a plan.

The weeks — a blur of aimless walks and abstract

conversations — had felt like one long improvisation, or maybe a series of one-act plays. Panzi still wasn't sure if he was an actor or the audience. They'd roamed the city, stopping to chat with seemingly everyone — street vendors, policemen, beggars, old women returning with vegetables from the market. They gave away their pears to strangers on the 113 bus and ate sesame seed cakes after midnight. Xiao Song occasionally disappeared for a few unexplained hours in the afternoons, but by and large they spent the formless days together.

Panzi never knew what to expect next from Xiao Song — an anxiety that became an addiction. His brain ached from the constant activity, from her almost militant restlessness, but he had already grown to crave it. Anyway, he couldn't resist it even if he wanted to; in his mind, he was already a passive Number Five.

"Ooh, violent past. Definitely," Xiao Song said one mid-February afternoon. They were playing the game they always did when they rode the subway together — inventing backstories for nearby passengers.

"What about her?"

"She went to Africa last year for a safari and got diarrhea," she whispered.

"You do him next," Xiao Song said, pointing her eyes toward the door.

"He plays, uh, jazz saxophone," Panzi ventured. "But only for his grandmother."

At first Panzi thought the game was an amusing diversion, a bit of levity on a crowded train. But Xiao Song took it seriously, scrutinizing their targets, even when they stared back. Every time they played, Panzi couldn't help but wonder what *they* might have thought about them: a bleached-blonde Chinese girl wearing a sundress in winter and a skinny kid in dark-rimmed glasses looking around nervously for her.

"We should choose *futures* for all these people," Xiao Song said suddenly.

Panzi wasn't sure what this meant. "Uh, okay. You go first."

Her eyes swept around the train and settled on a thin, heavily made up girl wrapped in some kind of gray fur. Xiao Song opened her mouth as if she were about to start commenting but stopped herself.

"The future is just a more perfect understanding of the present," she said abruptly. The words sounded like they were being recited from a book. "If you pay close enough attention to the present, it can tell you your fate."

"I thought we were playing a game."

"You believe in cause and effect, don't you?" she said impatiently. "Well, that's all the present is: little causes scattered everywhere, like tiny clues to a giant mystery."

"But the present is always changing," he said, sensing the game was over. Sometimes with Xiao Song, Panzi got the impression that she didn't believe in any of her wild theories; she was only trying them on, like pairs of high heels.

"Well, you don't need to worry about the fate of *everything* that will happen in the future, just the big stuff," she went on. "You only really need to worry about your own fate, so that you can hit your cues."

"Your cues?"

The train's doors opened, and they exited at the Zhangzizhong Station.

"You know, your cues. The handful of moments that

really define your life. You'll miss out being shaped by them if you're not paying attention to the present."

"What does this have to do with telling people's futures?"

"Because you'll never know your future unless you pay attention to the present and find the clues. Look. Stop for a second." Panzi obeyed; what else could he do? Xiao Song gestured to a flight of stairs and escalator side by side. "You have to practice. We've got stairs and we've got an escalator. Do you think I'm really *fated* to go up one or the other?"

"Um, no."

"Good. Me neither. Maybe that choice is fate, maybe it isn't. The important thing is it doesn't *feel* like fate, right? Going up the stairs or going up the escalator; it just feels arbitrary."

"It is arbitrary."

"But what about the more important moments in life?" she went on as they climbed the stairs. "Those choices don't feel arbitrary, do they? You feel a tug, and if you don't read the situation right, you can't fulfill your destiny. You miss your cue."

The pat illogic annoyed him. Panzi thought about how whenever he asked Xiao Song some serious question — about her studies, her family, her future plans — she just brushed him off. She didn't have time for any of it; living in the present was that important. What did he even know about Xiao Song? He collected her peculiarities and obsessions but never felt like he was getting to know her in any real sense. He knew that her favorite food was candied haws and that she didn't own a pair of jeans. He knew about her obsession with Marilyn

Monroe, the insomnia, the personality numbers. Money didn't seem to be a problem for her, but then again, they never spent much of it. Was she supposed to be in school? Who was Xiao Song, really?

He had already shown the apartment where they were staying to a half dozen prospective buyers. One of them was bound to snap up the apartment soon. And then what would happen to the two of them? Would he and Xiao Song stay together? Panzi didn't know; he *couldn't* know! With Xiao Song it felt taboo to bring up the future.

Or maybe he just hadn't collected all the right clues, Panzi thought bitterly. Here's a better way to divine someone's future: ask them what they're going to do.

"If you miss your cue, then it isn't fate," he said finally, as they neared the exit. "Look, if everything is determined by fate, then it doesn't matter if we hit our cues or not; the end result is all the same. Either our choices matter or they don't."

"That's not right," Xiao Song said. "I think some of our choices matter and others don't. I think you believe that too. You *feel* it. And when you feel that a choice matters, that's your destiny trying to pull you closer. But you have to pay attention to the present. Otherwise you won't feel the tug. If you don't pay attention, you won't feel anything at all."

* * *

Xiao Song never seemed to get a full night's rest. Sometimes Panzi would go to the bathroom in the middle of the night and find her sitting in her bedroom, papers fanned out on the floor. Her plastic folder — Insomnia Methods — was stuffed with torn pages from health magazines and handwritten notes from fortunetellers. She pored over the scraps of paper, arranging and re-arranging them on the floor in new combinations.

Panzi rolled his eyes at many of them. They seemed too superstitious, even for a girl who claimed to have grown up next door to a Buddhist temple. Stone circles on the floor? Warm cucumber water? Reciting the digits of pi? It was all too much. But he did marvel at how there was never even the slightest glimmer of self-pity on her face when he found her on the floor in the middle of the night staring at the ceiling, crickets and harp music seeping from her cell phone.

Xiao Song said there were two types of insomnia. Sometimes when she woke, she knew there was a chance she might drift back off to sleep as long as she kept her eyes closed and relaxed her shoulders. But then there were other awakenings — in a way, equally calming in their certainty — that appeared like a man's silhouette in the doorway. Those were the nights when she would slip outside, cross Zhangzizhong Road, and walk in the quiet shadows of the Duanqiruifu grounds to clear her head.

The Duanqiruifu complex was like nowhere else in the city — a collection of hundred-year-old European buildings in the heart of Old Beijing. They'd been erected as headquarters for the Qing dynasty army at the turn of the century. During the Republican period, they housed the presidential offices, including for Duan Qirui — the warlord-politician the grounds were named after. The Japanese had occupied Duanqiruifu in the 1930s, the Kuomintang in the 1940s, and the Communists after that.

But the buildings, grand and peeling as they were, didn't put on airs about their history. Their second-floor balconies and dramatic archways were crammed with boxes, bird cages, discarded furniture, construction scraps — the detritus of the living, not the dead. Sweaters, hung on clotheslines between columns, dripped water onto the intricate stone facades. For the few dozen families that lived there — in dim, drafty quarters inside the compound's three Tudor-inspired buildings — Duanqiruifu's chief virtue wasn't its history, it was its calm.

There was an unsettling if beautiful aura to it, Panzi thought — the broken streetlamps, the overgrown pathways. But Xiao Song shrugged these omens off; she said she loved to feel the stillness at the center of the massive, teeming city.

He hadn't even known about the midnight walks until the night he woke and found Xiao Song missing from their apartment, her bed cold and cell phone laying on the nightstand. Panzi called her name into the empty rooms and, as the minutes passed into an hour, the image of her face seemed to grow faint. That familiar, sinking feeling returned, the one he felt every time Xiao Song was away — that she had left forever, had been spirited away on the same current that brought her to him a month ago.

That night, Panzi waited for her in the dark, replaying every bit of conversation he could remember from the evening, certain Xiao Song was gone forever. But then he heard the apartment door's shallow creak and felt embarrassed for the melodrama the dark had conjured. That embarrassment soured to shame, which soured to anger. Panzi and Xiao Song fought that night for the first time. Actually, he fought with her while she emptied flower buds from her pockets — compact, fuzzy things — and told him to calm down, calm down, calm down. Spring was coming. Don't be angry, spring was coming.

Before he could voice another worry, she crawled under the covers of his bed and fanned her cool hair across his chest. She fixed her ear in the hollow of his sternum while her fingers began wandering down his leg.

"Don't be upset," she whispered.

He pushed her away. "What are you doing?"

"I was just thinking."

Panzi's mouth felt extremely dry. "About what?" he finally grunted.

"About spring. About how the whole world is coming back to life."

Panzi could feel the heat of Xiao Song's body through her clothes. He remained on his back, eyes closed, trying to focus his anger, as she stirred him to life. Her touch was much different than he'd expected, than he'd imagined in the shower — not frank and hungry at all. Soft hands, plush skin. When she took him in her hand, he could feel her still-cold nose against his neck, a dizzying warm-cold sensation he worried might take him over the edge. He reached out and stroked her back, something to distract himself with. His fingers made it underneath the straps of her dress when she stopped him.

"No, like this."

She slid down her underwear and carefully rolled on top of him with her dress still on. He felt her electric warmth but couldn't see anything. Panzi remained on

his back, arms pinned behind his head while Xiao Song
guided him inside her, wordlessly.

"Do you want this?" she asked after he was already
inside.

"Uh-huh," he gasped.

Pure, warm pleasure. But when it was over and he
began replaying it in his head, the entire episode felt
forced. Did *she* want this? Did she have any genuine
feelings for him at all or was this just another sponta-
neous life experiment? They had sex three more determined times over the following week; and oddly Panzi
felt more distant from Xiao Song after each time. They
never talked about the sex. She never let him see her
body. At first, he thought she might be ashamed of being
a little overweight, but as he lay awake after their fourth
time, he knew that couldn't be all it was. She may have
chided him for closing himself off, but Xiao Song could
hide when she wanted too.

* * *

A peal of shrieking tires jolted Panzi awake. He shot
upright and looked out his bedroom window toward the
direction of the sound. He saw Duanqiruifu's crenelated
tower, rising from behind the compound's red front gate
and its broad Chinese scalloped-tile roof — everything
completely still.

Xiao Song was gone. Minutes of deafening silence
passed before an animal instinct crawled up his spine.
He shoved house keys in his pocket and tramped outside
in his coat and a pair of plastic sandals.

Despite his bare feet, the February night felt warm

as he rushed toward the street, the heels of his sandals clapping against his soles. The street seemed empty. Had no one else heard the noise?

When he turned the corner, he saw it — a mangled bright-red sports car, its crumpled hood against one of the concrete columns in front of Duanqiruifu's main gate. As he ran across Zhangzizhong Road, the scene seemed to grow redder and redder. The red car. The red columns. The red wooden doors to Duanqiruifu thrown wide open.

And a girl in a white dress on the pavement. He knew; he knew even before he'd made it to the other side of the road. Panzi rushed over to her and saw that Xiao Song's body was splayed, twisted at some horrible angle beneath the ruined fender of the car. The sight froze him for a moment before he recovered and managed to yell out her name.

Panzi yelled her name again when he made it to her side, fumbling with her still-warm wrist. Her legs were mangled but there was hardly any blood. *Was she just unconscious?* He gently shook her shoulders and yelled again. He rolled her over; she was still breathing.

Panzi looked up, frantic now, still on his knees, and realized he had no way to call for help. *He had to call for help!* No, he couldn't leave Xiao Song like that. He managed to stand. No traffic on Zhangzizhong Road. *No one anywhere.*

He looked back toward the car and realized that the driver's-side door was open. No one behind the wheel. Panzi took a few steps forward and saw there, hunched forward in the car's front-passenger seat, a motionless body. The interior light of the car was still on; Panzi saw him very clearly. It was a boy, about his own age. His head lay on the dashboard, his disfigured face turned toward him. Short-cropped hair, round cheeks, a silver necklace, and two closed eyes projecting calm and obliviousness. Blood dripped down his chin and pooled on the floor mat, a yellow stallion and the word "Ferrari."

Panzi looked away, back at Xiao Song, instinctively, and felt something loosen inside. *Go call for help.* He turned to run back to his apartment; but as he did something caught his eye, a tall figure in a black T-shirt standing ten meters away. Panzi ran up to him.

"Hey! Hey!"

The man had his back turned. He was leaning against one of the stone lions that flanked the gate of Duanqiruifu, holding a cloth against the right side of his head. He remained motionless until Panzi ran up behind him and grabbed his arm.

"Hey! Call an ambulance! Do you hear me?!"

The boy — he seemed younger than Panzi — lolled his head toward the voice, revealing two black, laconic eyes. A few strands of his swept-back hair had become unglued and dangled to his eyebrows. He stared back at Panzi without comprehension.

"Call for help!" Panzi yelled again. "Give me your phone! They could die!"

Finally, as if to answer, the boy in black removed the cloth — a rumpled white dress shirt — from his face for a moment, and Panzi saw the large crimson gash on his chin. The wound was dark and wet and traced his jawline like half of an exaggerated smile.

"What did you do to them?" Panzi screamed. Tears were streaming down his face now.

The driver stared past him and outstretched his hand, gazing out at something distant at the road's vanishing point. Panzi ran back around the car and inside Duanqiruifu to look for help but had made it only a few steps when he caught a glimpse of flashing red lights approaching. No sirens.

An ambulance pulled up next to one of the stone lions and four men in street clothes emerged from the back, rolling a gurney behind them. A fat bald man commanded them in a gruff voice.

Panzi watched the bald man survey the scene for a moment before muttering something into a walkie-talkie. The medics worked quickly, lifting Xiao Song's limp body atop the clean white sheets as Panzi hovered around them, hysterical with questions that he repeated with increasing intensity: Is she alive? Where are you from? Where are you taking her? No one responded. Desperate, Panzi shoved one of them.

"She's going to the hospital!" one of them snapped. Like the others, he wore street clothes and had a blue surgeon's mask that hid his mouth. Panzi could see only his eyes.

"Which hospital?! Which one?"

But the team had already begun wheeling her toward the back of the ambulance. Panzi followed them, helpless, pleading. The last thing he saw before they loaded Xiao Song inside was that she was still taking shallow breaths. The entire operation had taken about two minutes.

Panzi could hear the men conferring inside the ambulance before one of them hopped out and approached the Ferrari. The man crawled through the open driver's-side door and dragged the lifeless body back out with him by the armpits — its black boots leaving red smudges on the cobblestones — and lay it face-up on the ground. Panzi stood over the kneeling men as they applied a few cursory bandages and compresses to the most visible wounds. This boy, the car's passenger, didn't seem to be breathing. After they had installed this body in the ambulance with Xiao Song, the bald man with the walkie-talkie slammed shut the rear doors and smacked the back window twice with the palm of his hand.

Just as the ambulance took off, a frenzy of new vehicles arrived. A white tow truck parked in the same spot where the ambulance had been. Behind it, two gray vans pulled up next to the curb and maybe a dozen sanitation workers in reflective orange vests poured out of the side doors, wielding straw brooms and sloshing buckets of water. This crew moved more slowly, as if just woken.

The bald man with the walkie-talkie was standing near what remained of the Ferrari's front bumper, guiding the tow truck's swinging iron hook.

"I need your help," Panzi pleaded with the man. "I need to know where you took my friend. I need to be there for her. Which hospital did you take her to? Where can I find her?"

The sanitation workers swarmed around them, picking up shards of red plastic and sweeping up glass.

Unlike the medics, this man responded immediately. He was potbellied and didn't mask his impatience with the situation.

"Don't worry," he told Panzi, in a thick Beijing accent. "We're taking them to a hospital. Right now, I need you to —"

"Which hospital? Where can I find her?"

"It's close by. A very good hospital. You don't have to worry. We'll get in touch with you."

"*How* are you doing to contact me!" Panzi screamed over the tow truck's beeping.

The man remained focused on the slow-moving back end inching closer, waving at the driver, yelling instructions. Finally, he shouted "Okay!" and truck's pistons released a loud hiss.

"Okay. Give me your phone number," he said. Panzi recited the numbers.

"Don't worry. I will send you a message."

The mechanical arm of the tow truck swung toward the hood of the car. One of the sanitation workers pulled a sopping wet rag from a bucket and took to the blood-splattered column the car had rammed into, wiping back and forth over the worst of the mess.

"I want *your* phone number," Panzi said.

The man wrote down some numbers on a scrap of paper. Because of the angle the tow truck had taken, three workers had to push the Ferrari off of the now-wet concrete column before the hook could be fitted under the front axle. The red metal groaned when it was dislodged. The man with the bucket splashed some gray water on the black mark left from the impact and the excess trickled down the incline between the grooves in the stones.

"What about *him*?" Panzi yell, gesturing toward one of the gray vans. The boy in the black T-shirt, the Ferrari's driver, was in the front seat with his head resting against the doorframe. "*He's* the one responsible. We need to call the police."

"We will take care of it," the man mumbled. "You should go rest."

Panzi watched — suddenly overcome by exhaustion — as they towed away the wreckage by its front fender. From the back, the car was sleek and unblemished. The gleaming roof plunged downward to the word "Ferrari" and a stallion logo between the taillights. There was no license plate.

The sanitation workers filed into the back of the van, and the door slammed shut. Panzi stood slack outside the gate, watching the tow truck and vans disappear west beyond the traffic lights. Bits of windshield glass glittered on the ground. A scuff mark. A few faint speckles of blood on the column, those too high for the workers to reach with their rags. Beyond these minor details and the wet cobblestones, little looked out of place.

Panzi rushed back to his apartment and dialed the number on the scrap of paper he'd been given. He was looking at Xiao Song's high heels lined up against the front door when the recording played back to him: *The number you are trying to reach does not exist.*

* * *

Panzi was standing outside the Dongcheng Police Station with Xiao Song's ID card at eight forty-five, bleary-eyed and in the same clothes as the night before. When the office opened, a young, uniformed secretary wrote out his statement in the boxes of a police report form — grunting annoyed questions at him. Then Panzi was left alone in a waiting room with two semiretired patrolmen reading the same newspaper. He waited for two hours.

A man who introduced himself as the district vice police chief finally emerged and asked Panzi to follow him to his office. He wore a light-blue uniform and peaked cap, which he removed and set carefully on the desk.

"I've read over your statement," he began, face expressionless. "I understand you were a witness to an automobile accident last night."

Panzi launched into the details of what had happened, but the officer just held up his hand.

"We are well aware of the situation and have already begun to investigate the matter."

"Okay, that's good," Panzi said. "But there are a few other details I think you —"

"Now," he interrupted, "we are already in the process of investigating the accident and assessing the extent of property damage to the Duanqiruifu gate."

"But Xiao Song was the one who —"

The man held up his hand again. This time, he picked up a sheet of paper and recited exactly three sentences:

> An automobile accident occurred at the gate of Duanqiruifu on the night of February 17, caused by the inexperience of a new driver. Property damage was caused. No injuries were reported.

The shock lasted a few seconds. When Panzi recovered, he tried pleading. He showed the officer pictures of Xiao Song on his phone and her ID card. He could hear his voice growing shrill and frantic. He was an eyewitness!

They needed to find her! But the vice police chief never lost his calm. If Panzi wished to file a missing persons report, he would be happy to assist.

Panzi wandered out of the police station an hour later into a world that felt hyperreal. He stood at the building's entrance for some time, feeling like nothing more than a collection of sensations. A bicycle clanked. Basin-water splashed on the pavement. A dog wheezed. A man with a cart called for wastepaper. He felt a distant communion with all of it, as if his own life had been spilled out into the world, making it vibrant and himself completely numb.

When you're overwhelmed, you fixate on tiny details and observations, to ground you.

Panzi couldn't think of a single place to go. Eventually, he hailed a taxi and heard his voice tell the driver the address of his mother's house.

"You never answer your phone!" his mother shrieked when he appeared in the doorway. "C'mon, we're about to eat."

Panzi followed her inside, listening as more words poured off her.

"It's good you're here though," Qinyan went on busily. "I told the buyer we'd meet him there around three. After that, I want to go see that new development out at Fragrant River, okay? Prices have dropped to forty thousand...."

Panzi felt his pulse rising in his throat. He took a breath and exhaled. "Mom, I need to tell you something. Yesterday —"

"I know," she said, cutting him off. The comment dazed

him until he realized what she'd meant; they had closed on the property across the street from Duanqiruifu yesterday. The sale seemed like a lifetime ago.

"No, that's not it. I was going to say —"

"Will you call Grandpa down for lunch? It's ready."

Panzi gritted his teeth and climbed the gunmetal spiral staircase leading to the roof. He found Grandpa fussing with a large plastic tarp. Every spring Old Li took down the winter tarps on the pigeon coops, an event, he claimed, the birds looked forward to. For the first time all morning, Panzi thought he might burst into tears as he helped Grandpa down the stairs, feeling the old man's thin arms even though they were layered in two sweaters and a coat.

Panzi wasn't hungry, but his mother placed a large bowl of stew on the cardboard table for him anyway. It steamed, untouched, as he told her and Grandpa about Xiao Song, the Ferrari crash, the strange ambulance and cleanup crew, the surreal visit to the police station that morning. Grandpa stopped eating, eyes wide with alarm. Qinyan slurped from her bowl quietly. When he'd finished the story, Panzi took off his glasses and rubbed his eyes.

"So, this girl," his mother said carefully, "she was *living* with you in the sales unit?"

"She's gone, Mom. I don't even know where they took her."

"She was your girlfriend?"

"Mom!"

"This is important to know! How long had you been together? What was your relationship with her? The police will need to know this information."

"You're not the police. Look, maybe if we went to police headquarters they could help."

Qinyan took a deep breath and set her spoon on the table. She spoke in the gentle voice Panzi remembered hearing as a boy.

"In a time like this, calm is most important," she began. "We need to think clearly. This Xiao Song is your girl-friend, is that right?" She collected herself and began again. "This is a tragedy. A tragedy. But would the result change if we ... well, if we ruffled too many feathers? I don't like the sound of this, Panzi. I don't know anything about Ferraris. The police said they were investigating. Why not wait to see what emerges? Then we'll —"

Panzi stormed out of the room. What did he expect coming home and telling her anyway? He had made it to the bottom of the stairwell when he heard Grandpa's voice call for him to wait. Panzi stood in place, face flushed, scraping at cement grooves of the brick wall with his house key.

"I'm going to buy cigarettes," Old Li said when he'd made it to the bottom of the stairs. "Come with me."

Panzi reached for this grandfather's arm and they headed down the alley. Grandpa looked even older than he had on the roof, stooped forward and shuffling along in soft cotton shoes. His toes must be freezing, Panzi realized, a thought that almost choked him up as they walked. *He* was the one who should be taking care of Grandpa, not the other way around. Old Li paused to catch his breath, and Panzi saw the spot on the pavement where, six weeks ago, they had burned an offering for his father. Gone. Xiao Song, gone. Grandpa would be gone soon too.

"You know, your father had big ears like you," Old Li said suddenly. Panzi looked up from the spot on the pavement.

"He was proud of them," the old man smiled. "They used to make fun of him at school, you know. But your dad always boasted that he could hear things that no one else could. His classmates used to gather around, just to watch him." Old Li smiled to himself.

"Your dad would close his eyes and tell all his classmates to shut up. He was trying to listen to the radio he'd kept on in his bedroom. 'You can't hear it? You seriously can't hear it?' he'd say."

Old Li allowed himself another melancholy smile. He looked as if he might say more but didn't.

"Did they believe him?" Panzi finally asked. "The classmates."

"I think most of them knew there was nothing to hear. But they all stopped and listened, at least for a moment. I think they wanted to believe him."

"I'm not making up the story about the Ferrari, Grandpa. It really happened."

"I believe you," Old Li said. "And I believed in your father's radio too. I'm old enough to know there are whole worlds out there that I know nothing about."

SPRING

5

The Boss of Houhai

THE Boss of Houhai sat at the mahjong table trying to concentrate. The clack of tiles, Fat Liang's drunken rambling, and harsh halogen lights buzzed around him as he fished a Zhongnanhai cigarette from the drooping breast pocket of his flannel pajamas. He stared hard at the meager hand just dealt to him, notching the filtered tip into one of the gaps in his bottom row of teeth. His fingers hurt from the cold.

"Now *Cuban* women...." Fat Liang went on, almost shouting to a man at the next table over. "When we called to the port in Havana, you could see their asses swaying from the deck of the ship!" he cackled.

The three tables of neighborhood regulars gazed into the green felt, pretending they weren't listening to him. They all lived nearby — solid-looking women in their forties, old codgers in wheelchairs, two migrant workers from Hunan who rarely spoke. Everyone wore coats in the bare, unheated room and sipped hot water from thermoses brought from home. Fat Liang's pocked cheeks seemed to get redder as he worked himself up. He helped himself to the Boss's pack of Zhongnanhais on the table.

The Boss had already pocketed some sixty kuai tonight, but this hand would not end well. The Boss was expansive as a winner, which he had been up until twenty minutes ago, before Fat Liang had burst in reeking of *baijiu* and bad luck.

"You can't afford your own fucking cigarettes?" the Boss growled.

Fat Liang's dirty fingernail scratched around inside the pack; if he heard the Boss, he didn't let on. They had known each other their whole lives as neighbors on this hutong; few boundaries remained between them. The Boss knew everything there was to know about Fat Liang; he was a blight on the neighborhood, an uncultured drunk with no steady job, no business connections, or anything else to offer society — nothing but loud provocation and rude libido. The Boss couldn't imagine life in Beijing without him.

Fat Liang lit the cigarette, and the Boss sighed again at his tiles. He glanced at the clock on the wall. He should get going anyhow.

"Fatty! You want to step in here? I'm leaving."

Fat Liang had two hands held up, cupping imaginary Cuban breasts. The Boss stood to leave and threw a wad of ones and fives on the felt. He shook his pack of Zhongnanhais.

"Did you hear me?!" the Boss yelled again, this time his blood rising with a touch of anger. "And buy your own damn cigarettes!"

The Boss didn't care about the cigarettes or the money but snapping at Fat Liang sent a needed warm jolt through his body as he swept away the plastic flaps hanging from the doorway and stepped out into the cold night.

"Are you going for a girl?" came Fat Liang's impish voice from inside. "Because there's only one thing you could be going out for at this hour!"

"Go back inside, you —"

"A man has his needs!" Fat Liang sniggered. "I haven't been out with you to see the girls in a *long* time. But you're getting older. Maybe a man's needs change as he gets older. Maybe he's *powerless* to control parts of his body."

The Boss ignored the idiotic voice as he shuffled toward home in his flannel slippers. His lungs ached with each breath of the crisp air. March was still this fucking cold. A deep rattling cough consumed him halfway down Jingyang Hutong, and the Boss had to stop for a moment, double over, and spit a large gob of phlegm on the pavement before he continued. He should be taking better care of himself — get a massage, soak his feet, eat some porridge.

His two cars — the Honda and the BMW — were parked on either side of a hundred-year-old cypress tree opposite the dark entrance of his shared courtyard home. Seeing them both wrapped in snug vinyl covers against the dust warmed him a bit more. He continued inside, past the piles of boxes and construction scraps.

His wife was watching television alone on the couch, a space heater glowing orange on the floor beside her.

"Where are the keys to the BMW?" he asked by way of greeting.

He didn't wait for a reply, crossing over to the adjacent bedroom to change out of his pajamas. The Boss closed the bedroom door so that he could look at himself in the full-length mirror that hung on the inside. As he unbuttoned his shirt, he tilted the pate of his head toward the glass, reflexively, scrutinizing the thin but still-black rivulets of hair. He turned his head and ran his fingertips across his chin. Only fifty-eight years old, the Boss looked closer to seventy, his body an offering to the only lifestyle he'd ever known — heavy drinking and smoking, occasional cocaine and ketamine. And sex, which the Boss reckoned had aged him the worst of all.

But the dark circles under his eyes were looking a little better, he decided. Maybe the acupuncture was working. The Boss unscrewed an unlabeled jar of dark-brown balm and smeared some on his forehead, his cheeks, and the soft tissue under his eyes. He inhaled the scent of bitter herbs and star anise, and examined his naked, hairless chest — breasts sagging and shriveled purple nipples that pointed toward the floor. He buttoned up a dress shirt and pants over a layer of long underwear before returning to his hair. On this pass, he pulled a foldable comb from the pocket of his pants and rearranged a few stray strands. *Not bad.*

He reached for another small, unmarked bottle of herbal body lotion and placed it in his purse. Then he aligned the thick gold chain already around his neck and opened the door to find his wife unmoved, still transfixed in the pale-blue glow of the television.

"Are you deaf?" he said. "Where are the keys?"

The Boss's wife looked up at him, eyes blurred. She had purple eyebrows and a shock of frizzed hair that he hated.

"They're probably right where you left them. I haven't been anywhere all day," she said. "You smell like a pharmacy, by the way."

The Boss didn't dignify that comment. He walked over to the coffee table only a few feet away from his wife and swiped the keys off the glass surface. On the floor inside the front door was a cardboard box brimming with yellow duty-free shopping bags from the airport. The Boss rummaged around until he found a fresh, unopened pack of Chunghwa 5000s — the ones he always brought for business meetings — and tossed his half-pack of Zhongnanhais on the table.

* * *

It was Old Xue, the owner of the Sea of Clouds, who had first dubbed Xiao Dongxuan "the Boss of Houhai" two decades ago. In the nineties, you would have found the Boss out in Houhai — the city's raucous nightlife lake district — seemingly every night. He worked, in those days, at a state monopoly selling dairy products, run by his older cousin. Xiao Dongxuan's official job title was "business relations director," which meant entertaining retail buyers visiting the capital from the hinterland. Nearly every night the Boss led his charges — their village dialects growing more incomprehensible by the bottle — on odysseys through private dining rooms, darkened hotel lobbies, and red-light massage parlors, and, inevitably, to Houhai.

The dairy company had privatized years ago, but the Boss kept Houhai for his office. Everyone knew him there, and the Boss always knew the right spot. The Bronze Bell was big and rowdy — perfect for wide-eyed country bumpkin clients visiting from out of town. Gold Coast Coffee and Tea had high-end teas for afternoon meetings with the old government cadres.

The Sea of Clouds had an expansive view over the yellow lights strung along the lake's east shore. The place was nothing extravagant and god knows not quiet, but the Sea of Clouds was discreet enough to talk business with a city government official not wanting to be recognized.

The problem was the young people; Houhai had been infested with them for the better part of the last ten years. The music bars had metastasized, with their sappy ballads and tape-loops of electronic pounding. The Boss watched as the old guard had gradually been replaced. He had tried getting to know some of the new owners of the music bars, invariably young transplants from out-of-town money and zero business experience. He'd introduced himself as the Boss of Houhai, as usual. The young people usually laughed at this and asked him if wanted to drink something called a mojito.

At least the Sea of Clouds had managed to stay the same, the Boss thought as he lounged alone on the bar's second floor. It had had its only facelift fifteen years ago, at the behest of Old Xue's then mistress, who fancied herself an interior decorator. Most of the purple and silver rings hung on the walls had since become unglued. Cheap plastic globe lamps marked a path across the room toward the bar. The hallway toward the toilet was lined with gilded-frame paintings of topless ethnic minority girls holding water jugs. The heavy purple satin curtains held five years' worth of dust. It was a comfortable place.

The Boss gazed outside, down on the hawkers flashing green laser beams at people passing by. Noise bled in through the window — winsome ballads, classical guitars, retirees singing, a jackhammer. Out of habit, the Boss ran a finger along the prominent purple-black birthmark that extended from the corner of right eye like a fat tear.

He caught sight of Director Li crossing the humpback walking bridge below, his drab trench coat thrown into sharp relief against the sea of youth. Li clutched a black briefcase and looked flustered — green, red, yellow lights reflecting off his large, smooth head. The Boss remained perfectly still, waiting until the man disappeared from view and emerged at the top of the narrow wooden stairs.

"The driver dropped me off at the other end of the lake," Director Li puffed, waving off the waitress trying to take his coat. "It's freezing!"

"Sit, sit. Waitress! Bring a bottle and some snacks!" the Boss yelled. "Have your driver pick you up at the Drum Tower, it's closer from here. Take one." The Boss held out his box of Chunghwas toward Director Li and flicked open his metal Zippo lighter in the same motion. "Keeps you warm from the cold."

The waitress returned to mix the Chivas and sweet green tea at an adjacent empty table. Both men settled into a cloud of smoke as Li rubbed his hands together for warmth. She poured them each an amber highball and placed the hard-plastic pitcher at the center of the table before retreating downstairs, leaving them alone.

"I'm surprised it's taken us this long to meet," Director Li finally began. "Everyone seems to know you."

The Boss's cracked lips parted into a smile; he was a sucker for flattery.

"So, what do you do? Real estate, is it?"

"No, not me," the Boss replied. "I'm already old, almost retired. My nephew has a construction company that I help out with here and there."

Were this a different kind of meeting, the Boss would have reached for his black leather zip-purse on the table. Inside, his eight different business cards suggested he did any number of things.

"How are things at City Planning these days?" the Boss asked.

"Lots of changes, lots of new projects," Li replied with a shake of the head. "The merger, of course. You might say it is a time of great uncertainty for a lot of people." He glanced up and caught the Boss's eye but, getting no real reaction, looked out the window again.

The Chivas had already taken the edge off Director Li, it seemed. Shallow grooves appeared from the corners of his mouth as he swallowed and flashed his ruined teeth, the candlelight casting new shadows. To the Boss, Li suddenly appeared as a well-fed Guangdong businessman having his fortune read.

"Sure, there are rumors," Li was saying. "Everyone fighting for their jobs. Frankly, it makes me glad that I was able to make it out of district government when I did. But you must know all about this. I understand you follow Beijing politics closely."

"I just like knowing what's going on in my neighborhood. You could say I'm the local gossip."

"What about City Planning?" Li asked of the commission he directed. "Heard any interesting gossip?"

The Boss took a sip of his drink.

"Oh, I've heard a few things about the district merger as well," he began. "I've also heard there is someone new there, a young man that came up from Dongcheng District. Sun something. Uh, let's see," the Boss rubbed his birthmark in mock concentration. "Sun Zhenhua, I think it is. I heard he was sent there by Vice Mayor Chen Yihui."

Director Li allowed a solemn nod at the mention of the vice mayor.

"It sounded pretty interesting anyway," the Boss said. "This Zhenhua is quite young. It seemed rather ... *significant* that a vice mayor would get involved for such a minor appointment. He is a talented writer, at least from what I've heard. What's your impression of Zhenhua?"

Director Li uncrossed his legs and leaned forward for a fresh cigarette. The placid look on his face was gone.

"I haven't really noticed him. He seems like every other young person at the office — inexperienced. Zhenhua has a lot to learn." The lighter clicked in Li's hand. "What about Vice Mayor Chen, then?"

The Boss shifted his weight in the chair to get comfortable. He was beginning to enjoy himself.

"Young people," the Boss sighed, as if he hadn't heard the question. "They've never had to eat bitterness like our generation, eh? They don't know how to persevere; everything is just handed to them. They have time to get into all kinds of trouble." The Boss stopped there, but Director Li seemed to miss the innuendo.

"I understand you are quite close with Vice Mayor Chen," Li persisted. His face had already begun to flush with the alcohol.

"Well, Vice Mayor Chen has been very busy," the Boss replied. "They say he's being shortlisted for Party Secretary."

Director Li frowned. He wasn't getting his point across.

"There's a rumor about the vice mayor's son," Li said. "An accident with a Ferrari." Li paused, avoiding the Boss's eyes, took a breath and started anew. "It is a very sensitive time right now — the merger, the upcoming plenum, the anti-corruption campaign. It's a sensitive time for the Party as well. People don't believe in the Party anymore; they don't have faith in it. We need good leaders, moral leaders, leaders the people can look up to. So, this business with the vice mayor's son...." Li gazed into his glass. "The Party needs moral leaders, that's what I'm saying."

The Boss almost burst out laughing but was saved by the waitress returning to refill the pitcher. Director Li fitted another cigarette between his lips, and the Boss leaned back, marveling at the faux-earnest performance he'd just witnessed. Party morality!

"So, you're not in contact with Vice Mayor Chen, then?" Li asked when she was gone.

"Well, I'm afraid he doesn't have much free time for his old friends these days."

* * *

In truth, it was the Boss who had been avoiding Vice Mayor Chen since the night of the crash, a month ago. The cover-up had been risky to arrange — the ambulance, the street cleaners, a tow truck hauling an unregistered Ferrari, all in the center of the fucking city! The Boss didn't have great existing contacts in the police department; it required a work-around. But the Boss didn't hesitate to send Fat Liang to clean up the scene the moment he got the call from Chen's assistant in the middle of the night. It was for Vice Mayor Chen, after all.

The Boss had first met Vice Mayor Chen twenty years prior, back even before he was "the Boss of Houhai." Chen was a minor official at the Food and Drug Administration at the time, but the Boss sensed immediately that the young cadre was destined for great things. Chen knew everything about the Boss's dairy company — its leaders, its finances, its upcoming investments. Chen could drill down to every cadre from the FDA as well — reeling off their allies and enemies, their prospects for promotion. Chen's father had been a three-star general in the PLA. It was obvious — someday Chen Yihui was going to run Beijing.

Chen and the Boss had maintained a loose symbiosis for years after that. They were not friends, not business partners, not family. The Boss had never visited the villa he'd helped Chen's wife discreetly buy on the outskirts of the city. The vice mayor never joined the meetings brokered between the Boss and other influential officials. The two had never exchanged anything as vulgar as money in exchange for favors.

Even one month ago, when the Boss doled out envelopes of cash from his own pocket to the tow truck owner, the ambulance driver, the street cleaners — he never expected a cent from the vice mayor in return. The currency of their relationship had never been money. Vice Mayor Chen was the Boss's investment, due to mature when Chen was named Beijing Party Secretary in the fall.

That had been the plan, anyway. But the Ferrari crash had devastated Vice Mayor Chen. For the last month, he wept in meetings and cancelled appointments. He spent hours locked in his son Shishan's hospital room, whispering to his son to wake up from his coma.

By default, the Boss became an uncomfortable confidant, taking Chen's calls at odd hours, listening to one of the most powerful politicians in Beijing talk dreamily about beach vacations and family picnics from years ago. It was embarrassing.

"Shishan didn't do anything wrong," Vice Mayor Chen would sob. "It wasn't his fault." Each time Vice Mayor Chen called, anger simmered in the Boss. *Do you think that matters? Do you think anyone would care that it wasn't his Ferrari?* Shishan was a good kid, the Boss had heard. But details wouldn't matter if the public or the Party ever found out about the crash. "Ferrari" would be the only word they heard. And when they did — poof. The end of Vice Mayor Chen's career.

It took the Boss too long to admit, but he had to cut his losses. It was time for him to cash out for what he could get before Chen was worth nothing at all. Vice Mayor Chen was unstable; you could hear it in the timbre of his voice. How long until he spilled to someone about his comatose son? How long until the entire cover-up was exposed? How long until he started throwing around the Boss's name?

The Boss needed to protect himself. And if he turned a bit of a profit, well, that wasn't personal, just business. He didn't owe Vice Mayor Chen anything. You don't always get to pick your business partners — like the donkey of a man sitting across the table — you had to keep your eyes open and follow the opportunities.

"I like a man who speaks directly, the way you do," the Boss said to Director Li finally. He had a smile plastered to his face. "I agree that the city needs moral officials, but it needs other improvements as well. Better quality buildings, for example."

Before Li could jump in and hammer away again at the topic of the vice mayor, the Boss began naming a handful of property development projects of interest around the city. The project he'd been eyeing for months, the Moon Tower Office Complex project, had still not been approved by Director Li's commission. At least three property developers wanted the project, but none of them had the stamped permits. If a building contractor like the Boss's brother-in-law could deliver such approvals, developers would be falling over themselves to sign.

Director Li's eyes darted around as he groped for the scattered details to the Boss's queries, like a schoolboy struggling to remember his times tables. Eventually, he resorted to the papers in his briefcase, reading the figures from them while the Boss leaned back and smoked, silently calculating the price of Chen Yihui's scalp in square meters.

* * *

The Boss laid face down, forehead and chin pressed against the massage bed's round, padded opening, waiting for No. 43. His pale, hairless legs jutted out from gauzy, throwaway pajama shorts. He didn't bother wearing the top half; the room was warm. A paper cup of hot water steamed next to an empty ashtray on the nightstand. Waterfall *guzheng* music played from the ceiling. Voices and footsteps murmured outside his room.

"The old man in room three," a voice said from the hallway. "The one with the smelly medicine."

A few moments later, No. 43, a seventeen-year-old girl from Sichuan with hair pulled back in a neat bun and long bangs, entered the room. She was short and wiry, with flared cheekbones and small, rough hands that left red marks on flesh.

"Boss! You're back," she exclaimed.

The Boss only grunted; he'd seen her last Tuesday.

Like all the numbered girls, No. 43 came straight from the countryside. Most evenings, the Boss liked chatting with her as she worked his back in the warm, red room. Tonight, though, the "old man" comment he'd just overheard from the hall had soured his mood. Once No. 43 adjusted her towels, the Boss simply pointed to the bottle of dark-brown lotion on the table and gruffly told her to get started. She squeezed some of the Boss's herbal tonic into her palm. Soon the pungent smell of wormwood and ginger filled the room as she worked the dark, gummy ointment in.

"Where are you from again?" the Boss finally asked after they'd been silent for more than twenty minutes.

He knew the answer but was ready to hear her talk now. The Boss enjoyed listening to her lilting Sichuanese accent describe her far-flung home village in the mountains — how hot the weather got, what crops were grown, what kinds of foods they ate. Everything was cheaper there, she would always say. He made No. 43 reel off the prices of everything — rice, meat, houses — fantasizing about buying the entire village himself. That was a pleasant daydream: buying every single house in a remote mountain valley and living like an emperor.

"It's very poor, very backward," she summarized.

"But it's also beautiful, right?"

"No, it's too poor."

"How long will you stay in Beijing?"

"For a few years to make some money. Then I'll go home."

"I thought you said it was too poor. Why do you want to go back?"

No. 43 smiled at the Boss as if he'd asked the most world's most obvious question. "My family is all there. It's my home."

The Boss watched No. 43 unlatch a small wooden box at her feet and remove a glass jar, forceps, cotton balls, and a business-card slab of flint. She swabbed the jar, lit a brief, swirling blue flame inside, and suctioned the hot opening to the bottom of his foot. Each time she broke the seal, wrenching the jar from his foot, there was a resounding *BOP!* pulling impurities and toxins with it.

She stood next to the bed, rubbing his back and shoulders before moving to the backs of his legs. Her fingers slid just under the cuff of his thin shorts, grazing his inner thighs. The kneading was workmanlike, non-sensual, but the Boss stared at the floor trying to summon a faint thrill of arousal anyway, remembering

Fat Liang's taunts on the alley. That son a bitch thinks he is such a man because he still goes out whoring every other night. Just because you don't have a hard-on every hour of the day doesn't mean you aren't a man.

The Boss readjusted his body on the bed and shut his eyes in concentration. Still nothing. Then he did something he hadn't done in years. He grabbed No. 43 by the wrist and led her palm across his belly and down below the drawstring of his shorts. She felt her arm tense up; she wasn't that kind of girl, she said. But the Boss emitted a low growl, and the girl finally buried her fingers gracelessly in his tangle of dark hair. The Boss laid on his back staring angrily at the ceiling as No. 43 rummaged around for a few minutes. The *guzheng* music had stopped some time ago; the room was silent except for the rustling of cheap fabric.

The Boss waved the girl off. She didn't know the first thing about how to please a man, he said. How was he supposed to get aroused with those ugly blunt fingers fumbling around? Eventually No. 43 bowed out of the room and fled. The Boss heard the quick patter of her footsteps disappear down the hall.

As he angrily dressed, the Boss consoled himself with thoughts of Fat Liang's pathetic life. The man still lived in the same four-square-meter hovel, alone, with yellowed newspapers covering the walls. Eating cheap oil-soaked food. Nicotine-stained teeth. Arms covered in cigarette burns. Venereal diseases, surely.

The spa's manager was already standing near the front desk, head slightly bowed when the Boss emerged. He was perhaps twenty-two and wore a cheap black suit and earpiece whose cord snaked down his neck. He had one job: to ensure his VIP customers were happy. The Boss had never learned his name.

"Here." The Boss held out a wad of hundred-yuan notes.

"Sir?" The boy replied. "We can deduct today's massage from your VIP account."

"I won't be back," the Boss said angrily.

Panic spread across the boy's face as he began to register what this might mean for him. He gently pushed the Boss's money away.

"I'm glad you stopped by the front desk," he stammered. "In fact, we've prepared a small gift for you." The boy tugged at the black cord near his neck to radio back for someone to bring out a gift, but the Boss stopped him. The groveling did lift the Boss's mood, in fact. He put the bills back in his wallet and gave the room a once over.

"This place is not as good as it used to be," he said. "You need to make improvements."

"Please forgive me! Please forgive me!"

The manager stood on his toes, ready to move mountains for his unsatisfied VIP. The Boss summoned a few vague comments about the lighting and the small size of the rooms as he headed toward the exit. When he got to the doorway, he paused once more.

"And get rid of that No. 43. I don't want to see her again."

6

Struggle

Yanmei looked up from her notebook and swept a strand of hair out of her face. Gusts of April wind whipped past her on the highway overpass, mussing Guang Fei's blanket of goods — plastic combs, nail clippers, headbands, and decks of cards. He had tried pinning down the corners with some of the merchandise, but nothing was heavy enough to keep it in place.

A steady stream of weekend foot traffic filtered past without paying much attention to the odd threesome: a young girl with a reporter's notebook; a whiskered man perched on a wooden cart; and a patchy, brown mutt with his head on the pavement.

Yanmei reached down and stroked the dog's white neck.

"He's pretty calm today," she observed. "What did you say his name was?"

"I call him Momo since I don't know his real name. I found him outside the Stars Hotel a few weeks ago. I thought he might be sick. He still doesn't move around all that well." Guang Fei gazed at the creature for a moment. "They won't let him inside, so I feed him whatever's left from breakfast." Guang Fei looked down at Momo with affection. "We need to fatten you up, don't we?"

Yanmei smiled and glanced at the clock on her phone. The dog, the wind, the roaring six lanes of traffic below — nothing seemed to faze him. She'd followed Guang Fei up here an hour ago, and he hadn't stopped talking since.

Maybe this was a bad idea, teasing out this "color." Yanmei already had plenty of material — a half-dozen interviews, even a few visits to shelters around the city — to pitch her editor at the *Beijing Evening News* a feature about homelessness in Beijing. Why, then, was she so compelled to chase down the story of the Idiot? Since she'd come across the color photo of him at an art gallery two weeks ago — deranged looking, tragic, eating a bowl full of dirt — she knew instinctively she needed that image, that story, for the feature she wanted to write.

The photographer of "Eat Dirt" knew nothing about his subject, she'd learned. A few of the men staying at the homeless shelters had recognized the man in the photo — "the Idiot" everyone called him — but no one had seen him recently. She had been showing the photo at a shelter near Beijing Station when Guang Fei rolled his wooden cart over to her and said, matter-of-factly, that he knew the Idiot. The Idiot had saved his life.

"So, Mr. Guang," Yanmei began again. "Can you tell

me exactly how you met him, the man I mentioned to you back at the shelter? The one from the photograph."

"I'm getting to that."

"But I don't understand exactly how he saved your life. Can you start from the beginning? Where were you when you met him?"

"I'm getting there," Guang Fei repeated. He smoothed his blanket of trinkets once more and tucked his hands into his coat sleeves.

"A lot of people think life is always hard for a cripple," Guang Fei began. "But back in my home village, things weren't always that bad. I had a place to sleep; I had food to eat; I had shelter from the cold. My family received a stipend from the government twice a year to take care of me. Between that and the money my brother brought in doing construction, it was enough for us to get by, as long as we were careful.

"My mother had been sick for as long as I could remember. She never complained about the pain; but sometimes when only the two of us were home alone, she'd shut herself in the bedroom and I'd hear her moan from the next room. That was her struggle: cancer, though we didn't find out about it until later. When she left this world, I moved in with my brother and his family.

"How can I describe those years? They were the best of my life. The four of us — my brother, his wife and son, and me — we were a family. My nephew called me 'Uncle Cripple.' I spent the mornings wheeling my cart around the village, running errands, and the afternoons inside with the television while everyone else was busy with school and work.

"But all that changed when my brother decided he

would go search for work out on the coast. There were steadier, better-paying construction jobs in the big cities. It was too poor in our village, he said. He'd return for New Year, he promised, and send back money when he could manage. After a few months, his wife and their boy joined him.

"They didn't leave me completely alone. My brother decided he would have our next-door neighbor, Auntie Peng, look after me while they were away. I was afraid of Auntie Peng, to be honest. Sometimes at night I heard her yelling at her husband, threatening to cut off his fingers if he ever hit her again. I told my brother that I could take care of myself, but he wouldn't hear of it. I needed help, he insisted, even if it was from an angry old woman.

"I don't think Auntie Peng ever understood that just because my legs were paralyzed, that didn't mean my mind was gone. She didn't like the thought of me wheeling myself around the village, going about my normal routines. She locked me inside the house and brought over wilted vegetables once a week. It was for my own protection, she always said. When I tried to reason with her, she just yelled at me like a child. She threatened me with worse if I ever spoke ill of her to my brother. For the three months I spent under her thumb, I didn't leave the house. Auntie Peng was the only person I saw.

"So, I watched TV. I liked the war dramas best — the heroic Red Army, the Long March, the wicked Japanese imperialists — those sorts of shows. Maybe it's because I've never been able to use my legs that I always felt drawn to the action — running alongside Chairman Mao, yelling ahead that the Japanese devils were advancing.

The triumphant music played, and the actors repeated the same words over and over: struggle, sacrifice, martyrdom, endurance, honor.

"When the speeches on TV ended, I would wipe away my tears, look down at my legs, and remember the padlock on the front door. I sat on the couch and smoked. My mother and father were gone. My brother would never come back. What was I going to do, spend the rest of my life like this, alone like a prisoner?

"Our family kept bottles of pesticide in the corner of my brother's old bedroom. One afternoon, when I finished a pack of cigarettes, I wheeled myself over and held one of the bottles in my hands. There had been others in my village who had done it this way, I knew. It would take only a few swigs.

"But just then, on TV, I heard Chairman Mao — well, the actor playing him — start to speak. On the screen he was giving a victory speech from atop the famous rostrum on Tiananmen Square. Below him, a sea of adoring people waved. The music played. I knew all the horror and violence of the war; I'd watched the whole series. But there were no traces of it on Chairman Mao. His face looked beautiful.

"The Chairman continued with his speech: struggle, hardship, victory.... And all of a sudden, I was sure he was talking to me. He was promising a taste of glory at the end of my own bitter struggle. My heart swelled. I turned off the television set and sat on my cart, thinking. I finished a cigarette and thought: Why shouldn't I travel to Beijing to see Tiananmen Square myself? It would be my own Liberation, my final triumph.

"And after that, I would end my own struggle. I would

find a quiet place, drink a bottle of *yanghua leguo* and join my parents."

* * *

Yanmei sat on a page of newsprint, knees pulled to her chest, long ago having abandoned taking notes on Guang Fei's story. The sun had migrated along the North Second Ring Road and was now hidden behind a giant glass building to her left. Maybe ten yuan in small bills had accumulated on the blanket; Guang Fei had sold three plastic combs.

"So, ... the Idiot," she said gently.

"It took two full days to get to Beijing. You don't want to know how I got here! I had to break out of the house and get myself to the train station! That's another story. But I made it to Beijing Station. Some city management thugs picked me up and dropped me off at the Stars Hotel.

"You've seen the Stars Hotel already, haven't you? *Hotel!* My god. It's just a shelter, a big, cold concrete room where they throw all of us. Anyway, on the day I arrived in Beijing, even the Stars Hotel looked welcoming. I was filthy and bloody and starving, but I had made it to Beijing!

"The Idiot arrived at the Stars Hotel that morning. He had been roughed up somewhere during the night and probably should have been in the hospital. The manager of the Stars Hotel just started waving his hand when he saw the Idiot. Take him anywhere else, he yelled! The hospital, the police station, he didn't care.

"The Idiot was barefoot, his clothes in shreds, but he was still grinning, I remember. The only thing that looked out of place was his hair, which was caked with dirt and blood but otherwise a perfect bowl, a 'mushroom cut.'

"No one knew the Idiot's name. He didn't have an identity card. The two students who'd found him had tried calling the police, they said, but when the Idiot realized what was happening, he began shrieking. The manager kept his arms crossed until one of the exasperated students opened his wallet. They haggled for a few minutes, and finally the manager stuffed the bills in his pocket and yelled at the Idiot to go inside to sleep.

"Instead, the Idiot shambled over to where I was eating and sat down on the ground. His head lolled up and down, but something in his eyes told me he was hungry. I pointed to the group still huddled near the entrance.

"'Go up there and get some food if you're hungry,' I said.

"The Idiot made kind of a whinnying sound and his eyes remained fixed on me as his head bobbed back and forth, bangs dangling. I turned away to ignore him, but he whinnied again, this time louder.

"'Right over there! Food!'

"I had a long day ahead of me. It might take me all day to make it to Tiananmen Square, but I was ready to fulfill my purpose. I slung my green satchel over my shoulder and winced as I planted my hands on the ground — they were raw and sore from the previous days. I took a deep breath and reminded myself that I would need to struggle only little while longer. I pushed myself across the floor toward the entrance.

"'Hhhuuuugh!' The Idiot was on his feet, honking at me like a goose.

"'What? What is it?' I yelled at him.

"'Hhhuuuugh!'

"'The buns are right over there! Go get one!'

"I moved a little further but couldn't exactly make an escape from him. The Idiot followed me through the entrance of the Stars Hotel, still gurgling and honking. I looked around for the manager to get the Idiot away from me, but he was gone. No one else was paying any attention.

"'Go back inside,' I said. 'I can't help you. Look at me! Does it look like I can help you? Go inside; get a bun while there are still some left and go to sleep, okay? Do you understand?'

"The Idiot just stared back at me with that unhinged grin and stupid haircut. He couldn't understand a word I was saying.

"I began crawling down the street, but the Idiot caught up to me without delay. I didn't know what to do, so I just continued on with the Idiot shuffling behind me. It was slow going and I stopped to rest often. Every time I did, I could hear angry bicycle bells and motorcycle horns behind me. No one offered any help. Every once in a while, the Idiot would wander away from view and I thought maybe I might begin the solemn, heroic journey I had imagined. But then he would appear again, staggering toward me, barking.

"We continued on that way through the morning, and I began talking to him. I knew he couldn't understand me, of course, but I'm a talker. Sometimes I think that after spending those months alone, locked in the house by Auntie Peng with no one to talk to, I was making up for it somehow. Anyway, I told the Idiot some of the same things I'm telling you now: where I was from, where my brother and his family were living. I told him about my favorite PLA generals and great military battles. I told him about my own Long March as well, and how I intended to end it just as gloriously. What did it matter? He was an idiot.

"How can I describe seeing Tiananmen Square for the first time? As I approached, it seemed impossibly vast. It was noisy — traffic and people everywhere. I stopped talking to the Idiot as we inched forward. I wanted to concentrate on every detail of the Tiananmen Gate as Chairman Mao's portrait came into view. The Idiot himself must have felt the change as well. He stuck close to me and stopped making noises. Finally, up close to the gate, I caught only fleeting glances of the rostrum between the legs of tourists. Then both of us were shooed away by guards.

"We crossed a road as wide as a river and stopped near an iron gate surrounding the Monument to the People's Heroes. There I read the inscription from Chairman Mao that I had already learned by heart: *The People's Heroes Will Live Forever.* I looked across the giant square, waiting for my feeling of triumph. I sat and waited a little longer. But it never came; I was too exhausted.

"I shut my eyes for a moment, and when I opened them the Idiot was running away from me, screaming and honking again. He returned a few moments later with a young girl. She looked about your age but was a bit fatter. She had yellow hair, which looked odd to me. She was holding the Idiot's hand.

"'Excuse me, did you come here with him?' the girl asked. 'Where did you find him?'

"'His mind has problems,' I replied. 'I don't know who he is.'

"'He says he knows you.'

"'What? He doesn't even speak human language!'

"'He says he came here with you.'

"'Who are you?'

"She told me she had been looking for the Idiot for months. He'd run away from the Stars Hotel a month ago and she hadn't seen him since. Why was I out here with him?

"I told her everything I knew, which was nothing. The girl called a taxi and the three of us headed back to the Stars Hotel. From the car, the buildings and streets flew by. In no time we were back where we started. The girl bought dumplings from across the street and sat with us, waiting for the manager to return so she could berate him.

"As we ate, I watched with some amazement as the girl 'talked' with the Idiot. Her words were slow and carefully formed — the same way I'd talked to him — yet when she told him to pick up the trash he dropped or asked whether or not he wanted water, he listened and responded. The Idiot would occasionally grab a fistful of dirt and crumbled brick and put the whole thing in his mouth, thinking it was food. She would make him spit it out, smacking him on the back, but she never yelled at him.

"She asked me a lot of questions: Where was I from? How long had I been crippled? Why was I in Beijing? It may have been the exhaustion or that I hadn't really talked with anyone in a long time, but I felt like I could trust her. She had a good heart. Before I knew better, I found myself telling her my real reason for coming to Beijing — Tiananmen Square and the end.

"Both of us watched the Idiot playing with the girl's cell phone for a few moments.

"That's when she told me the Idiot's real name: Song Gang. I should have asked her name then, but I never did.

"'Life does seem unfair,' she said. 'Some people have lives full of pain, but others' — she was gazing at the Idiot — 'they don't seem to feel it. But you don't learn anything until you're in pain. You don't understand that eating rotten food is bad for you until it makes you sick; you don't understand how much you need water until you're dying of thirst. Of course, someone could tell you about it, but that's not same as understanding it. Some people don't feel enough to understand anything.'

"'Those lucky people,' I said.

"'No, it's the opposite. You're lucky if you can feel pain.'

"'That's nonsense.'

"'We are responsible for those people, the ones who never feel it, because there is so much they will never understand. We have to look after them.'

"I just called the girl 'Little Sister.' She stayed with us until the other men began arriving in the evening. I could hear her arguing with the owner, accusing him of negligence, but I think she knew that the Stars Hotel wasn't responsible for any of us, really.

"That night, I woke up in the middle of the night, throat dry and face drenched with sweat. The Idiot was curled up next to me on my left. I laid there staring at the ceiling and suddenly remembered that I was supposed to have killed myself already. I watched the Idiot breathe for a while. I could see crimson cuts on his forehead with his bangs all swept to one side. My satchel with the *yanghua leguo* was on the other side of him, and I decided I didn't want to disturb him.

"The girl returned in the morning as promised, carrying a wooden plank with four small wheels for me, this same cart. She visited me and the Idiot at the shelter every few days for a month or so, joining me as I rolled myself farther and farther from the Stars Hotel. I started to learn the street names and cheap places to eat. The Idiot always tagged along with us. I realized after a few weeks that the two of them were the only reason I couldn't seem to go through with my original plan.

"And then one day, about a month ago, I woke up and the Idiot had disappeared. I wheeled myself around the entire neighborhood, circling the same alleyways over and over, worried what Little Sister would say when she found out. I'd lost him! I was miserable but had no idea what to do. I went to a convenience store and bought a few sweets that I knew she liked. I waited for her at the Stars Hotel that night, hoping she would appear with the Idiot, but she never did. The Idiot never came back either. I waited for them both the next day and the day after that. I waited with those sweets for a long time."

* * *

Yanmei entered the newsroom the following day, mind still reeling from Guang Fei's story. The sleek new offices of the *Evening News* were empty most days. Department heads and editors still met every morning for an eight o'clock editorial meeting, but reporters mostly filed stories from home and texted their editors. Yanmei and the five other *Evening Focus* reporters met in the office only once a week, on Wednesdays, to pitch story ideas and assign tasks. But today's meeting was special, Section Editor Deng had warned them. *Everyone be on time!* she had texted. *Tomorrow the new chief editor will join us!*

Yanmei's section, *Evening Focus*, which produced longer features, was located in the back of the newsroom. Junk mail was piled up on an open desk. There were five unused desktop computers and one landline telephone shared by the section.

"The exact same, really! Even his eyebrows!" Yuanyuan was murmuring when Yanmei put down her backpack. She was two years older than Yanmei, squat, with a short androgynous haircut. She kept a blue cartoon elephant humidifier on her desk so, from her own chair, Yanmei could see only the top of Yuanyuan's crown and a white column of steam.

"What's the same?"

Yuanyuan didn't reply, but a few moments later, once Yanmei had started up her own laptop, a message window popped open on her screen, from the other side of divide. There were two headshot photos: Ge You — Beijing's bald, ubiquitous film actor, and another man she didn't recognize.

"Look!" Yuanyuan said, emerging from the white fog and sidling up next to Yanmei. "Chief Editor Ge. The new editor!"

"Um."

"Look at them! Both surnamed *Ge*! I bet they're related somehow!"

"They don't look alike at all. Listen, Yuanyuan, we've got a few minutes before the meeting, I'd like to —"

"Annie!" Yuanyuan called.

Annie, their *Evening Focus* colleague, appeared from around the corner. She brushed a pile of unopened mail out of the way and sat on Yanmei's desk. Annie — she only went by her English name — wore tight, fashionable jeans and contact lenses that turned her eyes a creepy shade of light blue.

"*Wa!* They're the same!" she agreed.

Yanmei needed to concentrate; she had only fifteen minutes to make some sense out of the shotgun notes she'd taken of Guang Fei's story. *Look! The ears aren't right!* Yanmei slid down further in her chair. Her pitch about Guang Fei's story needed to be *clear.* That was what Section Editor Deng was always carping on. *Ge You must be older; look at those wrinkles near his eyes.*

"Hey! Can you guys just give me a second to think?" she pleaded.

Annie rolled her eyes enough that Yanmei could see the whites. "Geez, Yanmei, sorry to *bother* you."

Section Editor Deng was waiting in the conference room when Yanmei, Yuanyuan, Annie, and the others filed inside. Deng had a severe haircut and short fingernails, and affected a brusqueness in meetings meant to show that she was leading. In her late thirties, Deng was fifteen years older than any of the reporters in her section. Next to her was Editor Ge — *the* Editor Ge — in a slim-fitting pink dress shirt and navy trousers. He smiled kindly at the five assembled *Evening Focus* reporters but said nothing and was not formally introduced.

"Where's Longlong?" snapped Deng.

"She's got a thing," someone mumbled.

"Where? We are having a meeting."

Section Editor Deng stared hard at her charges, as if waiting for one of them to conjure Longlong from a corner of the conference room. She glanced at her phone, picked it up, and set it back down.

"I'm just here as an observer," Editor Ge volunteered. "I just wanted to sit in on regular meetings to get a sense of how things work."

Yanmei was last to present her story pitches. She spoke slowly, *clearly*. Her first idea was profiles of three sisters with Alzheimer's she had met recently in Beijing. Yanmei introduced some statistics she had researched from the World Health Organization, while Deng nodded carefully at each number. No one said anything when she finished. Unsure, Yanmei plowed ahead with Idea No. 2: an underground kindergarten on the outskirts of town that served children of migrant workers in Beijing. She was describing the school's abysmal conditions when Section Editor Deng cut her off.

"Yanmei, you need to think clearly about the *feasibility* of such stories," Deng said. "The ideas are fine, but they will take a lot of effort to report."

Yanmei gritted her teeth. She had tried pushing back against Deng's critiques in the past. Now, with Editor Ge sitting beside her, Yanmei knew that her boss would never praise a story idea unless it was her own.

"Okay," Yanmei soldiered on. "My last idea is a feature story about homelessness in Beijing. I found someone with an incredible story now living in a shelter. He's handicapped and came all the way from Shanxi Province with a plan to kill himself —"

"Enough! Enough!" yelled Deng. She looked at Editor Ge as though she might blush.

"Yanmei, I'm not sure what to say to you."

Yanmei waited for Deng to say it.

"Think *clearly* about these topics, Yanmei. Disease, run-down schools, suicide — are such topics really suitable for the *Evening News*? We're aiming for stories that are more ... inspiring."

"He didn't kill himself in the end," Yanmei protested. "He says someone saved his life." Deng's lips tightened into a sour expression.

In the end, Yanmei, again, was assigned stories to write for the coming week. The most pressing was a full-page spread on the best places in Beijing to eat porridge (one thousand characters). Other assignments were a calligraphy exhibit opening (three hundred characters), proper posture at the office (three exercises, two hundred characters each), and a summary of a recent Harvard psychology study (four hundred characters).

After the meeting, after Deng and the others had left the room, Yanmei lingered, jotting down her list of responsibilities. A man's voice caused her to look up. Yanmei realized with a start that Editor Ge was still sitting comfortably, straightening the corners of his notepad with his fingers.

"How long have you been here?" he asked.

"Six months. I'm a trainee journalist."

Ge nodded and smirked. He *did* look a little like Ge You. "Ah, the porridge beat."

Yanmei laughed at this.

"I came from the national affairs desk at *Global Times*," Ge said. "Before that, I worked in the South. Newspapers in Guangdong."

"*Southern Weekend*, right?" Yanmei had looked up

Editor Ge's CV online. The weekly paper had a reputation as one of China's most independent and investigative publications.

Editor Ge offered her a tight, cryptic smile and nodded. "What happened to him, the cripple?" he asked.

Yanmei was taken aback. "Well, he says someone saved his life. Two people, actually. He's still searching for them."

"Do you know who they are?"

She told him about the research and the interviews, and he nodded again. Yanmei could sense that Editor Ge was warming to the idea. She slipped a photo of "Eat Dirt" from her notebook.

"That's him, the person he's searching for. He says his name is Song Gang."

Editor Ge studied the image for what seemed like an eternity.

"Keep working on this story in your free time," he said finally. "Show it to me directly when you've got a draft together, okay?"

Yanmei felt her heart pounding with a new giddiness but she kept her voice even. They chatted a few more minutes until Yanmei's phone buzzed with new message: Deng asking where she was. They would need to start reporting immediately if they were to visit five porridge restaurants by tomorrow. She excused herself and left Editor Ge alone in the room.

Back at her desk, Yanmei told her fellow trainees nothing about her run-in with Editor Ge, despite the fact that he remained the topic of gossip for the rest of the afternoon. It was her conversation with him, replayed over and over, that buoyed her spirits as she loitered in the entrances of porridge restaurants around the city, stopping groups of confused, hungry seniors with the same question: "Hello! Sorry to interrupt. I'm a reporter with the *Beijing Evening News*. May I ask you a question? Do you prefer savory or sweet porridge?"

7

An Enthusiastic Educator

DAVID's heart started to sink just inside the frost-ed-glass entrance. Five-year-old boys chased each other up and down the orange hallways. Parents slouched on cheap plastic chairs, arms crossed, angrily sleeping. A cell phone rang and rang unanswered. He proceeded down the main hallway of Silicon Valley English, two glass walls that adjoined the classrooms. As he passed the animal posters, the writing essays plastered to the walls, the bright alphabet letters snaking above doorways, dread filled his mouth.

David hadn't stepped foot inside an English school like this for five years, not since a gig teaching oral English at a medical college on the outskirts of the city, his first job in China. He'd been nervous before classes began, sure that the bright university students would see through him and his non-existent qualifications. But

David caught on to the farce as soon as the semester began. The school's English department was a joke; there were no textbooks, no curricula, no supervision. Instead, he downloaded pro forma lesson plans and dialogues from the internet, and spent most of his classroom time kibitzing between the Cherries, Stars, and Janes, correcting their r's and w's.

Sure, there was a stigma of English teaching — any native English speaker could do it — but David didn't care. He needed some easy money. His agent refused to answer his calls, and for the past few weeks, whenever he phoned any of his TV-industry contacts, introducing himself brightly as Gao Fushuai, he got little more than confused silence on the other end.

David had already left his designer Sanlitun apartment without notifying the landlord. His new apartment, a concrete-bunker walk-up was dark and had rattling door handles. The kitchen smelled permanently of cooking oil. He had unpacked his clothes and nothing else, as if to convince himself that his stay would be temporary.

The meager proceeds from selling the "Eat Dirt" photograph were almost gone already. The buyer had been a slight, effeminate young Chinese artist with a mustache and round 1920s-style spectacles who David had found online. After the man confirmed the artist's signature in the corner of the photograph, he leaned the print next to a dozen others against the far wall of his art studio and reached into a desk drawer crammed with cash. He counted out twenty thousand yuan while David hungrily watched. Twenty thousand — less than half of what he'd originally paid.

That afternoon, back in a taxi heading toward the city

center with his pockets stuffed with cash, David stared out the window with idle, violent thoughts. How easy it would have been to smack that fucking hipster around a bit, empty the drawer into a bag, and leave. There had been no one else in the studio; no one would have seen. That money would have been enough to get him set up somewhere else, far from China.

"So, Carl says you're from America."

A prim woman in her forties was sitting across her orange desk from David. The gold plaque on her desk read "Principal Yue Qiya." Next to him, Carl, a clean-shaven Brit wearing a crisp button-down shirt, who'd posted the job ad online, sat smiling gamely. David was horrified, at first, to find himself trawling the want ads for English-teaching jobs, but he didn't know what else to do. Carl's family had a vague family emergency back in Manchester. He expected to be gone for three months, long enough for David to fill in, make a bit of money, and find his feet. Yes, it was English teaching, David thought bitterly, but at least it would be easy and temporary.

"Did you happen to bring a copy of your CV and ESL certification?" Principal Yue asked. David was caught off guard by this and told her that he had neither. He recovered somewhat, waxing about his teaching days years ago in Beijing, his methods for getting students engaged in discussions, and his favorite tongue twisters for pronunciation. Principal Yue nodded along and smiled. When he finished, she politely asked for a word alone with Carl, who looked like he'd stepped out of some brochure. David lingered outside her office for a few minutes — long enough to hear the cloying marketing video playing in the lobby repeat itself three times — while Carl and the principal presumably negotiated his candidacy.

Principal Yue called David back in and warily asked him to bring his passport and university diploma to the school the following day. She would allow him to teach a trial class — an unpaid hour of supervised teaching to assess his abilities. If he scored well enough, she'd allow him to teach at Silicon Valley English. David, teeth gritted, glanced at Carl and found him triumphant. Principal Yue presented David a binder with both hands: Adult Learning — Lesson Six.

David was ten minutes late for his eight p.m. trial class the following evening. Ten college-aged kids, a few businessmen, and Principal Yue were waiting for him in one of the hideous glass-walled rooms. He had skimmed the lesson binder in the taxi and found the topic was music. Perfect. Easy. First though, it was always good to kill fifteen minutes with introductions. David walked the rows of desks, shaking hands and grinning at each of his pupils like an unhinged politician. Principal Yue scratched something in her notebook.

"All right," David continued, clapping his hands. "Today's lesson is about music. Can you tell me what your favorite kind of music is? How about you right here? What. Kind. Of. Music. Do. You. Like?"

David became aware of the too-silent room and pressed on, asking an acne-scarred girl named Jane the same question. The pen stopped twirling in her fingers; she looked up at him with alarm. The girl sitting behind her whispered something in Chinese that David didn't catch. Soon the room was giggling.

"She said she likes you. You're a famous man. *Gao Fushuai.*"

The whole room laughed again. David felt his face begin to flush and cut them off, commanding them to practice speaking in pairs. Jesus, how much time had passed? Was this almost over? Soon, robotic chatter filled the classroom as Principal Yue sidled up to him.

"Come to my office after class."

Once she'd left, David sat on the teacher's desk, resting his legs and rubbing his eyes. The painkillers he'd taken for his headache were beginning to wear off. Suddenly he remembered the classroom's glass walls and sprung to his feet, but thankfully no one had been watching.

Principal Yue declared David "an enthusiastic educator" in her office afterward, but one who needed major improvements in his time management and lesson preparedness. She sat behind her orange desk, ticking off her classroom observations, one by one, as David gripped the armrests of his chair. Once she finished critiquing David's performance, she shifted to a more conciliatory tone, almost bashful.

"To be honest, I thought it might have been you, but I wasn't sure. On television, you were always wearing Western suits, so I didn't recognize you. So, will you be filming again soon?"

David knew what he had to say. He loathed it, loathed himself, but he was desperate. He was down to his last few hundred kuai. He was exhausted and humiliated, and his head was pounding. This was his only job lead, and he wasn't sure if Principal Yue might still take it away. Since when had English schools been so fucking demanding?

"Honestly, I just realized that I missed being in the classroom," he said. "I'm not going back to television." David smiled across the orange desk, his cheesy stage-actor smile.

Principal Yue smiled back. She was willing to give David a chance, though he'd need to teach two unpaid classes, supervised by a more experienced teacher, which would be a great opportunity for him to improve his "in-class tool kit." Did he have any questions or comments for her? David was fuming but only thanked Principal Yue for her keen observations and vowed to do better next time. They shook hands. He would start on Wednesday.

* * *

David left Silicon Valley English with less a thirst for beer than an urge to flood himself with it. He climbed into a taxi and instinctively told the driver to head toward the Sanlitun bar district. It wasn't until he began texting a few friends en route — Trish, Phil, Marco, James — that something tripped a wire and he remembered his solemn thirtieth-birthday vow from two months ago. Start a new life, a new decade. Why had he just thought of that? David paused, phone in hand, looking out the taxi windshield, searching the landscape for guidance. Then he dialed his friends. His new life could wait.

Sanlitun Back Street was doing its usual Friday-night glowing and writhing when David arrived at the south entrance. The street was a jumble of shabby bars and massage joints built on top of each other, all pushed out of eyesight from the nearby shiny shopping malls embarrassed by it. The main drag was always packed. David pushed his way slowly through the groups of high school students, girls shrieking through windows, a couple fighting on the curb, a guy sitting on the sidewalk near a pile of vomit, a table of Africans in suits and cravats smoking thick cigars, women selling balloons, women selling roses, three old white men sitting on a balcony, singing a Queen song. Mani Pedi. Tarot Reading. Mojito Man. *Vietnamese Food! DVD!* The smell of chicken grease and stale beer on concrete.

Even as a dive bar, Baller Bar was bland. The main clientele was underage American kids from international high schools and ex-fraternity brothers still clinging to their frayed ball caps. The tabletops were streaked with carved initials, and American movie posters lined the wall. Above the doorway, the bar's motto "Ball So Hard!" was spray-painted in dark blue. Yet, of all the bars David could think of, Baller Bar still had the cheapest drinks, only fifteen kuai for a Beijing draft, the same price as the year he arrived in the city; there was a small comfort in that.

The group was already assembled around a dark wooden booth when David arrived, unwinding his scarf. A fizzing beer was already waiting for him on the table. He sat down without acknowledgment.

"But if you *know* that ninety percent of all liquor in Beijing is fake, how can you still drink it?" Phil was saying.

"You would rather drink *Yanjing Beer*, which is made with *tap water*, than fake alcohol?" said Marco. "At least with whisky you know that the bacteria have been killed."

"But at least your body *digests* bacteria. Think of the

chemicals that go into fake alcohol — mercury, lead, formaldehyde, probably."

Marco was just about to start his rebuttal when Trish cut him off.

"Look, David's here. David? What do you have to say for yourself?"

David had known Trish since his second year in Beijing, when the two had lived as roommates in a two-bedroom walk-up near Beixinqiao. She was a stout West Londoner with a handsome face that seemed to attract balding graduate students. They had bonded years ago over Thursday wine nights at home, which coincided with the end of Trish's work week at her kindergarten-teaching job (David was never needed in the studio before noon).

Trish was a legendary complainer — she hated the kids, the parents, the school and its cheery stickers — and her horror stories grew wittier and more acerbic on the second bottle. Trish could be a damn funny drunk. She also had a habit of holding court, surrounded by inferior men, and calling on them to speak like the teacher she was. She was the closest thing David had to a sister in the city.

"Let's drink up," David remarked.

He drained the contents of his glass and wiped the foam from his mouth with the back of his hand. There was zero chance he would tell any of them about what had happened at the TV show, moving apartments, the English school. Especially the English school. It was true that David had been seeing more of Trish and her cohort this past year; he had been too busy before then. They weren't a glamorous bunch, and none of them spoke

Chinese like he did. He liked telling them stories from the front lines of China's show business industry though, watching their faces light up with admiration and envy.

"Christ, you've got that look of destruction tonight," Trish observed. "Can we at least go down to that new cocktail bar, Mirella? This place," she looked around for effect, "I think I got herpes the moment I sat down."

"*Can* you get herpes twice?" Phil wondered aloud.

Everyone laughed at this but David.

"Go anywhere you want, but I'm staying," he said. "Anyone else ready for one?"

"Charming," Trish said, as David walked away. "I'm counting on you then, James. Give me something interesting or I'm leaving. You drunks are a waste of my time."

As he elbowed his way through the crowd for a fresh beer, David's resolve began to weaken. He suddenly didn't want to be here, didn't want to be around other people, didn't want the hassle of socializing and eye contact. By the time he returned to the table, his friends would be talking about work — their well-paid jobs in PR, media, and the arts. All of them had boring, steady desk jobs. Even Trish, a fucking kindergarten teacher, had been to the Philippines since the last time he saw her. Where had he been? What had he done?

He stepped outside and bummed a cigarette from a young migrant selling pineapple on a stick. Young girls with astonishing legs passed by; an old woman selling roses pestered a table across the road. What was he still doing in this hellhole? David stood smoking, gazing out onto the bedlam of Bar Street awhile longer, ransacking his brain for somewhere else to go, something else to do, but he couldn't think of anything. He dialed Cindy's phone number, but again there was no answer. David stamped out his butt and walked back inside, feeling more than ever like a ghost.

"Look, sure they *could* clean up the air when they really want to," Marco was saying, two hours later. "But it's not like there's some giant weather switch in Zhongnanhai labeled 'rain,' that's what I'm saying."

"You don't think it's a coincidence that it rains on June fourth every year? Or that the sky magically turns blue when there's an important delegation in town?" said David.

"If it was so easy, then why isn't every day beautiful?" said Trish.

David shrugged. He fingered the ring of foam left over from his fifth beer on the table. Baller Bar's brick walls seemed softer now, the room warmer.

"China doesn't want to clean up the air. Why cut off the pollution? It's big business. The coal plants and carmakers sell the problem. The green companies and hospitals sell the solution. And the government gets its cut of all of it. Who makes money when there's no problem?"

"Well, they've got to do something. People are fed up," said Marco, landing a fresh clutch of beers on the table. "They're going to start demanding clean air and clean food. It doesn't matter how much money the government is making then, if they lose the people. Did you guys see that *New Yorker* article about the woman who was locked up for doing lung exams in Hebei?"

"Another dissident bites the dust," David sniffed. He rotated his mug until the handle was at a satisfactory angle.

"No, she's American," said Marco. "They've had her locked up in some black jail for over a month. The embassy is freaking out."

As Marco sketched more details of the poor woman's case, the four expats took solemn drinks of beer, imagining themselves in her place.

"I'm telling you, we've outstayed our welcome," said David finally. "Look around. Cops knocking on our doors to check paperwork. Drug raids at the big expat bars. Visa crackdowns. They don't want us here anymore."

"God, here we go," said Trish. "No, China doesn't want *this*. Bar Street. They don't want drunk foreigners pissing in the streets."

"It's more than that," David countered. "Look, I'm not saying that we're going to be rounded up and put on trains; it's just that, you know, if times really turned dark.... Say, war broke out and the nationalism got really out of hand. Would you really trust your Chinese friends? You don't think they'd turn on you in a second? We'll never be accepted; we'll never be safe here."

"Yeah, David. You're such a pariah," she said. "All those sixteen-year-old girls that watch you on TV. Bashing your door down with selfie sticks."

"It's not just expats," Marco put in. "*No one* in this country feels safe. Kids buy houses they can't afford. Parents don't trust the baby formula. Corrupt officials send their families to Canada. Nobody trusts the government. No one feels secure. And why should they? Look at the history. The last fifty years of this pl—"

"No," David cut him off. "It's not the history." A parade of images materialized in front of him: Cindy's face, Principal Yue's orange desk, that fucking hipster artist, the entitled English students twirling their pens. They had ruined this city, he knew, made it so superficial and expensive and fake.

"No one feels safe because there *is* nothing to trust here. None of this is built on anything!" He must have been yelling, because he saw Trish look around for him, embarrassed.

"There's no structure, no security. And the reason there's no structure is because Chinese people don't care about ideas; they don't trust ideas to protect them. They're realists; they're *pragmatic.* Everyone celebrates that. Deng Xiaoping. The black or white cat. The stones across the river. Blah, blah, blah. Feeling the goddamn stones across the river is just another way of saying you have no idea where you're going.

"Everyone wants to be rich and powerful here, but no one asks why. You're not supposed to ask why, not supposed to ask where all these stones are leading. Just get rich. Just make enough money to protect yourself. Mistrust — *that* is the real incentive to get rich in China, not greed or materialism or ambition. You get rich and powerful or you get fucked. It's always been like that here, back to the emperors. You roll your eyes, but I'm serious, Trish."

"Did I say anything?"

"That look."

"It's just ... that's quite a speech coming from someone who was praising the government a few months ago."

"Praising the government? Oh, give me a fucking break. That was on TV."

"What about that article you sent me, the one about 'what if the U.S. had a one-party system'?"

"That's different."

"Whatever, I get it. China's a moral wasteland, et cetera, et cetera. Your outrage is noted."

* * *

An hour later the two of them stood together at an intersection, waving at passing taxis. David had said little in the last hour; his tirade had worn him out, and his mind was elsewhere. He could feel Trish's worried gaze on his shoulders as he cursed at yet another taxi that zoomed by.

"Maybe we should go down there," said Trish, pointing to the next intersection. Another taxi approached, slowed, and then sped off without them. The tails of David's dress shirt were pulled out, and the leather strap of his faux-leather briefcase dug into the back of his neck.

"It feels like we haven't talked in ages. I worry about you, you know," Trish said.

"I'm fine."

"Because you seem, I don't know, moodier. You're sure everything is all right?"

"The ranting."

"No, that's still pretty entertaining. It's just ... I don't know."

"How much longer are you going to stay here?" David asked, suddenly.

"In Beijing?"

"Yeah."

"Well, I've still got more than a year on my contract. I have some time to think about it."

"Do you ever feel like you're becoming one of those

people, one of those expats that talks about leaving all the time but never does? You just stay here and be bitter and complain about the pollution and traffic and bullshit politics."

"We're talking about me here?" she smiled. David gazed off toward the street. "Look, we *can* leave anytime we want to. It's not like we're trapped."

David was still looking off at some indistinct point in the distance.

"You know that feeling you get when you're standing on the subway platform," he said, "right before the train arrives — that angst, that crazy fear you might suddenly jump in front of it for no reason. Not that you want to, but that you're capable of doing it. There's nothing stopping you."

"Well, if it was *rush* hour...."

"Dammit, I'm being serious. We never jump, you know? We tell ourselves that we *could* do it, but we never do. We always hold back. Doesn't that mean something?"

"It means we don't want to die?" Unease crept into the final syllable, making it sound like a question. They continued walking, and when David didn't respond, she spoke up again.

"So, we're afraid of leaving China, that's what you're saying."

"I'm saying that we tell ourselves that we can leave anytime but it's not true. We *are* trapped here, but not for any diplomatic reason; we're trapped by something else. And we make it worse telling ourselves that we're free."

"God, that's pretty dramatic, David, even for you."

As Trish said this, a taxi finally pulled up to the curb and they both climbed in — David first, since he lived farther away. Here, sitting next to him, Trish could see the fine creases of his rumpled dress shirt and wayward strands of his wild hair, and she felt a touch of remorse for being so sarcastic. David's head lolled backward against the headrest, eyes half-lidded. He looked miserable. They rode through the wide, empty streets without speaking, only listening to the murmuring radio call-in show up front — a woman giving relationship advice in a low, buttery voice.

"Love is not just a feeling; love is a choice," she was saying.

Each time the woman on the radio finished a thought, an absolute silence hung in the car. Trish glanced over at David to see if he was listening; but his eyes were closed, mouth open. Funny, she never pegged him for a quiet sleeper.

8

Phoenix City

ONE of the first things Panzi's mother made him do when he moved into a new apartment was hang a cheap red-bordered portrait of Zao Jun, the Kitchen God, on the wall. Real homebuyers, unlike investors, always spent the most time in kitchens when they visited a property. They lingered there, not just to ask questions about appliances and counter space, but to truly imagine daily life — to sniff the air for future meals. It was a room of childhood memories and half-remembered advertisements. It didn't matter that Zao Jun was a drunk, a wastrel, a suicide — no one remembered that. The Kitchen God represented something else, and Panzi's mother knew it. He surveyed his domain, Technicolor gown flowing, and promised these uprooted families that at least here, next to the fire, nothing had changed.

The Kitchen God arrived at Phoenix City in mid-April.

The complex, whose full name was "Phoenix City: Phase I: The Sunrise," was a forest of identical ash-gray towers on the outskirts of the city. From the eighteenth floor, Panzi had a view of the dried-up pond and anemic willow trees that ringed it. The complex was five years old but felt older; none of the apartment's doors closed properly; the wooden floorboards were already buckled. Across the empty six-lane road, cranes and bulldozers were in constant motion, busy with what the scale model downstairs promised as "Phoenix City: Phase II: The Sunset."

There was nowhere to go without a car. A fifteen-minute walk could get you to a strip of dusty, makeshift shops selling bags of cement, cigarettes, snacks, and cheap mops and brooms. Panzi passed the days curled up on the plastic-wrapped sofa, reading novels and checking online bulletin boards on his cell phone's tiny glowing screen. Somewhere below, in the bowels of the building, the clang and whirr of renovation projects began each morning at seven. In the afternoons, he ventured out for instant noodles and fruit, before returning to watch the sun struggle across the grime-streaked windows in the living room.

He had canvassed every classmate he knew for information about Xiao Song but had gotten nowhere. Someone had heard her family had moved away from Beijing years ago, down to Hainan for her father's work. Another claimed both her parents had died; why else had she disappeared from their school after grade five? Panzi tried to piece these bits of information together like broken tiles of a mosaic, but no image ever emerged.

Online, his classmates called Xiao Song "Dumb Cat,"

the nickname she earned in primary school spending her recesses alone, crawling on her hands and knees, meowing at no one. Panzi sometimes woke up in the corner of the large, bare bed he slept on at Phoenix City thinking about this little girl. He remembered following the other boys in his class, terrorizing Xiao Song every day after lunch. Once, one of his classmates managed to loop a string under her Young Pioneers red bandana, the one they all wore, and prance behind her with a makeshift leash. "Walk faster, Dumb Cat!" her new owner commanded. They all howled at that one, Panzi too. But he also remembered how it was always unsatisfying to tease Xiao Song, because she never seemed to notice them. She seemed alone then, in her own world.

He'd thrown Xiao Song's pink backpack away, but Panzi still expected to see a pair of her high heels tossed near the welcome mat each time he returned to Phoenix City. He heard her singing in the shower, saw her chatting with restaurant owners out of the corner of his eye. These visions made him feel even worse; even if she were alive somewhere in the city, how would she ever find him here in this isolated wasteland? Still, he dialed Xiao Song's phone number every few days just to make sure it was still turned off. He kept her ID card in his front pocket, its unchanging photo a steadying force.

Panzi kept the apartment clean and unlived-in for the prospective buyers who visited every few days on short notice. He had a sales pitch — the lines he always used on first-time buyers, newlyweds, rural transplants. But after three weeks on this desolate, lifeless planet, Panzi couldn't muster them. He fumbled easy answers, as if trying to sabotage his own sale. Phoenix City was a huge step up in the world for many of the families, he knew, but he still didn't want them to live here. He didn't want *anyone* to live here. There was nothing for the Kitchen God to do but look on, helpless.

The arrival of his loneliness became part of Panzi's routine at Phoenix City. It gathered around him at dusk and whispered to him on the couch. He would never leave this room, would never find Xiao Song, it said. He was defective, just like his father, fated to remain alone. The voice seemed poised to say more, but whenever he started to hear it, Panzi fled downstairs, past the row of dusty, makeshift shops until he saw the red-and-white neon sign: internet bar.

It was proximity to people, even if they were strangers. One evening, he ducked inside the quiet, smoke-filled lair, walking by rows of young faces lit pale by computer light until he found an open seat near the far wall. A cigarette smoldered next to the mousing hand of a teenager next to him slaughtering waves of orcs with a glittering sword. The room was quiet save for an excitable virtual game show host shouting a stream of encouragement in English from somewhere: "Great shot! Perfect! You've got it!" On the wall above Panzi, an anime poster read: Do What's Never Been Done.

Panzi logged on and started an episode of a history documentary he liked.

He couldn't remember ever being alone back when he was still in school and living at home. There were always adult hands and faces surrounding him, looking over his shoulder, watching his every move. Every meal with Mother and Grandpa was huddled around a squat wooden table that had been pushed into the middle of the room. Panzi copied out his homework assignments at the same table while his grandfather listened to Shan Tianfang tell Three Kingdom stories on the radio. Panzi was an only child — he had his own desk, his own room. But he preferred the noise and commotion of family.

In the years after his father's death, Mom and Grandpa always headed off his bouts of sadness. They stormed into his room when they heard him crying in bed; they pounded on the bathroom door if he'd been inside for a suspiciously long time. Panzi was not allowed to be alone, not allowed to feel sad. There was no voice. There was only the passing of days.

One afternoon, when Panzi was nine, a boy at school called him a name and there was a fight. The boy was a grade older and the fight lasted less than a minute. *Go look on the streets for your dad, Dog Bastard, see if you can find him there*, the boy spat at Panzi as he sauntered away. Panzi sat on the street, holding his bleeding lip, and as he beat the dust off his pants and wiped away the tears, the oddest feeling came over him: the physical pain was real. He was feeling something.

"I *hate* Dad," Panzi complained to his mother that night, kicking in bed.

"Don't say that."

"They think I'm some kind of freak because of what he did."

She placed a hand on Panzi's shoulder. "You shouldn't think about that. Now, come on. Dinner's ready."

"I'm not hungry."

"Well, you're not staying here," she said briskly. "You're going to come sit with us." She stood up and the bed creaked.

"Do *you* hate him?" Panzi asked, looking up at her.

"You shouldn't think about it," she repeated. "Now, come on."

At home, there was always another meal, another homework assignment, another television show to distract him. But all that ended abruptly once Panzi started to work, two years ago, at eighteen. Since then, he'd bounced around the city, apartment to apartment, more or less alone.

At first the sense of freedom and constant movement was intoxicating. Whole apartments to himself! When he moved into a new unit, Panzi slept in a different bedroom every night. He woke early to novel sounds and learned the rhythms of neighborhoods — Maizidian, Fengtai Garden, Zhongguancun. Each apartment unit became a home; he liked to imagine where on the sofa he would curl up with his wife, imagine in which corner his daughter would practice piano.

But the fantasies slipped away; the houses became less haunted. The job became a steady procession of empty rooms and meals alone. A building crane. A car alarm. The pounding of renovation. The voice.

His high school classmates, all off at university now, rarely called. Occasionally a group of them got together for a meal to talk about, what else, university. They were all invariably anxious about finding jobs, buying houses, finding spouses. They complained about the lives they hadn't yet started. How nice it must be for Panzi! He knew they resented him — the college entrance exam failure with the most plum life of all — and that was why he hardly ever saw them.

Panzi slouched down in his seat at the internet cafe

and rubbed his eyes, still unwilling to return to Phoenix City. There were websites for chatting with strangers online, he knew. It might have been a solution, but Panzi could never seem to bring himself to log on — all the flashing icons, juggling of conversations, and awkwardness of introductions never seemed worth the effort. That was Panzi's dilemma: he didn't want to make friends; he wanted only old friends. And now he didn't even care about old friends; he wanted only Xiao Song.

Panzi looked down the row of computers and saw a number of people now asleep, earphones wrapped around their necks, their TV shows still blithely flashing onward. Before restarting his documentary, he glanced at the screen of the next computer over. The high schooler was still awake, still deep in some magical battle for meaningless points.

* * *

Panzi's mother, Qinyan, tapped her fingers lightly on the steering wheel of her Volkswagen Golf. She'd just finished her day's allotment of her favorite motivational speaker and was listening to light piano music murmuring over the air conditioning, a little treat for herself.

She glanced at the dashboard clock; still plenty of time. *She'd* be there with plenty of time to spare. Maybe she should call Panzi to make sure he wasn't running late. What if he forgot their appointment altogether?

Qinyan tapped her fingers again. No, stay calm; stay positive, like the tapes said. She glanced at herself in the mirror and smiled. Look, Panzi had agreed to start studying English again; that was clearly a positive sign!

Such a clever boy, so talented, she sighed. Most parents shied away from praising their kids, but Qinyan found this, like all superstitions, distasteful. No, you had to face the truth; no false modesty. If Panzi was the best violin player in the class, then she would tell him! What nonsense pretending it wasn't so!

But, yes, there were negative facts too. She could admit them! It was true that Panzi had a lazy streak, though she was sure he'd gotten it from his father. Qinyan had always needed an outlet for her enthusiasm — a classroom monitor in primary school and her school's loudest wailer at Chairman Mao's funeral in 1976. Years later, when she was on maternity leave from the milk factory, Qinyan wove so many baby outfits for Panzi that he hardly wore the same clothes twice. The walls of her apartment were still crowded with her embroidered cats. Five years ago, she'd discovered the most lucrative application of energies yet: flipping apartment units across the capital.

But you can't just magically transfer these abilities to your children. You can only focus on the positive. And, well, yes, now that she thought about it, that was negative fact number two: Panzi did not focus on the positive. He had a tendency to sulk. Like his father, again. Panzi's teenage years were full of brooding — closed bedroom doors and grunted conversations; it worried her so much. What was all that moroseness going to accomplish? that's what she wanted to know. She couldn't understand, he'd said. Couldn't understand what, exactly?

Qinyan glanced at the dashboard clock again. Positive. More than anything, she wanted to help Panzi. But it was like Old Li liked to tell her: you can't live the boy's life for him. But she would do such a great job! Ha ha. Even during that miserable last year of high school, when he was preparing for his disastrous college entrance exam, when she had to leave his dinner outside the bedroom door, like a prisoner, because he refused to talk to her — Qinyan liked to think her effort meant something, that he'd thank her one day. A mother mustn't give up! When your child smashes the egg timer you've set up for him, a good mother goes out and buys a new one.

This English class would be good for Panzi, she thought. They would close on the Phoenix City property in a week or so — it had certainly taken him long enough to make that sale! — and then Panzi would spend some more time at home, with her. English would be good for him, take his mind off his troubles. Well, not that she knew much about them anyway, his troubles. He never talked to her about anything, especially about that girlfriend of his who broke up with him. Yes, getting back in the classroom again would have a good influence, give him a bit of structure. Who knows, maybe Panzi would get inspired to start studying for the college entrance exam again!

But English first. Qinyan had found a special trial promotion at Silicon Valley English, a language school with branches throughout the city. She'd already bought Panzi a pile of books with titles like *Business English for the Future* and *China Real Estate Law: A Compilation*; but they never left the apartment with her son. Qinyan herself had studied a bit of Russian during her patchy school career, and she'd read a magazine article that said English was three times easier to learn than Russian.

And for a clever boy like Panzi, it should take only six months if he really applied himself.

And then, yes, there were the business considerations of having her son speak English. Qinyan pictured the gray-haired Europeans that lived on Zhuangta Alley. Whenever she ran into them at the Gongmenkou wet market, she liked to linger near the tomatoes, overhearing how the foreigners never managed to haggle down the price of vegetables. They didn't even return their empty Yanjing Beer bottles to the neighborhood store for their refund deposits! Once Qinyan learned what the Europeans paid to rent their largely un-renovated courtyard house, she grew adamant. Foreigners overpaid for everything! And she was losing out. Someday, she thought, Chinese people would have as much money as foreigners and maybe then they too could afford to be so extravagant.

Sure, she had money, about 16,530,000 yuan in the bank at last check, but that was not a lot of money, not by Beijing standards. Look at the true property developers like Wang Jianlin and Pan Shiyi — they were billionaires! Maybe if she had had better family connections or had gotten started earlier, she could have.... No, what would she even *do* with all that money, Qinyan thought excitedly. She allowed herself a few luxuries — a bottle of Chanel No. 5 perfume, a Louis Vuitton handbag, Lancôme facial moisturizer — and felt a pang of guilt after each purchase. She didn't *need* any of it. She might get sick, after all, and you'd be surprised how fast the greedy hospitals are once you're stuck there.

Qinyan pulled her sedan smartly into one of the school's parking spots stenciled off in yellow. Once she'd paid the attendant with a crisp ten-yuan note through the window, she reached for the small bottle of Chanel she kept in the center console. So expensive, this foreign perfume, but so fragrant! She sprayed and rubbed her wrists together, just like the woman in the Hong Kong duty free shop had showed her. The smell of sandalwood and vanilla filled the quiet car. There, she breathed. Now she was ready to go.

To her surprise, Panzi was waiting in one of the padded chairs when she arrived in the lobby.

"You're here."

"I'm here."

"How long did it take you to get here?"

"About an hour, more or less."

He looked thin, too thin for Qinyan's liking, so she told him. No, he hadn't changed, he insisted. Yes, of course he'd eaten. So odd, Qinyan thought, talking to my own son like an acquaintance. But it was marginally true; they had hardly spoken in weeks. Her boy wasn't just thinner, but darker and older somehow as well. He slouched, head bobbing forward, and she could see his spine protruding from his neck. White hairs had sprouted behind his ears. Panzi was starting to look a bit like ... but Qinyan banished the thought.

"Panzi?" said a smiling young girl in a pink polo shirt now standing in front of them. "My name is Cherry," she said brightly in English. "You can come with me."

Qinyan stood up with him.

"Oh, hello there." The girl hadn't registered that Qinyan was with him. "Great! Please follow me."

They passed through a glass-walled hallway and into a glass-walled room. They arranged themselves around a glass table. She welcomed them both and fanned the results of Panzi's English placement assessment on the surface. Cherry sprinkled her sales pitch with English words, usually the word "English" itself.

"So, we're here today to create a tailored *action plan* for you to realize all of your *English goals!*" Panzi slouched a little further into the chair. "I understand that you are primarily interested in our twenty-first century business *English* course." When Panzi didn't offer an audible response, Cherry ventured a look toward Qinyan, who was nodding vigorously.

"That's great!" Cherry enthused. "Based on our scientific assessment of Panzi, we'd would recommend him begin his *English journey* with our *basic English* and move on to *business English* after that." She made it through about four color bar charts on the paper before Qinyan cut her off.

"Well, that result doesn't sound right to me," she blurted out, meaning it did not square with her six-month timeline for Panzi. "My son studied at one of Beijing's best high schools, No. 23, and with foreign teachers. He can speak a lot of English already." Panzi sat next to her with his hands in his lap. A tight smile was fixed on Cherry's face.

"I think your son would benefit most if he were placed according to this assessment."

"Panzi, say something in English," his mother goaded. "C'mon! Quickly!" Cherry looked at him, embarrassed. Panzi said the first memorized phrase that popped into his head.

"The mosquitoes are most unfortunate, but I suppose nothing can be done," he said, in a cracked voice.

"You see?" Qinyan triumphed. "What can most people say in English? Halloo? Halloo? Nice-a to meet you!"

Cherry nodded slightly and looked down at the table, a gesture Panzi had seen a thousand times watching his mother negotiate apartment prices with buyers. It was a look of early capitulation. Cherry would resist awhile longer, point at a few more charts, but Panzi could tell she wouldn't last. His mother would never back down.

* * *

The girl who sat in front of Panzi in Business English, Rebecca, had failed the IELTS proficiency test at least once already. She kept a battered test prep book that was covered in red circles open on her lap during class. Panzi seemed to be the only one in class without an IELTS or TOEFL mock exam book close at hand.

Panzi and Rebecca were conversation partners, which meant he was the one she complained to about having less than a month to pass her test if she was going to make it to Britain for graduate school in the fall. She seemed to like that better than what they were supposed to be doing in class — parroting bits of dialogue back and forth about U.S. tourist sites and dated pop-culture figures.

Rebecca's spoken English wasn't bad — much better than Panzi's anyway — but she was usually too distracted or annoyed to finish their exchanges about Wall Street and Star Wars and the Alamo. How was Mount Rushmore going to help her get to London, she demanded? It was just some dumb sculpture on the wrong side of the ocean.

Their instructor, Teacher David, also wasn't from England, the first of his many flaws, according to Rebecca. He couldn't read the phonetic alphabet. He couldn't explain when *fish* was a countable noun either. Undaunted, she often approached Teacher David's desk during the fifteen-minute break between hours of class to ask him questions about commas. Panzi couldn't hear these exchanges, but he spied on the pair from his desk, watching how frustrated they grew with each other. Rebecca would narrow her eyes, stabbing her textbook with a finger while David waved his hands, eyes pinned to the wall clock. Neither of them wanted to deal with the other, but they seemed to have no choice.

Since Panzi wasn't under some extreme testing deadline, he didn't find Teacher David that offensive. He reminded Panzi of his American teachers in high school, who similarly fumbled over diagraming sentences but were generally friendly and open. Back in high school, English was Panzi's favorite subject despite terrible grades. He had studied it for eight years, which had meant memorizing endless lists of vocabulary.

Teacher David had a mop of frizzy light-brown hair that bobbed above his head like a cloud and shivered when he pantomimed dialogues in character. He arrived at the classroom (late, always) in a bulky brown coat that reminded Panzi of a caveman illustration he'd once seen as a child — shoulders heavy with animal skins.

"Clean ... tech ... nology ... is a ... lyn ... ch ... pin of —"

"Not *clean* technology," Rebecca snapped at him during dialogue practice. "*Green* technology."

Panzi was repeating the line again when Teacher David appeared next to him to listen. Up close, he could see dark circles under Teacher David's eyes. He looked ragged, worn down, as if returning back to the village empty-handed from the hunt.

"Teck-nah-lo-GEE," the teacher said. "Teck-nah-lo-GEE," Panzi repeated.

"He's not even a real teacher, you know," Rebecca groused to Panzi when Teacher David had wandered away again. "He's a foreign actor. He was on TV."

Panzi looked up and studied his teacher anew. Had he seen him somewhere before? Teacher David was engrossed in a newspaper, fingers twirling a lock of hair. He seemed pained. Panzi wasn't sure David was reading at all; he seemed to be only staring vacantly at the newsprint. When class ended at ten p.m., Teacher David remained fixed at his desk rather than bolting out the glass door as usual. Panzi gathered his books and papers slowly so that only the two of them remained in the classroom. Panzi had never really talked with his teacher one-on-one, but something tugged him toward David's desk.

"Teacher David, are you okay?"

He looked up at his pupil with a dreamy expression.

"Fine, fine," David replied in Chinese.

Panzi was relieved to switch languages. "What are you reading?"

"It's nothing."

Panzi read the headline of the two-page spread, upside down: "Searching for Song Gang."

"Your Chinese is very good," Panzi mustered. When David didn't respond to this comment, Panzi tried again. "Is it a good article?"

"I don't know. What's your question?"

"Oh, I don't have a question." Panzi waited a moment and then took a step toward the door. He stopped when he heard David's voice again.

"This photograph. I owned it. It was mine."

Panzi turned the paper right-side up and studied the image on the opposite page. It was a strange-looking beggar. Panzi leaned forward, looking at the man's face — his maniacal grin, his neat, boyish haircut, and a bowl of dirt held up to his mouth.

"Oh. I didn't know you were a photographer."

David's face reddened. "I didn't take the picture. A professional did. It's called 'Eat Dirt.'"

Panzi stood next to the desk and listened to David explain how he had bought the print two years ago, for seventy thousand yuan at a gallery in the 798 Art District. He'd just sold it, at a loss, back to the same gallery. And now it was in the newspaper. How the hell had that happened? Panzi said he didn't know. The way David spoke — the exact figures, the angry questions — gave Panzi the impression that he was the first person to hear them. He felt slightly embarrassed for his teacher.

"A photograph of a beggar was worth seventy thousand yuan?" Panzi asked, incredulous.

"Probably not."

"Why did you buy it, then?"

"I don't know," David sighed. "I just liked it. It made me feel something. I wasn't planning on selling it later on."

"I see."

They remained on either side of the desk — David sitting, Panzi standing — both staring at the photograph, as if the man in the photograph might speak. Instead, David's cell phone rang. He answered it, gesturing goodbye as he left the classroom. Panzi could hear David's voice ricocheting down the darkened glass hallway as he walked away.

There was something accusatory, even confrontational about the beggar's smile. *Go ahead and look*, it seemed to say. *I'm down here eating dirt so you don't have to.* Panzi's eyes wandered across the columns of text until he found himself at the beginning of the article. He sat down and started to read, slowly, taking steady breaths as the Cripple made his journey to Tiananmen Square. Every once in a while, Panzi looked up into the silent, motionless classroom to see if someone had arrived to kick him out, but he was always alone.

The three accompanying articles, all with bylines by someone named Liu Yanmei, were arranged around the picture of the Idiot staring dead ahead with his bowl of dirt. Along the right edge of the layout, there were infographics about homelessness and mental illness. In the upper-left corner, just below the headline of the main article, there was a small inset picture of Guang Fei on his wooden cart staring off the page, still in search of the man who "saved" his life.

Before picking up the story again, Panzi glanced back over to check on the unblinking Idiot. When the Idiot made his appearance in the story, Panzi looked at the photograph again. When he reached the description of the girl who had recognized the Idiot on Tiananmen Square that day — white dress, blonde hair — Panzi stopped and looked up at the glass walls once more. He took a few more shallow breaths and wrestled down a wild thought. He looked back at the Idiot, his stare still unbroken. Then he read the next line in the article:

She said that you're lucky if you can feel pain. You have to look after those who can't.

Panzi realized with an instant, shaking panic that the words were Xiao Song's. He heard her voice, saw her sitting on the ledge of Capital Mansions. She *said* these exact words!

The glass door creaked, and Panzi jumped to his feet.

"Still here?" Cherry was standing in the half-darkened doorway. "Time to go home. It's late."

Panzi nodded in her direction but kept his hands on the desk, trying to steady his trembling body.

"Yes, I'm going. I'm going."

But he lingered a little while longer once Cherry had gone. The Idiot kept his fixed, cockeyed gaze until Panzi folded the newspaper and stashed it in his backpack.

9

At the Lotus Club

THE Lotus Club had lost its aquarium tables decades ago, but the Boss of Houhai still remembered them every time he banqueted there. In the early nineties, back when the place was known as Magnificent Wave, the tables — hulking glass cylinders stocked with nurse sharks — provided just the spectacle and ostentation that a formal gathering demanded.

Mr. Bai, the owner of Magnificent Wave, didn't bother regularly cleaning the tanks, so you could never see much of the listless beasts circling in the murky water. Visiting cadres in town on junkets to the capital would titter in delight nonetheless. They rapped on the glass and shouted at the sharks and stomped their butts into nicotine-grime grooves in the white-tile flooring. Magnificent Wave served hearty northeastern fare and never had a slow night.

But that was more than twenty years and three Party crackdowns ago. Once the campaign against "conspicuous consumption" was launched, Mr. Bai had no choice but to relegate the shark tables to a few special private rooms. That compromise lasted another four years until the edict on "excessive entertainment" banished the remaining tables to the trash heap. Business waned. Mr. Bai sold the place and returned to Harbin.

A new management team flew in a Hong Kong chef and rebranded as an upscale seafood restaurant, affixing a giant neon shrimp to the gray brick wall facing Beilitu Road. Glorious Shrimp did very well for a while; the Boss was a regular, holding court over raucous banquets that went on until the floor was covered in fish bones. There were whispers that the restaurant did *too* well, so well that one of the investors fled to Hong Kong with the company's seals and bank account details.

That was around the time of the "strengthening the motherland's culture" initiative, which probably would have been the end of Glorious Shrimp anyway. Traditional courtyard architecture was to be venerated, the Party had decided. The building lay fallow another two years — weeds sprouting in the cracks of the courtyard's cobblestones — before it was reincarnated again as a handsome Qing-era private club — the Lotus Club.

The new-old Lotus Club was understated and historically reverent. It had only one large dining room, at the north side of the courtyard, appointed with high-backed rosewood chairs and soapstone panels, circular wooden doorways, reproductions of "running grass" calligraphy scrolls. Water burbled. *Erhu* music whined from hidden speakers. Compared to its aquarium days, the Lotus Club served a third of the people and made ten times the money.

"What do brass hinges sell for these days?" the Boss asked Hou Dexin, the man next to him.

The two men sat together inside the entrance, near a display of luxury car magazines. The Boss's eyes had been scanning the walls as he tried to remember how much he'd profited brokering construction supplies to the club's owner during the latest renovation years ago — not a small project. What was it, seven years ago? Eight? There were margins in the doors, the Boss remembered that at least. His company had installed eight of them leading to the courtyard.

"Barely anything. The sub-contractor handles all that," replied Dexin. His head was bowed toward the glow of his cell phone clock. Bits of sunflower seed husks covered his lap. He was in his early forties and had long eyebrows with hairs that quivered when he was nervous.

"They're late. You're sure you said seven o'clock?" Dexin asked.

Five kuai apiece, maybe? Prices must have doubled since then though. The Boss lit a cigarette and ignored the question from his brother-in-law.

"What kind of contractor doesn't know the price of his building materials?"

Dexin was bouncing his leg up and down on the ball of his foot. He wouldn't sit still, and it drove the Boss mad.

"Barely anything," he muttered again.

Dexin brushed off his pants and walked over to the window. He rolled up the papers in his hand and began tapping them against the glass — *swish, swish, swish* — studying his reflection. He inspected his chin, ran his free hand through his bristled hair, and turned to inspect his profile. *Swish, swish, sw—*

"Sit!" the Boss hissed. "There's nothing to be nervous about! Just fucking sit down!" Dexin stopped; he was accustomed to such outbursts. But instead of obeying, he walked down the hall toward the restroom, leaving the rolled-up construction contract in the empty chair.

Though the Boss wouldn't have admitted it, part of him missed the shark-tank tables and tile floors. The old place had no grace but at least it had some life. This — the Boss's eyes swept down the red-trim hallway — this place felt as quiet as a Qing tomb.

He picked up the paper left on the chair and idly flipped to the last page, studying the red circular stamp of Beijing Huaxing Property Co., Ltd. It had been an easy negotiation, rushed as it was into a single week. When the Boss and Dexin arrived at Huaxing's office two nights ago with the pro forma contract and figures left blank, there was some last-minute resistance, but, in the end, the Boss wrangled a figure that was eighty percent of what he asked for. Dexin had watched, slouched in a black leather chair and silent as a child.

The Moon Tower Office Complex was a two-billion-yuan project, and Dexin's construction firm secured a 150-million-yuan contract as the project's building contractor. The Boss himself would secure six million once the signed government approval documents were in Huaxing's hands.

But there was something joyless about it, the Boss decided. Huaxing wanted the Moon Tower, every developer in the city did. A kill without the chase. At six million yuan, it was a decent payout for himself, the Boss had to admit. It was more difficult to make that kind of money in the old days. Negotiations used to stretch on for days — trench warfare, espionage, strategy. Whenever the Boss used to close a deal, he felt the swelling pride of being the last man standing. More than the money, he savored the exhaustion and pride. Tonight, the Boss just felt exhausted.

He was still seated alone, rubbing his birthmark when the two young hostesses flanking the restaurant's entrance shouted "welcome!" in unison, startling him. A parade of dark suits filed through the threshold, as if they'd been assembled outside. Dexin materialized by the Boss's side, hands soaking wet from the restroom.

Director Li was the first one inside. He paused for a moment at the sight of Dexin's dripping hands before shouting, "Well, it looks like we're all here!"

The hostess led the group into the central courtyard, weaving around two spindly trees and into a single dining room along the far side. They passed large banquet tables, each covered with embroidered tablecloths and jade sculptures at the centers. Their party sat only ten, a minor moon in orbit of those planetary bodies. The Boss folded the Huaxing contract lengthwise and slipped it inside his jacket pocket, along with the unaltered police report detailing the Ferrari car crash from February.

He took a seat next to Director Li at the round table and tried to mask his annoyance at the size of the group. What were so many City Planning officials doing at this private meeting? This was supposed to be low-key.

"Take your seats!" said Director Li, who remained standing. A dozen cold dishes were spaced perfectly equidistant atop the glass lazy Susan. Miniature wine glasses for *baijiu* stood at the right hand of each place setting, though the Boss didn't see a bottle anywhere.

"We are at a critical juncture both in Beijing and at the City Planning Commission," Li began. The table of middle-aged men quieted while waitresses placed white napkins on their laps. "Our city is facing unprecedented challenges — economic challenges, housing-pricing challenges, *moral* challenges. It's important that we, as government officials, are able to keep the lines of communication open with citizens of the city! We are having this dinner tonight with a pillar of the Beijing community, Xiao Dongxuan!" Director Li gestured toward the Boss. "I'd encourage you all to reach out to him for suggestions on ways to improve our work and our standing in the eyes of the people!"

Their glasses still empty, the group began awkwardly clapping. No one seemed quite sure how to respond to Li's address. The Boss plastered a smile to his face; he had absolutely no idea what was going on. He looked back at Director Li, still standing, and could find no trace of guile or cunning on his beaming, idiotic face. Li seemed ready to lead the table for a toast but instead sat down and commanded the table to start eating.

Porcelain chopsticks rattled against plates. The chandelier's light overhead glinted off the spinning glass tabletop, while a young woman in costume began plucking a *pipa* in the corner. A bottle of *baijiu* appeared and toasts were made. The cadres murmured in low voices about the food. The Boss settled into his high-backed chair, surveying the table. Now that attention had shifted away from him, he felt less exposed but still furious. They all had heard about him before, the Boss thought;

he could tell by the way they whispered and glanced. What the fuck was Director Li doing introducing him like this? His mind spun with contingencies. Was it some kind of message?

Director Li looked almost jovial sitting next to him, praising the freshness of the tree fungus he'd just sampled. To his left, the Boss overheard his brother-in-law straining to make small talk with the young official seated next to him. They were both examining each other's business cards.

"Sun Zhenhua. City Planning," read Dexin. "You must be busy!"

"Yes. Very busy." Zhenhua read the card in his hand. "Uh, how's business been lately?" He plucked a radish slice soaked in soy sauce from one of the dishes.

"Busy, busy," Dexin answered. "Prices are rising, as always."

Neither could think of anything else to say. They picked at the dishes in silence until Director Li's voice cut across the table.

"Zhenhua, you're drinking far too little!" The individual conversations fell away and all eyes fell on the youngest person at the table. Zhenhua's high forehead was already bright red with drink. He looked frail without his glasses, which were already on the table. A hopeless lightweight, Zhenhua was Director Li's favorite target.

"Waitress! Pour him another drink."

"No, no. That's enough for me," Zhenhua stammered, covering the rim of his glass with his palm.

"You're not going to drink anymore?" teased Director Li. "You're going to make City Planning lose face in front of our distinguished guests? You're the youngest one here. You should be able to drink more than old men like us!" Director Li continued to bully and cajole, which turned harsher the longer Zhenhua refused.

So, this was Zhenhua, the Boss thought. At least the young man didn't whine or make excuses.

The rest of the table seemed bored with this exchange; they had seen it many times before. This Sunday night dinner would go on for at least another hour — cold dishes, soup, mains, fruit. They were not sure why they were there. Every banquet had its purpose, but not everyone present at it did. The seven middle-aged men had paid close attention to Director Li during the first round of toasts and proclamations, trying to divine their significance. Yet once Director Li began coercing Zhenhua, the banquet snapped back into a familiar tedium, and their minds wandered. At least, they consoled themselves, they were not the ones being picked on.

Finally, Zhenhua relented, allowing the waitress to pour him another shot. He drank it down by himself in three slow, shuddering gulps. The table breathed a sigh of relief and went back to the warm dishes, which were steaming on the table.

"You still have a lot to learn, Zhenhua," Li said, after his subordinate had finished his drink.

Watching this exchange relaxed the Boss. Director Li was no conniving mastermind; he was a bully. This banquet wasn't some veiled threat directed toward the Boss; Director Li was gloating. He was going to take Vice Mayor Chen Yihui down, and he was going to humiliate Zhenhua and all the other Chen supporters along the way.

Zhenhua began piling stalks of asparagus onto his

plate in a show of normalcy. A few moments later he disappeared to the restroom. Director Li dug into the food with gusto, saying little. The Boss leaned back in his chair, smoking and sipping green tea. Eating such a heavy meal so late at night was bad for digestion; no wonder these cadres were so overweight and pallid. Director Li leaned toward him, spitting chicken gristle on the tablecloth, and blathered aimlessly about the Soul of Beijing, new subway lines in the works, and the city's recent air quality.

It wasn't until the Boss mentioned their "unfinished business" that Director Li stood and led them into an adjacent room. They stood alone among the empty banquet tables.

"Have you brought what you promised?" asked Li. The Boss tried to ignore the round oil stain, still slick, that was spreading under Li's white collar. The Boss despised this man's smug frankness. He just wanted to get this over with.

"Let me see it."

The Boss reached inside his jacket and handed over the documents. Li unfolded them and began to read out loud, like a halfwit. He was a paragraph into the police report, when the Boss saw the red-trim door behind him begin to open noiselessly and Zhenhua's flushed face appear in the doorway. The whole thing happened so quickly the Boss couldn't react. Some small part of him marveled at how well the door was built; it hadn't made a sound.

"Feeling better?" the Boss called out.

Director Li spun around and regarded the intruder.

"Get out of here, Zhenhua," Director Li snapped.

"We're talking business. There's a couch in the other room if you wish to lie down."

"No need," Zhenhua mumbled. He backed out of the room the way he had entered. The Boss turned back to Director Li, furious at the man's recklessness. What the fuck had he been thinking, reading such confidential information aloud? What if someone else had been listening? What a pointless risk to take! But the Boss swallowed his rage.

Director Li grinned at the Boss, oblivious. "The contract will be signed when the milestone is reached," he said, folding the papers again. "You've done a good deed, handing over this information, Mr. Xiao," he added formally. "The Party thanks you for your vigilance against the specter of corruption."

Director Li held out his hand, gesturing for the Boss to return to the banquet hall, but the Boss had no intention of staying any longer than he had to. Now that the documents had been handed over, he told Li to go on without him and headed in the direction of the bathroom.

* * *

The Boss ended up in the courtyard instead, staring up at the moon from under the flowering branches of a jujube tree. He could hear the clatter of plates and Director Li's voice seeping out from the warm glow of the dining room. He was thinking of the Lotus Club's old owner Mr. Bai and some of his early days with Vice Mayor Chen, some of them spent right here, back when the place was still a dump. The Boss was inspecting a few notches cut into the trunk of the tree when he caught a shift in the darkness out of the corner of his eye. He turned and saw a silhouette step out from behind a brick-wall corner — Zhenhua in a black suit.

"How do you feel?" asked the Boss.

"Oh, I'm fine. The air outside feels better."

"Take one," the Boss said, holding out his box of Chunghwas.

"No, no. Thank you ... thank you, Teacher Xiao. I don't smoke," Zhenhua said, pushing away the open pack thrust toward him in a way that suggested polite refusal.

"Don't be so formal. You don't need to call me 'Teacher Xiao.' People don't call me 'Old Xiao' either." He pocketed his cigarettes and lighter. "Most people call me the Boss of Houhai."

"The Boss of Houhai," repeated Zhenhua, rolling the syllables around in his mouth. "So, you and Director Li?"

"Friends before we had hair," the Boss lied. "We just like getting together to chew the fat. I like knowing what's going on in my neighborhood, that's all." He pointed toward the dining hall. "Just now we were going over some development plans in Xicheng District." The Boss glanced toward Zhenhua to gauge his response to this, but the young man only nodded.

In the growing silence, the Boss could tell that Zhenhua was looking at his face. The large dark blotch below his eye. His crooked nose. The deep grooves running from his nose to mouth. The Boss had studied every millimeter of it himself.

"You'd be surprised. I'm not as old as I look."

"Oh, I wasn't —"

"It's okay. You?"

Zhenhua took a step forward. "I'm not forty yet."

"You're young for your position," the Boss observed.

"Well, it's been only six months. Director Li...." Zhenhua sighed. "I still have a lot to learn."

The Boss laughed at the reference. He liked this kid.

"There will always be Director Lis," he said, blowing a plume of smoke. "What have you learned so far?"

"Well, there's a lot happening right now — lots of projects, lots of changes. I suppose most people are focused on the merger in October. Everyone is preparing for what might happen."

"You can spend a long time preparing for what might happen."

His words hung in the tree branches. They were silent until Zhenhua spoke again.

"May I ask you a question?" He swayed slightly and tried to focus his gaze. "We're putting together a comprehensive white paper on city development. We've settled on four pillar values to guide development: 'Innovative, Green, Lawful, Harmonious.' You've lived in the area your entire life, what is your impression of those pillars?"

The Boss winced at this sincerity. Zhenhua seemed like a sharp, diligent cadre; but none of that would help him in the coming weeks and months. Once Director Li brought down the vice mayor, Zhenhua would be ruined as well. Would he even realize what was happening, the Boss wondered? Would he remain hard at work, beavering away at some meaningless document all the way up to the end, right up until the moment someone called to tell him he'd been demoted to some far-flung suburban district? God, it was like watching a dog get put down. It was always the sincere ones that were least equipped for survival.

"Whose pillars?" the Boss asked.

"Pillars for Beijing's development, for the people of Beijing."

"For development or for the people?" The Boss cracked a smile.

Zhenhua looked as though he might launch into a longwinded exposition, so the Boss spoke first.

"You work in historic preservation, right?" he began. "How's your history?"

"History?"

"Did you know Pujie once lived here? Right here in this courtyard."

Zhenhua looked around. "The brother of the last emperor?" he asked.

"Good," the Boss said. "Pujie was still living here when I was a kid. He'd married a Japanese woman, so we neighborhood kids would hang around the door and curse them. We used to call this place the Japanese devil house." The Boss sighed, almost wistfully. "We didn't have anything else to do in those days. How old did you say you were? Forty? You weren't even alive then.

"Pujie and his family never let us hooligans inside the gate, of course, but we plotted an invasion once. Some of the older kids said there were jujube trees planted inside the Japanese devils' house, which were the absolute worst kind of tree as far as we were concerned. They said the Japanese loved jujube trees; so, naturally, we hated them," the Boss laughed. "Think of that! A counter-revolutionary old man, a Japanese woman, and a jujube tree all in one place! That got our blood boiling! We were going to sneak inside, lock up old Pujie and his wife, and demolish these Japanese devil trees.

"On the night of our attack, we hoisted the youngest boy up on our shoulders and he made it on top of the roof and over the wall. It seemed like an eternity before we heard him unlock the padlock from the other side. We were inside! It was quiet in the courtyard, the rooms dark, I remember.

"The older boy of our detachment, the leader, had brought a small hacksaw, and he knelt by the trunk. He got three or four good strokes in...." The Boss touched the trunk. "But then a dog from inside one of the rooms started howling. We were already spooked, and it sounded ferocious. We bolted out of the front door and didn't look back."

Zhenhua stood still, half-rapt by the rambling tale. He looked up into the branches.

"Jujube trees ..." he finally murmured.

"I'm glad we didn't chop it down," the Boss added. "Everything else in this city gets torn down and built up again, but you can still recognize old places by their trees."

"They've seen a lot."

"Everything else changes," said the Boss, as if entranced. "They've needed a lot of luck to survive this long. But they did. Look, they've even grown tall."

"And they weren't evil after all," Zhenhua suggested.

As he said this, a chill passed over the Boss's neck that made him feel exposed. He heard sounds from inside the dining room and the footsteps of the banquet party approaching.

"No, they're just trees," the Boss said quickly. "Some of them survive and others don't."

SUMMER

10

Some Delicate Owl

"No, it was a girl in *Evening Focus*."

"A Level *One*? Fuck!"

Yanmei held her breath, listening to the pair of *Evening News* sports reporters shout back and forth in the cafeteria line. She slid her tray farther down the parallel steel bars, edging its molded lip as close to the voices as she could. She leaned forward slightly, straining to hear their conversation.

"I bet I could get a Level One too if I spent that much time on my knees in Editor Ge's office!"

The two jackasses laughed again, and Yanmei felt her face turn bright red. She glared at her tray, watching her thumbs turn white. When she was sure they were preoccupied paying the cashier, Yanmei looked back at the two of them, memorizing their faces. They might not recognize the face of a trainee journalist like her, but she would remember them.

Yanmei took a seat alone at one of the cafeteria's long, sleek metal tables and ate quickly.

Jealous, they were all just jealous of her, she decided. That morning, the latest quality bonus scores were posted. Every article and photograph the newspaper published got a score, one through five, from the editors. The scores were posted on a large bulletin board on the fourth floor, like college entrance exam scores at schools, for all to see.

All morning, Yanmei had drifted around the newsroom, lingering near the board, waiting for someone to congratulate her. "Searching for Song Gang" had fetched a Level One, the top score of the year. Rereading the article, holding the copy of it she secretly kept in her desk drawer, still invigorated her. She was proud of it.

All of Yanmei's other menial reporting chores had continued unabated, but "Searching for Song Gang" was a bright beacon, a glimpse into the future. *This* was the kind of writing she should have been doing. *This* was what she would be doing one day, exclusively.

Yanmei gazed at the cafeteria's television, sipping her yogurt — war footage in the Middle East. The next time she looked up, she saw dramatic flyover images of Beijing at sunset scored to a swelling string arrangement. A deep voice intoned: *Beijing: Innovative. Green. Lawful. Harmonious. The Soul of Beijing!* By the time the smiling, waving family appeared at the end the commercial, Yanmei had already looked away again, back at her phone. She pictured Editor Ge's face and felt another flush of anger.

For the rest of the afternoon, Yanmei couldn't concentrate. Yuanyuan and Annie, who usually filed their stories from home, were in the office that day, which meant near-constant running commentary. Worse, today's topic was Yanmei's "mysterious admirer," someone who had called the *Evening Focus* department last week looking for her. He had called the newspaper's landline phone at the center of their four desks, so when Yanmei talked to the strange voice on the other end, the other girls could overhear her conversation completely.

The caller — Panzi, he called himself — was persistent and sounded on edge. He'd asked her a dozen questions about her article on Guang Fei and the blonde-haired girl who had helped him. What did she look like? Where did she meet him? When had Yanmei last seen her? Yanmei had sat at her desk, avoiding Annie's and Yuanyuan's teasing gazes and told the caller, over and over, that she knew nothing about the girl, not even her name. All the details she knew were already written up in "Searching for Song Gang."

"Sorry, I have to ask," she had said last week, exasperated, "what does this have to do with you?"

"It would take too long to explain," the strange voice had replied. "And I'd rather not say over the phone. If we met, I'd be able to say more. Why don't you give me your phone number?"

That was the line — God, why had she even told Yuanyuan and Annie about it? *That* line was the source of today's speculation and hilarity.

"Yanmei, he sounds kind of sexy, like a spy, right?" Annie's voice dropped to a whisper. "Darling, it will take too long to explain. We must meet in person."

"Darling!" Yuanyuan chimed in gamely. "I can't say too much. The phone isn't safe. It's better to meet face-to-face. No, not in the daytime. Meet me at midnight."

The girls looked toward Yanmei and tittered.

"What are you so mad about? I wish *I* had an admirer," said Annie. "It's exciting."

"He's not an admirer," Yanmei insisted. She refused to look away from her computer screen to acknowledge them. "I think he's looking for someone."

Yet even as she said this, Yanmei wasn't completely sure. Was this why she had agreed to meet him tonight, the strange caller? There was something strained and earnest in his voice, she decided. He didn't sound dangerous. Perhaps he was crazy or perhaps someone in the sports department was playing a joke on her. But Yanmei realized, listening to this stranger ask about the minute details of her article, hearing someone pore over her words, line by line, that part of her *wanted* to meet him.

On her way out of the office, Yanmei took the elevator up to the seventh floor and found Editor Ge perched on the corner of his desk, legs dangling, reading a newspaper. His door was open, as usual, and he didn't hear her approach. Editor Ge had a vain streak, the office whispered. Yanmei could see royal purple socks peeking out from his cuffed linen trousers. She couldn't detect a single crease in his blue Oxford despite it being the end of the workday. His shaved head gleamed below the halogen office lights.

Seeing Editor Ge reminded Yanmei of the snide comments in the cafeteria. Why *had* he taken such an interest in her story, she wondered? Editor Ge had done so much for her — helped arrange interviews, pushed back against Section Editor Deng, and even edited the text when the time came. Didn't he have more important things to do than help a lowly trainee journalist like her?

"Have you seen this?" he asked Yanmei when he finally noticed her in the doorway. He held up a page of the *People's Daily*. "The Soul of Beijing!" he mock announced. "I've had six meetings about it this week already. We're supposed to give it wall-to-wall coverage. Let me ask you something —"

"I saw my Quality Bonus Score," Yanmei blurted out. Editor Ge folded the newspaper neatly into quarters.

"Of course. Congratulations about that."

Editor Ge watched her evenly. He interlaced his long fingers over his knee. Perfect cuticles. Was there something lecherous about him, Yanmei wondered? No, when had he ever said anything, done anything to make her think that? Still, she tried to push the thought from her mind but couldn't manage to. Maybe he was gay.

"Thank you for your help with it," Yanmei said. She looked around his office. "I just wish...." Hearing the whine creep into her voice, Yanmei stopped herself. What was she trying to say?

"It was a good article, but it wasn't great," Ge said finally, still sitting on his desk. He picked up his newspaper again and resumed his idle reading. "Don't pay any attention to those quality bonus scores anyway. You need to aim higher than that."

Yanmei nodded. "What was it you wanted to ask me?"

"Oh, nothing." He kept his eyes trained on the newsprint. "Now go find another story and then write it. That's the job."

* * *

Yanmei stood, contorted, at the center of a subway car-
riage on line one. She tried — arm bent thirty degrees,
wrapped around a nearby pole — to bring her phone's
display closer to her face. Body heat pressed in on her
from all sides. Someone coughed on the back of her
neck. Each time the train stopped, passengers inside
and out shoved and jostled toward the fleeting opening.
Groans and grumbles. Curses under breath. The machine
beeped its warning and the doors slid to close, inevitably bouncing off bags and body parts still bridging
the threshold.

Yanmei didn't even need to hold the bar. At rush hour
there was nowhere to lose your balance; bodies braced
bodies. They swayed in unison like underwater plants
as the train rumbled through the dark underground.
Like everyone else, Yanmei hated, dreaded, and finally
wearily accepted the subway as the low point of her day.
She lingered late at the newsroom to avoid it, normally
heading in the opposite direction — eastbound — from
the newspaper's office at Dongdan Station toward her
shared apartment in Sihui. Today she rode west.

Cell phones were the only escape from such misery; seemingly everyone had a glowing screen inches
from their noses, games and sitcoms to distract. Since
Yanmei couldn't reach hers, she closed her eyes, trying
to imagine what Panzi looked like. His voice sounded
young, maybe her own age. Non-smoker. Rolling *rrr*s
of a local Beijinger.

He had promised to be waiting for her at the subway
entrance of Xidan Station but hadn't mentioned which

exit. When she messaged him to clarify that afternoon, it went unanswered. Perhaps this whole meeting *was* some elaborate practical joke. Maybe Yuanyuan and Annie would be waiting at the top of the escalators doubled over with laughter when she emerged.

When the cooing subway recording called out her stop, Yanmei squeezed through the entrance. She walked a few moments freely, feeling sweat trickle down her back, before heading up the stairs to swipe her subway card. She followed the crowd through the tunnel and onto an escalator that lifted her slowly toward the neon light of Xidan Commercial Street.

Four people were waiting at the mouth of the entrance, three with their heads bowed, engrossed in the glow of their cell phones. Yanmei knew the fourth person was Panzi immediately, though she couldn't say why. He was thin and long, with short-cropped hair and ears pushed so far out they seemed alight from the neon flashing behind him. He wore a gray T-shirt with a canvas satchel slung over one shoulder. She moved closer and saw his eyes widen with recognition. They were honest.

As they walked together through the bright shopping mall district of Xidan toward the restaurant Panzi had picked out, she played journalist, peppering him with questions. Where was he from? What school did he go to? What did he do for a living?

"So, it's a real estate agency?" she said.

"It's sort of a middle-man agency. Family-owned."

"So, that's why you called me? You're interested in a property of some kind?"

"What? No! Turn left here."

They walked thirty meters into a well-lit alley and

entered a small Guizhou restaurant, a steam-and-smoke-filled room with six square wooden tables, half of them occupied. They sat on stools opposite a large copper pot. Moments later the owner emerged from the kitchen. He was Buddha-shaped and had a southern accent that lilted like music.

"You're back!" he exclaimed, recognizing Panzi. "It's been too long. When did you get back?"

"Just visiting," Panzi smiled. "How's business?"

"Ahhh!" The man's face crinkled into a sour expression. "So-so. But I'm not starving." He laughed at his own joke. Then the owner held up one chubby finger. "One specialty spicy dry pot?"

Panzi looked perfectly at ease across the low, cramped table. Yanmei saw the two of them as the owner might have; maybe he assumed they were old friends or that they were on a date.

"Can you take spice?" Panzi asked her.

"Sure," she replied, handing the laminated menu back to the owner, who waddled toward the kitchen.

"So, you used to live in this neighborhood?"

"The building over there." Panzi pointed over his shoulder. "I lived there last summer, for about three months." Yanmei resisted asking yet another question. Panzi went on: "I came to this restaurant pretty much every day. They usually have tables set up out on the street."

"So, did your office move or something?"

Panzi took a sip of hot water. "We don't really have an office. My mom buys and sells secondhand apartments around Beijing. Some of them are hers, others she manages for friends and clients. I live in them and show them to buyers. She doesn't have a Beijing *hukou*, so she's technically not allowed to trade properties as much as she does. I don't really understand how it works. But she says it's safer if someone is living in them when we sell, someone she's familiar with."

Yanmei could hear a wok sizzle from inside the kitchen. "But there are local agencies that can do all that."

Panzi shrugged. "They take a percentage, and there's more paperwork."

"So, you have to live in all these apartments yourself?"

Panzi nodded. He didn't seem comfortable talking about business. He said he couldn't explain how and why his mother did things the way she did. The owner suddenly burst through the swinging kitchen door holding a copper pot with two gray rags wrapped around the handles. It steamed thickly on the table — a medley of red peppers, ginger slices, vegetables, and chunks of meat — glazed and fiery. A handful of cilantro stalks and black peppercorns rested on top. It was enough food for four people. "Rice?" grinned the owner.

They settled in, picking at the dish and wiping their noses with tissues from a small plastic dispenser. Two tables of patrons left and a new group of four sat down next to the fogged window with characters that read backward from inside. Panzi and Yanmei were halfway through their meal when he set his chopsticks across the lip of his bowl and a worried look spread across his face.

"Your article," he began. His words were uncertain, clipped. "You wrote about someone. Xiao Song. I'm sure it's her."

"You mentioned that on the phone."

"You printed something she said. About being lucky to feel pain. Only Xiao Song said things like that."

Yanmei saw that Panzi was staring back at her, waiting. She dropped her voice to match his.

"Look, I talked to Guang Fei, the Cripple I wrote about, like you asked me to," she said. "He didn't remember anything else about the girl. He hasn't seen her since February. He wants to find her too, if it *is* the same person. But I don't know what —"

"Can I talk to him?"

"Who? Guang Fei?"

Panzi nodded, and Yanmei looked up at the table of four sitting near the window. Both women leaned away from the table, engrossed separately in their cell phones while the men sat adjacent, elbows on the table, talking loudly about politics. There were four empty green bottles clustered around the nearside table leg and two half-full bottles on the table.

"There was a car crash," Panzi said. "It happened in February; I was there. They hit Xiao Song; that's the last time I saw her. I'm not sure if she's just missing or she's.... All I know is that they took her away in an ambulance."

Panzi paused and took a drink of water, set his glasses on the table and rubbed his eyes. His face was flushed from the spicy meal.

"And there were two of them in the car," he whispered. "Second-generation rich kids. They were driving a *Ferrari*. I think one of them may have died; but the other one — the driver — was still alive. They took them all away. They just cleaned up everything; there was nothing left."

Yanmei felt the hairs on the back of her neck rise. *Searching for Xiao Song.* The headline leapt up at her immediately. She watched Panzi's face for traces of deceit, but her voice remained calm.

"So, this girl is your sister?"

"No!"

"I'm not sure I follow."

"Everything," Panzi repeated, almost in a whisper. "They made it all just *disappear*." Yanmei looked away again to steady her nerves. Two more green bottles had been added beneath the table. The Buddha owner now sat backward in a chair from a nearby table, chatting with the group. They laughed at one of the owner's jokes. What was she doing here? Who was this boy staring at her, waiting for her to say something?

"I don't understand why you're telling me this. It sounds crazy, but there's nothing I can do to help you," Yanmei finally said. "You need to talk to the police, not a journalist."

There was a clatter of beer bottles on the concrete floor; the owner had accidentally kicked them over. He laughed again and hoisted his arm toward the men — beer glass raised. The glasses clinked, and as they did, overflowing beer splashed on the table.

Panzi appeared to be weighing something in his mind. She watched as he produced a folded page of newsprint from his pocket and spread it across the table. A part of Yanmei hoped that it would be a copy of her article and felt a twinge when she saw it wasn't. Panzi smoothed the newsprint on the table. It was a *People's Daily* editorial dated the previous week. The headline read "The Time Has Come for Cadres to Explain Their Unexplained Luxury Assets." Panzi had circled a paragraph in the body of the text:

The phenomenon of "unexplained luxury assets" is now growing to critical levels, and it threatens the very fabric of society and society's ongoing trust in the Party. It is not enough for the Party to demand such trust. The Party must *earn* the public's respect by living personal lives worthy of such respect. Every "unexplained luxury asset" held by high-ranking officials — be it a Ferrari on the streets of Beijing or a mansion in the countryside of Canada — must be reckoned with. The time has come. The public and the Party deserve the truth.

"Something is coming," he said. "A crackdown."

"Okay," she said with a quick finality. She leaned back from the table. Time to go.

"I've spent a lot of time online, searching for clues," Panzi went on. His eyes widened in a way that set off bells in the back of Yanmei's head. "Certain names, names of officials, keep coming up. I think one of them may be the Ferrari's owner. Look." Panzi turned the tattered paper over. There were six names scrawled in the margin, two that Yanmei recognized as high-ranking city government officials.

"What is this?" she said, agitated. Yanmei pushed her stool back from the table. She glanced around the room a final time, suddenly paranoid that someone might be watching her. "What am I supposed to do with this?"

Panzi looked baffled at the question.

"I need your help!" he pleaded. "I can't find out any

more about these people by myself. You're a journalist; you must have resources."

The newsprint felt hot in her fingers. Panzi touched her hand, sending an electric shock through her. She reached for her purse and concentrated on steadying her voice.

"I don't know what you're talking about. I have to go. I'm going, now."

As Yanmei stood to leave, she heard him pleading. "I'm not asking you to write about all this. I just need to find her. She is a good person and doesn't deserve what happened to her. Look, will you take me to meet the Cripple? He may know something about what happened to her."

Yanmei paused for a moment, trying to imagine what Xiao Song must look like. She saw a slender beauty with long silky hair walking through a beautiful landscape — lush grasslands, maybe. Why else would Panzi and Guang Fei go to all this trouble to find her? Panzi remained seated at the table, his enormous eyes shining like those of some delicate owl.

* * *

Yanmei wouldn't make any promises. Guang Fei may well have already gone home, she warned Panzi as they approached the Dongzhimen overpass. In truth she knew exactly where Guang Fei would be; she had learned his daily routine. Ever since they first met, Yanmei sought Guang Fei out whenever she found herself in this neighborhood with time to spare. There was something soothing about hugging her knees next to his blanket of trinkets, watching the people pass, and being swept along Guang Fei's river of words.

The man talked constantly — about his hometown in Shanxi, about history, about Momo the dog, about his impressions of Beijing. At first, she brought her reporter's notebook, listening for the perfect lead for a follow-up article. As the weeks passed, however, a different dynamic emerged between them. Yanmei began bringing him store-bought food and calling him "Uncle."

When she and Panzi found Guang Fei at his usual perch, he was sitting on his cart, gazing at the rushing lanes of traffic below. His usual dark-blue blanket was strewn in front of him, wrinkled.

"You're still out here," Yanmei remarked when she and Panzi made it to him. It was around seven in the evening. "How's business?"

Guang Fei grunted.

"I brought a friend to talk to you."

Yanmei glanced at Panzi standing next to her; his bright eyes were fixed on Guang Fei.

A new arrival like Panzi should have set him off on a long, rambling battery of questions, but Guang Fei only stared off beyond the bridge. He had changed, darkened physically, Yanmei noticed. A patch of his gray beard near the chin had been pulled out. Dark circles ringed his eyes. Guang Fei never talked about killing himself anymore, but Yanmei had also learned that his new, modest life was a fragile thing.

"Uncle, hello," Panzi put in. "I'm a friend of Yanmei's. I read her interview with you in the newspaper. You're famous!"

"That's right!" Yanmei said brightly, as if talking to a child. "I brought Uncle ten copies of the article." Her voice trailed off; Guang Fei had barely acknowledged them.

Yanmei gave Panzi a helpless look; she knew he was anxious to talk about Xiao Song but Guang Fei didn't seem right. She attempted a few more lines of small talk, without effect. Then she asked him where Momo was.

Guang Fei looked up at Yanmei as if his heart might break. It took some prompting, but little by little Yanmei pried the details out of him. Momo was gone. Last week, two sanitation workers had thrown the dog in the back of a three-wheel cart and set off while Guang Fei yelled at them on the side of the road. They didn't even bother responding. The bigger of the two laughed at him, Guang Fei said.

"Who was I?" he went on, angry in a way Yanmei had never seen. "Just some crippled person on a wooden cart in a dirty army coat. I could hear him yelping as they peddled away. He was clawing against the metal. I called inside for help, but no one responded. Finally, someone came to the door, but he just stood there looking at me."

Yanmei watched Panzi's face as Guang Fei grew angrier, watched his eyes go soft, as if recognizing something.

Suddenly, Guang Fei was almost shouting. "Why *should* they care? They look at the dog and see that it's weak. They look at me and see I'm weak. I can't offer them anything, so why would they help me?"

Yanmei looked out over the endless lanes of traffic, feeling numb. After a few minutes, Guang Fei's indignation began to ebb. He looked worn out, soul-weary.

He stopped speaking, and the three of them sat together in a stunned silence, watching the legs of white-collar workers return home, each lost in separate thoughts. Finally, Panzi couldn't hold back any longer.

"Uncle, I need to ask you something. I'm searching for a girl, and I think you know her. She goes by Xiao Song."

"Panzi, maybe now isn't such —"

"You told Yanmei about a young girl who helped you and the Idiot. You met her on Tiananmen Square. You remember her, right?"

Panzi pulled an ID card from his front jeans pocket and held it up for both Yanmei and the Cripple to see.

"Her. It must be her that you met."

All three inspected the ID's tiny headshot, a little larger than a thumbnail. Yanmei was surprised to find a rather plain-looking girl staring back at her — plump face, wide nose, and short-cropped hair. The ID card had her birthday and hometown.

Guang Fei took the card out of Panzi's hands and brought it close to his face, almost touching his nose.

"She disappeared," Panzi said gently. "She disappeared after New Year, in February. That's the last time I saw her."

Yanmei saw that Guang Fei was gripping the edge of his cart with his free hand, knuckles white.

"Panzi," she pleaded softly.

"What happened to her?" Guang Fei asked.

"I don't know. That's why I wanted to talk with you. Did she tell you anything about herself? Where her family is?"

Guang Fei refused to look away from Xiao Song's ID.

"I don't know anything about her," he said finally. "I didn't even know her name, no one at the Stars Hotel did." Guang Fei looked as though he might start crying but didn't. "But they all knew her. After she disappeared, everyone just started calling her *Xiao Guanyin*, 'Little Goddess of Mercy.' Where was Little Goddess of Mercy? everyone asked me. When was she coming back? I couldn't even tell them a name. But we were waiting for *her* all this time.

Panzi began to explain the details of the accident and his search. As Yanmei listened, a low jealousy took shape. Panzi spoke in a hushed, reverential tone, as if Xiao Song herself were in the next room trying to listen in. Guang Fei broke his stunned silence to offer a few distant anecdotes about the time he'd spent with the girl as well — her quirks, habits. Yanmei took Xiao Song's ID card from Guang Fei's fingers and looked at the picture again. Little Goddess of Mercy.

Then Yanmei remembered the dog; she imagined the misery of that helpless animal and felt ashamed. She should be happy. Now, talking to Panzi about their missing friend, Guang Fei already seemed in better spirits than when they arrived.

11

Knock, Knock, Knock

THE room was having trouble concentrating. Lunch had just ended, and City Planning's entire office was uncomfortably hot. The central air conditioning had been shut off ever since all government departments had been "encouraged" by the Party Secretary's office to cut down on electricity consumption over the summer months. The vice directors, wearing identical short-sleeved white dress shirts, squirmed and fanned themselves with large envelopes. Zhenhua's fellow researcher at City Planning Yang Hong stood near the projector, wicking away sweat from his forehead as he read. Director Li sat at the head of the long, rectangular conference table, fiddling with his cell phone in his lap.

Zhenhua craned his neck for a better view of the PowerPoint slide projected at the front of the conference room. He sat on one of the folding chairs lining the back wall, next to the secretaries and assistants, listening to Yang Hong read from a stack of papers in his hand. From where Zhenhua sat, the slide, titled "Key Near-term Soul of Beijing Restoration Projects," looked like an abstract painting.

It was, in fact, a map of Beijing's old city center, hemmed in by the Second Ring Road. Zhenhua squinted, able to make out only the blotches of paint — red, yellow, orange, green — that spilled across neighborhoods, each color representing a different level of historic conservation. The Palace Museum, Tiananmen Square, and the Summer Palace were cordoned off in a deep forbidding red, their surrounding hutong neighborhoods splashed in yellow. Farther from the center, city blocks had been washed clean, save for a few paint drips marking the odd temple or ancient residence of interest. Bold purple numbers marked the proposed restoration projects.

Yang Hong was reeling them off in order: project name, proposed start date, investment amount ….

Director Li cut him off. "That's enough. Why is the investment for Project No. 7 so high?"

The investment amount of Project No. 7 on the list, the Duanqiruifu Luxury Restoration Project, was twice that of the second-largest project. Zhenhua fidgeted while Yang Hong fumbled for an explanation without notes he could read from. Someone with another sheet of paper chimed in to read more statistics. The Duanqiruifu project would require relocating forty-four families. The buildings' construction grades were rated "poor" or "very poor," which would require higher renovation costs. There would be excavation for underground parking.

"That's still too high," Li pronounced. "Let's reduce

that investment figure." Someone sitting at the table began writing down the comment in a notebook. "Also, the timeline for that project is too long."

"How old is the Duanqiruifu site?" he asked the room. "Qing dynasty?"

"The architecture is from the Republican era," Yang Hong replied, beaming. He knew that answer.

"Republican-era buildings are not as old as Qing buildings," Li declared. "Therefore, the renovation shouldn't take as long."

The comment was recorded in the notebook. The projector panted. Zhenhua waited nervously to see if anyone was going to correct Director Li. What kind of idiotic logic was that? City Planning had helped restore hundreds of traditional Qing-era courtyard homes; they knew the design principles and building materials inside and out. But Republican-era buildings with European architecture? They weren't even comparable!

"Pardon me, Director Li," Zhenhua croaked from the back row. "Perhaps we need some more details for Project No. 7 before we set a budget. The building quality is quite diff—"

"Were you listening, Zhenhua?" Li snapped. "The construction grades are 'poor,' but the buildings are not as old as Qing buildings. A 'poor' grade building in the Republican era is not the same as a 'poor' grade building in the Qing dynasty, am I right?" Yang Hong nodded vigorously.

"There are just many consid—"

"Did you call this meeting, Zhenhua? Talk to Yang Hong about it afterward. If you have comments, you should have voiced them before the meeting started."

The room waited to see if Zhenhua would respond and, when he didn't, Yang Hong wiped his forehead again and tapped a key on his laptop to change slides. Zhenhua slumped back in his chair and wiped away a few sweat droplets under his glasses with the handkerchief from his pocket. No one looked at him for the rest of the hour.

Zhenhua had been disappearing for weeks already. Yang Hong and Ma Jun no longer invited him out for lunches. Work assignments, even the banal work reports, ceased arriving without explanation. His name vanished from the contributors' page of the Soul of Beijing Report he'd essentially written himself. Even when he arrived at the City Planning's office in the mornings, his colleagues averted their gazes, as if afraid of eye contact.

It took time — *too* much time, Zhenhua chided himself — for him to understand why he'd become an invisible man at City Planning. He'd read the four *People's Daily* editorials — the ones about "unexplained luxury assets" — without realizing what they meant. None of them mentioned Vice Mayor Chen by name; the language was always intentionally vague.

But the rumors became more specific. A police report had surfaced showing that Vice Mayor Chen's son had been involved in a high-speed sports car crash. The vice mayor was on the verge of being hauled away on corruption charges by the Party. It was only a matter of time, people whispered.

Zhenhua had watched the storm clouds gathering around Vice Mayor Chen with a removed sense of awe. Zhenhua was certain that he was too new, too insignificant at City Planning for any of the drama to filter down to him. Sure, his colleagues at City Planning would ostracize him for the time being — the October merger was only four months away after all — but that would pass.

"Besides, I only met Chen once," he groused to Rui one night. His wife was curled up next to him on the sofa, feet tucked under her legs. "Why should I be punished for what some old man did, much less his stupid son? I don't even know him."

Rui reached toward the table and poured him another small glass of beer. Two bottles of Yanjing per night was their new routine.

"He was the one who promoted you, Dear," Rui said. "You have to expect that what happens to him will affect you too."

"I just want it over quickly. The sooner Vice Mayor Chen falls, the sooner this can all be over, and it can get back to normal."

Suddenly Rui was interested in the floral pattern of the sofa cushions. "Back to normal?" she asked.

"Of course. It's not like I did anything wrong, Rui. Look, I can understand why everyone would want to stay away from me right now. October is only four months away; it's too sensitive a time. But this is temporary. Once the whole commotion passes, I'll still have my abilities. I'll still have the quality of my work. They need me at City Planning; I'm the only one capable of getting the work done! You should have heard what Director Li was saying at this m—"

"Are you sure things will ever get back to normal?" Rui blurted out. She still wouldn't look at him.

"What?"

"I mean, once Chen goes down, you don't think it'll impact your career? Not just now but, you know, forever?"

Zhenhua threw back the glass of beer and laughed.

"Dear, you don't understand politics. What matters is —"

"Pick the right leader; help him with his work," Rui parroted. "But Zhenhua, you didn't pick the right leader. You don't know what is going to happen next. Who else is going to support you?"

Zhenhua's face hardened. "Well, you're right about that. I don't have any support at City Planning and don't have any here either, apparently."

"Zhenhua."

But he had already grabbed the beer bottle and was walking toward the bedroom. That night, Zhenhua fell asleep quickly with his bedside lamp burning and his back turned toward her. Rui slipped out of bed and studied her husband's sleeping face a moment before clicking off the light. He looked relaxed for the first time that night — forehead smooth and mouth slack. One of his thin legs was pulled on top of the thin sheet. He looked like Zhenhua.

* * *

When Director Li wanted to get Zhenhua's attention at the office, he liked to approach his desk from behind and knock on it like a door. *Knock, knock, knock.* Three short, dread-packed raps. Zhenhua knew exactly what to expect when he heard them: his boss standing with his bowlegs spaced apart, hands jammed deep in his pockets, smiling. The knocks usually occasioned Li delivering a smug, five-minute lecture about nothing before heading back to his own office.

"Qiaoqiao is out today," said Director Li at nine one morning. Qiaoqiao was City Planning's office administrator and secretary. "I know that you don't have much work to do these days, Zhenhua, so help me file these, won't you? It'll need to be done by the end of the day."

Li dropped a stack of papers on the spot where he'd knocked. Zhenhua could feel his colleagues watching him, listening to the exchange. An indignant anger rose in him, but he only nodded.

"Where should I file them?"

Li waved his hand. "Building Five or Six. I don't know. The keys are downstairs." Zhenhua grunted an acknowledgement and turned back to his computer screen.

Knock, knock, knock.

"Zhenhua, we'll need that done today."

He managed to wait until he saw Director Li's office door close before letting out a stream of profanity under his breath. Zhenhua snatched up the stack of papers, sending his office chair into a spin. On his way out, he thought he saw a few wry smiles from the people he passed, but the room remained deathly quiet, at least until the elevator doors closed.

City Planning used its old office buildings for storage — a handful of weathered but handsome six-story brick walk-ups scattered around its main office tower. The buildings were arranged like a small campus and had frescoes of peeling lotus flowers between the windows. Inside Building Six, Zhenhua stepped around heaps of campaign banners, gift bags, brochures, and pallets of plastic-wrapped government reports. The room's musty smell had a calming effect. In a way, Zhenhua was relieved to be out here alone.

He spent a few minutes puzzling over how the filing cabinets might be organized before realizing they weren't. He thumbed through the documents Li had given him — back issues of architecture digests and glossy design magazines — all junk. No one would ever need to see them again. Another menial task. Another humiliation. Zhenhua opened a metal drawer at random and thought about tossing the entire stack in at once. Might Director Li come all the way down here to check on his filing job, just to find something worth criticizing? It was possible.

As he moved the stack of magazines back out of the drawer, a single sheet of white paper fluttered to the floor, its round, bright-red official stamp winking at him. Zhenhua's eyes swept over its contents quickly, and he realized what he was holding before he reached the end of the document. It was a letter drafted by Director Li, dated the previous week, seeking candidates for the role of City Planning researcher. The department had only three researcher positions, including Zhenhua. One of them was being replaced.

Zhenhua stared at Director Li's letter, feeling his ears turn hot. He pictured the other two City Planning researchers — Yang Hong and Ma Jun — and he grew angrier still. How could Director Li get rid of *him*, the only one of the three who did any damn work in the first place? Zhenhua imagined Li's toady face gathering the entire office together to announce his departure — legs apart, hands in pockets, shit-eating grin.

Then a second, more enraging, thought surfaced: What if Li had given him the paper on purpose? What if he had *meant* for Zhenhua to read it? Zhenhua kicked the metal filing cabinet hard and listened to the sound disappear into the room. He stormed toward the door, clutching the document, leaving the stack of old magazines fanned out across the floor.

Outside, his rage began pulsing with shame as he ground his heels into the sidewalk. The hideous white-tile octagon glowered down at him, reminding him of the late nights he'd spent there. He saw himself inside drafting reports, studying blueprints, poring over academic books. He thought of the hours wasted in banquet halls, drinking down coerced shots of *baijiu* to please Director Li. He remembered all the times the vice directors dropped by his desk after meetings, asking him to deliver extra work that their own hires couldn't handle. He shouldered it all — the thankless work, the venom of his bosses. It made him angry of course; but, in a way, Zhenhua had expected all that. Doing good work always made you a threat to someone.

But for the first time, as he started his second circuit around the basketball courts, Zhenhua had a new, disturbing thought: maybe he wasn't a threat at all. He wasn't being pushed out of City Planning because Director Li was afraid of him. He was being punished for *nothing*.

He was a non-entity. The more he thought about Li's letter and the scandal engulfing Vice Mayor Chen, the smaller he felt, as if his career were a bit of debris, swept in and out with the tides, and now, finally, being washed out to sea.

Zhenhua's phone was ringing. God, what would he tell Rui? Would Yuqing have to change schools? The scrum of high school boys playing basketball, the street sweeper whisking along Nanshili Road — they all seemed like actors. The amphitheater of office towers leaned in on him, crowding out the cloudless sky. His phone rang again, but Zhenhua didn't answer it; the unknown number could be anyone. It could be Director Li looking for him. He felt an urge to keep moving, keep walking until he reached home, and then past his apartment, past the last reaches of city's sprawl, past the cornfields and the factories. Get far away from all this.

To run away, he thought bitterly. God, listen to this. He was so weak! *This* was why Director Li could so easily screw him over. At the first sign of trouble, what did he do? Run away. Pathetic. How many other low-level researchers like him — talented officials — had been driven away by the first sight of nasty politics? Was it any wonder the city was sliding a little further into incompetence?

When Zhenhua arrived at the basketball court's corner, he did not hesitate. He turned right once more, circling back toward City Planning's office. The heels of his dress shoes clicked louder than before. Director Li's face was clear in his mind's eye. He went back to work.

* * *

"Honestly!" Rui half-whispered from the tenth row. She was exasperated with the old man in front of her standing and taking photos. "Sit down!" she hissed. "Sit down!"

"Let me," said Zhenhua, reaching for her phone. "I can film from here. She's clear."

Zhenhua settled back in the seat next to Rui's father and watched his daughter file onto the auditorium stage through the screen on his phone. He saw Yuqing yank at the tight collar of her *qipao* dress and scratch her arm under the hot stage lights. She followed the girl in front of her until she arrived at her *guzheng*, which was lined up in a perfect row with the other seven.

"Welcome to the Little Mozarts Summer Class Concert!" her teacher announced.

The eight tiny girls bowed together as the audience applauded. After a few more remarks, the teacher nodded at them to sit. A faint keyboard drumbeat sounded from the side stage — the familiar whispering drumbeat — and the girls began plucking "Song of the Homebound Fisherman" in unison.

"Zoom in on her!" Rui whispered.

"I know, I know."

Zhenhua smiled at the sight of his daughter on stage but he was sick to death of the "Homebound Fisherman." Yuqing had been practicing it for weeks, usually as he washed the dishes after dinner. Two hours of practice every evening, on top of summer school, that was the rule. Yuqing's summer schedule seemed just as busy as during the school year.

"My mother didn't push me hard enough," Rui said when Zhenhua asked if they might want to ease back on Yuqing's grueling summer schedule. "Music education is good for her."

That summer, Rui was consumed with the minutes of her daughter's days, in a way Zhenhua had never seen before. Yuqing was rarely in a room alone for more than a minute without her mother. Rui padded around the apartment after her, calling for her to pick up her coloring books, get ready for bed, wash her hands for dinner — the tactical commands of parenting. It was exhausting work; but when Zhenhua volunteered to help, Rui didn't seem interested.

It was hard to tell if Yuqing enjoyed playing the *guzheng* at all. She said she did, which was suspicious. She bounded around the apartment with the metal nails fixed to her fingertips and raced through her compositions on muscle memory.

Zhenhua had seen his daughter's face light up exactly once in the last month: the time he walked in on her during one of those precious moments she had to herself. Her hands were hovered over the strings, head cocked at a demure angle. Zhenhua watched her from the doorway as Yuqing remained frozen in the pose for a few beats, dreamily humming to herself and plucking the air. It wasn't until Zhenhua saw the Disney storybook open at her feet that he realized Snow White was seated at the *guzheng* in exactly the same pose. Zhenhua felt twin surges of affection and sorrow for his daughter, but before he could call out to her, Rui slipped into the room behind him. *Why don't I hear music?*

Zhenhua, too, cultivated a secret world away from Rui, albeit less magical. He hadn't told her about Director Li's letter or his coming dismissal. The whole thing wasn't worth explaining, he'd decided. Rui wouldn't understand, wouldn't support him. She'd probably tell him to give up and quit.

For nearly a month, Zhenhua had been leaving the office at six and walking the streets alone for an hour before returning home around seven thirty. When he returned home each night, Rui hardly made eye contact. Neither had much to say, it appeared. She cooked, he washed. She helped Yuqing brush her teeth, Zhenhua tucked her in. Rui often fell asleep early while he read on his side of the bed. That suited Zhenhua just fine; he had hardly been sleeping at all.

Only once had there been a break in the clouds. One evening the previous week, Zhenhua returned to their bedroom after putting Yuqing to bed and paused at the threshold, hearing what sounded like soft sobs coming from inside. He stood outside the cracked door, hearing only faint sounds — crinkling paper, sniffling. When he entered, Rui made no effort to conceal what she was doing. She hardly looked up and acknowledged him.

Zhenhua sat next to her on the bed and picked up one of the pages Rui had been reading; it was a letter he'd written her in their university days. He put a hand on Rui's knee and asked why she was crying, to which she murmured something about her father's illness. Zhenhua took off his glasses and stared at the old letter, wondering whether or not he should confide in Rui, tell her about what was happening to him at City Planning. But he didn't say anything in the end. Rui was already upset; there was no sense in making it any worse.

* * *

After the concert ended, the whole family walked through the damp neighboring sidewalks in search of ice cream, Yuqing bounding ahead in her tiny silk dress. Rui called out to her daughter to watch out for puddles of dirty rainwater.

Zhenhua and Rui's father closed ranks, slowing their pace. He could hear the old man's labored breath as they made their way up Xindong Road. Rui's father — long and gangly — stooped when he walked, which made him seem older than he really was. He loved walking, covered five miles a day in his healthy years. When he started the chemotherapy, Rui's father never complained about the pain or nausea or hair loss. The worst part of the treatment, he said, was that the doctors made him stay at home all day.

"How have you been feeling?"

"I'm fine."

"Really?"

"I'm an old man. I'm not supposed to feel good."

"You're not even seventy yet."

The light changed and they crossed the road toward the shopping mall. When they made it through the pedestrian crossing, Zhenhua spoke again.

"Are the new pills still giving you dreams?"

The old man made a weary gesture. "Memories."

From his own insomniac perch in the living room, Zhenhua often heard low moans coming from the bedroom in the middle of the night. The first night he'd heard them, Zhenhua opened the bedroom door and listened to his father-in-law murmuring in a frightened voice, pleading. *Let me go, let me go! I don't know him!* When Zhenhua tried to wake him, gently, the old man grabbed his wrist so hard it left red marks. Eventually, his eyes flickered open in the dark and he stared at Zhenhua in an uncomprehending way that gave him chills. Then the old man fell back into a quiet sleep.

When Zhenhua told Rui about the dreams, they fought over what to do next. Look, he'd told her, Yuqing loved sharing a room with Grandpa, and the dreams hadn't bothered her; she slept through it all anyway. But Rui had already made up her mind — it wasn't good for Yuqing to hear someone having nightmares. Suppose he yells out and scares her? Grandpa should move across the hall to the third bedroom, which was empty anyway.

Zhenhua wanted to argue further. *Yuqing doesn't need any more changes in her life right now,* he'd wanted to say. But Rui wouldn't have known what he was talking about.

"The doctor said for you to rest often," Zhenhua said, opening the glass door of the ice cream shop. "That will help."

Inside, Yuqing was racing back and forth in front of the glass case of flavors, streaking the glass with her hand.

"Chocolate, Strawberry, Green Tea, Banana...."

"Which one are you going to get, Sweetie?"

"This one, this one, this one, this one, this one," she said jabbing her finger at half the flavors in the freezer.

"So much! You won't fit in your skirt anymore!"

They sat down in four neon-colored bucket seats and watched Yuqing eat her ice cream. Whenever a white dribble trickled down her wrist, Rui swooped in with a paper napkin to wipe it away. Yuqing giggled and stood up every so often to dance out her excitement.

"You're *that* happy, eh?" smiled Rui. "Sit down and eat or you're going to get a stomachache."

When Yuqing lost interest and the ice cream began

to melt, Rui and Zhenhua alternated bites until it was gone. Once they finished, Zhenhua surveyed his family and felt a twinge in his chest. Rui was smiling at Yuqing licking her fingers. Grandpa sat comfortably with his hands on his bony knees, gazing at them both.

What would happen to all of this once he lost his position? What would happen to the private music school? The cancer specialists at the City Government Hospital? What would happen when they'd be forced to move back into district-level housing and there'd be no third bedroom for Grandpa at all?

Back when he still confided in Rui about problems at work, she used to console him. *It doesn't matter what position you have or where you are. Your family is by your side. I'm by your side. And I'll be there no matter where you're standing.*

But reality was more complicated; surely she must see that. The man Rui claimed to love was not some fixed, unchanging star. Of course it mattered where he stood! The last few weeks — the quarreling, the lack of sex, the sleepless nights — proved it. How much worse would it get between them once he actually lost his job? What would Rui say when she found out he'd been keeping it from her for so long?

Zhenhua had to do something if he was going to save all this. He would call Vice Mayor Chen the following morning and offer to do whatever he could for Chen to keep his post. What other choice did he have?

"Okay, everybody ready to leave?" he said.

Did Rui perhaps sense this sudden moment of resolve? As they stood, he glanced at her from across the table and she was smiling.

12

Gold

DAVID stood waiting outside next to a gold-sphere sculpture and watched another car pull into the underground parking garage. The young guard, dressed in coattails, saluted the Porsche Cayenne and the mechanical arm rose. The boy glanced helplessly at David as he marched back to his post next to the tall bronze art deco door, under an inscription that read, in French: Palais de Violette.

Someone would be right down to let David in, a voice had told him, but he'd already been waiting ten minutes in the humid June heat. Who was he even waiting for? Likely some rich brat, judging by the cars and foppish guards. Principal Yue had told him only that her friend's kid needed an English tutor. He was a college-aged boy who would study abroad in the spring and "just needed to tune up his conversational English," as Principal Yue had aggravatingly put it. She had already recommended David personally, she added, as if this was supposed to flatter him. She could tell him nothing else about the job, of course — how much it paid, for instance.

Not that he had much of a choice anyway. When Principal Yue had approached him earlier that week with this side-teaching gig — grinning at him from behind her hideous orange desk — she *wanted to make her expectations clear.* David had shown great improvement in his three months teaching at Silicon Valley English, but she still had some concerns — not criticisms, not complaints, she beamed — only *concerns.* She was still waiting for him to prove he was willing to go above and beyond, she said, to be a *mentor* to students, not just a *teacher.* That afternoon, David's fingernails made little crescent moons in his palms as Principal Yue provided the address — way up north past the Fifth Ring and Olympic Park — time, and a phone number to call if he couldn't find the friend's house. Introduce yourself as "Gao Fushuai" when you get there, she urged. They'll be expecting you.

Gao Fushuai. As David wiped away the sweat on the neck, he suddenly realized why he had been pimped out personally. *Gao Fushuai, a foreigner television star!* That must have been Principal Yue's promise to her friend. Have a famous foreigner be your son's personal English monkey. David rolled up the sleeves of his white dress shirt and spat on the pavement. The guard turned his nose.

Just then, an older man in loose-fitting light-blue clothes approached from somewhere inside the gate. He hurried toward the guardroom in his soft-soled cloth shoes, spoke quickly, and an industrial buzz sounded, opening the gate. The man — some kind of kung fu butler? — didn't respond to David's greeting, only swept his arm in the direction he'd come from, indicating that David follow.

David had to nearly trot to keep up with his guide as they wove around three of the eight identical buildings, each one twenty stories and topped with a narrow tower that made them look like USB drives. They entered an ornate glass-and-bronze lobby on the first floor of one of the buildings and stood on either side of a tall black vase bursting with gaudy flowers. The elevator door was already wide open, but the old man didn't move. David stood by, confused. He asked why they were still waiting, but the old man just shook his head helplessly. Was he maybe deaf? David reached out and rubbed a petal between his thumb and forefinger: fake.

A second set of elevator doors opened and when they entered, David realized why they had been waiting. There were no buttons on the inside, only a small black box that his guide pressed a plastic card against. The doors closed and, after a few noiseless moments, opened again directly onto a foyer on the building's penthouse.

Gold. The entire room appeared as a single glinting piece of golden tinfoil, reflecting and refracting still more golden light pouring down from a massive chandelier at the room's center. David stepped out of the elevator onto polished checkerboard marble as the old kung fu master in blue disappeared down the hall, still without a word. The heads of two Tibetan antelope, completely golden, down to their impossibly long antlers, stared out from the wall. Corinthian columns. Gleaming vine motifs etched into the already-golden wallpaper. The vision was dazzling. David would, in a few short seconds, begin processing how hilariously, staggeringly tacky the apartment was, but for a few brief moments, standing next to the elevator, he was dazzled, the way a bird would be.

He took a few more steps inside and called out hello. He surveyed the foyer, living room, and attached open kitchen, but David didn't see any signs of life. He had made his way into the living room when he heard footsteps — harder, rubber soles — approaching from the hallway. A boy appeared — tall and lanky, wearing a baggy hip-hop sweatshirt and black ball cap with a flat brim.

"Hello," David said, in English.

The cap brim nodded.

"I'm Gao Fushuai."

If the boy was supposed to recognize David by his Chinese stage name, he didn't appear to.

"Did my mom send you here?" the boy said, in Chinese. He hadn't moved from the hallway, as if wary of this stranger.

"The principal at my school told me to come here. She said you wanted to practice your English."

The boy rolled his eyes and trudged down the hallway. David hated him instantly. Alone again, he walked over to the grand piano, hoping the room would shore up his spirits again. Billowy curtains the color of red wine swept down to the floor behind it. He turned back and sat down on one of the high-backed stuffed burgundy thrones and studied the woodwork. Everything in the room looked edible, made of chocolate.

"What's your name?" David asked when the boy returned.

"Dai."

"You don't have an English name?"

The boy was rummaging around kitchen drawers and didn't respond. Bedroom, study, kitchen, living room — Dai couldn't locate a single pen. David told him to sit down anyway. They could just have a chat. Up close, David could see a long prominent scar running down the right side of the boy's face, tracing his jawline. Dai had thick eyebrows, partially obscured by the brim of his hat. His cheeks were sunken.

"So, you're going to Australia?"

The boy gave an assenting grunt.

"When are you going?"

"*Jiuyuefen.*"

"'September,' you mean."

Grunt.

"Why don't you try saying it? Sep-tem-ber."

They staggered on like this for some time — twenty questions and monosyllabic answers. As he droned on, David cycled through a range of feelings — visceral hate, confusion, absurd amusement, empathy, resentment. Silicon Valley English was filled with kids like Dai — little spoiled pricks who spoke zero English but whose parents paid their ways to study in the West. Dai was no different, David was sure, an entitled, apathetic, arrogant punk. Still, David was vaguely impressed that even after a half hour, Dai still seemed genuinely mystified as to why he was sitting here fielding questions from a strange foreigner. He didn't look at home here in the Palace of Versailles.

There were no breaks, no offers for a drink of water. Neither of them had any idea how long "Gao Fushuai" was supposed to stay. Finally, after about an hour, David slapped his knee and said they could stop here for the day. Dai remained morose and superior the entire time.

"So...," David said, switching to Chinese again. "There's the matter of the tutoring fee."

"How much is it?" It was the longest string of words Dai had said for the last hour.

"Five hundred," David said immediately. He'd come up with the number, high but not stratospheric, sitting on the couch. It was clear Dai had no clue about the lessons, and his family had the money. If he was going to spend time with this brat all the way out here in Tutankhamen's tomb, David was at least it was going to be paid well.

Dai handed over the bills, and David immediately regretted not asking for more. David asked about returning next week; maybe they could meet for two hours next time since the location was a bit hard to reach. Dai shrugged.

"Okay, so that would be one thousand kuai for two hours next time."

Dai offered only another maddeningly apathetic look back. David wanted to smack the hat off his head. Fuck these people.

"Plus another fifty kuai for transportation to and from your house," he added.

* * *

June was a rainy, monotonous blur that David spent

equally at Silicon Valley English, Dai's house at Palais de Violette, and his apartment with bottles of Yanjing Beer and downloaded American movies. Even if he'd had money, David had no real desire to go anywhere else, to socialize or meet people. Well, he'd made a little money, hadn't he? Between his job at the school and tutoring Dai on Saturdays, David had stepped back from the precipice at least. Still, having a little money felt worse than being flat broke. David thought about squandering it all in one go, getting rid of it, but spending a few thousand kuai meant making decisions, thinking. Why go anywhere? Beijing's weather seemed to understand this, at least.

In truth, he was also a little depressed since a Skype conversation last week. Through an old contact of his agent's, David had tracked down a television producer working in Los Angeles. No one especially important, but someone who had produced a few sitcoms. David knew that this life in Beijing — teaching fucking English — was not sustainable. He needed a way out, and he had a few film credits after all.

The LA producer had never heard of *The Art of Peace* or *The Valley of the Heart.* Had David done any films in English, a co-production at least? Well, no, but David was looking to relocate and, with his language skills, he might be useful to have on set at a co-production. He was in the middle of a sentence, when the internet connection in his apartment began to crap out.

"Hello? Hello?"

"Hi, are you still there?"

"Hello?"

The connection dropped and David redialed. "Hi. Can you hear me now?"

All told, the interview lasted fifteen minutes, ending on a string of chopped words: "'ough market ... agent can ... 'ead shot."

David tried calling a third time, but no one answered.

He knew he had to keep trying. If anything had become clear to David during the last month it was that he had to escape China — escape the shitty internet connection, the pollution, the gutter-oil food. But he'd prefer escaping to *something* back in the States. He just needed to keep life steady until he could think of what that was.

So it felt like an intrusion when Dai texted him a few hours before their planned lesson one Saturday asking to meet at David's apartment instead of the Palais de Violette. Yes, it was easier for David not to leave his apartment, but that wasn't the point. It was needless change; Dai didn't offer a reason.

Their one-hundred-and-twenty minutes together that afternoon was especially excruciating. Dai spoke even less than usual, only grunting out a few lines from his textbook, word for word: *I believe that climate change is the defining global crisis of our lifetimes, and you?* The minutes dragged on; David hadn't even eaten dinner yet. He pointed to another line on the page and listened to Dai mangle it slowly, word by word.

What were they doing here, David thought that night? They both hated it. Dai would go to Australia and not understand a word spoken in the classroom. He'd find a way to pass the English proficiency test — pay a test-taker, skirt the admissions rules somehow. He would get to Australia and learn exactly nothing for four years. Then he'd return to Beijing and go into business and never have to speak English. Why even study it in the first place?

Dai never tried because he knew, deep down, he didn't have to. He hadn't faced a real challenge his entire life, David was certain. He had never been lost, desperate, struggling through a Skype conversation half the world away. He had never been broke, drinking watery five-kuai Yanjing beers. And for whatever reason, seeing Dai's whole act — the apathy, the sullenness — in his own dark, one-bedroom apartment infuriated David even further.

When Dai finally left the apartment after ten, David ordered in noodles and took a shower. He set up his laptop on the coffee table in the living room, split a pair of disposable wooden chopsticks, and collapsed on the couch. As he did, he felt something hard jab him. David twisted an arm behind his back and produced a black cell phone. He had seen the soft black leather case enough times to know it belonged to Dai. Shit, he'd left it here.

David weighed the sleek thing in his palm for a moment and then set it on the coffee table next to his plastic container of fried noodles and started to eat. Dai would realize he was missing his phone and return any minute. The little punk was so lucky he'd dropped it here, somewhere safe, David thought. How many cell phones had *he* lost? How many phones had he lost in the back seats of taxis or snatched from his pocket on the subway?

How many bicycles had been stolen from him in Beijing over six years? Five? Six? At least one per year, David thought. Expensive mountain bikes with expensive locks, cheap Flying Pigeons that weighed almost as much as he did — none of them ever lasted. The neighbors, police, friends — they all had zero sympathy. That's just the way it was.

Five bikes. Three phones. Five hundred kuai each, let's say. Beijing owed him at least four thousand kuai, David reckoned. He picked up Dai's cell phone off the table once again. The silver-black surface returned his reflection. Why shouldn't he go sell it in the morning? He could probably get twenty-five hundred kuai for it. Why not just lie to Dai about having it. Let the brat go out tomorrow and buy a new one. Dai had the money; what did it matter to him? If he were back in St. Louis, David would have returned it without question, but why should he here? Why be honest when no one else was?

David pushed the oil-streaked plastic box to the center of the table and stretched out on the couch, pleased with his decision. It was only eleven o'clock, but he felt an overpowering urge to sleep.

Instead, he absently slipped the back cover off of Dai's cell phone and blew on the battery. When he reassembled it and tried turning it on, the device responded with a vibrating jolt and the screen flashed to life. The battery seemed to be fully charged. Had it only been turned off? On his back, David held the phone up at arms' length, idly scrolling through the games, contacts and call histories. There were thirty missed calls from Dai's father. In fact, there didn't appear to be any incoming or outgoing calls for months.

When David opened the photo gallery, he saw something very different: two young naked Chinese women bent toward a glass-top table about to snort thin lines of white powder.

David squirmed upright and zoomed in, starting with the women. One was bent toward the camera, her long hair a curtain that obscured her face. David eventually examined the other, clothed, figures in the room. Silver and satin decor — a private room in a club somewhere. David swiped through more pictures that appeared to be taken from the same night — same group of Chinese kids at a dance club, crooked ties and lazy eyes, rail-thin women who could pass for models.

In more than a few of the photos, Dai had turned the camera on himself, arm heavily draped around one woman or another. David almost didn't recognize him without the hip-hop getup. Dai was dressed up — a silver dress shirt with a skinny black tie, swept-back wet-looking hair. The photos had been taken only months ago, the files read, but something was off about Dai's face; it was too clean. His thick dark eyebrows looked the same, as did his faint mustache. It took David a few more moments before he realized what was missing: Dai didn't have the large scar running down his jaw.

David clicked on a video trained on a semi-dressed girl.

"I bet you have!" the man's voice behind the camera called.

"No, I haven't before!" she purred back. "You have to teach me!"

"All right. You have to come closer. Here … no … even closer.… What are you so afraid of? You can't be afraid to touch it!"

She crawled over to him as he reclined on the black couch and unbuttoned his pants.

Bass-heavy music pounded in the video as she took

him into her mouth. David watched, aroused, momentarily transported.

Then the video suddenly slipped away from the screen, and David stared uncomprehendingly at the word "Dad" emblazoned on the screen. The phone began to chirp the opening bass line to a pop song. David held the device in his frozen hand, mind completely blank.

David did nothing. Soon, the noises and vibrations stopped, and the screen returned to a black head of hair bobbing up and down. A rush of goose bumps swept across the nape of his neck and down his back. The phone's menu bar read "31 missed calls." David's right thumb crawled up to the side of the phone and powered it off.

* * *

Even through the tangle of strobe lights, David spotted him immediately. Dai sat alone with his elbows on a high bar table. Black slacks and white V-neck T-shirt that read "MAYBACH." He was slouched forward over the empty tabletop, a heavy silver watch dangling from his thin wrist. David paused next to the glass staircase, peering at Dai through the gaps in the steps like a seasoned voyeur.

David was as prepared as he would ever be — he had already copied all of contents of Dai's cell phone onto his computer, studying the pictures with a mixture of shock and jealousy. Now there was no more time for research, only action. A wash of synthesizer strings rushed through the lounge music playing overhead as David straightened his back and strode up to the table.

"Hey, Dai!" he exclaimed, as if they were old friends.

Dai lifted his eyes to meet his teacher's.

"Have you been waiting long?" David spoke to him in Chinese.

"Just arrived."

David placed Dai's black cell phone in the center of the round table as a token of goodwill.

"I only found it late last night and didn't know how to reach you. Otherwise I would have returned it. You didn't call."

Dai shrugged. "I don't use it anymore."

David puzzled over the meaning of this for a moment. "So, are you partying tonight?"

"It's a bit early."

Only a few of the tables were occupied, and the room was too cold, refrigerated against the body heat not yet being generated. David nodded and tried to ignore the spider of worry crawling across his mind. Did Dai suspect something?

"C'mon, let's get a drink." David had only three hundred kuai on him, but there was nothing else to say.

"I'm not drinking."

An uncomfortable silence settled between them again. David tried to remember whether or not he'd seen a Maybach from the photos. In one of them, Dai and a half-dozen of his high school friends and their fathers stood in front of a lineup of gleaming Maseratis, Ferraris, and a black Lamborghini, with its vertical doors jackknifed like the wings of an exotic beetle. They appeared to be standing in the parking lot of a private club somewhere. The boys posed slightly, wearing sunglasses. The middle-aged fathers stood squarely behind their sons, shoulders slouched forward, arms slack.

David could feel Dai looking at him more closely now. He scanned the room for another topic. David had vowed to himself not to bring up English lessons; he didn't want to be Dai's teacher tonight, he wanted to be … a friend? A business partner? He wasn't sure yet. The only thing he'd decided so far was that he wasn't going to sell Dai's phone. Its contents had to be worth much than a few thousand kuai. David just needed to feel Dai out for how much more.

"C'mon, one drink!" David pressed.

He stood up from the table before Dai could respond and made his way to the bar, careful not to open his wallet until he was a safe distance away. Sixty kuai for a vodka-and-Red Bull! And Dai hadn't even offered to pay. Since when were Chinese people at dance clubs so stingy? During his first year in China, David had never paid for a drink. You could walk into any club and some beaming young guy in a tight-fitting purple T-shirt would have his arms around you in seconds, steering you toward a table of blended Scotch and ice in a plastic cup.

As he waited for a boy in a bowtie to pour his drinks, two girls tottered by in high-heels and fishnet stockings to a table close to the dance floor. One wore a strapless iridescent short dress that seemed to flash at David as she brushed by. Was it just him, or did their gazes linger on him for an extra beat? Were they judging him? David glanced beneath the glass bar top and saw his dull-black dress shoes staring back. He was the oldest person in this room.

Dai loosened up a tiny bit once the drinks began to flow, mercifully. The Thursday night crowd began filling up the club in earnest around midnight. Two of Dai's friends materialized and sat with them — Benny and Fish, they called themselves. They were high school classmates of Dai's — both, what, nineteen years old? They were subservient to him in subtle ways, clinking glasses with Dai at a lower angle, lighting his cigarettes, not speaking without being prompted by him. Both wore clothes a bit too ostentatious to be truly rich. Neither were in any of the photos David had seen.

"How about those girls?" David said, gesturing toward the pair of young girls he'd seen earlier.

"Too old."

"What do you mean too old? Look at them!"

Benny tapped his upper arm with two fingers, a gesture that David didn't understand. David strained for a look at the girls' arms, but they were turned the wrong way.

"Too old," he repeated. "See their arms? Those little scars on their arms are from vaccines when they were young. They are girls born in the 1980s. Young girls don't have them."

Dai was just as arrogant here as he was during English lessons. Every time the conversation drifted toward brands of watches, apartments, or luxury cars, he doled out joyless, correct opinions. By the third vodka-and-Red Bull, the conversation devolved into Dai scoffing at everything Benny said. *You thought Tag Hauer watches were made in Germany!* David nodded along to it all and wiped away rings of condensation from the table with his palm. He was down to one-hundred-and-thirty kuai — two more drinks, if he was lucky. Tomorrow ... well, David strained to push it out of mind.

David kind of liked Benny and Fish. There was a familiar eagerness to them compared to Dai's jaded, accounting view of the world. They were nineteen and seemed to recognize that they hadn't figured it all out yet. They laughed and said, "I don't know." They both complimented David's Chinese, even if they hadn't recognized him from TV.

"I didn't study English hard enough in school," Benny confessed.

"The language environment is very important," said Fish. "If you lived in America, you would use English every day. You would learn it quickly."

"Well, that's why Dai is studying English. To study abroad, right?" David said. Dai didn't look up from his phone.

"Brother Dai!" Benny finally called. "When do you leave for Australia?"

"Soon." The distracted, icy look was back on Dai's face. He was bored of these people. David felt a tipsy urge to grab him and beat the entitlement out of him.

"I need to go home," Dai said finally, pocketing his phone. "Where are you going?"

There seemed no hope of pressuring Dai to stay any longer, so David accepted the unexpected offer of a ride home. They left Benny and Fish at the table and walked by the glass stairs and out of the club. Rain angled down in the streetlights. The sky had a reddish hue, lit up by the city lights or pollution — David had never figured out which. He surveyed the parking lot; obscene sports cars were lined up along the curb. The taillights of a black sedan flashed silently ahead, and David felt a twinge of disappointment. It was only a BMW.

"How many days per week are you studying English?" David asked, once they were in the car. He hated himself for bringing up English lessons, but he couldn't think of anything else to say.

"I don't like English."

"Okay," David sighed. "Aren't you going to Australia though?"

"Yeah."

"Well, then you *have* to study English, right?" Dai fiddled with the windshield wipers.

"Yeah, I have to," he finally said.

What the hell was he doing here with this little puke? He'd spent nearly the last of his money pretending to be Dai's friend, all for what? He'd learned nothing useful over the course of the night. What had he expected? As they continued west, David thought about all the obscene photos and videos on Dai's phone and got angry all over again. It wasn't until they'd almost arrived at David's house that he broke the silence.

"What about that scar on your chin? Get in a fight?"

"Car accident."

"Must have been a serious one."

"I was lucky. My friend wasn't."

"My best friend from high school back in the U.S. died in a car crash. He was seventeen," David lied.

Dai kept staring ahead. David took a breath. It was now or never. "Who was your friend? Was it one of the guys in the photos, standing in front of the cars?"

For the first time in the car, Dai turned to face him. "What?"

"Nothing. I was just saying that your friend dying is the same as my friend from high school."

"No, you said something about a photo. What photo are you talking about?"

David stared ahead, pulse pounding. Dai pulled the BMW to the gate of David's apartment compound, near a large pile of dirt on the sidewalk. He did not unlock the car doors.

"What photo are you talking about?" Dai repeated, louder now.

"You and your friends...," David said weakly. He suddenly wasn't sure where he was going with this.

Dai was turned toward David, and the scar on the right side of his face disappeared into shadow. He was glaring at David, hair gleaming.

"Okay, okay," David tried soothing. Outside, the mist swirled in the car's unmoving headlights. "I'm not going to tell anyone about them," he said carefully. "I mean, don't you think I deserve something for that?"

"You don't know anything about me and my friends," Dai said. David heard the car door snap unlocked, and he reached for the handle.

David climbed out, and the BMW pulled away from the curb. David let out his breath, feeling an electric heat — fear, excitement — even though his teeth were chattering. He had hit a nerve! Dai *must* be worried about those photos. David zipped up his rain jacket and set off toward his building, leaving wet footprints in his wake.

13

The Soul of Beijing Volunteer Corps

THE Soul of Beijing Volunteer Corps was napping when Yanmei and her photographer from the *Beijing Evening News* arrived at Ju'er Hutong. Three volunteers — retirees with red armbands pinned to their T-shirts — dozed on folding chairs inside the neighborhood committee office. An electric fan swung across them, rustling newsprint on the table. Yanmei waited at the doorway until a heavy, grayed woman with pendulous breasts emerged from the underground stairwell and demanded to know who she was. The woman's face was cockeyed, nearly winking. Yanmei hurried to explain herself. The woman, Auntie Wang, said to follow her downstairs. The Corps did not stir.

The walls of the neighborhood committee office were covered with glossy posters of cartoon children offering residents advice on a range of topics. Daily Habits to Improve Hygiene in the Kitchen. Fire Prevention Starts with You! Breastfeeding and Your Child. Identifying and Reporting Terrorists. A long red banner tacked to the wall above a whiteboard proclaimed: Raise the Moral Standing of the People.

Downstairs, a woman in her late twenties introduced herself to Yanmei as Meng Yuan, another neighborhood committee member. She had a round face and wore glasses and dirty pink flats with white bows on the toes. Most of the Soul of Beijing Volunteer Corps had returned home already, Meng Yuan explained, but she'd be happy to answer questions. Yanmei looked at Auntie Wang, who was standing next to the photographer, asking how much money he'd paid for his camera.

"Let's go outside, where there's more light," Yanmei suggested.

Since July, every neighborhood committee in the city had formed its own Soul of Beijing Volunteer Corps. State media heralded the groups as "grassroots," even though neighborhood committees, as always, were officially administered by the Party. To earn their red armbands, volunteers were supposed to take oaths to "uphold and improve the Soul of Beijing;" but at least on Ju'er Hutong, they had been handed out to the first ten retirees who had wandered in the office on the day the box arrived.

Yanmei needed smiling photos and a few pull-quotes by three o'clock, and it was already past noon. Normally, she could send in her stories as late as ten thirty the day of publication, but this was a special article. The *Evening News* planned to run four pages of volunteer profiles under the headline "Soulful Beijingers."

Once the foursome returned outside, Meng Yuan helped rouse one of the napping volunteers inside as the photographer paced around looking for an acceptable backdrop. She emerged with an eighty-year-old man who blinked at the afternoon sunshine with narrow, beady eyes. He had a brush cut and wore a stretched purple T-shirt that read "Fashion Child" across the front, in English.

"This female reporter would like to interview you!" Meng Yuan yelled into the man's ear.

She tugged at his arm, helping him down the stone stairs. His legs were so thin that his long white tube socks bunched at his ankles.

"What interview?"

"An interview with the newspaper!" Meng Yuan yelled back.

"Stop wasting time!" chided Auntie Wang. Her feet were firmly planted next to Yanmei. "It's for the newspaper!"

"Why don't we find a place to sit?" Yanmei proposed.

"I'm fine standing!" declared the man. As if to prove this point, he straightened his back.

"All right," said Yanmei, flipping open her notebook. "What is your name?"

"Zhang Weimin," he replied.

"I see. That's a very good name for a volunteer," Yanmei commented brightly.

"What?"

Auntie Wang sprung to action. "SHE SAID, YOUR NAME SOUNDS LIKE A VOLUNTEER'S!"

Yanmei asked a few more questions so she might sketch a biography of the man before her. As Zhang Weimin talked, Yanmei's photographer stalked around him, muttering that the light was too bright. Auntie Wang kept a running commentary on each of Zhang's responses until Meng Yuan politely hushed her.

Zhang Weimin was born in Beijing before the founding of the People's Republic, one of three brothers (that was a small household then!), sent to Qinghai Province during the Cultural Revolution (western China is too poor!) and taught high school mathematics (No. 23 is one of Beijing's best high schools!) until retiring in the 1990s. Yanmei took notes in her notepad. When she turned the interview toward his deeds as a Soul of Beijing volunteer, though, Zhang Weimin got confused.

"I helped a foreigner find the Bird's Nest once," he said. "He was looking for the Bird's Nest. I told him it was that way." Zhang held a crooked finger toward north.

The group pondered this reply for a moment.

Then Auntie Wang shouted "THAT WAS DURING THE OLYMPICS! THAT WAS YEARS AGO!"

"I'm an Olympics volunteer!" Zhang protested.

"Old Zhang," Meng Yuan interjected. "Why don't you say that you help our community with public safety? You help with the neighborhood watch."

"Our residence compound is too chaotic," Zhang declared. "Outsiders can just come in as they please.

Before, everyone knew each other. Now there are bad eggs everywhere, like the Henanese."

"Old Zhang," Meng Yuan tutted. "You can't say 'The Henanese are bad eggs.'"

"How about helping people?" Yanmei tried. "Have you helped anyone in need, like children or the homeless?"

Zhang thought a moment. "Beggars? They shouldn't be here during the Olympic Games!"

"THIS ISN'T FOR THE OLYMPICS VOLUNTEERS!" yelled Auntie Wang. "THESE ARE THE *SOUL OF BEI-JING* VOLUNTEERS!"

Meng Yuan suggested they take a break. The photographer asked Zhang Weimin to stand by the ivy-covered entrance of the compound. The group debated what acts of soulfulness might be staged for a few action shots. Auntie Wang picked a glass bottle out of the trash and set it on the pavement for Old Zhang to pick up and throw away again. A baby and mother were produced so that Zhang might smile alongside them. Auntie Wang herself borrowed a three-wheel pedicab and pedaled it toward Old Zhang, who stood near the entrance holding out a flat palm, motioning her to stop.

Yanmei's mind was already composing text. *Zhang Weimin, retired schoolteacher and old Beijinger, is one of Ju'er Hutong neighborhood's Soul of Beijing volunteers. Previously an Olympics volunteer, Zhang helps oversee public safety....* Her eyes scanned the top edge of her notebook where she had written the four so-called Soul of Beijing pillars: Innovative. Green. Lawful. Harmonious. For the following day's spread, the *Evening News* planned to organize the Soulful Beijinger profiles by pillar, devoting a full page to each of the four. Yanmei looked back up at Zhang Weimin — leaning in front of Auntie Wang's pedicab, arm extended. His red armband now drooped past his bony elbow by the last remaining safety pin. Yanmei circled the word "Lawful."

* * *

The city begged for autumn, but July dragged on like a single endless afternoon in which nothing moved but the mosquitoes. The plane trees bent forward, their thin branches grasping for a breeze. Office workers wilted after lunch, splayed across their desks in high-rise towers. Perhaps twice a day an old man emerged from his front door, sniffed at the air, and forecasted rain; but he was always wrong.

Yanmei sat in the back seat of a taxi, staring out the open window. The driver refused to turn on the air conditioning and now, in gridlocked traffic, dense, stagnant air filled the car. Sweat glued her bangs to her forehead. She stared at her notes on the luminous life of Lawful Zhang Weimin, picturing him bent at the waist and slightly dazed by the myriad voices around him. The old man's face brought to mind her own grandfather's, back in Shandong Province — creased, weathered skin, deep-set eyes, and a thatch of steel-wool hair.

She recalled a stray detail about Old Zhang and scratched the words "liberation shoes" at the bottom of the page. Old Zhang had been wearing the same shoes her grandfather swore by — army-green canvas shoes with black plastic soles. That entire hardened generation still dressed as if war might break out in the country at any moment. They had endured years of privation, hunger, and turmoil, and couldn't quite give themselves over to these fat years, couldn't quite be convinced that there was no more revolution to come.

She absently flipped through a few more pages in her notebook, stopping on a page with five names in a column — the city government officials Panzi suspected of being responsible for his fateful Ferrari. Two months of haphazard digging and nothing to show for it, really. She had investigated their family members and sifted through what limited financial documents were available, carefully plotting each new fact on hand-drawn relationship maps that she kept in the bottom drawer of her *Evening News* desk. The digging was torturous, obsessive work, but she found she enjoyed it immensely. Each new discovery seemed like a gleaming coin hidden from the rest of the world.

Still, two months of research and she was no closer to finding a red Ferrari.

Yanmei told no one in the office about her pursuit, not even Editor Ge, not even when he stumbled upon her late one night at the office. She was studying a recent Beijing bond prospectus — another shiny coin — when he appeared from the dark corridor that led to the elevators. He seemed immaculate from across the room, as if he might have just returned from a fancy dinner. When he got closer, Yanmei could smell alcohol on him. He installed himself at the desk opposite her, hands on his knee, and asked what she was working on.

Yanmei stammered out a lie, something about wanting to learn about finance. She trusted Editor Ge, but not enough to confide in him her secret project. Editor Ge leveled his gaze at her. They both knew that most of the *Evening News*' business and economics articles were simply reprinted from China's main business dailies. The *Evening News* didn't even have a business correspondent. Besides, Yanmei's beat was culture.

"I don't know numbers, but anything I can help with?" he asked.

She got the sense that night that Editor Ge didn't want to return home. After they chatted for a while longer, he began talking about himself, unprompted. He said it had been fifteen years since he'd moved his family to Beijing. It wasn't easy; he still thought about the old days, he confessed. He told her about his old paper, *Southern Weekend*, his biggest investigative scoops, the newsroom camaraderie — *real* journalism, *real* journalism, he kept repeating.

"The stubborn ones stayed, despite the crackdowns, even after *Southern Weekend*'s editor was put under house arrest," Editor Ge told her. "But what was I supposed to do? I wasn't like them. I had kids to feed. Yanmei, you understand me; I know you do," he pleaded. "I know they resent me even though they would never say anything to my face. But I didn't have a choice."

Yanmei was taken aback, unsure of what to say. What was Editor Ge looking for, she wondered? Forgiveness? Recognition? An affair with her?

But before she could open her mouth to respond, Editor Ge stood and straightened his tie, as if sensing her pity. He told her good night and walked away.

* * *

Yanmei and Panzi had grown closer in the months since they first met — the initial surreal rush of his car-crash conspiracy giving way to steady text messaging and the odd meal together. At first, they met only when Yanmei's research had found some new lead, but by their fourth dinner together there was nothing new to report. The topic of the crash breached like a whale — heavy and half-hidden — before submerging again for long periods in colder waters. Panzi had begun affectionately calling her Big Sister.

Panzi lived in three different apartments that summer but spent most of his time on the city's outskirts, running errands or scouting properties. Yanmei rode new subway line extensions to meet him after work. She peered out the windows of the aboveground cars that ran along wide highways already swimming with red taillights. They met at subway exits and set off together through the wide planned streets of new neighborhoods and half-built apartment blocks, usually in search of somewhere to eat. They probed the contours of the city and revisited his favorite haunts. Neighborhoods emerged. Bridges were named. As the city expanded, it also grew more intimate.

She mostly followed Panzi's lead. He seemed bent on paying attention to everything. She waited while he chatted with restaurant owners, waitresses, old men waiting on benches. He took inordinate pleasure in these dull conversations, she thought. As they ate, he asked Yanmei the intimate details of whatever story was working on, however mundane. What *was* the difference between China's best-selling soy sauce and the rest of the brands? *Why* was Qingdao considered the country's most dog-friendly city? These puff pieces meant absolutely nothing to her; why did he care so much?

At first, she thought he was only being polite, but the longer Yanmei spent with Panzi, she began to suspect that all of it — the small talk, the endless battery of questions — was a kind of distraction. There was a fragility to him; she caught glimpses of it when their conversations brushed up against certain topics — his family, the apartment buyers he encountered, and, of course, the night of the Ferrari crash.

Once, over a meal of chicken wings, he nearly broke down crying when she asked a polite question about his grandfather's health. He rubbed his eyes so hard they turned purple. Panzi seemed so young then. Too young! Was he really only two years her junior? Yanmei fought down an instinct to reach across the table and touch the arm of the boy.

She liked Panzi, liked his smile and the thin blue veins that showed beneath the skin of his temples. Mostly she liked having some place to go besides the *Evening News* office and her own apartment. Whenever she saw her phone light up with a message from Panzi in the afternoon, she felt a little thrill. *Sure, I don't have any plans tonight. What time?* He would text back some far-flung subway station she'd never heard of before, and she would spend the next ten minutes consulting the map on her phone, wondering what new territory they'd explore that night.

This particular night, Yanmei exited Guomao Station and made her way north along East Third Ring Road. The dark angles of the China Central Television building rose above the construction wall on her right, pinpricks of red light flashing red in unison on its roof. Across the overpass on her left, the city's central business district lit the inky sky. Ten minutes of walking along with traffic toward the CCTV building and it didn't seem any closer.

When she arrived at the bus stop, their meeting place, she nearly didn't recognize the figure with his back to her, talking on the phone. When he turned and saw her, Panzi gave her a helpless smile. He'd shaved his head!

"No ... no.... I can't," he was saying. "I'm meeting some-one right now. Look she's already here.... No, she's.... Listen, she's here."

Panzi rolled his eyes for effect while Yanmei waited another minute. She peered back up at the CCTV build-ing, the angles far more dramatic here at the base. Every-one likened the building to a giant pair of pants, but here it reminded Yanmei of the Sphinx in Egypt. She heard Panzi's words tapering off to spare monosyllables, and then he hung up.

"Sorry, my mother's coming. I need to grab a new apartment key. We can go eat after that."

"What did you do? You look like a monk!"

It wasn't just his buzzed head; Panzi looked thinner than he had only a week ago. He wore a baggy T-shirt and shorts that hung off his frame. Panzi rubbed a hand over his head.

"It's too hot."

They turned east and walked along the sidewalk, leaving the noise of the Third Ring Road behind them but making little conversation to compensate. The silence was a comfortable one, at least to Yanmei. Panzi walked a few paces ahead, muttering softly to himself, preoccupied. A black leather belt barely held up his baggy shorts, bunched up at the waist, and his bare legs looked pale and skinny, in a way that reminded her of Lawful Zhang Weimin.

Waiting at a stoplight she glanced back at the CCTV building, now at the opposite angle from her initial approach. The building looked like someone on his knees praying, maybe begging. The light turned and she followed Panzi across the intersection.

They entered a housing compound — a loose collection of three-story tan brick buildings — where Panzi said they had to wait for his mother. The buildings must have been at least twenty years old, with rusted bars over tiny windows and notices for handymen and air conditioning repair plastered around the entrances. Nearby, a television murmured beside a lean-to fruit stand. The buildings were run-down and darkened with age in a way that made Yanmei nostalgic.

"So, you bought a place here?" she asked.

"Upstairs, I think." Panzi was standing next to an open iron gate, fiddling with his phone. He looked up at the third floor. "Mom won't be happy when she sees it."

"It reminds me of where I grew up, in Jinan," she said, looking around. "Though I guess we didn't have this much open space between the buildings —"

"*Wei!* Mom, where are you?" Panzi yelled, cutting her off. "I'm standing at the gate. The front gate! No, you don't need to park. You can just hand me the keys."

He hung up the phone and a few minutes later, a compact middle-aged woman emerged from the compound's entrance. She approached at a brisk pace, a bright-red designer purse dangling from her elbow. Her permed hair didn't seem to move.

"What a terrible place!" she exclaimed. "Fifty thousand per square meter?" Her mouth appeared puckered, and then her eyes swept over the girl.

"Mom, this is Yanmei." Panzi's voice had dropped to an almost inaudible whisper. "Big Sister, this is my mom."

Qinyan gave the girl another efficient look before fixing her eyes to the barred third-story window. An air conditioning unit dripped near their shoes, a rust-colored trickle staining the tan brick wall. Panzi and Yanmei followed his mother up three flights of concrete stairs. Inside, the apartment looked just as worn as the building's exterior — water-stained walls, a flaking ceiling, a torn couch covered in a layer of black dust. A familiar sickening smell of sewage permeated the white-tile bathroom. The kitchen sink stood, unconnected to any pipes, in the middle of the living room.

Yanmei lingered near the entrance while Panzi's mother stalked in and out of rooms, ranting at every new abomination she discovered. Through one of the two narrow windows, Yanmei noticed the outline of a new office tower under construction a few streets away. The building was tall and oblong; it took up nearly the entire window frame. Through the gauzy construction cover, crosshatches of steel and discs of cement rose upward toward the curved peak. Welding sparks winked at her through the scaffolding. *This is Yanmei, my Big Sister.*

"Do you know what that building is?" she asked Panzi when he reappeared. He shrugged and joined her at the window.

"Sorry about all this. She'll leave soon," he whispered.

"It's fine. There's no rush."

Yanmei turned back to the tall building under construction just in time for a shower of sparks to fall from one of the upper floors. She realized that Panzi was staring at the same scene, mesmerized, transported elsewhere. Panzi's neck looked thin, almost delicate in this light. Warmth spread through her.

Qinyan stormed back into the room, vowing to call the seller that evening. Fifty thousand, she kept muttering. Panzi finally procured the apartment keys from her and ushered everyone out the door and downstairs. They walked Panzi's mother toward her car, which was parked with two wheels jacked up on the sidewalk. Panzi stood by, awkwardly formal, while his mother eventually pulled away, speeding through a yellow traffic light. Yanmei watched the tension leave Panzi's shoulders as soon as his mother was gone.

The two of them settled on a donkey-meat restaurant not far from the compound. It was a simple, local place, opened by a family from Shanxi Province, with hard seats and pixelated photographs of animals in pastures on the walls. A Guo'an soccer match played on a television in the corner, though none of the dozen restaurant patrons paid any attention to it.

"Sorry about that," Panzi said.

Yanmei shrugged. "She's your mother. She's well-intentioned."

Panzi sighed, and his gaze drifted to the animals on the wall.

"You know, back when I was still in school, she had this egg timer," he began. "She used to set it on the desk when I was doing review exercises for the college entrance exam...."

He paused and sighed heavily again.

"I was falling behind at school; we both knew it. She said I wasted too much time, so she started following me around the house with it. Ten minutes for a shower. Twenty minutes for supper."

Yanmei looked down at the table, half-embarrassed, half-delighted. The sandwiches and beer appeared. She had never eaten donkey-meat sandwiches before, but the meat was thinly sliced and tasted like beef. It was delicious.

"God, that sound," Panzi went on, eyes still set on a pixel of the Photoshopped field of donkeys. "They aren't clocks, you know? They just grind and grind and *grind*. I was sure that was the sound of my chest tightening. I had to lock myself in the bedroom. Is that even normal?"

"It's the college entrance exam," Yanmei said. "Parents go a little crazy; but they're just trying to help. My parents wouldn't let me watch a minute of TV for months before the exam."

"I was so relieved when I found out that I'd failed," Panzi said without hesitation. "It was the worst thing that could have happened. And so, when it did, there was this enormous weight lifted off my shoulders. I couldn't disappoint her any more than that. It was over."

Yanmei set her sandwich down, genuinely surprised to hear this.

"You weren't ashamed?"

"Of course I was! The day we got my test results, the two of us sat down in the kitchen, and my mom cried and cried. She kept saying she was such a failure; she didn't even seem mad at *me*. I had to sit at that table a long time and console *her*."

They picked at their food for a few moments in silence. At the *Evening News*' office, Yanmei endured endless stories from Annie and Yuanyuan about their dating escapades. She imagined walking into the office the following morning and casually mentioning she'd been on a date to a donkey meat restaurant with a college reject the previous night. The thought made her laugh.

"What's so funny?" Panzi asked.

"Nothing.... I was just thinking about that luxurious apartment your mom owns now," she said, gesturing back toward the residential compound. "That's some consolation."

They laughed and clinked glasses.

"Seriously, you're really going to stay there? It's such a dump."

"For a while," he sighed. "Or one of the other places she's bought."

"Why can't you just rent your own apartment?"

"It's complicated."

Surely Panzi's family was wealthy enough to afford buying a property for him, she thought.

"I've gotten used to moving around a lot," he went on. "Every place has its own charm if you look hard enough."

"That place didn't even have running water! You call that charm?"

Panzi took a sip of beer. "It's more interesting this way. Moving around. I like leaving it up to fate."

"Fate, meaning your mother."

"I guess you could say that."

Panzi's expression changed. Small furrows appeared on his forehead. The last three bites of his sandwich remained untouched in the basket.

"Maybe not fate, maybe just letting go of control. I see my mom trying to control everything...."

His voice trailed off. Yanmei watched his face contorted in thought.

"It's all a lie, really, right? We want to believe we have control; that's what we tell ourselves. But there's so much we can't control. And for people like my mom, she just ignores everything she can't control. Like it's not real."

He paused, looking intently at the plastic table. Yanmei felt a tightening in her stomach; she knew instinctively that these were Xiao Song's words.

"So...."

"So, you have to give up some control to see the bigger picture," he said. "When I go back to that awful apartment tonight, I'll see and hear things I never would have if I were the one choosing."

He began to blush. Panzi looked so comically serious as he said this that Yanmei couldn't help herself.

"God, you really are turning into a Taoist monk!" she cried.

Panzi looked up at her, his dark eyes magnified by his glasses, ridiculous ears outstretched. She looked away; his face was unbearable. Yanmei hated what she was about to say next but couldn't stop; it was a scab she had to pick.

"Let me guess," she said quietly, looking at the wall. "Your missing girlfriend, the one from Duanqiruifu told you all about that." She hoped her cheeks weren't as flushed with beer as they felt.

"Big Sister, what do you mean by that?" Panzi sat up straight again.

"It's just ... didn't she teach you all about the secret harmony of the universe or whatever?"

He began to protest, but Yanmei cut him off.

"It doesn't matter," she sighed. "It's none of my business."

14

Carapace

IT took nearly an hour every night, fighting rush-hour traffic along Chang'an Avenue, for Zhenhua to get from City Planning's office to the city government building on Zhengyi Road. As his taxi inched eastward, he occasionally looked up from his paperwork in the back seat, as if hearing a distant voice, and studied the faces of the other souls trapped in cars in the next lanes. They were all invariably engrossed in their phones — even the drivers — trying to distract themselves from gridlocked reality. He never caught anyone looking especially upset, only resigned. Many of them were heading home after all, toward supper and a few more blissful hours of escape from all of this. But Zhenhua was not going home; he was going back to work.

His job moonlighting at the vice mayor's office was simple: write. Editorials, essays, reports, reflections, speeches — thousands of words lauding Vice Mayor Chen Yihui's track record in Beijing's government. Quantity of achievements was the main thing. After a few weeks of this, Zhenhua's mind sloshed with torrents of statistics. Foreign investment was up. Dog-biting incidents were down. Technology patents were being registered at a record pace.

Each night, he sat at an open desk next to Rong Baiheng, Chen's secretary, who worked his contact list and faxed Zhenhua's editorials to newspapers and publishing houses. Baiheng was a distant relative of the vice mayor and younger than Zhenhua by nearly a decade. Beyond that, Zhenhua knew little about Baiheng or Vice Mayor Chen's situation in general. It didn't feel appropriate to ask directly, and there was no one else around to triangulate such questions. Most of Zhenhua's interactions with Baiheng came hunched over oily takeout boxes of eggplant-with-garlic-sauce and shredded pork or standing outside the men's restroom near the stairwell, smoking cigarettes afterward. Even then, there were no introductions, no strategic meetings, no explanations of what was really going on.

But listening in on Baiheng's increasingly harried phone calls, Zhenhua could tell time was running out. Vice Mayor Chen rarely emerged from his office anymore. His first days on Zhengyi Road, Zhenhua could hear Chen *thundering* on the other side of the wall — bluster, outrage, fists pounding desk. But in the weeks since, the walls had fallen silent. Now Zhenhua could tell that Chen had ended a phone call only when he heard a loud, bemused laugh. It was the self-satisfied laugh of a martyr, the laugh of someone who'd given up.

Zhenhua printed out a copy of his most recent glowing editorial, rapped softly on the vice mayor's door, and entered. Chen was sitting with his elbows on the desk, yelling at someone. Zhenhua could make out dark bags under his eyes and the long strands of black hair — meticulously plastered across his bald head when Zhenhua first met him a lifetime ago — that had now become unglued. Chen's office smelled rank, lived-in.

"Tell him to call me back tonight! Well, then you have to find him.... I don't care!" Chen hung up and gestured for Zhenhua to sit.

"What's this one?" Chen asked, taking the paper from Zhenhua's hand. "Culture Thriving at the Flourishing Peacock Arts Garden," he read. His eyes swept over a few lines of text and then he flicked it back toward Zhenhua with an annoyed grunt. "Fine. Have Baiheng send it out."

Zhenhua stood to leave, feeling worse for having seen the vice mayor up close. He made it to the door when Chen called him back to sit.

"I want to say something to you," Chen began when Zhenhua had taken his chair again. Chen's gaze seemed to bore holes right through him. A bit of dried white spit was crusted to the corner of his mouth.

"I want you to know that I will not forget your loyalty. When things return to normal, you will have my support. We are comrades in arms."

Zhenhua said his nervous, requisite thank you.

Chen finally broke eye contact and looked down at a newspaper laying on his desk, an editorial alluding to him. He stabbed it with his finger.

"This is a coordinated attack, you understand that,

don't you?" said Chen. He laughed his martyr laugh and cleared his throat. "And as we all know, it's not brute strength that brings success in war; it is unity. You've read *The Art of War*, I'm sure. That's why loyalty is so important. That is why we are comrades in arms."

"These are political attacks, Vice Mayor Chen," Zhenhua said, squeezing the words from his mouth. He arranged the papers of his peacock garden on the desk, hoping to escape. "Everyone knows the attacks are nonsense. The truth will come out."

"Look at it," Chen said, eyes flashing toward the desk again.

Zhenhua looked down and saw a sheet of white paper, hitherto concealed beneath the newsprint. He picked it up, flipped it over and saw that it was a madman's pencil scribbling — names, arrows, circles scrawled all the way to the paper's margins.

"There must be an impetus, an original force behind what has happened. This is what I've been contemplating, trying to balance myself properly, so that I might see clearly the cause of this new imbalance around me. To think clearly, you must maintain a balance, seek the harmony...."

Zhenhua stopped listening, eyes fixed on the paper. There must have been fifty names on it — x'ed out, underlined, circled. None of it made any sense. Dread filled Zhenhua's stomach as Chen droned on. He'd known the vice mayor was having a difficult time, but this — this was deranged. He was still staring at the words when he realized Chen had stopped talking.

"Well, in any case, they're not true anyway, the attacks," Zhenhua squeezed out. "The truth will come out."

He stood to leave.

"Zhenhua," the vice mayor called, "what matters is finding the source of imbalance and getting back to the way things were. And what matters is that we are comrades-in-arms."

* * *

At eleven that night, Zhenhua and Baiheng left the office to get drunk at a snug, wooden Japanese restaurant around the corner. It was Baiheng's idea, but Zhenhua needed little convincing. He felt restless after his talk with Vice Mayor Chen.

Rui would already be asleep by the time he got home anyway. At first, she had waited up for him with a cup of tea and the promise of small talk whenever he returned home after his second shift. When she complained to him about the long hours, Zhenhua reminded her that *she* was the one who first insisted that his career was tied up with the vice mayor's. The vice mayor was responsible for his promotion; now it was time to repay the favor and show loyalty. But lately, even when Rui was awake by the time he made it home, there didn't seem to be much to say between them.

By the time Zhenhua and Baiheng arrived, the restaurant was empty. The waitress stood a large bottle of sake in front of them, retreated to the corner table, and fell asleep with her head buried in her arms. Both men drank off the first three cups without saying much. Then Baiheng removed his glasses and started in.

"I was too naive," he sighed. His face was already crimson, and his glasses had left white marks near his temples. "Chen doesn't have any real talent; I can see that now. He was just lucky, that's all."

Zhenhua murmured something encouraging.

Baiheng looked down at his sake cup, weighing whether or not to give all the way into self-pity.

"They're going to announce the investigation any day now. I talked to a friend at Party Discipline. Two weeks, at the most, he said. It's already started."

"What did Vice Mayor Chen say?"

Baiheng laughed bitterly. "You think I bothered telling him? *You* saw him today, didn't you?"

Zhenhua thought back to his conversation with Chen and felt his face turn redder.

"What else are our options?" he said weakly. "There's nothing we can do besides keep at it." They clinked porcelain cups again. "And look, even if you're right. Even if Chen's career is through, there will be other opportunities. We're both still young. Look at you; you're not even thirty yet! Just work hard, stay clean —"

"Stay clean!" Baiheng let out another bitter laugh, louder. "We're all dirty now. We're 'jackals from the same lair.'"

Baiheng held up another dribbling shot of alcohol. He downed it as Zhenhua tried focusing on his face.

"What do you mean 'we're all dirty'?"

"Why are you here, Comrade Sun?" Baiheng asked. He seemed amused. "Do you even know why you're here? Why you're writing about fucking peacock gardens in the middle of the night?"

"I know about the rumors," Zhenhua said defensively. "I mean, I probably know as much as you do."

"Bullshit!" Baiheng pounded on the wooden table,

stirring the waitress from her nap. If he were an older man, Baiheng would have stopped there, but he couldn't resist saying more.

"You know as much as I do, do you? Do you know what Chen is doing in his office all day?"

"The coordinated attacks," Zhenhua mumbled.

Baiheng burst out into toxic laughter. "You think he's in there trying to save his career? Save *our* careers? Trying to find some 'balance'? Balance of what? Chen is in there calling the *hospital*. He calls them every goddamn hour to check on his son. I got a call from them last week — *me* — asking if I could get him to stop calling. But you knew that, right? You knew *I* was the one who had to tell his wife. The night it happened. You knew *I* was the one who had to arrange everything. Cleaning it up, making it disappear. You know as much as I do, don't you?"

"So, they're true, the rumors," Zhenhua said when Baiheng had exhausted himself.

"Some of them. Not all of them. It doesn't matter. Someone out there has the truth, and you can build a lot of lies with the truth. Whoever has the details about Chen's son won't just come out with it."

Baiheng drank off the rest of his cup.

"Chen was fucked the moment we made the call to clean it up. Some favors are too great. That goddamn Boss of Houhai had us by the balls after that."

Zhenhua stared at the table for a moment, trying to recall something.

"Wait, the Boss of Houhai? The old man with the birthmark on his face? What does he have to do with this?"

"Goddamn traitor."

"He was the one who leaked the truth?" Zhenhua asked.

"Half-truth. How else does it get all the way to the *People's Daily*? He fucked us, sold out Vice Mayor Chen to the highest bidder. Some friend."

"They're friends?"

Baiheng snorted. "Chen's known him for years. I've never liked him, fucking snake. Probably sold Chen out to Vice Mayor Tang, so *he* could take Party Secretary." Baiheng watched the last few drops of sake drip from the bottle into his glass.

"No, that's not who," Zhenhua said, eyes widening. Stray memories were clicking into place. "The Boss cut a deal with Director Li, at City Planning," he said quickly. "I overheard them talking about it months ago! I'm sure that's who it is!"

"Well, there you go," Baiheng smiled, unimpressed. "Looks like you do know something that I don't, Zhenhua. You should tell Chen that; it'd save him a lot of time on his scribbling."

Both men looked down at their empty glasses for a beat. Zhenhua felt himself grow more and more angry at the vice mayor, remembering the old fool's conspiracy theories, his nonsense about disharmony and imbalance.

"Why are *you* here?" Zhenhua finally asked. "Why have you stuck with Vice Mayor Chen through all this?"

"I don't know." Baiheng looked down at the table again and didn't continue for a few moments. "I should have left some time ago, but he's family. You've seen him; he's broken. I feel sorry for him. It's not like any of this is his fault anyway."

"Not *his* fault?" repeated Zhenhua, furious. "It's not his fault that his son was driving around in a Ferrari?"

"Calm down. It wasn't the kid's car. You think Chen would be stupid enough to buy his son a Ferrari? Not that he wanted one in the first place. Chen's son was a good kid, a studious kid. Polite. A good heart. I never understood why he hung around with all those worthless rich classmates of his."

"But the papers, they're accusing Chen...."

"A few truths, a few lies — what does it matter?" Baiheng shrugged. "It all amounts to the same thing."

* * *

Later that night, once he'd sent Baiheng home in a taxi, Zhenhua found himself wandering back toward Zhengyi Road though it was well past two in the morning. Inside the government building, he paced up and down the dark, empty halls, trying to imagine the rooms filled with civil servants busying themselves with the city's affairs. He wanted to join them, find some productive outlet for the restlessness that still hadn't subsided.

He stopped at a dark rosewood bench at the end of the hall, slipped off his shoes, and stretched out. The wooden slats pressed against his shoulder blades, but after a few moments their hardness began to feel comfortable, soothing. His thoughts turned from Baiheng to Director Li to the Boss of Houhai. He remembered the Boss at the Lotus Club months ago talking about jujube trees. *Some of them survive and others don't.* Survival. It was a warning.

And how was he going to survive? Zhenhua shifted

his weight. Write meaningless propaganda articles until the walls came tumbling down around him? He felt another sting of shame spread over his face in the dark. A hundred articles in the *People's Daily* wouldn't save Chen. A hundred white papers on the Soul of Beijing meant nothing to Director Li. Zhenhua returned to the same vision of himself he'd had two months ago at the City Planning office: an insignificant bit of flotsam caught in the waves, washing in, out, in.

He was going to drown. The thought appeared before him with a sudden and terrible clarity. He wasn't floating; he was drowning. Whenever Rui reminded him that he didn't have the heart of an official, this is what she really meant, he realized. She was telling him he would drown. He didn't belong out in the dark, icy waters, circling the deep wellspring of power.

Zhenhua dug his shoulders deeper into the wooden bench. He wanted to feel hard like rosewood, to absorb its rigidity like a carapace. He could sleep right here. Rui would hiss at him if he showed up at home now anyway, reeking of booze and cigarettes. She was always complaining about something. No, this bench was much better. The hardness felt *right*.

If the Boss had sold Chen out to the highest bidder, what was it that Director Li offered him, Zhenhua wondered? Cash? Favors? Zhenhua shut his eyes, trying to recall every detail he could from the night at the Lotus Club, months prior. Hadn't there been another man with the Boss, some dullard who worked in construction?

Zhenhua climbed off the bench and slipped back on his shoes, remembering the collection of business cards kept in his desk drawer. When he entered the department, he saw light spilling out from the vice mayor's closed office door. Zhenhua stood outside until he heard a light *ping!* of metal on wood. He called the vice mayor's name and, hearing no response, let himself inside.

Chen was seated at his desk and didn't look up. He was hunched over three copper coins lined up in a row, his barcode comb-over splayed in all directions. At his right wrist, a notepad was filled with tallies. The desk-lamp light illuminated ten thousand creases in the vice mayor's rumpled dress shirt, and towers of newsprint cast long shadows across the desk. Chen's face, also half cast in shadow, was twisted in an eerie concentration.

"Vice Mayor Chen?" Zhenhua said cautiously. "What are you doing? It's late."

Chen remained motionless, a wide unhinged smile spread across his face, as if listening to an inaudible frequency. Zhenhua watched him consult his tally sheet, nodding at some calculation. Only when he was finished counting did he acknowledge the other soul in the room.

"You're here early, Zhenhua."

"I ... I left but just came back. I was out with Baiheng. What are you doing?"

Chen brightened at the question, picking up the copper coins.

"I Ching. Divination. The future. I'm getting closer to an answer. You see, the first hexagrams —"

"Vice Mayor Chen," Zhenhua said impatiently. "There's something I need to tell you. I talked to Baiheng about the political attacks against you. I know who is behind them." Zhenhua waited, eyes wide, for the vice mayor to look up again, to greet the important news. Instead, he kept writing. Zhenhua's ears turned red. He felt the sake warming in his stomach.

"Vice Mayor Chen?" A strain was rising in his voice. "Sir, you don't need the I Ching. I know who is behind th—"

"Political attacks." Chen finished the sentence wearily. "No, that's not what this is for."

For a moment, Zhenhua felt as if rage might take over his whole body. He gripped the seams of his pants to steady his hands.

"What are you doing, then?"

"I'm asking a different set of questions. Health-related questions. You see, my son is in the hospital."

As if by way of explanation, the vice mayor picked up the copper coins once again and tossed them on the table. One rolled along the wood's grain — perfectly upright, turning over and over, tracing a long arc bent toward the desk lamp — before wobbling under its failing momentum and collapsing into ever tightening spirals, ringing against the wood. When the sound stopped, Chen began to explain what the arrangement foretold about his beloved son, but his office door was wide open, leading to the darkened, empty department.

* * *

They moved in pairs and clusters — shuffling, pausing, slurping, gawking, photographing. The walking street, Nanluogu Xiang, was a kind of carnival strip compressed to eight meters across, a sensory overload designed for high schoolers. Shop fronts on either side hawked large skewers of orange barbecued meat, fried octopus, yogurt, ice-cream-covered fried dough, lemonade, stinky tofu, cotton candy. Since it was night, street vendors had descended as well, laying out their gimcrack toys, souvenirs, and novelty T-shirts. Green laser beams bounced overhead. Loudspeakers lined opposite sides of the street, launching salvos of Cantopop into the fray.

Zhenhua tried his best to charge past the throngs of young people clogging the street, but he never made it more than a few steps. He weaved around two girls in matching cat-ear headbands stabbing at fried balls with toothpicks, trying to remember the lines he'd rehearsed for his meeting with the Boss of Houhai, but it was impossible. Waves of barbecue smoke and noise mingled with sticky night air, producing a powerful nausea in him.

It had taken some rummaging through desk drawers before Zhenhua dug out Hou Dexin's business card. The man clearly had no memory of Zhenhua from their banquet months ago at the Lotus Club, but he was warm and effusive nonetheless once he heard where Zhenhua was calling from. He rattled off the digits to the Boss's cell phone in one breath, and soon Zhenhua was listening to the Boss's growling voice on the other end. The Boss sounded oddly delighted to hear from Zhenhua. Of course they should meet, the Boss insisted.

And then what? How could he confront the Boss of Houhai, the person responsible for this entire mess? Baiheng had been no help at all.

"You're going to *meet* with that son of a bitch?" he had said when Zhenhua confided in him. "Tell me you're bringing some friends to beat the hell out of him."

"To negotiate."

"Negotiate! Zhenhua, you're even dumber than I thought."

"He's the only one who can put a stop to all this, before Vice Mayor Chen is taken in."

"That son of a bitch is the one who put a *start* to all of this! Besides it's too late, Zhenhua. It's out of the Boss's hands now. It's over."

"Then there's no reason I shouldn't meet him."

Baiheng shook his head. "What are you going to negotiate with, huh? Promise to write his biography?"

Zhenhua did have a plan. It had taken countless laps around the walking paths of the Party School, but the details gradually assembled themselves. It was a desperate, improbable plan, one that might have been improved by a second, sharper mind like Baiheng's. But hearing the young man's sarcastic, strident voice, Zhenhua realized instinctively he wouldn't tell Baiheng about it. He wouldn't tell anyone. He didn't want to be indebted to anyone anymore.

He spotted the Boss sitting on a wooden bench opposite a small hamburger stand on Jingyang Hutong. The old man held a large green bottle of Yanjing Beer and wore faded blue cotton pajamas with the legs rolled to his knees. Not exactly a formal setting. The birthmark under the Boss's right eye seemed bigger than Zhenhua remembered. Zhenhua approached and spoke the Boss's name.

"Sun Zhenhua!" the Boss roared back. "It's been too long! You've put on weight! Have a seat, unless you're in a rush to get somewhere."

Zhenhua obeyed, sitting on the wooden bench next to the old man in his pajamas. The Boss dispatched the man next to him — Fat Liang, he called him — to fetch a beer for Zhenhua. Fat Liang stood uneasily and weaved a few steps across the narrow hutong to the burger stand. The owner, a young man with hair pulled back in a ponytail, was working the grill, so Fat Liang just walked inside, opened the refrigerator, and helped himself. He popped the top off with his teeth and handed the icy bottle to Zhenhua.

"Fuck me, it's hot!" yelled Fat Liang.

"It's not hot," countered the Boss. "For a lard-ass like you, of course it will feel hot. It's a nice night. Watch your language, this is a high-ranking official that just sat down!" He turned to Zhenhua. "Sorry about him. He's got no culture." The Boss messily slapped Fat Liang on the shoulder with an open palm.

"Who are you saying doesn't have fucking culture!" slurred Fat Liang. "I travelled to more than sixty countries when I was working the boats. How many fucking countries have you been to?"

Zhenhua felt beads of condensation collect around his fingertips as he listened to the two drunken men arguing. He looked away from them to compose his thoughts. The drunkenness, the pajamas — he hadn't expected any of this. Clumps of young people filtered past in their lensless plastic glasses and bright-colored shoes — a herd shuffling toward more lights and novelties, shedding paper napkins, wooden skewers, and plastic bags in its wake. It seemed like one giant organism, one whose antennae didn't detect the three older men against the wall.

The other person being ignored, Zhenhua saw, was a beggar floating through the crowd like driftwood. He shambled pigeon-toed, parting groups of people with his outstretched iron meal bowl. He didn't seem aware of his surroundings, never pausing long enough for anyone to put anything in his bowl. Zhenhua watched him bob from bank to bank as he came closer. The man's face was ringed with grit — someone must have tried washing it recently. He wore a pained but uncomprehending expression, one that reminded Zhenhua of Vice Mayor Chen more than a little. Zhenhua reached for his wallet.

"What the fuck do you want?" Fat Liang spat at the beggar once he'd arrived. Even in his late forties, Fat Liang retained a restless, almost adolescent need to provoke. All three men on the bench now regarded the new arrival.

"Get the fuck out of here!"

The beggar didn't move.

"Get lost!" yelled Fat Liang again.

"He doesn't understand," the Boss observed. "He's retarded. He's an idiot."

Fat Liang jumped up from the bench, brandishing a green bottle over his head as if to strike. The beggar flinched and fell to his knees cowering. He curled up on the cobblestones near the legs of the bench, his blackened bare feet pointed at Zhenhua. Fat Liang stood over him, legs parted like a boxer dazed from a sudden knockout. He yelled down at his feet again, but there was less violence in his voice now. The beggar didn't move.

"Knock it off, Fatty," said the Boss. "What's wrong with you?"

"Boss," urged Zhenhua. "I need to talk with you. It's about Director Li."

The Boss turned back toward Zhenhua. His bright eyes were glassy, filled with drink.

"He's your friend, right?" Zhenhua went on quickly. "Well, he wants me out of City Planning. I didn't think much of it at first. I figured he was just being hard on me."

"I'm sorry to hear that," the Boss replied absently. "Politics is a tough —"

"Ever since this thing with him and Vice Mayor Chen started, it's only gotten worse."

"What does Vice Mayor Chen have to do with anything?"

Zhenhua looked up at the Boss and took a silent breath.

"The Ferrari crash," Zhenhua replied calmly. "The vice mayor's son, the police report, all that."

The Boss took a swig from his bottle and wiped his hand on his flannel pants.

The beggar was still curled into a fetal position, head buried in his arms. Fat Liang was muttering, nudging him in the ribs with the toe of his white sneaker. A small group of passersby was gathering to stare at the spectacle. The Boss, too, kept his eyes trained on the Idiot, trying to clear his head.

"I don't think I understand," the Boss said evenly.

"Well, as you know, I'm caught in the middle of all this myself because of Vice Mayor Chen," Zhenhua added. "That's why I wanted to meet you. I need a favor."

15

The Duanqiruifu Luxury Restoration Project

A DOZEN people were gathered around Fat Liang still standing over the Idiot, pouring beer on the ground near his body.

"Get up!" he yelled. He dribbled closer and closer toward the unmoving target, turning the gray stones dark with each splash. "Do you think I'm joking?"

His movements were gleefully dramatic now. The audience had formed an arc at a safe distance from the spectacle and watched.

The nervous energy of the crowd annoyed the Boss; his neck suddenly felt hot under his flannel collar. Zhenhua's little monologue had sobered him up; he hated surprises.

"I'll be honest with you," the Boss lied. "I've heard that Vice Mayor Chen is in some trouble, but I only know what I read in the papers. Hasn't Party Discipline already gotten to him? I think I read that."

"No, not yet."

"Well, I'm not sure what I can do for you. What are you looking for? Advice?"

"Protection," Zhenhua replied.

The Boss laughed despite himself and tried to clink bottles with Zhenhua.

"Protection from Director Li *and* Vice Mayor Chen," Zhenhua said gravely.

"You flatter me," the Boss chuckled. "But I don't understand anything about politics. I'm just an ordinary guy." The Boss looked down at his flannel pajamas for effect.

"Oh, I think you're capable of a lot," Zhenhua said. "At least that's what Baiheng says."

The name of Chen's assistant froze the Boss for a second. How the hell had Zhenhua connected with him?

"He's the one who called you the night of the crash, right?" Zhenhua added when the Boss didn't respond. The Boss gritted his teeth.

"You seem to be implying that I had something to do with whatever happened, which is ridiculous."

"Maybe you didn't," Zhenhua shrugged. He reached into his shirt pocket for another cigarette, lit it and waved away the smoke.

The Boss turned and studied Zhenhua anew. Hadn't he said he wasn't a smoker? The man's glasses and smooth forehead reflected the neon streetlight. He looked older, sallower than he had that night under the jujube tree only months ago.

"There's something else," Zhenhua said, "something you may be more interested in. Have you heard of the Duanqiruifu Luxury Restoration Project?"

The Boss started as a loud scream sounded from the sidewalk, and the Idiot — beads of beer rolling down his matted bangs — jumped up and scampered north on the walking street. He fled so quickly that the crowd was still standing around, gazing at nothing but a wet stain on the stones. Fat Liang shrugged theatrically.

The Boss couldn't tell whether his pulse was racing because of the beggar's scream or what Zhenhua had said. To calm his nerves, he cast his mind across town, summoning the Moon Tower construction site. Huaxing would start digging later this month. He and his nephew had already put money down on equipment, started feeding the workers. Huaxing had all the permits; they'd signed with the developer. They were safe. It was too late for City Planning, for anyone, to change his mind about the project.

"The Duanqiruifu Luxury Restoration Project," Zhenhua repeated in a low voice when the crowd had dispersed. "You may have heard of it already."

The Boss said nothing.

Zhenhua described the project's details — buildings were gutted, fixtures refurbished, trees planted. Republican-era coffee shops, five-star hotels and open-air restaurants were opened. Business leaders took evening strolls under lamplight around the grounds. It was a brand-new hub of historic Beijing — understated but luxurious, modern but historical. The total investment amounted to three hundred million.

"A massive project," Zhenhua summarized. "City

Planning has earmarked the necessary funds for it, but they are still seeking a developer to partner with. The tender is coming up, and no one knows the details of the project better than me. Not even Director Li. I could be a useful resource for anyone interested in bidding on it."

"Resource," the Boss repeated absently. The nine-digit figure had dazzled him for a moment.

* * *

No. 32 worked the Boss's neck and back as he lay face down on the padded bed. She could feel in his shoulders that he was still too tense for the massage to do any good, but it was no use telling him to relax again. The Boss just got like this sometimes, that's what the other girls said. They told her she should be careful, keep quiet, and not disturb him if she could help it. No. 32 had learned the entire landscape of the Boss's body but had no idea what could be on his mind.

Nothing. That's what the Boss said two days ago when she'd worked up the nerve to ask. He wasn't thinking about anything. Since his encounter with Zhenhua the previous week, the Boss had spent each night here, at Tang Relaxation Massage, forcing himself to forget it.

Everything was going according to plan. His sources said Vice Mayor Chen had only another two more weeks until Party Discipline began investigating him, which would be the end. Once Chen was under investigation, Director Li, as agreed, would issue final approval for the Moon Tower project and the Boss would receive his six million.

Yet as the Boss lay on his bamboo-slat-covered bed each night and stared at the dark ceiling, the missing details of the Duanqiruifu project gnawed at him, as if part of a half-remembered dream. He tried to focus on the logistics of the upcoming construction at the Moon Tower but called his contacts to ask about details of Duanqiruifu instead. He'd confirmed that the project did, in fact, exist and that it would be one of the largest historic restoration projects in the city. Massive promised investment. Hundreds of millions. But no one knew who the developer was or when City Planning would approve it. Perhaps Zhenhua was telling the truth.

The young man's face appeared to him with maddening frequency. When the Boss pictured Zhenhua, it was as he appeared on Nanluogu Xiang last week — smoking, wiping his mouth with the back of his hand. Where had all this chutzpah come from?

He had to admit, with a grudging respect, Zhenhua had come a long way. Sometime in the past six months, the kid had learned to take matters into his own hands. He even had a slight air of authority to him. If he put on a little weight and lost his glasses, he might pass for a real cadre in ten years' time. It was a shame that such a promising political career had to be collateral damage just as he was getting a nose for politics. In another few years, Zhenhua might have become someone useful to know. But Zhenhua didn't have that kind of time; once Vice Mayor Chen was hauled in the week after next, Zhenhua would be gone too.

Vice Mayor Chen — that was another face that emerged in the dark small hours. The Boss pictured the Chen he'd known in the early days, twenty years ago — the slight, bookish cadre at the Food and Drug Administration. There was nothing to him: owlish glasses and a vast forehead flaming red with drink. In Chen, most people saw a policy wonk for life. He was a world apart from his superiors at the time, who were all rough, semiliterate men with ties to the army. They mocked Chen's glasses and delicate fingers, and sat him next to unmarried girls at banquets, bullying him. "Comrade Chen! Why don't you ask Ms. Fang if she is married?"

The Boss thought back to one of their first private meetings, twenty years ago, in the old Houhai. Chen nursed a single watery highball of whisky and reeled off astonishing strings of rumors, gossip, and theories about the inner workings of Beijing's government to the Boss. He saw all the imperceptible connections and divined the future from boilerplate *People's Daily* editorials. When Chen finally figured out how to make use of his gift, to throw his weight around in the right way and play hard, he rose fast. No one did politics like Chen. Well, the Chen of old. What a waste to have cracked up and fallen apart now, when he was *this* close to Party Secretary.

"That's enough," the Boss finally growled at No. 32, who was still pressing her hands into his fleshy shoulders. She left the room.

Was this what was bothering him? the Boss wondered. His relationship with Vice Mayor Chen, two decades in the making, had petered out to *this*. Six million yuan. It seemed an absurdly low figure for twenty-five years of work. What would six million buy the Boss that he didn't have anyway? Another house? Another car?

He might make a few investments, but he could think of nothing specific. He didn't have anyone to support.

Six million yuan. He recalled Zhenhua's description of the Duanqiruifu Luxury Restoration Project — its gleaming light fixtures and five-star hotel — and for the first time, the Boss pictured himself there. He sat alone, at the center of a lavish hotel lobby, drinking tea and smoking. It was all his. He controlled everything he saw; he could do whatever he wanted with it. Now *that* would be a worthy culmination of twenty years' work. *That* would be a success that no one would be able to deny.

No, no, it was just greed that was digging at him. The Duanqiruifu project was too uncertain. There would be endless approvals, negotiations, and deal-making. The City Planning director would need to approve it, which would mean dealing with Director Li. Simmering rage consumed the Boss each time he imagined Director Li drunkenly bragging about their secret agreement. Is that what had tipped Zhenhua off in the first place?

City Planning approval would be only the beginning. After that, families — dozens of families living on the grounds — would need to be relocated. That might delay the project, perhaps indefinitely. It might never get off the ground. No, *relax*, the Boss thought. Do nothing.

There would always be new projects and new partnerships once Vice Mayor Chen and Zhenhua were gone. The Boss would be alone for a while; but then he'd find new partners, new assets. Of course he would be alone! The successful ones were always alone. You couldn't well have loyal friends if you were going to be successful; they would betray you the first chance they got. That's just how it was. Better to make deals with useful fools like Director Li than make foolish bets on the future with someone like Zhenhua.

The Boss's hips creaked as he sat up in the bed. He looked around the dim, empty room, imagining himself two weeks in the future. Chen had been apprehended. The six-million bank transfer had come through. The Boss saw his future self standing outside his courtyard home in the dark. His wife was inside watching television; she cared nothing about business. Fat Liang was nowhere to be seen. He had no appointment in Houhai. What would he do next?

The Boss imagined himself returning right here, back to this room, regaling No. 32 with his latest business success. *Six million yuan*, he even heard himself tell her. No. 32 smiled and asked him some flattering question. Then the future Boss of Houhai watched No. 32 walk out of the room again, leaving with her little Japanese bow, and there he was, just as now, alone.

* * *

On the walk home from Tang Relaxation Massage, the Boss had to step around stacks of sidewalk tiles being dug up by a group of migrant workers under a dangling light bulb. They were ragtag and wore dirty camouflage pants. These street repair crews worked only in the middle of the night, arranging the new cobblestones on wet sand and pounding them into place with rubber mallets.

The Boss paused for yet another cigarette, watching them work. Their movements were slow and methodical. The crew was all from the countryside, and they smoked and chatted as they worked — tile by tile — as if aware that the job was one long, senseless distraction. The workers returned to the capital every summer, like seasonal birds, to dig up the same sidewalks they had laid the previous year. The Boss never understood why the city repaved all the sidewalks every year; but the arrival of the workers was comforting, one of the annual rhythms of the city.

The Boss's legs carried him toward home; but when he arrived at Jingyang Hutong, he realized he wasn't ready to end the night yet. He set out west, toward Houhai, for a drink at the Sea of Clouds. Along the hutong near his house, he could hear a group of foreigners talking loudly behind the brick wall of a courtyard-cum-beer garden. New bars and cafes for young people and foreigners were opening every day, seeping into remaining gaps between the carnival strip of Nanluogu Xiang and Houhai. These discoveries usually riled him; but tonight, the Boss felt calm. The temperature outside was pleasant, and his mind raced with reveries set in the Duanqiruifu compound, away from all this change. Maybe he could open a health spa there. Daily hair treatment. Deep-tissue massages.

When the Boss arrived at the Sea of Clouds, the door was closed. He peered through the window and saw all the tables and chairs were missing. Old Xue was inside and unlocked the door when the Boss knocked.

"You didn't tell me you were renovating!" the Boss said from the doorway.

"Not renovating. Closing," the old man replied, walking toward the bar. He went back to organizing dusty glasses.

"What do you mean closing? You're moving?"

"Retiring," Old Xue said. "I found a buyer for the place. Got a good price. Eight hundred thousand."

The Boss was supposed to give some knowing comment on whether Old Xue got a good deal. On some shelf in his brain were a few recent prices for Houhai commercial property that he could reference. But instead, the Boss sat down on one of the two remaining bar stools and looked over the empty room. There were piles of paper garbage along the wall and a stack of bricks near the purple curtains. A wooden beam leaned against one of the tacky paintings left hanging on the walls. The floor was covered in dust. The Boss had sat right here as recently as last week and Old Xue had never mentioned retiring. The Boss had been a loyal customer to the Sea of Clouds for years, and Old Xue just decides to shutter, just like that?

"So, you're really going."

"Business is bad. Plus, I want to spend some more time with my grandson," Old Xue said. "This place is no good anyhow. It's too old and run-down."

"How many years?"

"He just turned six. I'm going to teach him how to fish."

"I meant the bar. How many years has it been open?"

"Oh. Well, more than twenty years. You've been here most of them, I guess."

A heavy sorrow crossed the room and settled on the Boss's shoulders, anchoring him to the chair. Old Xue continued packing the box of glasses, looking, for the first time, like a frail old man. His small bony hand reached inside each glass with a rag, twisting to wipe away the filth. A lump formed in the Boss's throat, and he cursed himself for being so sentimental. It was only a fucking bar. When he reached for his cigarettes and lighter, he realized his own hands were shaking. He remained fixed on the barstool, terrified of moving.

"Have one last drink?" the Boss finally asked.

"I've only got this left," Old Xue said, holding up a half-empty bottle of blended whisky.

"Doesn't matter."

Old Xue poured the Boss two fingers into one of the glasses he'd just cleaned.

"You won't drink one with me?" asked the Boss. "For old time's sake."

"You know I can't."

"Right."

The Boss was looking forward to feeling the warm burn of alcohol in his throat, but from the first swallow the whisky didn't taste strong enough. He wanted to feel something hotter, blindingly hot, a purifying fire that would burn off all this self-pity. There was nothing useful about it, he knew. It was pointless; none of it helped you accomplish anything. It was inevitable that the Sea of Clouds would close one day, just as it was that his relationship with Vice Mayor Chen would expire. There would always be new bars, new owners, new work contacts, new building projects. He still had time.

* * *

The Boss pulled down his sleeping mask and blinked at the darkness. Yes, faint cell phone music was tinkling from the living room. His wife breathed heavily next to him, undisturbed. The music started again. The Boss groaned and rocked himself out of bed.

He opened the bedroom door and a rush of cold air drew goose bumps on his naked arms. Fuck, she had left the air conditioning running out here all night. He trudged, shivering, toward the table by the front door where his phone was still alight and jangling. The phone's display was a blur without his contact lenses.

"What is it?"

"Dongxuan?" asked a voice. "Can you hear me?"

The Boss held his breath, recognizing Vice Mayor Chen's voice immediately.

"Dongxuan, are you there? Hello?"

The Boss made a noise.

"I know you don't want me to call, but it's Shishan," the vice mayor said. "He's.... I don't know what I'm going to do."

"Where are you?"

"301 Military Hospital. Room 14. He doesn't have much time left. The doctors are saying...." Chen's voice trailed off again.

"Is anyone else there with you?" the Boss asked.

"No," Chen replied softly. "I didn't know who else to call. Will you —"

The Boss hung up and powered off his phone before Chen could finish the question. He sat for some time in the dark, rubbing his birthmark and letting the frigid air lap against his skin. He was wide-awake now. He stood up from the couch but then paused, as if confused by the surroundings. He ... well, he wasn't going back to bed. The goddamn room was as cold as a tomb; he needed to get out, take a walk.

The Boss dressed, and by the time he was outside he had changed his mind again. He peeled the dust cover off the Honda and tossed it in a heap inside his court-yard door. He flipped on the headlights and pulled onto Di'anmenwai Avenue.

The Boss stopped at a red light and glanced at his reflection in the rearview mirror. There was no movement in any direction, save the rolling LED lights inside a darkened bank. Vice Mayor Chen would be a wreck. The conversation just now reminded the Boss of how wistful and shattered Chen sounded during all their phone calls over the winter — the red-raw grief, the sobbing, the long silences. It was unfortunate, but nothing could be done. No amount of crying was going to bring Chen his son back.

It wasn't until the Boss arrived on the fourth floor of the hospital that he remembered how much he hated them, even nice ones like 301. The hallway smelled faintly of urine; his shoes squeaked on the disinfected floor. The Boss passed through the near-empty hall, past large machines on wheels, with cabinets and hoses and wires. The walls were lined with framed propaganda posters of young saluting soldiers. He peered inside each dark window, even though he knew room 14 was at the end of the hall. Blue television light. A young woman curled up sleeping in a chair. A body inclined in a bed, wrapped in bandages.

When he arrived at room 14 and peered through the slender window, the Boss saw that Vice Mayor Chen was not alone. In the far corner, the Boss could see Zhenhua and Baiheng sitting side by side, each looking at his phone. What were they doing here? Had Chen summoned them after he'd called him? A panic passed over the Boss; this was a mistake.

The angle of the window didn't permit the Boss to see anything more of Chen's son than two feet under the blanket. Chen absently ran his hand up and down the boy's leg. He looked terrible; dark circles ringed his eyes. A doctor stood near them, studying a flashing monitor.

The entire tableau looked as if it had been staged for him to see. No one moved, said anything. The Boss looked away to quiet another swell of panic, but he couldn't pull himself away from the window. The boy must have made some new, horrible sound, because now Chen and the doctor were all gazing at the same point, where the boy's face must be.

Any moment now one of them would look up and see him standing at the window, the Boss was sure of it. Eyes would widen with surprise. Then they would all turn toward him and open the door, exposing him completely in the doorway. *What are you doing here?* they would demand. Perhaps in anger, perhaps only in shock. What would he say then? What *was* he doing here?

But no one looked up. The Boss left the window of room 14, exited into the hospital's courtyard, and pulled out his phone. Zhenhua's groggy voice answered.

"Come outside," the Boss said. "I'm on a bench in the courtyard."

The Boss lit a cigarette and tried to clear his head. He had planned to call Zhenhua the following day, but talking to him face-to-face was better, now that he thought about it. Tonight was as good a night as any.

A handful of crickets chirped from a large willow tree near the parking lot. The world around him seemed heightened — the crickets too loud, the night air too cool, the cigarette too strong — the exact opposite of his recent night at the Sea of Clouds. He felt like he'd taken drugs, like the old days.

A few moments later, Zhenhua emerged from the automatic glass doors and approached along the brick path toward the bench. He sat down next to the Boss, lit his own cigarette, and the two men gazed up at the hospital building. A room light on the third floor switched off.

"What are you doing here?" Zhenhua said. He looked tired and doughy. The Boss felt a surge of confidence; he'd been right to come out and do this tonight. The crickets chirped again and again.

"I needed to talk to you about the Duanqiruifu project."

Zhenhua sighed.

"City Planning still needs a developer, doesn't it?"

Zhenhua shook his head in disgust. "Chen's son is dying upstairs and you —"

"You need a developer," the Boss said firmly.

Zhenhua straightened his back and composed himself. "Like I said the other night, City Planning is starting the selection process."

"Good."

"But, as you know, Director Li —"

"*You* need a developer, yes?" the Boss repeated.

Zhenhua stared at the orange glow of his dying cigarette. The Boss waited for the young man to ask what he meant; he could almost hear Zhenhua straining not to. But Zhenhua resisted. Impressive.

"I don't know how involved Director Li will be with City Planning going forward," the Boss said finally, letting the smoke curl toward his eyes. "I've been hearing rumors. Something about a police raid at his house. It seems that he got his hands on a police report he shouldn't have. About a car crash, I believe. It sounded like a serious breach. I know the police aren't happy about it."

Zhenhua blinked once, twice.

"Wait, you mentioned a car crash the last time we met, didn't you? Something about Vice Mayor Chen and Director Li, right?"

"You," Zhenhua finally said. The single syllable barely squeezed out of his mouth. "You were the one that arranged the whole —"

"I heard Chen's assistant got his hands on that police report," the Boss continued. "Young kid, a rising star. Baiheng, they called him, I believe. He helped cover up the whole thing and then tried to blackmail his own boss. Really ugly. I hope I'm wrong; that's just what I hear."

Zhenhua cast a panicked glance toward the hospital room where Chen and Baiheng were still waiting. He stood up and took an uncertain step toward the hospital door.

"I wouldn't," the Boss said. His voice was back to its lower, growling register. The theatrics were over.

"There's nothing for you in that room, Zhenhua. Vice Mayor Chen is done. Baiheng is done. Director Li is done. But you're not. You don't have to be, anyway. That's what you wanted, wasn't it?"

16

Thwack

Old Li liked to watch television with the volume turned high. He sat completely still on the couch, hands on knees, heavy lids half-closed to the flashing blue light. On screen, a young singer with gelled hair and sequined black pants belted out a love song to a live audience waving glowing orange sticks in unison. Panzi appeared in the living room just as the song was building toward its deafening climax.

"Grandpa! Turn it down!" he shouted.

Before he could get a response, Panzi began rummaged through the papers piled on the coffee table for the remote control as the shrieking grew louder, pressing close against his skull. A stack of papers fell to the floor.

Three weeks ago, Panzi's mother had sold the last of her properties and made no new acquisitions, leaving Panzi nowhere else to stay but here. She was working on something major, but he didn't know the details. She appeared in the doorway every so often with an armful of newspapers and computer printouts — anything written about historic building restoration in Beijing. *Read these*, she commanded, dropping the stack on the coffee table. Before Panzi could even ask why, Qinyan would have returned to her bedroom to stand near the window with the outlet, where she could make calls with her phone still charging.

By the time Panzi had managed to turn the TV's volume down, the applause on screen was finished. He reached for the scattered papers on the floor, glancing at the headlines. He had read more than a few of the articles, in fact; what else was he going to do? The city government was pouring money into historic building restoration — that was the gist of most of them. Old courtyard homes were being rebuilt, historic shopping streets overhauled. Gray brick facades and red wooden doors were back in style. Heritage, history, Chinese culture — it was certainly a contrast from the futuristic marketing slogans plastered around half-built towers on the outskirts of the city where he'd spent most of the spring.

Panzi looked down at his grandfather as a flu medicine commercial jingled on the television. Panzi knew he couldn't leave Grandpa alone, but he had to get out of this apartment. Old Li looked innocent and exposed, like the calm, fixed axis of a loud, spinning world.

"Grandpa, let's go outside for a walk."

They set out into the sticky September night. Old Li had the legs of his cotton pants rolled to his knees and mopped the back of his neck with the towel draped over his shoulder as they weaved through the familiar crumbling alleyways of Xicheng District. They treaded slowly through the small-scale construction noise, the white dust, the methane smell of public toilets, chatting about pigeons and the weather.

They turned a corner and came upon a group of men huddled around a Chinese chessboard in a pool of streetlamp light. Half of the crowd was shirtless, and a few stirred the listless air with paper fans, casting shadows on the wooden board. Old Li offered one of his Hongxi cigarettes to an acquaintance and took one for himself. Panzi hovered over the board with the others, listening to the banter and smacks of wooden tiles. Two dirty white Pekinese dogs panted underfoot. Both players sat in small folding chairs brought from home, and the rest of the crowd squatted or stood over them. The older man of the pair was winning and kept a running commentary of the game, to the bemusement of the crowd.

"You want to take my horse?" he goaded. *Thwack!* "I'll give you something to take. Bring that cannon a little closer, and I'll show you. *Thwack!* He thinks he can get my elephant if he moves there. See that? See that? *Thwack!*"

Panzi drew a deep lungful of the humid, smoke-filled air and began to relax. He fantasized about this sometimes, living like an old codger deep in some ancient hutong. God, how weird was that? It was only here in the hutongs that the heat and boredom drove the whole neighborhood out into the street after supper.

Grandpa's acquaintance said he had a new coin to show Old Li and led them both into the dark courtyard

entrance nearby. Panzi followed the twin trails of cigarette smoke through the warren of rundown buildings inside. Tinny shrieking of Peking Opera seeped
out from a window. The silhouette of a cat jumped
between roofs.

When they arrived at the man's narrow room, Panzi
waited outside while Grandpa and his friend talked and
passed an old bronze coin back and forth. The man's
room was typically minuscule, hardly large enough to
accommodate two bodies at once. The floor space not
occupied by the man's bed was piled with boxes, a suitcase, a boxy television, and an electric hot plate with an
iron bowl of dirt-encrusted potatoes on top.

The adjacent units were similarly rundown, stuffy,
ill-lit, and cramped — Panzi knew all the common complaints. Ask anyone living in this courtyard, any man
standing around the chessboard, and they'd be the first
to tell you how poor the conditions were. Make them
the right offer and most residents would trade up to a
"modern" apartment tower, somewhere with a bathroom,
with new furnishings, with more space and fewer people.

Panzi had sold a handful of modern apartments to
people just like them, hutong dwellers. They usually
called him back months later to complain. The shiny
faucets had begun to rust; the bedroom doors didn't
close right; their nameless neighbors were too noisy on
the weekends. At their new homes, they became fixated
on small problems that never would have registered
back in the hutongs. They seemed restless. After less
than a year, a few told Panzi they were already in the
market for a new apartment; they wanted to trade up for
something bigger, quieter, more isolated. That seemed

to be the end goal: a place to wall their families off from the outside world completely.

Hutong life was the opposite — filled with discomfort and intrusion. *Hutong communities*, that was the euphemism in the articles scattered atop the coffee table at home. One was by an academic, a preservationist, bemoaning the destruction of these old one-story buildings in the hutongs. It wasn't just irreplaceable architecture, she argued, it was the *hutong communities* that were being destroyed each time residents were shipped off to anonymous high-rises in the city's suburbs.

But hutong communities weren't formed by choice, they were forged out of inconvenience — forged squatting side by side in the public toilets; forged by the meddling Auntie who barges into your house uninvited; forged gossiping about the loud row overheard last night. People were sensible; if someone handed over enough money for you to be comfortably isolated, you took it. But until then, until you had the means to escape, you were the hutong community. You were cold in winter and mosquito-bitten in summer. You listened to Peking Opera through the walls. You learned your neighbors' names not because you liked them but because you had to see them every day. You were not restless; you had to accept things as they were. And you were never alone.

A new chess game was just about ending when they returned to the alley. The surrounding men watched in silence, waiting for the loudmouth winner to say something. Panzi glanced at Grandpa and saw that a light had returned to the old man's eyes. A few more intermittent *thwacks* and the game ended to half-mumbled commentary. Those bent over straightened, those squatting stretched their necks. The board was reset without discussion and the winner made the first move: *Thwack!* Only Panzi and Old Li took their leave, stepping past a pile of bricks in the direction of a neon-lit noodle shop.

"The neighborhood still hasn't changed all that much," Panzi remarked once they had walked awhile. "Mom doesn't talk about moving anymore, does she?"

"If she wants to move, she can move by herself!" They both laughed at this; the chess game had enlivened Old Li. "She knows that your dad will never agree to it."

Panzi sighed. "Grandpa, Dad has been gone for years already."

Grandpa stopped in the middle of the alley and shook his head. "He hardly ever comes out of his room anymore."

It was no use to argue; Old Li got confused like this all the time now.

"He's got food to eat; he's got a house and a son," Grandpa went on. "Why all the talk about 'feeling useless' all the time? He should be happy."

"Stop talking, Grandpa. You're confused."

"I don't understand why he's so sad all the time." Old Li looked directly at his grandson. "You should talk to him."

Panzi steered them both toward home. In the silence, he tried to think of anything other than what Grandpa had just said. When they arrived back at the apartment, the television was still playing to the empty room. Panzi's mother appeared from the bedroom. He wanted to tell her about what Grandpa had said, but Qinyan sat down on the living room sofa and began to shuffle through the papers covering the coffee table. She was smiling.

"I need you to come with me tomorrow," she told Panzi.

"Where?"

"Oh, close by," she said quickly. She could barely contain herself. "You should get some sleep."

"What's with all the secrecy? Can't you just tell me where we're going?"

She was nearly grinning. "We're meeting Wu Wei at nine." Wu Wei was Qinyan's real estate agent. "He says there are four families interested in selling, all at below market rate! I wasn't sure if I could believe it at first."

Panzi's interest had already begun to slip. His eyes dropped to the surface of the coffee table covered in newsprint.

"So, it's some kind of restoration project?"

"Oh!" Qinyan exclaimed. "I haven't even told you the details yet! Yes, four units at a place called Duanqiruifu. Old buildings. There's going to be a big restoration project —"

"Wait. What?"

"Restoration project."

"I know that." Panzi glared at his mother. "Where did you say we're going?"

"Oh, it's a place near Zhangzizhong Road."

"I know where Duanqiruifu is!" Panzi shouted. "You've been working on a deal *there* all this time and you didn't tell me!"

Qinyan looked at her son for the first time, rebuke in her eyes. Panzi could tell she wanted to scold him for raising his voice but was now unsure. Seeing his mother's blank expression made him angrier yet, face turning hot. He scowled at her.

"Tell me you remember," he said in a low voice. They stood like this, suspended, for a few moments.

"The missing girl," Old Li called finally, still staring at the television.

Panzi turned to his grandfather, stunned. How could he have remembered? Qinyan seized the moment to break eye contact and look down at the papers in her hand. He knew she felt no shame or embarrassment. She didn't remember anything of what he'd been through.

"Well," she said finally. "We should leave before eight thirty."

"I'm going to bed."

Panzi's old bedroom was kept more or less the same since he moved out four years ago — a steel-framed twin bed, whitewashed walls, and a stand-alone clothing rack with a dustcover emblazoned with cartoon sheep. It was windowless and small. He flipped off the room's only light, a halogen bulb overhead, laid down, and stared at the ceiling. He wasn't tired. He checked his phone for messages; there were none. The television in the living room blathered on and on.

He shut his eyes tight.

Why all the talk about "feeling useless" all the time? He should be happy.

Grandpa's words out on the hutong sent a chill through Panzi, and he covered himself with a blanket.

Was that the root of Dad's ultimate sorrow, "feeling useless"? What did that even mean? Could that have driven his father to do what he did all those years ago? No, there was no reason, no grand explanation. Dad was just lonely and depressed.

Panzi thought back to New Year's Eve, atop Capital

Mansions. He had told Xiao Song about his dad's suicide that night. *Let your feelings in*, she had told him. But weren't feelings the whole problem? Suppose *he* was lonely and depressed too, he had wanted to yell at her! Why let *those* feelings in? Why push any deeper into that dark, terrible jungle, the one his father had never returned from? What good were feelings when you had no control over where they'd lead you?

* * *

Panzi stared out of the window of his mother's Volkswagen the following morning. He tried concentrating on the stereo, tuned to Joy 87.6, some talk show, but his mother wouldn't stop chattering at him. She did this whenever she was nervous, this prattling, and Panzi took some small consolation in ignoring her.

"Are you listening to me? You can't find properties like this for fifty thousand a square meter! But we don't have much time. Wu Wei said they're going to announce the restoration project any day now. Panzi, do you hear me?"

Panzi refused her again. He knew his mother hadn't given a second thought to their argument last night. Qinyan paused and glanced at her son.

"Panzi? I need positive thoughts from you, okay?"

Their car neared the red gate of Duanqiruifu, and Qinyan pulled over alongside one of the two stone lions to call Wu Wei. Panzi gazed out his window at the lion's gaping mouth, its large paws. Right *there*. His eyes swept over the rest of the gate — the columns, the cobblestones, the chipped red doors — nothing about it looked out of place. It looked ageless, neither old nor new. He tried to imagine the carnage of the Ferrari wreck but couldn't. Before long, his mother had put the car in gear, and they were inching their way up the stone ramp inside.

Wu Wei was standing in front of a blue corrugated metal fence, under a red banner that read "Welcome the Restoration of Historic Beijing." Behind him, the stone facade of the grounds' principal building was enveloped in green construction gauze.

Wu Wei was wearing his usual work uniform — white button-down shirt and a waxy blue tie that hung like cardboard. He had a job for a large Beijing-based real estate intermediary but made a small fortune sourcing deals for Qinyan off the books. He was only a few years older than Panzi, with scraggy hair that caught inside his collar. He had the intelligent gleam of an entrepreneur in his eye and spoke the same language as Panzi's mother.

"They're ready for us in unit two," he said by way of greeting. "Park here. It's better that they don't see you drive in."

The three of them set off down a stone path bisecting the grounds' four main historic buildings, and Panzi listened to his mother and Wu Wei review a few remaining tactical details, following them up the steps into the dark foyer of the south-facing building. Inside, they proceeded down a long hallway lined with cooking stoves and tile countertops on either side. They passed a shared bathroom with concrete dividers between latrines, and Wu Wei knocked on the next door to the left. An old man in a gray shirt opened the door, just as his cell phone erupted. He gestured for them to enter and cupped his mouth with the hand his lit cigarette was in.

"Okay, okay," he mumbled on the phone. He stood at the window, back to the room. The three arrivals remained in the doorway, and Panzi watched his mother's eyes work over the room, already inside her thoughts: paint flaking from the ceiling, old windows, mold spreading in the corner next to the dresser. The room was spare and tidy — a carefully folded quilt at the foot of the twin bed with a single pair of slippers aligned underneath.

"Sorry about that," the man said finally.

He dug out a tin of cigarettes with the image of St. Basil's cathedral on the front and lit one for Wu Wei and another for himself.

"What kind of cigarettes are these?" Wu Wei asked. He was very good.

"From Russia," the man beamed. "One of my old students brought them back with him." They puffed for a beat, but no one was introduced. Qinyan opened by asking a few neutral questions she already knew answers to: How many square meters was the room? How high were the ceilings? Panzi knew she was warming up to the criticisms to drive down the price.

"This is an extremely good apartment," the man contended. "This kind of European architecture is extremely rare in Beijing. The atmosphere is extremely peaceful." He paused, looked up, and grinned at the peacefulness.

Qinyan was smiling and nodded at each *extremely*.

"We're all retired professors," he went on. "I taught Japanese language for thirty years." The professor went on with his life story — his years teaching, the death of his wife last spring, his not having any children, and finally his plan to return to his mother's ancestral village back in Japan. He looked around the room wistfully, as if seeing memories.

"There are many things about this place you can't find anywhere else in Beijing," he added. "It's an extremely good apartment."

"Still, the overall conditions are not very good," Qinyan replied. "For instance, the sanitation. There's no bathroom here, and the cooking stoves are out in the shared hallway. That's not very convenient."

"Also, it must cost a lot to heat this place in the winter," Wu Wei observed, tapping the window.

"The windows are double-paned glass!" said the man. "It's very warm in the winter." As the three of them went back and forth cataloguing the merits and flaws of the room, Panzi wandered toward the sidewall to look at the old photographs hanging in dark wooden frames. Three black-and-white portraits, all of the same young man with round spectacles and a pencil mustache. In the middle one, he stood, full-length, with a girl in a light-colored *qipao* under a flowering tree. Plum blossoms, maybe. The couple stood shoulder-to-shoulder, a sliver of daylight between them. The woman's chin was angled demurely toward the parasol in her hand while the man smiled squarely at the camera. "Tokyo, 1924" was scratched in white ink in the bottom right corner. This must be the man's parents?

"So, what do you think?" Qinyan asked her son.

The question caught Panzi off guard. The timbre of his mother's voice had changed. He turned from the photographs and met three sets of eyes trained on him.

"Do you like the apartment, Panzi?"

"Uh, I ... I think there are some nice features —"

"He is getting close to marrying age," Qinyan interjected. "We'll need to find him a suitable apartment before he settles down. It's not quite like our generation, is it?" She nodded toward the old photographs on the wall. "Apartments are getting more and more expensive for young people just starting out, aren't they?"

Qinyan sighed dramatically, and Panzi watched the property's owner face soften ever so slightly. The real purpose of his presence dawned on Panzi; he was a prop. He shoved his hands in his pockets and glared at his mother.

"How are the nearby elementary schools?" Qinyan asked.

"Schools are all very good inside the Second Ring Road."

"Hmm. Well, we all know that the best elementary schools are in Xicheng District."

"Schools here in Dongcheng District are also very good," the man replied.

Childless, what did he know about schools? Qinyan only offered him a tight smile and sighed again. "So much to think about!"

Panzi turned toward the photos on the wall once more, to steady himself. Mother kept talking and talking, endless words, endless lies. He shut his eyes to stop himself from screaming. Look at her nodding at the old professor like that. Fake! Everything fake! Panzi looked at the old professor once more, with his ragged sweatshirt and glasses hung from a string around his neck.

"I don't feel well," Panzi said evenly, taking a step toward the door.

"Are you okay?" Qinyan asked her son sweetly. God,

the look on her face…. Rage poured off of him, but Panzi made it out of the room without responding.

He tramped down the darkened hall and ducked out the entrance into the morning sunlight, which dazed him for a moment. He scanned the scene, looking for something to hate. Magpies swooped from rooftop perches into the trees. An old woman in a bright-red sweater pushed her husband in a wheelchair. Panzi set off without a destination, watching his feet as he stomped forward, fuming, yelling at his invisible mother.

She was a monster; he was certain of it now. There was only her own meaningless success, money, vanity. She didn't even *see* other people, not him, not Grandpa. Panzi thought once more of the black-and-white portraits hanging in the room and then of the retired professor, frail and alone in the world. A university professor with a Japanese background — the horrors he must have lived through. Tears welled up in Panzi's eyes as he walked.

Before long, he found himself back at the entrance to Duanqiruifu. He sat on the stone steps at the edge of the construction site and gazed at the red gate. Through the narrow entrance and across the lanes of traffic, Panzi could make out the blank white spirit wall, twelve meters long, on the other side of the road. It was designed to protect the entrance of the compound from threatening spirits, but he had never noticed it there before. It looked brilliantly white in the morning sunshine, like a movie screen. Cars passed in front of it, along the slipstream of Zhangzizhong Road. Three middle school girls in tracksuits loped past on the sidewalk like actors without a backdrop.

"Panzi!"

He didn't turn around. If he even looked at his mother, he was sure he'd explode.

"Come on, we have work to do," she breathed when she made it next to him.

"I'm not going anywhere with you."

"We have three other units to visit!"

"Go by yourself."

Qinyan sat down on the steps next to her son and gazed in the same direction. The renovation work on the building behind them had started up again — voices and buzzsaws.

"Aren't you ashamed?" he finally asked.

"Of what?"

"How you scheme and manipulate people!" Panzi yelled. "You use people. You use me."

"You're my son!" Qinyan half-shouted back. "Didn't I raise you? We're family."

Panzi felt another wave of revulsion and had to stand. A cruel thought entered his mind, as if beamed there. It slid up his throat and then out to the tip of his tongue. A worker behind him was hammering on a steel pipe.

"You're going to end up like him, that professor, you know, alone in a room," Panzi said.

"You don't talk to your mother like that. We're family —"

"Family! Family!" Panzi shouted back. He could hear his voice going shrill but couldn't seem to stop the momentum building behind him. "You don't want a family! You want a secretary! I can't stand being around you. And Dad, maybe he was the same."

Her palm smacked his cheek fast and hard, so quick that he seemed to hear the blow before he felt it. Qinyan had never laid a hand on her son, so both mother and son looked at each other for a moment, uncertain of what came next. Panzi's face began to throb. Qinyan was the first to recover.

"Family is all there is," she said severely. "You may not understand that yet, but you will."

Panzi stared at the white spirit wall, eyes watering.

"Didn't I raise you by myself? Didn't I put you into one of Beijing's best high schools? And you squandered it. Didn't I give you a job? And you resent me for it?"

"You would have done that for *anybody*," he said. "You don't care about *me*. You only care about me because I'm your son."

"You *are* my son! Are you crazy?"

"Never mind."

"You don't know how good you have it," Qinyan went on. "After everything I've given you.... I ask so little in return. God, I've spoiled you." She gestured toward a construction worker on the other side of the green gauze, sawing a pipe. "That's what you'd be doing if it weren't for me! And you get upset because I take you along to a few meetings?"

"You don't understand."

"What is there to understand?!"

The conversation was useless. They sat facing each other, listening to the high-pitched whine of the saw until Qinyan stood and walked away. Panzi sat back down on the steps and let the construction noise wash over him in waves. Finally, he got up and followed the path his mother had taken, back into Duanqiruifu. It wasn't surrender, he told himself; he just couldn't stand looking at the red gate any longer.

17

Tighten the Rope

Hot afternoon sunlight poured in over the swooping curves of the Galaxy Soho outdoor shopping mall, bright enough that David could make out the grime and dust clinging to the white edges of the building.

He and Trish stood in the shade, clutching plastic cups. Behind them, two rows of craft beer and local food vendors were selling gourmet sausages, couscous, and gelato — a promenade of white tents leading to the rear staircase. A large crowd of young foreigners and Chinese — bare legs and arms, sunglasses, and glowing necklaces — squealed and laughed and milled nearby. On stage, a mediocre blues band, all wearing black T-shirts, plodded through a cover of "Everyday I Have the Blues."

David scanned the crowd once more, recognizing a few faces but no one he wanted to talk to. Who were all these young expats? Where did they come from?

"They all taste like boiled cabbage," said Trish, frowning into her cup. "I thought they weren't even going to have a beer festival, after the police last year."

"Yeah," he said distantly. David looked back up at the rim of the building overhead, at the scrum of drunken foreigners dancing and shouting at each other. It'd be so easy for the police to swoop in and take them all out, boxed in like this. Send in the riot police. Crack some *laowai* skulls. They would have nowhere to run.

"*Yeah,*" she mimicked.

"What?"

She sighed. "You're still thinking about the brat."

"It just doesn't make any sense," David said. "Why would Dai just drop his plans to go to Australia, all of a sudden?"

"He probably failed the language test. You said his English was shite."

David shook his head. "No, it's something else. He said his dad wasn't making him go anymore. 'It's safe to stay now,' he said. What does that mean?"

"So, who knows why? The kid stops lessons. You're out of a job. So what?"

"The photos."

Trish finished off her cup with gulp. She was bored. "Okay, the photos. So, what are you going to do?"

It was a question David had been turning over and over for days already. Dai had been in some kind of trouble, David was convinced. *It's safe to stay now.* His change of plans didn't make sense any other way. And if had been in trouble, David was holding something very valuable — those radioactive photos.

They were all damming evidence of *something*. David's

mind circled back to the idea he'd been toying with and thought he might as well tell Trish, just to hear how it sounded spoken out loud.

"I'm going to ask Dai if he wants them back," he said nonchalantly.

"Ask him."

"Well, I'm not just going to *give* them back. If he wants them back, we can talk about the terms."

"Blackmail, you mean. Americans call that 'blackmail' like we do, right?"

The band crashed to the end of a song, and the crowd yelled back its drunken approval. Soon, waves of people were approaching, thirsty for refills and respite from the sun. David and Trish shifted to stand near one of the white tents, out of the way. *Blackmail.* David rolled the word around in his mouth.

"Listen," said Trish. "You don't know anything about this kid, really. You're telling me he has all kinds of Ferraris and Lamborghinis. That doesn't sound like someone I'd want to blackmail. Sounds like he's got a powerful daddy."

"I *hope* he has a powerful daddy!" David said, a bit too loudly. Once, at the Palais de Violette, David caught a glimpse of Dai's father, a blurred figure entering a bedroom at the end of the hall, but saw nothing distinct. He'd asked Dai indirectly about his father but was put off each time. The only thing he really knew about Dai's father was that his son seemed to ignore him.

"Look, you read about how all these rich, entitled kids in China fuck up all the time," he went on. "Crash their cars. Get kicked out of school. Knock up girls. Do any of them really get in any trouble for it? No. Daddy always finds a way to pay and make it go away. You know how China is. When your kid fucks up, you just pay people off. When your kid kills someone, you pay off the family. When your kid flunks out of school, you pay the school off. This is exactly the same. Dai fucked up. He must have done something. Why shouldn't I get paid off?"

"But you're not a victim, David. Besides, you don't even know what he did —"

"David?!"

Trish stopped mid-sentence and they both watched a tall, slender blonde girl approach. She wore a dark-green tank top, ripped jean shorts, and oversized dark sunglasses. It was only when she flashed her perfect teeth that David recognized her. She threw her arms around him; her hair felt hot against his cheek and still smelled like shampoo. David, remembering Trish next to him, began to panic.

"How *are* you?" she sang.

David grimaced and turned to Trish. "This is Jessica. We work together."

"Television, possibly?" she deadpanned.

On the set of *Outstanding Talents*, the crew loved Jessica — fussed over her golden hair and delicate Suzhou-accented Mandarin. Jessica was twenty-four, and David remembered how the make-up artists liked to crack jokes about if Gao Fushuai was supposed to be so handsome, why did they have to spend more time covering up his wrinkles than they did doing Jessica's makeup? She was from Texas, and her voice almost twanged now. Did it come out more when she was drinking? Was she playing it up? David glanced at Trish, whose face was expressionless.

"The show just got extended for another year," Jessica was saying. "'Course I'm not sure if I'll be there."

"No?" David perked up at this. Maybe the show had gone to hell after he'd left.

"It ain't official," she beamed, "but I may be down in Anhui then. We're shooting a biopic of Pearl Buck. Tom Hanks is playing the father!"

"That's amazing!" Trish blurted out.

"Thank you!" Jessica squealed.

David wasn't going to congratulate her. He and Jessica had the same agent when they were both at *Outstanding Talents*; he had *introduced* Jessica to him. How had this drawling clown gotten a movie with Tom Hanks? She had no experience and mediocre Chinese. She was young and beautiful — that's all that mattered in show business in China.

"So, what about you?" she asked David. "What've you been up to? I thought you left."

David felt Trish's gaze burning a hole in the left side of his face but ignored it. He'd never told her that he'd been fired from the show. Tutoring Dai, he'd told her lamely, was just something to tide him over until the new season.

"No, I'm still here," he said coldly.

"Oh-kay," she sang. "So...."

"I may be leaving soon though. I'm still getting everything together."

"Well, like I said, everyone misses you on set! You were just so funny!"

Jessica said it with a dreamy, half-drunk, indisputably happy voice. David gritted his teeth once more but only took another drink from the plastic cup. He wanted to ask about Cindy but knew he couldn't. When Jessica had skipped away again, he turned back to Trish — fat, dull-haired, funny-T-shirt Trish — and started to say something.

"Don't," she said. "I get it."

David returned to his apartment that night with a trail of dead bodies in his wake. On the bus ride home, slightly buzzed and needing to urinate, he strangled the driver laying on his horn; he smashed sedans with idiotic drivers blocking the intersections; he demolished blocks of hideous concrete buildings; he smote every retiree taking up precious bus seats, every cutesy teen-ager who jostled him as they exited. Somebody needed to pay for this, all of it.

The text message David sent to Dai's phone number that night was brief and hastily conceived. Call it black-mail, he didn't care.

> Hello. You should still remember me. I have kept copies of all the photographs and videos of your cell phone, for my own protection. I would like to return them to you. I have friends in the media who are very interested in these kinds of matters, so I hope you will respond. Thank you.

David stayed awake most of the night, waiting to hear his own phone vibrate with a reply. He dozed off around three. When he woke at eight the next morning, his mouth was horribly dry, but there was still no reply.

* * *

It wasn't David's first brush with blackmail, technically speaking. Two years ago, he'd been cast as Otto, a rapacious German officer bent on stealing China's treasure in wake of the Boxer Rebellion. Otto learned the ropes of looting from the British in Beijing before being sent to down to Qingdao, where he seduced a local princess and used their illicit affair to extort riches from her family. One scene in the middle of the film showed David laughing maniacally in candlelight, running his fingers through bags of coins. Had the Communists existed then, Otto surely would have been apprehended and summarily executed. But there were no heroes around at the time. Otto never faced justice, only the final shocking realization, on the steamship back to Europe, that his bags of silver taels had been swapped with metal scraps by the clever rickshaw boy.

But Otto never blackmailed by text message. What was the tone supposed to be? Formal? Menacing? When David looked up the word in his Chinese dictionary, for a hint, it returned two possibilities: *qiaozha* — literally "overcharge and swindle" or *lesuo* — "tighten the rope." Tighten the rope. This wasn't blackmail; it was *lesuo*. He searched online for sample *lesuo* letters for inspiration. He read Chinese-language forums on people's experience with *lesuo*. Perhaps there was some element of local psychology he was overlooking.

In an odd way, David hadn't felt this engaged in the language in years. He agonized over the wording of the four texts in total he sent to Dai, each one, he hoped, calibrated to sound more threatening than the last. David didn't identify himself at first. Perhaps Dai had read those unsigned messages and believed someone was spamming him?

David's third text was almost apologetic; he wrote as if the whole *lesuo* ordeal was a big inconvenience for him as well. It wasn't as if *he* wanted to make Dai's pictures public; he just didn't have a choice. David wasn't worried; even if Dai went to the police, he was the one holding the evidence.

In a fit of frustration, one night, David dialed Dai's cell phone directly, heart thumping, just to see if the number was still connected. It rang and rang. He took a trip out to the Palais de Violette too, walking around the compound's outer wall in the dark, like some amateur cat burglar. The lights in the penthouse were still burning. Dai was inside, he knew it. His final text read:

> I'm tired of these games. I am going public with your photos next week. Either you give me a response by tonight or you will see the consequences. I am not joking around. Teacher David.

He waited in his apartment all afternoon, eyeing his dark phone for life every few minutes. Perhaps there was no cell signal inside his apartment? But no, around six he received a message from Trish, which he ignored.

That night, David sat alone at the quick-fry restaurant around the corner from his apartment, trying to console himself with a few Yanjings but still thinking of money. His finances had taken a hit since he stopped tutoring the little punk; it would take him another four months to save enough money for a plane ticket home and a new start back in the United States.

Yes, he was leaving China! This was the great nourishing thought that buoyed him through the summer and into fall. David was surer than ever he had to get out of this country. For so long he'd been hesitant to leave Beijing because he couldn't envision a new life for himself in the States, couldn't place himself in his own daydream. But that didn't matter, he realized now. He just needed to get out. He didn't need savings or a job lined up back home. He'd rip off the Band-Aid, figure out all of the details of his new life after he arrived. After all, that was precisely what he'd done when he'd arrived in China years ago.

And the fucking pollution! Even his mom agreed with him on that. For months, his chest had felt tight, had ached with each breath. Like everyone else, David had an app downloaded on his phone that spit back hourly numbers of how much particulate matter was in the air. But the apps were all bullshit, David was convinced, controlled by the government. How else was he so short of breath when the pollution level was only at 120? How vile was a government that lied to its own citizens about poison in the air? Fuck this country. He was out of here as soon as he had the money.

As David finished his rice at the restaurant, he noticed a middle-aged man sitting alone in the corner. Fake-leather jacket, bad haircut — he looked like the plain-clothes thugs dispatched across Tiananmen Square, ready to pounce on protesters. The man picked at a bowl of beef noodles and caught David's eye more than once. Each time their eyes connected, the man looked back down at his newspaper in a suspicious way. When David stood to pay, the man followed him out of the restaurant.

Outside, David quickened his steps toward home, feeling the man behind him. The thug remained fifteen meters away — not gaining pace but not falling behind either. Inside his apartment compound, David slipped into a darkened stairwell, sure that the goon hadn't seen him. He stood in the dark, arms slack, scalp tingling. The thug appeared at the gate, not all that tall, David realized; he would fight if he needed to. He had the element of surprise.

The man approached, unlit cigarette in one hand, newspaper in the other. He paused, shoulders turned away from David, lit the cigarette, and looked up at the apartment building (at David's unit?). Then he walked toward the opposite gate. David remained frozen in the dark, holding his breath, until he was sure the man was gone. Then he scampered upstairs and locked the door behind him. Adrenaline coursed through David's veins as he stood inside his front door, mind racing. *Either you give me a response by tonight or you will see the consequences.*

David considered telling Trish about his encounter with the thug from the restaurant but didn't. She would only overact, he knew, only remind him that he was in over his head. She'd tell him to come clean to the police. The police! As if they would do anything for a *laowai*.

He wasn't in any real danger from Dai, though, come to think of it, the little puke did know where he lived. And, true, Principal Yue — who was more or less to blame for the whole situation — seemed to look at him differently at school. When David called

in sick to work for a few days after the incident —
who wouldn't? — Principal Yue was on him more
than usual. She said she was "concerned about your
lesson preparedness" and "putting you on probation."
That was convenient: right after he'd stopped tutoring
her rich friend's kid.

He'd spent those days away from school perched at
his bedroom window, overlooking the complex's main
gate. He ate his delivery food there — the contents of
the plastic clamshell box fogging the glass — scanning
the apartment grounds six floors below for movement.

Sometimes at the window, he fantasized about Dai
texting him back, asking how much he wanted for the
photos. That would be a delicate situation, David knew
— determining his asking price. He had been through the
entire catalogue countless times, devised a dozen ways
to calculate its value. Six figures, at least. With some
luck, he would be able to take a trip through Southeast
Asia before he settled back in the United States.

* * *

Two weeks after David returned to Silicon Valley English,
he was in the middle of a lecture on space exploration
when he heard a knock on the glass door and saw Principal Yue lead a new body inside.

A man, perhaps in his early forties — shaved head,
rail-thin — stepped in front of her. His face was all
hardened angles. *Please, go sit back there*, she whispered
to him in Chinese.

"A new shipmate on your English journey!" Principal
Yue announced to the class. David shuddered.

When she left, David called loudly toward the new student in the back, in English. "What is your name?"

"Grin."

"Grin?"

The man stared back with his dead eyes. He was not grinning.

"Grin," the man repeated once more. "*Lesuo*," he said in Chinese. David stood very still, swallowing down an electric panic. The man stared back. "*Lüse*," he repeated, pointing to the green jacket hung on his chair.

"*Green*, you mean."

Teacher and student regarded each other for a few blank moments. This was no language learner; David was sure of it. Two girls in the front row spun pens around in their fingers. David's brain sent a new signal: Do not show fear.

"Okay, *Green*," David repeated, conscious of how loud his voice was. Another chill sent him toward the whiteboard.

It was impossible to riff on Mars colonization and asteroid mining with Green's bullet head gleaming from the back row. The new arrival stared at the wall, his desk, the back of the head of the kid in front of him without comprehending a word. When David put the students in pairs for conversation practice, Green was the odd man out and sat fiddling with his cell phone beneath the desk. David made no effort to include him, only wandered the same route between the pairs of desks, ostensibly listening, skirting Green's desk each time.

David knew he was safe as long as there were other students around. But after class? Just look at him sitting there, biding his time. What had Dai instructed him to do, exactly?

A mere fifteen minutes had passed. The pairs of students, finished with their dialogues, grew restless, bored. They checked their phones and talked in low voices. David kept pacing up and down the rows, willing the panicked seconds forward and keeping Green in the corner of his eye. He knew it was time to start in on the new unit, but it felt better to keep his legs moving, to stay mobile.

"Teacher David!" whined Rebecca. "A question!"

He felt himself glide over to her desk; a strange weightlessness had come over him. Rebecca started in on her list of past participles. As she did, Panzi, the skinny kid with the ears sitting next to her, was talking on his phone in Chinese, whispering through a cupped hand.

"No Chinese!" David snapped him. His voice was too loud again. Panzi looked up, confused. Since when had Teacher David cared about students speaking Chinese in class?

"Do you say, 'I *will not have had* the pleasure' or 'I *have not yet had* the pleasure'?" Rebecca was asking.

Suddenly, the bell chimed overhead, which didn't seem right. David was the first one out the door. He glanced back at Green, who was slipping on his windbreaker one arm at a time. Not a single muscle on his face moved, as if he wore a mask.

Bursting into Principal Yue's office, David slammed the door behind him. Green wasn't a good fit for his class, he wheezed. His spoken English level was far too low so he couldn't understand what was being said which was not good for the classroom environment and he knew that Principal Yue was most focused on providing the very best level of education which he was trying to do but it would be impossible if some students in the class were at a very different level than others so it was vital that Green be moved to another class maybe a Basic English class that was taught by one of the Chinese instructors.

Principal Yue took off her glasses. David remained standing, rubbing his palms on his pants.

"David, are you all right?" She seemed suspicious.

"He doesn't understand me," David replied, as clearly as he could.

"David," she said again gently, as if speaking to a child. "What did I say after our chat last week? What I want — what I *need* — from you is to show a bit more initiative in the classroom. You should treat this as a challenge!"

He studied her face for signs of deceit. Principal Yue knew Dai's family after all. Had they put her up to this?

"Adult education is an important —"

The chime rang in the hallway.

"Well, we can pick this up later," she said.

David stared at her for a beat, loathing her raised eyebrows. A look of impatience. Fuck her, fuck this school. David stalked back down the glass hallway, fists clenched, ready for the first flash of a green windbreaker. Yet, when he made it back to the classroom, there was no sign of the thug. Green's seat was empty.

"No more Chinese!" Teacher David roared at his students. "And no phones! This is an English class! Everyone is supposed to speak English!"

The classroom was silent.

"Okay," David said, sitting on the edge of his desk.

He ran his fingers through a tangle of hair behind his ears. His chest ached from the all the yelling. Twenty students stared at their desks.

"Just ... practice the dialogues."

The rustle of paper. A dropped pencil. Low voices. The room seemed to swallow rather than produce noises. David remained in front of the whiteboard, eyes shut, fingers pinching the bridge of his nose. Just walk out. Just fucking go. No, what if Green were outside waiting for him? He imagined Green following him down the stairwell, footsteps echoing off the walls.

"Teacher David?" Rebecca called again.

As he shuffled over to Rebecca's desk, he again caught a glimpse of Panzi's cellphone glowing beneath his textbook page. Panzi scrambled to pocket it before David noticed it, but it was too late.

"Give it to me."

Panzi looked back, pleadingly, a final time before handing his teacher the glowing device. David glanced at the screen and dropped the phone back on the desk, as if it were hot to the touch.

EXCLUSIVE: THE LAST HOURS OF
VICE MAYOR'S PLAYBOY SON

Below the headline, there was unmistakably a photo of Dai, his arm around another kid who looked vaguely familiar. David managed a few labored breaths before looking wildly at Panzi. What was a picture of Dai doing on this phone? What the fuck was this?

"Teacher David?" Panzi said. They were all staring at him, as if about to close ranks. "Are you all right?"

"Get away from me!"

David picked up the phone again read the headline. Last hours? Dai was dead? It didn't make any sense. He reread the photo caption, explaining that the boy on the right was dead. David studied the pudgier face on the right. He recognized it from Dai's cache of photos as well.

A slight breeze began blowing in his mind, stirring the fog. Dai was alive. The other boy was dead. Wait, who was this? The vice mayor's son?

He pointed out Dai's face to Panzi.

"Is he still alive?" David asked. He wanted to hear someone confirm it.

Panzi looked confused again but nodded. "Teacher David, do you know him?"

David stared at the photo and then began to scan the article's text for Dai's name. There didn't seem to be any mention of him.

"Have you seen him before?" Panzi asked, pointing at Dai's picture again. "I'm looking for him," Panzi went on. "I've been looking for him for months. Do you know him? Do you know where he is?"

David thrust the phone back toward his student and took a panicked step away. Where the hell was Green? What the hell was this, some kind of ruse set up by Dai?

"No, Teacher David," Panzi started over again. "You don't understand. I've been looking for him for months, with my journalist friend. We need to find him."

David looked over the kid's face, searching for traces of deceit. Panzi's eyes were wide, expectant. *Journalist friend?* None of it made any sense. But David knew instinctively he didn't have much time. *Where was Green?* He shuffled around rows of desks and to the door while the rest of the class watched. Rebecca's mouth was still open when the door closed behind him.

"Teacher David!" Panzi called. The boy had followed him out into the hallway. "Where are you going?"

The elevator door opened, and David jumped inside. Still no sign of Green; he must have been inside Principal Yue's office. The last thing David saw before the dull metal elevator doors closed was Panzi darting down the orange hallway toward the stairwell. David jabbed the ground-floor button over and over, knowing he needed to beat Panzi to the bottom.

18

Smoke

THAT October, the city kept catching fire. It started in Changping District, far northwest of the city center, when a high-rise apartment under construction burst into flames in the middle of the night. Four dead, thirteen injured. Days later, a gas line exploded on the west side of town, blowing off the last of the ginko-tree leaves at Babao Cemetery. One dead, seventy-two injured. Then, a chemical fire broke out at a plastics factory, in Fengtai District, which quickly spread to a workers' dormitory nearby, engulfing three floors of bunk beds in minutes. That fire happened just after lunch, when workers were napping, and the bosses had a habit of locking them inside "for safety." Thirteen dead.

In the pages of the *Beijing Evening News*, the tragedies were treated like natural disasters. The paper reprinted the same cursory three paragraphs that appeared in every other state media outlet across the country — lives as statistics. In the days after each new calamity, Yanmei was dispatched to the scorched neighborhoods to seek out stories of heroism or, failing that, heartbreak. She interviewed a street sweeper from her hospital bed, badly burned and still in her reflective orange uniform. She met a young boy who talked to her from the same piano bench he'd been sitting on when a shard of window glass flew into his ear.

Most of the victims were furious. She filled her reporter's notebook with their anger and frustration. They blamed corrupt property developers cutting corners on safety; they blamed the government for avoiding payment of compensation. One showed her a homemade video that she thought back to often — silhouettes of workers clinging to the charred scaffolding, backlit in dramatic fiery red.

There was no place for any of it in print, she knew. These were supposed to be *Profiles in Tragedy*, Section Editor Deng groused, reading Yanmei's first draft, not *Profiles in Anger*. What could Yanmei do but neuter her stories? What were any of them supposed to do? So Yanmei spent her afternoons flipping through pages and pages of angry interview notes, hunting along the margins for material that wouldn't be left on the *Evening News*' cutting room floor.

When Yanmei's article about the street sweeper was finally published, it appeared on page three, just below the fold. Above the spread, a photo showed an overweight, hollow-eyed man in a prison jumpsuit sitting behind a wooden desk in court — "former City Planning

Director Li Panglai stands accused of serious disciplinary violations," the caption read.

At first, Yanmei was surprised to see the stand-alone photo floating in space. Director Li had been swept up in some anti-corruption probe, some political scandal a month ago, she knew; he had nothing to do with the exploded buildings and gas-line ruptures. But the longer she looked at it, she realized bitterly that no, the layout, not the text, told the correct story: a photo of a burning building, a sympathetic headline about "tragedy," and a man in handcuffs.

When Panzi texted her that afternoon about meeting for dinner — yet another dinner — she ignored it. A nameless frustration had been building for weeks, hovering over her, or maybe the entire city, seeping into everything. She was tired of the fires. Tired of the *Profiles in Tragedy*. Tired of research and reporting — what did it matter anyway? Tired of Panzi and this string of purposeless dinners. She was tired of being tired.

She left the office early, around three o'clock, just to be alone for a while. She began walking east along Chang'an Avenue, eyes never trained more than a meter or two ahead. She heard her phone buzz inside her purse with another message. Perhaps she would walk all the way home to Sihui from here.

It was the uncertainty that got under her skin. She was Panzi's what? His friend? His confidante? Something more? Toward the end of summer, she was meeting Panzi almost weekly. Sometimes, together with him, it seemed so obvious that she was nothing more than Big Sister. He complained to her about his mother, about apartment buyers, as if she were supposed to comfort him. Then he would laugh at something, reach across the table, and touch the back of her hand. He was by far the most sensitive person Yanmei had ever known. Maybe he was just shy.

It began to rain, and Yanmei ducked inside a subway entrance and rode the train the rest of the way home. When she walked in the door, her roommate, Lola, murmured something about it raining. Lola was Yanmei's classmate from university and never seemed to move from her perch in their living room, where she watched costume dramas on her laptop. They rarely spoke, and neither felt compelled to make an effort. This is why both were surprised when Yanmei sidled up to Lola on the sofa and haltingly asked her how she might find out if Panzi might be romantically interested. She had mentioned Panzi to her before but had never said anything like this.

"*Wa!*" Lola squealed, pausing her show. "Are you serious?"

"It's just…. I don't know…." She watched Lola try to fight down a bout of giddiness. Oh God, this was a mistake.

"This is amazing! How much time do we have?"

"What?"

"You're going to see him again soon, right?"

"Well, he invited me out for dinner tonight, but I haven't said yes yet."

"Okay, okay," said Lola, clapping her hands. Her eyes darted around Yanmei's face, scheming. "Text him now. And then come with me to my closet."

Lola's advice was unequivocal: dress up sexily and see how Panzi responds — a form-fitting dress, heels, earrings, a bit of lipstick. How oddly calming it was to have someone dress you, Yanmei thought, as Lola held up a ruby-red dress against her body in the mirror and then tossed it back on the bed, muttering. As she tried on Lola's clothes, Yanmei lost her nerve, imagining the surprised look on Panzi's face. He would be shocked. It would be awkward. It was so unlike her to do something this dramatic, this impetuous. Yet, in the end, it was that same logic that pushed her forward. She stood in front of the mirror in Lola's undersized, vaguely tiger-striped dress. Yanmei was tired of being herself but not whoever this was looking back at her.

Lola's black heels were already soaked in hutong-gutter rainwater by the time Yanmei reached the fried oyster restaurant and located Panzi at the corner table. It had been pouring outside for hours and she was thirty minutes late. The room reeked of cooking oil. Rain-soaked cardboard boxes lined the floor of the grimy restaurant. Pools of water formed under umbrellas leaning against table legs.

"Sorry I'm late."

"Doesn't matter. You're soaked!"

Yanmei gave him a helpless smile.

"Did you come from some event? You sounded busy."

Yanmei leapt at the excuse. "A cocktail party. For work." Absurd, but what did he know?

"Well, thanks for meeting with me. There's a lot to talk about."

Thanks for meeting with me?

Panzi flagged down a waitress and ordered two trays of garlicky fried oysters. Yanmei jammed her cold hands between her thighs for warmth. Not even a flicker of interest had registered in Panzi's eye, she was sure of it. She was invisible to him. At the table across from them, two middle-aged women were whispering and casting sidelong glances at her. Was Lola's makeup running? There was no mirror, no place to see her reflection.

"So, have you seen it?" he asked, barely contained.

"What?" She had barely caught her breath.

"The article about the vice mayor's son."

Before she could answer, Panzi had his phone in his hand. He pulled up the text and thrust it across the table at her. "The Last Hours of Vice Mayor's Playboy Son," read the clickbait headline. It looked like a blog post.

"It came out two days ago."

Yanmei read the first few lines.

> Chen Shishan didn't like to wait for anything. Cruising the streets of Beijing in his red Ferrari at night, he didn't wait for parking spots, didn't wait for pedestrians, and certainly didn't wait for red lights. Why would he? His father was a vice mayor of the city. What's the worst that could happen? But one night, earlier this year, Chen Shishan would find his life in the fast lane come abruptly to an end.

It went on to describe the crash in some detail. February 17. The Duanqiruifu gate. Chen Shishan. The sacked vice mayor, Chen Yihui.

Yanmei wanted to laugh. So that was the name she'd been looking for: Chen Shishan. She'd spent months digging for clues — poring over reports, teasing out relationships, working late nights — and all for what? All that time and effort, only for the story to miraculously appear one day, published as some sensational blog post. What a joke. Yanmei gazed at the metal tray of glistening oysters, feeling damp and nauseous.

"The article's not right," Panzi said gravely. "There's no mention of Xiao Song, no mention of the other guy in the car, the actual driver. It doesn't make any sense."

"It says the right date, doesn't it? February 17. A red Ferrari. Duanqiruifu. This is it, Panzi. Chen Shishan. That's who you've been looking for."

"No, no, look." He pointed at the photo accompanying the article. Two boys, about Panzi's age, stood together at some dance club with their arms around one another, smiling. The photo was clearly pulled from one of their social media profiles.

"They were *both* there. *He* was the one driving, not Chen Shishan."

"God, who cares!" she yelled. The women at the next table over looked up from their scallops. Yanmei stared back at them, furious, until they turned away again. "Do you think it matters who was driving the car? Do you think that's going to change anything?"

Panzi looked shocked and hurt by the outburst. His voice went soft. "Big Sister, I just want to know the truth."

"This *is* the truth, Panzi. You just don't like it."

Panzi looked down, as if he might cry, his huge eyes going dark. It made Yanmei angrier still. They swallowed a few bites of food in silence. Her feet were freezing. What an idiot she had been to come out and meet him like this tonight. How pathetic was she to try and impress him, to surprise him.

"There's something else," Panzi said finally. "My teacher, David, says he knows him."

"Who?"

Panzi gestured at his phone again. "The other one. The driver."

Yanmei set her chopsticks down across the lip of her bowl with great care. A very real and calming feeling of finality came over her. She would listen very carefully to whatever Panzi was about to say, because this would be the last time she would ever see him. No more dinners, no more uncertainty. He could go on sifting through the desert, searching for whatever it was he was looking for. And she would get on with her life. At least then she would have accomplished something tonight.

Panzi began to talk about an altercation with his English teacher the previous day. Somehow, this foreign teacher claimed to know the driver of the Ferrari.

"He has some photos," Panzi went on. "I don't know what they are exactly; he won't show them to me. He won't tell me anything else unless I introduce him to someone in the media. He says he wants to *sell* them."

Yanmei remained very calm and said nothing. Panzi scratched the back of his head nervously.

"To be honest, I don't think Teacher David's well. He's been acting really strange. But you sort of know him already; he's the one who sold 'Eat Dirt.' Remember? You're connected to him too, Big Sister." Panzi rambled on, glancing up at Yanmei's stony face every so often. "Look, I know the *Evening News* isn't going to buy any photos from him, but maybe you could meet with us at least and have a look? It wouldn't take long. Five minutes. He shows the photos, you say 'no' and that's it. Then at least we could see them. We'd know if they were real or not."

"You, not *we*," Yanmei said finally. "*You* would know if they were real."

When they had finished the meal in silence, Panzi called for the check and the two of them split it, as usual. Outside the restaurant, the rain had stopped; but large black puddles remained in the creases of the pavement. They turned at the intersection and made their way south toward the Dongsi Station entrance. It was after ten o'clock, and massive transport trucks, finally allowed inside the city, rumbled past them, spraying rainwater and diesel exhaust in their wakes.

The points of Lola's heels clicked against the sidewalk, one step behind Panzi. The toes of her damp, borrowed shoes rubbed against the blisters already formed. Yanmei dreaded the thought of returning to her apartment to face Lola, who would be hungry for details of the pivotal date. She just wanted to be alone in her bed with the covers pulled tight. What had she been thinking? Yanmei looked up and watched Panzi — walking a few steps ahead of her as usual.

They said a curt goodbye at the subway entrance and Yanmei rode the escalator down alone.

Her apartment was quiet; Lola was mercifully asleep. No Korean soap operas playing in the living room, no dog barking from the apartment upstairs. Yanmei pulled the purple curtains in her bedroom closed, shutting out the haze outside. She crawled into bed, still in Lola's clothes, and shut her eyes.

That night Yanmei dreamt that she was five years old, walking with her grandmother along the faded green concrete steps of her hometown. She saw herself skipping along in a white ruffled dress while her grandmother followed, a few steps behind, hands clasped behind her back and bent forward like a figure skater.

It must have been October because even in the city district, farmers had spread out ears of corn on the back streets to dry for harvest. Inside People's Park gate, Yanmei was spinning around with hungry joy, trying to take up as much space as possible. Her grandmother kept calling out "Go slowly!" when Yanmei twirled too far ahead.

Suddenly they were sitting, eating watermelon popsicles. Her grandmother pointed a swollen finger toward a white-breasted blue bird darting through sycamore branches and whispered, "Look! That's *you!*"

Yanmei's eyes expanded with wonder.

"That's a swallow, just like your name!"

The fluttering of wings and heart, the glint of sun around the tips of the tree. Her gaze followed the bird's robotic movements, her own body suddenly itchy, lifting upward, outward, higher with each beat of wing.

Yanmei turned to her grandmother and asked, "When will I be old enough to fly?"

"You can't fly now," she tutted. "There's too much smoke."

Yanmei looked back up past the tree branches and saw that the sky had changed. The hard blue dome was now rolling waves of black smoke, billowing toward her. Yanmei reached for her grandmother, but felt a larger, smoother hand take hers instead. Editor Ge took off a pair of stylish sunglasses and looked down at five-year-old Yanmei.

"It's another fire," he said calmly. "You need to prepare for the interview."

Yanmei reached into the tiny pockets of her dress, searching for a pen, but all she found were dozens of tiny balls of paper.

"I don't have anything to write with."

"It's okay. You just need to remember it."

The bank of smoke was much closer now, blacker, almost on top of them. Editor Ge stared back at it serenely before putting on his sunglasses again. Yanmei squinted as the wave overtook them, wisps across her shoulders, filling her nose and mouth. She closed her eyes and held her breath, letting the smoke completely smother her.

Yanmei startled herself awake, gasping for air. She jerked her head up and looked past the foot of the bed toward the vanity mirror above her dresser, breathing heavily. She needed to see herself. Her darkened bedroom was still; she could hear her pulse pounding in her ears. The room remained dark for a long time. It seemed to take forever before her eyes had adjusted enough to the dark to see her own reflection.

* * *

Yanmei's first impulse, spotting Panzi and a ragged-looking foreigner outside the *Evening News* building the following morning was to turn and run. Panzi stepped out of the shade and approached her, smiling, as if she hadn't seen him — hadn't *fought* with him! — the previous night. The south-facing facade of the *Evening News* building was long and bowed, glass panels catching and pitching back heat from the morning sun. Yanmei felt it on her face.

"What are you doing here?"

"I needed to see you. It's an emergency."

"What are you doing here?" Yanmei hissed again. Damn her calm. She focused her gaze past him, toward the building's entrance. "I have work to do."

"You won't answer your phone. What was I supposed to do?"

"You're supposed to leave me alone!"

When Yanmei tried to brush by him, their shoulders collided. Panzi grabbed her arm, sending an electric current through her. She glared at his hand and thought about smacking it away, but the foreigner was standing nearby, and she didn't want to make a scene.

"Five minutes," Panzi whispered.

Yanmei shook herself free from him.

"Look, I know you're upset," he said. "I know that I'm imposing on you but it's not up to me." His voice dropped to a whisper. "Teacher David won't show me the pictures otherwise."

"It *is* up to you, Panzi!"

"Sister," he pleaded.

His face was sweating, she could see. The hot sun beat down on them for a moment as she tried to muster another outburst. *It's not up to me.* How could he even say that! Panzi *wanted* to believe it wasn't up to him, that he had no control. How convenient for *him!*

Yet, in the next moment, seeing his flushed, pious face in front of her, Yanmei felt something soften, a familiar feeling. So many of her bouts of anger and frustration toward Panzi fizzled this way, when she could tell he wanted desperately to connect with her, to understand her, but couldn't. It wasn't his fault, Yanmei realized. She wasn't angry at Panzi; she was angry at Xiao Song. Jealous. *Little Goddess of Mercy.*

"Sister," Panzi repeated softly.

Yanmei looked away and took a breath. How petty and cruel — standing in the blazing reflected heat of the building — to blame him, to punish him out of jealousy, she thought. How selfish it suddenly seemed, to leave him stranded here, perhaps just six meters away from finding out his truth.

"I don't even know if our editors will be in today," she said finally.

The *Evening News'* dozen section heads and editors were just finishing their daily eight o'clock meeting in the conference room when Yanmei, Panzi, and David arrived in the open lobby. A few of the editors cast sideways glances at David as they filed out. Yanmei forced a smile and charged into the stream of bodies until she found Editor Ge, still seated at one of the white leather chairs. He was writing in his notebook when she approached. Yanmei called back to Panzi and David, still waiting outside, and the four of them assembled around the short end of the blond-wood conference table.

Yanmei introduced David to Editor Ge as the photographer of "Eat Dirt," the photograph from her feature on Guang Fei and the Idiot, way back in May.

"He is a talented photographer," Yanmei stammered. "And he has some additional photographs that he thought the *Evening News* might be interested in."

"Good," said Editor Ge, rising from the chair with an

I'm-busy smile. "Take him down to see Su Su. I hope it works out."

"Ah, well, Su Su is not in today," Yanmei muttered. "So, I was hoping I might show you some —"

"I'm not a photographer," David blurted out. A week's worth of red-brown stubble covered his chin. His blood-shot eyes were focused away from the group, toward something out the window. Yanmei watched Editor Ge watching David, sure that he had now noticed the spot of white crust on the shoulder of David's gray sweatshirt.

Editor Ge's eyebrow was cocked. "Well, then I...."

"I didn't shoot these photos myself," David explained, "but I came across them recently, and I believe they are newsworthy."

With surprising swiftness, David had Yanmei's laptop open on the table and a blue USB drive inserted. Computer-screen light bathed his pallid face. Without another word, David opened a folder containing twenty images and began to flick through them.

David lingered on each image for exactly five seconds, which he had calculated was just enough time to pique maximum interest. He silently counted off the seconds — *one one thousand, two one thousand* — before tapping the arrow key forward. David had spent an inordinate amount of time curating and ordering the images so that they grew in salaciousness — from disco-lit revelry, sex and hard drugs, to the final Ferrari-and-Lamborghini highway drag races.

Looking at the photos yet again, it was hard for David to spot many new details. A new snake tattoo on the bare shoulder blade of girl ... *four one thousand, five one thousand*. A black leather wallet half-opened at the corner of a table ... *five one thousand*. A squinting middle-aged man standing next to the red Ferrari ... *five one thousand*. David's middle finger struck the arrow key a final time — an audible *snap!*

David shut the lid of the laptop, pulled out his USB drive and pocketed it. The four of them remained in a stunned silence for a long time.

"These are a few of the photos I have to offer. I have many more," David said.

Editor Ge was the first to regain his composure. "Where did you get these?"

"That's not important." David had been waiting for the right moment to bring up his asking prices and now seemed as good a time as any. "What's important is that your newspaper is interested in these, I'm sure. You may decide to publish them or *not* publish them. The choice is yours. I am selling them for one million yuan. All of them." Gauging no response at this line, he hastened to add "or individual photographs for one hundred thousand yuan each."

"You're selling these photos."

David took this as a positive sign. "You have my promise that you will be given the only copies. Once you buy them, they will be your property only."

Editor Ge closed his notebook and stood up.

"I don't know who you are, and I don't know if these are real, but you need to be very careful. This is not some game." He and David stared at each other for a smoldering moment before Editor Ge walked straight out of the conference room before David could get in another word.

"Yanmei, with me," he called over his shoulder.

"Just get out of here," she hissed at Panzi. "Both of you."

"Big Sister, I need to talk to you."

"Go!"

She disappeared from the open doorway, and two cleaning ladies in sea-foam uniforms rushed inside and began collecting tea mugs and food wrappers.

Editor Ge was standing behind his desk when Yanmei knocked to enter.

"Close the door. Sit," he said.

Yanmei did as she was told, folding her hands in her lap. Editor Ge's voice didn't sound ominous; it sounded energized.

Ge stood up again, agitated, and began to pace, though his office was large enough to accommodate only a few steps. He was still in the throes of the feeling — that familiar quickening of pulse, a kind of lust stuck in the back of his throat — that the stream of photos had brought on. He hadn't realized it at first, it'd been that long, but his body responded before his mind had caught up: he was staring at a scoop. It was a massive, career-defining investigative scoop like the kinds he fantasized about when he was down south, doing actual investigative journalism. God, that last photo showed half the mayor's office!

Back at the old *Southern Weekend* what would they have done with this cache of photos? Ge imagined the expressions on the faces of the old guard, mouths agape. God, how he wished to share that moment with them! He knew exactly what they would have done — cordon off a conference room, spread out the pictures across the surface and pore over every one of them until daybreak.

The *Evening News* could do absolutely nothing of the

sort, of course; it would never touch such radioactive stuff. Still, when he had glanced at Yanmei during the slideshow and watched her eyes darting around each flashing images, vacuuming for details, he read in her that same yearning. Her fingers were spread as if on the verge of grabbing control of the computer. She had good news instincts.

"What's going on, Yanmei?"

"Nothing," she protested.

"I know what you've been researching at the office," he said. "Your special research project. IT informed Deng Wen about it weeks ago. She came to me. You're lucky she did."

A jolt of panic held Yanmei's body deathly still in the chair.

"C'mon, Yanmei. You knew that your computer activity is monitored when you're here, didn't you?"

Yanmei stared at the desk, silent.

"I'm telling you that what you're doing is very sensitive. Corruption, luxury cars, now these photos. The *Evening News* isn't going to publish any of this. What's going on, Yanmei? Is this about the fires?"

Ge started pacing again, a welcome source of movement. When Yanmei looked up, she saw in Editor Ge's face that he wasn't threatening her; he was genuinely, journalistically curious. She relaxed a little.

"No, not that."

Yanmei took a breath and started at the beginning, with Panzi. By the time she got to the Ferrari crash cover-up, Ge had already stopped pacing; he was again sitting, engrossed. Yanmei told him about the *People's Daily* editorials, the names whispered in anonymous online forums, the research dead-ends, the half-true blog post, and finally, the parade of images they'd both just seen.

By the time she'd finished, she realized that Panzi was right — the story wasn't finished. She had begun pulling the thread to something much bigger, and now she didn't want to stop. Hearing the whole story out loud crystalized that in some important way. She thought back to the men in the photo, standing beside the cars. What were their connections to all of this? What connections did *those* connections have? She saw the lines crossing, overlapping, zigzagging, spiraling out toward the horizon.

Editor Ge already had a pencil in his hand, jotting the details into a skeleton outline on his desk. When she stopped, she waited a long time for him to say something. He took a final look at the paper, slashed an arrow across the margin and handed it to her.

"What am I supposed to do with this?" she asked.

"It depends. You can take it somewhere else and try to publish it or stay here at the *Evening News* and tear it up."

"You're firing me?"

"Did I say that?" He sighed. "Listen, Yanmei. You're a journalist, a good journalist. But we don't need journalists at the *Evening News*; we need 'news workers.' I've seen young reporters like you, the ones with real curiosity and ideals. I *was* one of them. If you stay, you'll get promoted or you'll end up in a lot of trouble — who knows? Either way, you'll be unhappy. But, no, I'm not going to fire you.

"I still have a few contacts who I worked with at *Southern Weekend*, in Guangzhou. Not the new *Southern*

Weekend, the old one. They are starting something new, a news website, with some Hong Kong investors. They haven't even published anything yet, and I've heard they were already raided by the police. The whole site may fold after three months; I don't know. But I do know that they will want stories like this. If you tell it right."

Yanmei looked at Ge's scrawling handwriting on the page.

"And if I stay?" she said slowly.

Editor Ge laughed.

"You'd be surprised what you can get used to."

19

Democracy

"THE car is already waiting downstairs."

"I know. I know. You don't have to keep repeating it. They're not going to leave without me."

Zhenhua stalked back into the bedroom in thin black dress socks, breathing hard. He checked inside the wardrobe a second time, then under the couch. He stepped around piles of clothes and two open suitcases on the floor. He had already woken that morning in an irritable mood from another night of fitful sleep. Now this. Where was his damn briefcase anyway?

He avoided Rui's glances each time he crossed back into the dining room. She sat, cupping a mug of tea on the glass-top dining room table, staring into space. Why couldn't he remember where he'd thrown his briefcase?

Zhenhua was back in the kitchen when Yuqing came running toward him.

"Daddy, Daddy!" she cried, holding his blessed brown leather bag by the strap.

Zhenhua grasped for it, relieved, but looked at his daughter severely. "Yuqing. You *cannot* take Daddy's things from him!"

"I was packing it for you!" she cried.

He felt his wife's eyes on him from across the room. He didn't want to say goodbye to them like this, but he was late.

"Just ... don't take Daddy's things, okay?" Zhenhua set the bag down and lunged for his shoes near the door.

"*You* left it when you came into my room last night!"

Zhenhua glanced over at Rui, as if to ask: *Are you hearing this?* Yuqing, however, stood her ground. His daughter looked proud.

"You woke me up and asked me where Grandpa was."

Zhenhua had his coat on already but froze at the mention of his father-in-law.

"Yuqing, you know that Grandpa left this world last month," Rui finally chimed in, crossing the room toward them.

"That's what *I* told *Daddy*."

"Oh, Sweetie," Rui said. She squatted so that she was eye-level with Yuqing, leaving Zhenhua standing alone with his briefcase. "You need to say goodbye to Daddy. We're not going to see him for a while."

"Why?"

Zhenhua looked at Rui, hoping to catch her eye, but she wasn't looking at him.

"I'm going to see you very soon," Zhenhua said. "You stay with Mommy until I meet you."

"When are you coming?"

Zhenhua looked up at Rui again but her eyes were still trained on their daughter.

"Soon, Sweetie. You listen to Mommy while you're in Jiangsu, okay?"

One month. That was how long Rui said she would need to stay in Jiangsu to take care of family matters following her father's passing in October. Neither of them could find any reasons to object, and Zhenhua was too busy with work anyway. The time apart might even do them good, they'd agreed.

"Give Daddy a hug."

Yuqing obliged, and Zhenhua felt the grip of her tiny fingers. Then she scampered off to her suitcase in the next room.

"So what time is your flight?" he asked quickly.

"It's okay," she replied. "I know you have to go." Rui hugged herself in a faded orange sweatshirt.

She finally looked up at him, and Zhenhua could make out tiny lines of worry above her eyebrows. He knew his wife well enough to know she was about to cry.

Zhenhua shouldered his briefcase.

"Have a safe flight," he said. "I'll call you when you get settled."

Rui swept a strand of hair from her face and crossed her arms again. Her eyes had already turned glassy.

"Don't call. Write me. A letter."

* * *

A gray Hyundai idled outside the gate of Zhenhua's apartment complex, white steam coughing from the muffler. City Planning's modest fleet of Audis and Buicks had been effectively impounded since October, after the latest government edict for officials to practice "moderate working lifestyles." That meant no more leather seats, no expensive wristwatches, no travel outside the country.

He was relieved to find he'd still made it to the city government building in time. Zhenhua entered the meeting room and took his assigned seat at one of the three long wooden tables arranged in a horseshoe. His place setting was identical to the others — a pink cardboard rectangle with his name printed on it, an empty white teacup and lid, a sharpened pencil, a thin microphone bent forward, and a fifty-page policy document. Zhenhua scanned the red lettering of the report's cover page: Beijing Municipal Party Committee Study Session (8th Session).

He was one of the first to arrive, and, to pass the time, he quizzed himself by reading the names facing him on the other side of the table. Gao Shibao, Zhou Jitong, Yang Zhengming, Guo Ping.... They were all heads of some Beijing government department or another, he knew, but which ones? No one's position was printed on the pink cards; no one would be formally introduced, which, come to think of it, was likely intentional. When all the men in identical baggy white dress shirts filed through that door, they were no longer supposed to be recognized as the heads of Beijing's most powerful municipal departments, they were all supposed to be students.

Zhenhua had attended study sessions before but never at this level, in this room, which, now that he really looked, was more austere than City Planning's own conference room. No projection equipment. No television screens. No decorations lining the walls. That was doubtless intentional as well. Television cameras would be filming this session to broadcast on the evening news. A red banner bearing the full name of the study session was stretched across the wall, at the horseshoe's opening. Zhenhua flipped through the thick report in front of him, trying to look busy. Then he changed his mind and aligned its corners back to its original untouched position, so it would look like all the others.

"Director Sun!"

Zhenhua turned in his chair and greeted the man standing behind him. He was older and had a smooth flat face. Three long hairs grew out of a mole on his neck. Zhenhua didn't recognize him.

"How are you finding it?" the man asked.

"Oh, fine. Busy as always," Zhenhua murmured.

There was a mischievous twinkle in the man's eye. He held Zhenhua's gaze a beat longer.

"I'm sure you're working hard," the man said. He seemed brimming with admiration. "But young directors like you still have lots of energy!"

Zhenhua felt as if his face might flush. He'd had a number of these conversations, which were less conversations than encounters. These men didn't so much want to talk with Zhenhua as stand close and look at him, to see if they might absorb a bit of his aura. It was very uncomfortable. Zhenhua told the man he was flattered, and they chatted for a few more minutes while the last of the cadres filed in and situated themselves. Then the man with the mole retreated to his station — Wang Yongping, his name turned out to be — and the

Beijing Party Secretary leaned forward in his chair and switched on his microphone.

"Welcome to the Beijing Municipal Party Committee Study Session, Eighth Session!" They all dutifully clapped.

Then, without another word of introduction, the Party Secretary began to read.

Everyone in the room, thirty-five middle-aged men, some gripping their standard-issue pencils, bowed their heads and followed along, word by word. Sentences stretched on for paragraphs, paragraphs for pages. Study sessions were a test of endurance and discipline more than anything. You had to sit still and concentrate, endure the tedium.

Zhenhua felt the man shouldering the TV camera move behind his chair but didn't dare look up. He straightened his back a little and underlined the first phrase that jumped out at him: "unswervingly implement reforms of the Warm and Close Beijing Family Campaign."

At larger, national Party gatherings, cameras sometimes caught officials yawning, sleeping, or worse. People online were already so cynical; they saw photos of dozing cadres and could only laugh. *What a comfortable life!* read a sarcastic comment Zhenhua had seen once, *Eat whenever you want, sleep whenever you want, ignore me whenever you want — I really envy the life of my cat!*

The life of a cat! Sleep whenever you want! Since becoming City Planning director, Zhenhua felt as if he hadn't slept at all. During the district merger in October last month — closing offices, disappearing whole departments — he'd spent it all in a kind of numb fear, alone. Everyone wanted face time with him — fellow officials, real estate developers, heads of industry associations. They seemed to lunge at him from all directions, as if *he* were the one orchestrating the city's entire reorganization.

He told nearly everyone he met the same thing: he wasn't responsible for the merger; he didn't have a say. But sometimes that wasn't enough. One night, a laid-off district cadre called Zhenhua's cell phone after midnight, drunk. The man's speech was slurred, but he otherwise spoke with a chilling calm, as if the two of them had scheduled a phone conference at that hour.

He stated his name, department, and position; then he threatened to kill Zhenhua and his daughter unless the city's plan changed.

The morning after the death threat, Zhenhua told the Boss of Houhai about all the promises he'd been forced to make, ones he knew he couldn't keep. Don't worry, the Boss assured him, promises weren't worth much in this particular economy. This is what you wanted, he reminded Zhenhua. You have your position, and soon you will be able to use it. For now, you just have to sit tight.

When he felt the cameraman move on, Zhenhua glanced up and around the room as the secretary general droned on. Here they all were, arranged around three wooden tables — the survivors. It was a miracle, it seemed, that the city survived October at all without any damage. When the merger was completed — at least the first, most painful phase — there were no congratulations, no celebrations. None of them got the day off. *Sleep whenever you want!* No, nothing to mark the occasion except another ride in the Hyundai, another policy document, another study session.

Zhenhua looked down at his stack of papers. "Warm and Close Beijing Family," that was the new slogan. It was a call for peace. After all the discord of the merger, the Central Party's office now wanted them all to join in a big, warm hug. Let the Party's propaganda department churn out whatever it wants, Zhenhua thought. No one sitting around these tables would ever be family. He wished it weren't so, but that was the sorry truth. The Boss wasn't right about everything, but he was right about that.

In truth, Zhenhua hadn't felt much remorse when Vice Mayor Chen was finally hauled in by Party Discipline and stripped of his position in September. Even if Chen's son didn't own a Ferrari, that didn't change the fact that Chen himself was a shell of a man, unfit for work. Whenever Zhenhua felt a pang of guilt over his former mentor, he recalled the night he'd walked in on Chen and his I Ching coins. Chen couldn't stay on as vice mayor in that state. The man was paralyzed, crippled.

The last Zhenhua had heard, Director Li had been sent to Qincheng Prison for corruption, political conspiracy, and "offenses against State Security." The whole affair hadn't taken long; Director Li had plenty of political enemies. His trial had been rushed to the last week of September, leveraged in some factional battle or another before the merger.

The city was better off without both of them, that was the main thing. Neither of them had the people's interest at heart; neither were really committed and able to do good. Zhenhua glanced around the room once more. The city's government was overrun with craven, ineffectual officials. Had he not gone to the Boss of Houhai in the summer, Director Li would be sitting exactly here. How much worse off would the city be then?

You had to make small sacrifices if you wanted to survive, if you wanted a chance to do good in the first place. Even Baiheng — Zhenhua didn't want to picture the young man's face at first but, no, there it was — even young, talented people like him sometimes had to suffer for the greater good. Zhenhua had pled with the Boss not to implicate Baiheng in any of the cover-up mess.

"He was only trying to save Vice Mayor Chen," Zhenhua had said. "Baiheng is extremely talented. I could use him at City Planning. Just let Chen himself take the fall."

But the Boss never let up, not even for a moment.

"I don't know why you're asking me. It's not as if I can do anything about it. All I know is what I read in the papers — that Chen's assistant is accused of selling secret police files to Director Li."

When he heard this, Zhenhua felt very small.

"Someone like that, it sounds like you're better off without him."

* * *

Ladies and gentlemen, we now formally announce the consultation process with residents of the Duanqiruifu community! Beijing's rich cultural heritage is an integral component to the Soul of Beijing. As a class-II protected cultural landmark, the Duanqiruifu Luxury Restoration Project will be restored

to glory in accordance with the relevant laws
and bylaws of the People's....

Zhenhua stopped skimming the written speech in his hand and glanced out the Hyundai's window, wishing he were going anywhere other than Duanqiruifu. He still had twenty minutes of peace, at least, before he arrived and the consultation started.

Relocation had always been the most sensitive issue of any new property development. Forced demolition, nail houses, self-immolations — so much could go wrong, and the central government knew it. In the last few years the rules had changed, and now residents had to be "consulted" before shovels went into the ground. Residents didn't own the land, of course, and they had little legal recourse to stop new projects. They were "consulted" but did not decide anything. But rules were rules; you had to hold a consultation meeting, which typically meant a lot of defiant yelling and chaos, clamoring for higher compensation.

Zhenhua had seen Director Li sweat through a few of them before he wised up and began throwing his subordinates to the wolves. At City Planning banquets they still joked about the time a sweet-looking granny in her pajamas took off her slipper and hurled it at Vice Director Dong. Much of the outrage was just posturing, Zhenhua knew. There was a lot of money at stake.

Middle-aged folks were reasonable people. They might shake their fists and raise their voices, but most of the heat was only smoke. They vowed they'd never leave, would never accept the government's compensation; but this was mostly a show. Money spoke loudly to middle-aged people. Zhenhua had plenty of money to offer; City Planning's budget had more than enough set aside for the Duanqiruifu Luxury Restoration Project. He had ensured that.

The elderly and the young — that's whom Zhenhua feared. When they refused to move, they were stubborn. When they said they didn't care about the amount of money for relocation, they meant it. Some had romantic notions about preserving the past; others held superstitions that made them wary of life in tall buildings. How do you negotiate with people like that, people who don't speak the language of progress? Many of them were too old to care, retirees with nothing better to do but play chess, gossip, sip tea, take walks in the park....

Zhenhua let the copy of his speech drop on his lap. He suddenly saw Rui and her father shuffling forward along a tree-lined path in Ditan Park. It was one of the last times he could remember the four of them together as a family, Zhenhua realized. That afternoon, Rui had dragged the whole family outside to see the autumn leaves. Yuqing was waving a plastic magic wand they'd just bought her.

That afternoon in the park, only a month ago, already belonged to another era. Everything since — his promotion, the merger, his father-in-law's passing — seemed surreal, out of body. At work, they now addressed him as "Director Sun," and Zhenhua would occasionally forget to reply. He went to business meetings with the Boss who chided him for doing things that no self-respecting director would — carrying business cards, answering phone calls from unknown numbers, speaking first in meetings.

"You'll learn," the Boss was fond of telling him, as he dispensed his advice. But Zhenhua didn't feel like he was learning anything. Was any of this really happening to him? He thought back to his daughter standing with his briefcase that morning. Maybe he *had* woken her up in the middle of the night? Or maybe that wasn't him; maybe that was only his body?

Zhenhua blinked in the Hyundai, and the vision disappeared. So strange, these little lucid memories that flitted by. He'd been having them more and more frequently. He needed sleep.

When his car arrived at the Duanqiruifu grounds, only the Boss of Houhai was waiting for him outside. He stood next to the stone steps at the entrance of the community meeting room. He wore a puffy orange down coat that looked a bit too fashionable for him. His freshly dyed hair gleamed blackly in the afternoon sun.

"S—," Zhenhua stopped himself before he could apologize for being late. That was another of the Boss's rules: directors don't apologize, for anything.

The men walked inside together, and Zhenhua looked over the crowd, counting middle-age faces. The group of fifty residents sat on peeling wooden chairs facing a large red banner hung behind a podium. The room smelled of mildew, and a cast-iron radiator lining the far wall let out a faint, high-pitched squeal. Mahjong tables had been pushed against the side wall. Many of the people wore goose-down coats or heavy padded jackets in the drafty room. Perhaps two-thirds were in their forties and fifties, a good sign.

Zhenhua's plan for the afternoon was to deliver his opening speech as quickly as possible, step down, and leave the "consulting" to working-level City Planning staff on hand. Ma Jun and Yang Hong had already erected an easel with fresh sheets of white paper near the first row of chairs. The first page of the large notepad had the words "Community Concerns" printed at the top. Zhenhua planned to stand aside and watch the crowd closely, taking note of any agitators.

Yang Hong stood at the wooden podium, which was festooned with a large bouquet of flowers, as if the event were a celebration. He tapped the microphone a few times and announced Zhenhua's name and position. Facing the crowd — dozens of blank faces peering back at him — Zhenhua felt his pulse rise to his throat. He gripped the edges of the dais. A baby, held in someone's lap, began to cry loudly.

"Good afternoon," he began. He read from his speech without looking up, trying to block out the deafening howls. The child's wailing seemed to grow louder with each reference to "relevant laws" and "sound development." No one hushed the boy. Zhenhua plowed ahead, reciting the words in a monotone until there was no more writing on the page. He muttered a brief thank you and returned to his seat, near the front of the group. There was no response from the audience at all. The baby continued screaming.

"Thank you, Director Sun!" enthused Yang Hong, now back in front of the group. He picked up a black felt-tip marker from the easel's tray like a kindergarten teacher and removed the cap.

"Now, we will formally begin the consultation portion of today's meeting! My name is Yang Hong — 'Yang' as in 'poplar tree,' 'Hong' as in 'red.' I'll be today's facilitator, along with my colleague Ma Jun. 'Ma' as in 'horse,' 'Jun' as —"

"You can't move us out!" someone yelled from the middle of the room.

Zhenhua looked behind him, in the direction of the outburst. A man in a gray coat with short gray hair and beady eyes was standing.

"We have rights! We have rights!"

Yang Hong flashed a benevolent smile toward the crowd. He slowed his speech and began over-enunciating.

"So, this gentleman has brought up the issue of community relocation. I will add that topic to our list of Community Concerns." Yang Hong turned his back to the crowd to write. When he stepped aside again, the word "relocation" was written on the large notepad. "Now, when I am finished introducing the project, we will have an opportunity to discuss other concerns! So, if I could —"

"What kind of nonsense is this?" yelled the gray-coat man again. "You can't develop new buildings on this site! This is historically protected." A few murmurs of support bubbled up from the group.

"This is a *restoration* project, not a construction project," Ma Jun put in. "Duanqiruifu is a class-II protected cultural landmark, which is managed under the auspices of the Beijing City Planning Commission."

Ma Jun was standing next to his colleague on the other side of the easel, and dressed informally in a pair of jeans and white sneakers. The outfit made him look like he'd just graduated from university.

"The historic buildings of the Duanqiruifu community

are old and dangerous," he went on. "The construction grade is very poor. There are multiple fire hazards."

"Duanqiruifu is part of People's University. It is not controlled by the city!"

"Now, it is administered by the Beijing City Planning Comm—"

"The compensation is too low!" yelled a woman from the crowd. She remained sitting, with her short legs crossed, and her hair pulled back in a ponytail. Before Yang Hong could respond, a third person, a woman from the back row, yelled at her from behind.

"What compensation? You've lived here for only a few months! What are you talking about compensation for?"

The ponytail woman turned toward the voice behind her. "I'm a resident here, same as you!"

"Nonsense! You're an outsider! You probably work for them!"

A shrill argument broke out. New voices seemed to erupt all at once. Suddenly, a separate cluster of retirees near the back was quarreling about the community's cooking gas supply.

"The property management company *can't* fix it!" someone shouted.

"Cooking gas is not the management company's problem! Everyone knows that!"

"Please wait a moment!" Yang Hong tried yelling over the din. "There is an order to the meeting! There are rules! Why don't we raise our hands to speak?"

"You've already wasted enough time!" spat the woman from the back. She wore a loose green sweater with the sleeves rolled up her arms. This woman lacked the palpable anger of the gray-coat man in front of her, but she was good at interrupting every time Yang Hong tried to yank back control of the meeting.

"Auntie —"

"These buildings are —"

"Auntie, let me —"

"— protected and not supposed to —"

"Auntie," Yang Hong pleaded, his voice trembling slightly with anger. "Yes! *You* say you want.... Listen to me, listen to me.... You say you want everyone to speak. So, we're all just going to yell? Let everyone ... listen to me ... let everyone have a turn to speak."

For a while, there was no form, no real chain of events or discussion — only an angry mob all shouting at once. Zhenhua sat still in his chair at the front with his eyes closed, letting the discord wash over him. He could still hear the child's screaming, cutting above everything else.

When the woman in the green sweater seemed to have exhausted herself, Yang Hong convinced a handful of people in the group to begin raising their hands before speaking. A woman with dyed curly hair raised her hand, waiting patiently like the teacher's pet. Yang Hong called on her formally and the woman stood.

"I have lived in the Duanqiruifu complex since 1973," she began. "We can all admit that there are problems living here. Am I right? Overall, the houses are very good quality, but we must admit there are some problems since they are so old." She gestured toward Yang Hong and his easel. "We can agree that we don't need their list, but we must remember that we need to work together! Am I right? Now, I raised my hand; we can all raise our hands!"

A smattering of applause broke out and then a

confused silence. Zhenhua looked behind his shoulder and saw the woman sitting behind him nodded her approval. She was knitting a scarf.

The group's intensity seemed to flag. Most people began raising their hands to speak, but occasionally the woman in green got antsy and had to blurt something out. Someone gave a long, defiant speech about the history of Duanqiruifu. Someone else began talking about problems with trash collection inside the community. Every time someone mentioned a new problem or comment, Ma Jun asked, "Does this belong in one of these categories or is it a new category?" Zhenhua quietly stood and moved toward the door. The last thing he saw before he slipped outside was a mind-map diagram beginning to take shape on the easel — spokes radiating out from the word "concerns."

The Boss was waiting for him outside on the stone steps, chatting with one of the middle-aged women from the meeting. He nodded to her a final time and slipped the woman's business card in his pocket before he and Zhenhua walked toward the Hyundai.

"Of course it was chaotic," the Boss told Zhenhua once they'd settled in at a restaurant not far from the Duanqiruifu site. "But anytime more than a few people get together in one place, it gets like that. There's nothing to worry about yet."

The men took drags from their cigarettes as the food began to appear — three home-style dishes and a soup. Zhenhua inspected the fatty pork belly without interest; he wasn't hungry. He poured himself another cup of jasmine tea from the pot on the table. He had thirty minutes to eat, thirty minutes until his next appointment.

The Boss briefed him on progress made lining up investors and retail partners. Zhenhua half-listened, nodding at regular intervals. It all sounded like good news, but his mind was elsewhere; he wished the whole Duanqiruifu project were behind him. There was no end in sight — endless meetings, the relocations, the drain on City Planning's budget.

No, it would all be worth it. The Boss was right; he *had* wanted this. Once the Duanqiruifu project was successfully underway and the aftershocks of the merger quieted, he would still be director. Whenever he had a few precious moments to himself, Zhenhua returned to his grand ideas for the future development of Beijing — not just more apartment blocks and shopping malls, but a *rejuvenated* city. He envisioned a calm, historic center of the city — clean streets and limited car traffic, parks and quaint shops — surrounded by state-of-the-art office buildings outside the Second Ring Road. There was so much to do.

"Do you think anyone will refuse to move?" Zhenhua asked.

"At Duanqiruifu? It's hard to tell," the Boss replied. "Probably a few of them. Most of them are on our side."

"That woman you were talking to? Who is she?"

"Just a local resident," the Boss smiled. "She told me she's in favor of the restoration. Such people are useful to know."

But that didn't help them with the old codgers, Zhenhua wanted to say. Most were retired professors from People's University — men of letters — with little ambition in life beyond maintaining the cramped, quiet homes they'd lived in since the 1970s. These academics paid the university a pittance for rent and resisted every new attempt at refurbishing the buildings. The university didn't have much leverage; the professors were well connected in national think tanks, and the university didn't have money for restoration and relocation anyway. For years, the Beijing city government had been pressuring People's University to sign over development rights of the area.

"Chaos is not the worst thing," the Boss observed. He stubbed out his cigarette and picked up his chopsticks. "Chaos has no direction. It's impotent."

Every time they met, it seemed the Boss had some new bit of philosophical advice to bestow. He had told Zhenhua whom he should meet, what he should say, how he should behave.

Zhenhua set down his spoon, thinking back to Director Li and his patronizing maxims.

"Well, it's unpredictable."

"So, you tame it. You make it predictable."

Zhenhua sighed into his soup.

"What do you think about democracy?" the Boss suddenly asked.

"What do you mean?"

"Democracy. Letting the people choose."

Zhenhua glanced at his watch; he had twenty minutes until the Hyundai arrived. "People aren't educated enough. It would be too chaotic."

The Boss shrugged. "I like democracy. It solves a lot of problems."

Zhenhua looked up at the Boss so he would continue.

"Suppose you have fifty families and you give them a choice. Either they can all be compensated and moved into nice, modern apartments or none of them can. They, as a group, can decide either way. *You* don't tell them what to do. It's *their* choice. That's democracy."

Zhenhua picked up his spoon again and thought a moment. Then he shook his head. "Don't you remember what just happened? It would only be *more* chaos! They could never all agree. In the end, they would never decide anything."

The Boss's lips parted into a cracked grin. "Oh no, they have to decide," he said. "That's why you make them vote."

20

An Ugly Sunset

DAVID wanted the cash dropped off at his apartment. No public places. No bank transfers. Twenty thousand yuan. It wasn't the million that he'd first demanded, but it was still a lot of money to Panzi.

How much was Panzi willing to pay for the truth about Xiao Song? Ten thousand? Fifty? Thinking about it, haggling over the price, made him sick. Each time David texted back some astronomical price for access to the photos, Panzi hated having to feign outrage. In the end, he told his mother that next year's tuition at Silicon Valley English was due.

When Panzi arrived at David's apartment with the two stacks of pink banknotes in a backpack on an early November afternoon, he didn't feel especially nervous until David let him inside. The apartment smelled like rotting bananas. Panzi took one step forward and heard his shoe peel away from the floor. He remained standing near the front door, next to a thick wooden stick leaning against the wall. Plastic take-out food boxes were piled in the kitchen sink, as if waiting to be washed. The countertop around it was a skyline of beer bottles.

Panzi unzipped his backpack and held out one of the blocks of cash as a show of goodwill. His teacher seemed uncertain handling it, riffling through the corners before placing it on the coffee table. David wore ripped jeans and a stretched-out white T-shirt with faded oil stains dotting the front. His hair was a tangled cloud, matted on one side.

"That's all of it?"

"I have some questions," Panzi said.

"What questions?"

"The ones I already asked you."

David's jaw muscles clenched but he said nothing.

"I need to find him. I need to talk to him."

"You don't want to talk to him. Trust me."

David led Panzi across the living room — weaving around more beer bottles and DVD cases — to the bedroom, which was nearly bare except for a mattress on the floor, a blinking wireless router, and a final green beer bottle on the windowsill half-filled with cigarette butts. Panzi felt a pang of sympathy; how long had his teacher been living like this? Before he could say anything, David swiped the blue USB drive off his bed and pressed it into Panzi's palm.

"This is the only copy of these files. You have my word," he said, stalking back into the living room, as if he had heard a noise. Panzi pocketed the thumb drive and followed him.

"Look," Panzi pleaded, "you *must* know something else about him. You don't have to tell me everything. It's just, as a friend, if you know anything —"

"You're not my friend," David snapped. He sat on the couch and began to count the second stack of pink bills.

"A name, a phone number, anything."

David stopped counting the money and looked up from the couch, his face a mask of disbelief. He snorted.

"This is only sixteen thousand," David said, thrusting the bills toward Panzi, incredulous.

"I know. Listen, I couldn't withdraw it all at once. We'll go down to the ATM together. I'll pay you."

"Fuck!" David yelled in English. Panzi took a step back toward the door.

David closed his eyes in frustration. "Fucking Chinese," he muttered. "Money is the one thing you people are supposed to understand."

During their silent procession together down six flights of concrete stairs, Panzi racked his brain for another way to ask David about the boy in the photos — the driver he had seen the night of crash — but came up with nothing. They crossed the compound's common area — David walking behind him, like a perp walk — and arrived at an ATM. Panzi stepped inside the glass booth while David waited outside, scanning the sidewalk in his white T-shirt. Panzi looked at the ATM's screen, checked his balance, and withdrew nearly all of it. The machine rattled and spit out the new bills.

When Panzi handed over the fresh stack of bills, David began counting them immediately. Halfway through, he stopped, looked up at his student, then counted the rest of the stack. Panzi had overpaid him by three thousand yuan; it was the only thing he could think to do, the only thing David seemed to care about. When he'd finished counting, David seemed lost in thought for a moment.

"Listen, Teacher David," Panzi said softly.

"Look, he's a dangerous person," David said, speaking Chinese again. "You don't want to seek him out."

"It's really important that I do."

David stuffed the last of the bills in his front jeans pockets. He crossed his arms for the first time, as if suddenly realizing how cold it was.

"His name is Dai. I don't know his full name, okay? I was just his English tutor for a few months."

Dai. His name is Dai.

"You've met him? Face-to-face?" Panzi asked. They began walking back toward David's apartment.

David nodded, scanning the sidewalk as if looking out for someone. "We met at his house. It's up north along line five." He told Panzi Dai's address at the Palais de Violette. He pointed to the blue USB drive in Panzi's hand.

"If you see him," David said, "don't say anything about me, okay?" David shivered a final time and walked up the concrete stairs alone.

Panzi left David's compound and immediately boarded the subway toward Palais de Violette. It was only one line change and thirty minutes away. Once the train emerged above ground, leaving Datun Road East Station, he tried to quiet his racing mind by fixing his eyes on the Olympic Park Observation Tower in the distance as the train hurtled north. He disembarked at Lishui Bridge South Station and followed a map on his phone, jaywalking across four lanes of traffic, and arriving at the main gate of the Palais de Violette.

He sat down on a wooden bench opposite the gate and took a breath. *His name is Dai.*

Panzi's heart leapt into his throat each time the doorman in a black suit opened the gate and a new person walked toward his car. The red Ferrari must have been parked right here, Panzi thought. He turned the blue USB drive over and over in his fingers while he watched.

After an hour or so, lights inside the apartment buildings began flickering on; the sun was already beginning to set. The gathering darkness brought with it a whole host of doubts. What was he going to do, wait on this bench all day, every day, in the hopes that Dai might appear?

And even if he found Dai, what would he do? What would he say?

* * *

Panzi flipped through Dai's photos perhaps two hundred times that November, stretched out on the twin bed in the professor's old room at Duanqiruifu. After a month of negotiations, his mother had ultimately bought five properties in the complex, but Panzi only stayed at the small room at the end of the hall. It was still stained the color of the professor's life. On the yellowed wall above the bed, there were three clean white rectangles where the black-and-white Japanese portraits had hung. The wardrobe's door was splintered along the bottom edge. Qinyan saw no use in furnishing it; the entire complex would be gutted come spring. It wasn't as if Panzi would need to show it to any buyers. Why stay in such a hovel, she wanted to know? Why didn't he just come home?

The first week of the month had been unseasonably rainy. From his narrow bed, Panzi had a view up into branches of waxy, almond-shaped leaves brilliantly yellow — a jujube tree, one of the neighborhood women told him. The first two nights, he had dreams of Xiao Song returning to his room, clutching a handful of those wet yellow leaves. In the afternoons, Panzi ambled around the compound with an umbrella, watching the flags, still out for the National Day holiday, drip in the doorways.

But mostly he stayed in bed. Panzi had uploaded Dai's photos to his phone and always swiped through them slowly, chronologically. He had been through them so many times that they had assumed their own rhythm — the timeline of Dai's life. Parents materialized, then friends. A new luxury car would arrive with fanfare — perhaps three dozen shots taken in a single afternoon, the gleaming metal shown at every possible angle — and then be replaced. There was a parade of women, all of whom looked about the same. One slim, fashionable girl after another appeared, posing in the exact same places — the passenger's-side seat, the blue-lit dance club sofa — as if reincarnated. It took Panzi some time to recognize that he was looking at a tedious, repetitive life.

He spent a lot of time examining the photos of Chen Shishan, the vice mayor's son, whose body he'd seen pulled out of the mangled Ferrari. He looked like a pudgier version of Dai and the others at first glance — short-cropped hair, silver necklace, well-groomed. But the longer Panzi studied the images, the more convinced he became that Shishan was out of place, uncomfortable somehow. He was always standing on the fringes of the action. He smiled his apple-cheek smile a bit too guile-lessly for the camera. In one shot, he was mopping up spilled drinks in the background. In another, he had a buddy's head placed gently on his lap. Dai was the one swigging cognac bottles to a cheering crowd; Shishan was on the margins, looking expectantly at him.

No matter how many times Panzi looked, there were no photos of the Ferrari crash. Five images, all dated February 17, led right up to the fateful moment — Dai and Shishan aping at each other in the front seat of the car. Dai was behind the wheel, his eyes hooded, then closed, then hooded again. Shishan looked happy, almost joyful. Each time Panzi swiped through this sequence he felt a tightening in his chest, an irrational guilt, as if *he* were the one causing what would come next. He felt the car speeding, swerving across Zhangzizhong Road. He was sure the next image would be the apparition of Xiao Song through the windshield, her ghostly white dress illuminated in headlights.

But the accident never happened. After the five photos taken inside the Ferrari — nothing. The next image in the stream was taken two weeks after the accident, the files read, from what must be Dai's bedroom inside the Palais de Violette — a muted, hazy sunset, taken at a stilted angle. Panzi stared at this image far longer than any other, desperate to wring it for meaning. Remorse? Depression? Relief? But the photo offered nothing other than what it was — an ugly sunset.

After the sunset, there were two dozen photos of a bleak-looking outdoor basketball court with high-volt-age wires and power station equipment behind it. They were all the same. To Panzi, the sunset was the end;

when he arrived at that image, he started back at the beginning again.

* * *

Panzi spent those wet November weeks studying the photos, the stained walls of the room, the jujube tree — waiting for something to happen. He had no desire to see his mother. Yanmei wouldn't meet with him. He might have remained in the professor's room for another month, but one morning Panzi woke and thought he caught a whiff of rotting bananas. Then he knew he had to go home.

Panzi found Grandpa on the roof of their apartment building, wrestling with a spool of chicken wire.

"It's almost winter!" Old Li called out when Panzi emerged at the top of the spiral staircase. "Come here and give me a hand!"

The two of them spent the morning fussing with plastic tarps and moving around cages — preparing the pigeon coops for winter. Old Li paced the edge the roof taking an inventory of the birds in his yellow notebook, like a manager on a factory floor. Panzi was heartened to see Grandpa looking healthy and full of purpose. He looked younger, which, in effect, he was. If the warehouse of Old Li's mind was slowly being emptied, the newest boxes were the first to go.

When Panzi asked Grandpa how he'd been during the past few months, Old Li had little to say. Instead, as they worked, Grandpa gossiped about people with nicknames Panzi had never heard of before — Little Monkey, Pockmarked Wang, Buck-toothed Po. The stories were disjointed and confused, so it took some time before Panzi realized that Grandpa was talking about kids from his youth. Yet even after Panzi understood that Grandpa wasn't making any sense, he didn't intervene. It didn't matter, really. The tales were detailed and aimless, perfect for filling a cold morning.

It made sense that traditions, most deeply ingrained of all, remained Old Li's bedrock. When he heard fireworks around noon — neighborhood boys setting off firecrackers somewhere — he grew anxious.

"We should start now," Old Li said.

"Grandpa, New Year is still months away," Panzi said gently.

The old man considered the white sky for a moment and then made for the staircase, muttering that they didn't have much time.

Panzi remained on the roof. The alley below was busy enough that there was always someone to watch — an old woman selling vegetables, a quarreling couple, a middle-aged woman walking her dog. Better to be outside of Duanqiruifu, up here, around people, he thought.

He watched the passersby for a few moments, each of them somehow resembling people he knew — Yanmei, Wu Wei, the family from Phoenix City.

Panzi was about to go downstairs when he heard Grandpa tramping back up the iron spiral staircase, clutching a sheaf of papers. When the old man finally shuffled up and onto the roof, he scanned the horizon.

"Hurry up!" he hissed.

Old Li fumbled with his cigarette lighter and commanded Panzi to start crumpling paper. The pages were all blank — ruled white pages ripped from a notebook. He must have confused them for joss paper, Panzi thought. Grandpa wanted to do their New Year tradition. Panzi stood by, watching Grandpa's swollen knuckles bring the trembling lighter toward the papers. Another smattering of explosions sounded to their left. When the flame disappeared again, Panzi offered to help but Grandpa brushed him off. Once the paper finally caught, Panzi watched Old Li's restless eyes.

"Grandpa, what's the matter?"

"This is good; everyone is distracted now. Fan the smoke around! They won't notice it that way."

"It's okay," Panzi sighed. "No one's going to bother us, Grandpa. It's okay."

"It's not okay," Old Li snapped. Worry and anger now creased his face. "You never understand how dangerous it is, do you? Give me the rest of the pages!"

"Grandpa —"

"Now!" Old Li commanded.

Panzi didn't want to fight; he handed over another fistful of blank pages. He watched a magpie perched on a telephone wire while Grandpa shook the lighter.

"You think you're some kind of scholar, writing this?" Old Li was muttering. He thrust out the papers as proof. "Foreign poetry! What if they found this? You think this is some kind of game?"

"Grandpa?"

"What if *Qinyan* saw this, this nonsense about 'my heart needs to be free'? Where would that leave the family? How could you be so selfish? You will never write this nonsense again! Do you understand me?"

Panzi looked at his grandfather, trying to plumb his confusion. Was Grandpa talking to his son? He looked down at the paper and tried to imagine his father's handwriting. Even then, at the height of Old Li's confusion, Panzi still couldn't bring himself to say stop. Part of him, the deepest part, wanted to hear it, all of it.

"I need to write it," Panzi ventured very softly.

"You don't know *what* you need. This, this ... poetry is *bourgeois decadence*," he hissed. "That's what they'll say. You want to ruin your family? Who do you think you're writing this trash to?"

Grandpa looked up from his smoldering paper, locking eyes with his grandson in a way that sent a deeper, shivering confusion through Panzi. Who were they talking about? Panzi swallowed and pictured Xiao Song's face.

"I need to write it to her. She's odd, but she's kind. And, yes, she's different than everyone else, but she's not dangerous."

"Are you crazy?" Old Li held out the papers again. He seemed genuinely unable to understand what Panzi had said. "There's no one to give this to. This isn't for anyone other than yourself!"

Panzi reached to wipe his nose and realized his cheeks were wet with tears. Enough. He didn't want to hear any more. He looked back up at the telephone wire, but the magpie was gone. At their feet, the last of the paper was smoking. Old Li swept away the small mound of ash with his foot, leaving behind a black smudge on the concrete. Grandpa looked dazed and shrunken now that he had finished scolding his dead son.

* * *

After Grandpa fell asleep on the couch that afternoon,

Panzi let himself out of the house and took line five back toward Duanqiruifu. Even on an early weekday afternoon, the train was half-filled. Panzi stood near the center of the car, holding a steel pole, searching the faces of the fellow riders, mind still swimming with the details of Grandpa's outburst on the roof.

He watched a migrant woman and her daughter from across the train. The daughter, perhaps two years old, sat on a bulging nylon sack — purple sweatpants and matching hoodie, with long hair and bangs to her eyebrows. Neither of them had a phone out, which was rare. Instead, the daughter stared serenely out the window of the train while her young mother kept her eyes closed. Panzi couldn't look away from the little girl; she seemed so tranquil. Was she making any sense of the city on the other side of the glass or was it all just flashes of light and color?

The overhead recording sounded, and the mother's eyes snapped open, breaking the spell. Panzi looked away from them, up toward the LED display: Lishui Bridge Station. Panzi rubbed the back of his neck; he had missed his stop some time ago. He would need to turn back.

When the train stopped, Panzi followed the mother and daughter onto the aboveground platform. He stepped behind them onto the long escalator, and, as it went down, he could see that the daughter had a bit of dried snot encrusted around her nostrils. As the escalator glided along, Panzi looked out over the raucous commercial street below and realized with a start he was at the subway station near the Palais de Violette.

He was looking out over the street when he felt something tugging at his fingers. He looked down and saw that the two-year-old had latched on to his fingers.

"Don't do that!" her mother chided when she noticed what was happening. The little girl dropped her arm to her side.

"It's okay," Panzi smiled.

When they all arrived at the ground floor, the woman and her girl disappeared through the subway exit. Panzi looked up the escalator that would lead him back toward the southbound train and paused for a moment. Then he exited the station.

Magpies were chirping along the wooden fence when Panzi arrived at the south entrance of the Palais de Violette. He sat on the bench opposite the front gate, the same one where he usually waited. The guards, still in their long black overcoats, were helping a woman with a stroller. They would notice him, the loiterer, soon enough, he reckoned.

Okay, he thought, *well, there it is.* He waited on the bench until the woman with the stroller got in a car and drove away.

Rather than returning to the street, Panzi wandered along the paths through the manicured garden outside the Palais de Violette's high bronze walls. The shrubs were already wrapped in green cloth for winter. The dead grass was so pale it almost looked white. Piano music seeped from fake rocks lining the path. No one else was around; Panzi walked slowly under the gray sky, looking at the trees and thinking not about Xiao Song or Dai but his father.

Why had he been writing poetry during the Cultural

Revolution? Was it true that he hadn't been writing it to anyone beside himself?

When Panzi turned right at the compound's northwest gate, the landscape changed. Tall, ugly power station equipment loomed overhead, its power lines swooping over dirt mounds and brittle trash. Megaphoned voices from the adjacent shopping complex bled through the trees. The residents of the Palais' northernmost apartment buildings must have thrown a fit when they saw this. Rather than a majestic southern view over Olympic Park, these buildings looked out over real Beijing: power lines, squat brick buildings, rows of idling city buses.

Panzi was about to turn back when, amid the twiggy brown and gray, a thin strip of bright green caught his eye. He continued along the north wall until he reached a basketball court. He stared at the bright neon-green backboard of the hoop for moment, wondering why the scene seemed so familiar — the court, the power lines, the conical spire of a commercial building in the distance.

With a start, Panzi took out his phone and began swiping furiously until he found them — the final set of images taken by Dai, the ones after the ugly sunset. Panzi held up the photo of the basketball court to the scene before him — an exact match. Panzi sat down on a bench next to the basketball court and looked closely at the photos for the first time, zooming in and out on stray details. There were more than twenty such photos. He swiped forward to another picture of the same scene — the same half-court, the same power lines — only this time, he noticed that the fallen leaves on the court were not quite the same. The next photo was slightly different still.

He'd been wrong; these photos were not identical at all; they weren't even taken on the same day.

Panzi looked at the file details of the photos and realized they'd been taken over the course of months. Dai had come to this exact spot, over and over, to photograph the same lifeless scene. Why?

Panzi had a sudden urge to call Yanmei; she would have known what to think about this. But before he had even the chance to debate whether or not to dial her, a figure approached over the small dirt hill.

Panzi watched with a growing panic as a young guy, about his own age, walked down the steps and approached. The newcomer — pale and drawn-faced — kept his eyes fixed on the path in front of him until he arrived at Panzi's bench and registered a stranger occupying his usual spot. The young man hesitated for the briefest of moments before continuing toward an adjacent bench near the backboard. As the figure passed by, Panzi caught a glimpse of a wide scar down his chin and he knew. Dai sat down without a sound.

Panzi stared dead ahead at the basketball hoop and jammed his icy fingers in his coat pockets. Would Dai even recognize him from the night of the crash? His stomach lurched. A minute passed. Should he just walk up and confront him? Was Dai dangerous, like David had warned him? *Say something!* Time was running out, but Panzi couldn't think of a single thing to say; his mind was a total blank. *Do not miss this!*

After a few moments, Dai glanced at Panzi for what seemed like the first time and stood to leave. Panzi, too, rose and stood in front of Dai, blocking his way to the stairs. What was he doing?

"I need to talk with you," Panzi said. "You know me, actually. You hurt a friend of mine." Dai didn't seem to hear him; he simply walked around Panzi, saying nothing. When his back was turned, Panzi shoved him with both hands, harder than he'd meant to. Dai fell hard on the basketball court.

"Are you a fucking psycho?" Dai screamed.

Panzi shifted his weight to the balls of his feet. Dai was shorter than he'd imagined, looking at the pictures, about Panzi's his own height. He was stockier as well, maybe twenty pounds heavier, with a puffy face.

"It happened after New Year," Panzi said in a voice that didn't sound like his own. "You ran her over. At the red gate at Duanqiruifu."

Dai looked at Panzi again. Was that a moment of recognition?

"You're fucking dead," Dai muttered, backing away toward the building.

Panzi lunged toward him and they tumbled onto the court, kicking, thrashing, grabbing handfuls of clothing. Dai shouted for help a few times; but no one seemed to hear. After some minutes, Panzi found himself on top of Dai with his arms pinned above his head. Neither had thrown a punch, but Dai's head had cracked against the ground at least once. Panzi wiped his nose and saw his fingers were red. Both were winded, and since Panzi didn't have a free hand to wipe his nose, it dripped fat red drops on Dai's chest.

"I know it was you!" he screamed.

Panzi felt his blood jangling; he was terrified. The wide scar across Dai's chin looked dull and red. Dai groaned. His eyes were closed. His entire face looked heavy and swollen, as if drowned. Once the tension left Dai's wrists, Panzi finally climbed off him, slumping toward the edge of the court. What had he done?

Dai propped himself up against one of the benches, dazed, and checked the back of his head for blood. His hand was dry.

"You took her away from me," Panzi said, still panting. "And it didn't even matter to you."

Dai was slouched; he said nothing.

"You recognize me from that night, don't you?" Panzi went on. "You know who I am. And you wouldn't help me."

Dai remained motionless, eyes cast downward on the white lines of the court.

"Say something!" Panzi screamed.

"You don't understand," Dai finally said.

Panzi felt another surge of hatred. He glared at Dai. "*I* don't understand?!"

"You don't know anything about me," Dai said.

Panzi was about to yell back, to contest this, but a fresh bolt of sadness came over him, thinking of the hours he had spent poring over Dai's pictures, imagining his life. Panzi knew *too* much about Dai, in fact, far more than Dai would ever know about him.

"What happened to Xiao Song?" Panzi said. "She left in an ambulance that night and I never saw here again."

Dai pushed himself more upright. He looked completely exhausted.

"The girl in the white dress," Panzi demanded.

"They told me she died at the hospital," Dai replied softly.

Panzi stared at Dai, waiting to feel a new wave of

rage, grief — anything, but it didn't arrive. His eyes were out of tears. He only sat there with his feet tucked under his legs, looking at the red-brown blood smears on his filthy pants.

"She's dead, then."

"It was an accident."

"Does she have family? Do they know?"

"I think so. I'm not sure."

Panzi took a deep breath and tasted metal. He turned toward Dai and noticed lines on his forehead for the first time. Dai's face looked so much older and heavier than it did in the pictures. The patch of discoloration on his cheek looked like a water stain from a leaking ceiling.

"What about him, your friend?"

Dai nodded slightly. "Shishan's dead too."

As soon as the words left his mouth, Dai's face collapsed into a horrible mask of grief, and Panzi had to look away. As Dai began to sob, Panzi set his jaw and stared at the power lines.

"Stop it."

"You don't understand! Shishan wasn't like me. He was good! He didn't deserve to die!"

"She didn't deserve to die either."

"They blamed him, but he didn't do anything! He was just following me, like always. But they blamed *him*! And now that it's all blown over, I'm supposed to be relieved but all I feel...." Dai stopped himself. He finished the sentence by hanging his head.

When Panzi looked at Dai again — face buried in his dirty hands, shoulders shaking — he knew instinctively that Dai had never grieved his friend. He had never confided in anyone about the crash, never confronted its aftermath. He was utterly alone.

Panzi felt a bit of tension leave his neck. He pictured Shishan as he'd appeared in the photos — making faces in the front seat of the Ferrari, grinning with his arm thrown around Dai. An eager face. Shishan and Dai probably knew each other their whole lives; they must have played basketball together on this court.

Panzi thought suddenly of the little girl in the purple sweatshirt from the train. He wasn't doing Xiao Song any good here. He got to his feet and took a deep breath.

"What am I supposed to do?" Dai pleaded.

Panzi began to walk away but turned back toward Dai a final time.

"I don't know," Panzi said. "But I do know you're lucky to feel something. Not everyone can."

WINTER

21

Gauntlet

A CROWD of three dozen expats was already waiting for him inside, milling near the Formica bar with glasses of wine and cocktails with orange straws. David paused inside the entrance of Square Bar, scratching his razor-burned neck. He scanned the faces and loosened his scarf. No one had noticed him yet; it wasn't too late to leave.

He had already taken a half-step back toward the door when Trish emerged from the pack in an expensive-looking striped dress. He could hear the points of her heels against the hardwood floor.

"You look nice," David said uneasily.

She eyed him with suspicion. "I wasn't sure you were going to show up."

"I said I would, didn't I?"

"That was two weeks ago."

David scratched his neck again. Whispering hand drums and crashing waves murmured somewhere overhead.

"All this is…. You didn't have to."

Trish sighed, surrendering. "At least you wore a bloody jacket. C'mon, I'll introduce you."

He followed her into the squall of bodies and was installed near the center. Trish dissolved somewhere off to his left. Every few minutes an acquaintance turned to David, smiled, and asked him how he'd been. Which day are you leaving Beijing? Where are you headed? Oh, where in the States? So, what are you going to be doing there? Mercifully, Trish reappeared, with a young girl who introduced herself as Rachel.

"He's the one who's leaving," Trish said. "It's his party." The girl nodded.

Trish turned back toward David. "Rachel studied with my sister in the States. She's only been here two weeks."

"Ah, new arrival."

"I promised her a lecture from one of the great, bitter Sinologists of our time," said Trish. "You'd better not disappoint."

David was supposed to give a witty repartee to this but couldn't think of anything to say. The room, the crowd — it was all overwhelming. Trish seemed to be speaking extremely fast. The girl, Rachel, began some kind of self-introduction monologue. How old was she? Twenty? She had a flat Midwestern accent and silky peach-smelling hair that David wanted to bury his face in.

"So, what do you do?" she asked. "Uh, what *did* you do, I guess?"

"I'm an actor."

"Wow! Really? Like, a Chinese actor?"

David shuddered. "Uh-huh."

Trish wandered away again, and the two of them found an open table with their drinks. It was a relief to sit somewhere with his back against the wall. Out of the corner of his eye, he spied on Trish, who looked much more relaxed with him sequestered from the group. She fit in seamlessly with the tailored, elegant crowd. Good for her. She'd insisted on this farewell party for him. Was she disappointed that he'd shown up for it?

"I'm not too worried about culture shock," Rachel was saying. "I was a Chinese major in college. I spent my junior year in Nanjing. Beijing is different though. The city is amazing."

David asked her what she was doing now, here in the amazing city.

"I'm working at the Guanxi Association, a non-profit that fosters closer U.S.–China understanding through cultural getaways."

"Cultural getaways?"

"Meetings, summits, offsite events."

"Trust falls, 'Kumbaya,' that kind of thing."

Rachel gave him a tight smile. "We have American professors come and give lectures on understanding American culture."

She spoke with the stiff, mission-statement efficiency of a newly minted intern. David took a slug of beer and felt his blood begin to warm, imagining her breathless emails back home.

God, how he wanted to puncture that balloon and set the record straight. If he didn't, they'd keep arriving

— waves and waves of Rachels — like refugees crowding the decks of giant steamships, clutching their Pleco dictionaries and bachelor's diplomas, thinking they'd be welcomed here. They were so eager, so polished, so *qualified* — David was certain Rachel's Mandarin was flawless. How could these Rachels not understand that China didn't want them anymore? The party was over. Maybe ten years ago there were places for all of them, but now China was only for the Chinese again, the way they'd always intended it to be.

You'll have a few years of little, funny conversations, David wanted to tell her. You'll make a few superficial friends. You'll find a job with a nice, thick glass ceiling. Then you'll go home without changing anything. Blather on as much as you like about "American culture;" all these rich peasants hear is how much better Chinese culture is. You think you're building bridges; they think you're kowtowing.

David sighed. He felt ancient.

"Gao Fushuai! Don't leave me!"

David turned toward the voice and watched Phil approach from across the bar, negotiating his way through the crowd with two green bottles of beer. He'd grown his hair out since the last time David saw him, nine months ago, but wore the same hiking fleece. He looked as out of place as David felt and as drunk as David wanted to be. The beers crashed down on the table, startling Rachel. Phil's face was already glowing red.

"Say it ain't so!" he grinned.

"'Fraid so."

"When do you leave?"

"Tomorrow."

"That's crazy! What about the show? Did you quit?"

David grunted something noncommittal and introduced Rachel to the flushed Asian face hovering over them. Rachel slid over in the booth, and Phil sat next to her, propping his elbows on the table.

"I mean, where have you *been?*" Phil's questions sounded like accusations after a few drinks.

"I've been busy, man. I don't know."

"And now you're leaving."

David felt an unexpected surge of affection for the guy. Goofy and sloppy and unrefined. At least one person at the bar seemed to care if he left. They clinked bottles.

"Yup. Now I'm leaving."

"What are you going to do?"

That question again. "I've talked to some producers in LA. We'll see."

"Awesome. So, you're sticking with the acting thing."

David grunted again and took a sip of beer.

"I don't know about down there, but half the Bay Area is Chinese. I'm sure you could find something. Chinese companies are probably hiring as well."

"They might send you back to Beijing!" Rachel put in. "Or, six months there, six months here."

What the hell was this? David thought. Weeks ago, when he'd told Trish about his departure plans, she'd effectively said the same thing.

"I think I'm done with China," said David.

"No, you'll be back," Phil grinned. "Everyone comes back eventually."

Why could no one accept the fact that he wanted to leave this place and not look back? Hadn't he earned the right to hate it?

As the night wore on, David drifted to the edge of the bar, watching the crowd playact their lives with equal measures envy and spite. Shiny, happy people. Don't scratch too hard at the surface, David wanted to tell them all. Enjoy your ten-dollar cocktails for as long as you can.

Bitter. He knew Trish well enough to know she wasn't joking. How could you not be bitter at this place? Six years of his life, his prime young adult life. He'd given so much of himself to China; what had this place given him? An abortive acting career. A going-away party with thirty strangers. Six thousand kuai — the amount he had left from Panzi's twenty-five thousand after a plane ticket to the U.S. and living expenses. He was thirty years old with one thousand dollars to his name. Why shouldn't he be bitter?

He still had his dignity, that was something. Leaving that campy television show, resisting Dai's threats, walking out of Silicon Valley English — the past year had been a series of trials, he now realized, a gauntlet. China had tried to break him, but he had withstood it. And it was better that he found out the truth about this place, however nasty. Imagine if he'd been hired for that Zhang Yimou film years ago! How could he have left China after that? No, it was better this way — better knowing the truth, better watching the lemmings from a distance than being one.

When Phil thrust a microphone at him thirty minutes later, David wanted to summon a sense of this. He stepped up on a sleek steel chair, and the bar's manager turned down the music overhead. The scrum nearest the bar continued talking. An elaborate modern light fixture — a kind of illuminated mobile with tinkling flower pedals and refracted light — hung just to the left of his head. David cleared his throat.

"So, I guess it's tradition when you leave China to make a big speech to tell everyone why," he began.

David paused for effect and looked out over the crowd of rapt faces. A few smiles. How comfortable it felt to be standing in front of an audience again! The light fixture was slowly rotating, he could see now. Shards of light crawled across the floor, like constellations. He passed the microphone between his hands and looked down, making eye contact with Rachel.

"But the real question is not 'Why do you leave China?' but '*When* do you leave China?' When do you know, deep down, that it's time to go?"

A few nods.

"I've got a theory about that. I don't think it's the pollution or the propaganda or the censored internet that gets you to that point. You can get used to all that. You lower your standards. You adjust. Someday China will fix all those problems, but people will *still* get burned out; people will *still* need to escape."

David looked out into the crowd and saw that he had lost a few people in the audience. He quickened his pace.

"When do you leave? You leave when you begin to see that all of China's problems are the same problem. Symptoms of the same disease. And there's no cure for it. It's terminal —"

"Okay! Let's get this guy another beer!" shouted Trish, spinning around toward the crowd.

A smattering of confused applause. David shook his head slightly and peered down toward the first row.

Trish had her back turned, but he could still make out her mortified smile. Every face he saw in the crowd enraged him now.

"I'm almost to my point," David snarled into the mic. "I was talking about the point when you decide to leave China...."

Below him, Rachel looked as if someone had kicked her in the stomach. David shut his eyes in concentration. His thoughts seemed very clear.

"People don't matter here. That's the disease. *You* don't matter. None of us do. Not the foreigners, not the locals. You're expendable. Your very life doesn't belong to you; they'll take it in a heartbeat if it means they can stay in power for another twenty minutes.

"But what can you do?" David mock-shrugged. "*Mei banfa.* There's nothing you can do but obey. You fall in line and hope for the best. You narrow down your hopes and focus on the world in front of your nose.

"And you're obeying them too!" he shouted at the crowd. "You might not admit it. You might not think about it much. You all have white-collar jobs and white-collar friends. But you are obeying them. And before long, you'll feel this little twinge; you'll start getting wound tight by all this obedience, even if you don't feel it at first. It builds in you. It gnaws at your soul — this hunger to stop obeying and really *respect* something. To *choose* to respect something, not just be told to...."

David opened his eyes, which were a bit blurry, and realized no one was listening to him anymore. His hand with the now-dead microphone dropped to his side.

The room was engulfed in lounge music again. David

stood awkwardly beneath the spinning light fixture for a few moments, adrenaline still pumping through him, before passing the microphone to Phil and stepping down from the chair. Trish stood with her back to him. No one made eye contact.

As David was about to leave, he spotted Rachel floating near the edge of the group and walked over to her. When he started talking, she wouldn't look at him either.

"So, I'm going to head off," he began. "Good luck with all the cultural —"

"You think you're so enlightened, but you're nothing," she blurted out. "You know what Trish told me about you on the way over here; she's sorry for you. You've been here all these years, but no one wants to be around you because you're so toxic. If China was so awful, you should have left earlier. But you didn't, did you? Because you were scared. Because you're just a loser back home."

David was too stunned to respond. Rachel disappeared once more, leaving him alone on the edge of the crowd. Time to go. He should find Trish and Phil and say goodbye at least. He stepped up on another metal chair for an aerial view of the room. There must have been fifty people now, arranged in groups. Everyone was engrossed in some kind of conversation. David surveyed the faces and found his friends; Phil and Trish were together, talking with some people David didn't recognize.

* * *

In the morning, fine-grained snow had begun to fall, drifting down and settling like wet ash along the bannisters and bare tree branches. David stood at the open window, considering the blank-white sky. The city performed its sounds — rumbling street traffic, crackling ice and water, a magpie croaking. Snow. Of all the days.

He turned back toward his living room and saw that the rush of cold air had dislodged two large dust bunnies from the foot of his bed. They drifted along the floorboards toward the kitchen door. David hadn't swept since the three Russian exchange students had come by to carry off the last of his Ikea furniture — the wardrobe, the stained love seat, the accordion floor lamp.

Though nearly all of his modest possessions were gone or packed, the room did not seem empty.

He showered and brushed his teeth; David's hair was still dripping when his landlord appeared at nine o'clock sharp, as promised, stomping his slip-on leather dress shoes in the dark entrance. The man shouted something into his cell phone and brushed by his tenant at the doorway, lit cigarette dangling from his lip.

The landlord was in his forties and wore a pink shirt and belt with a Playboy bunny logo on the buckle. David watched him stand at the threshold of the kitchen, back to the room, cigarette smoke rising as if his scalp was on fire. Bits of ash drifted down on the living room floor.

When the landlord finished his call, he darted from room to room, flipping light switches while David followed.

"So, when do you leave?"

"About five p.m."

"Where to?"

"United States."

The landlord brightened. "Ah! Where in the United States?"

"I don't know yet."

"I just got back from Los Angeles. I bought a house there for my daughter. She's studying to be a nurse," he went on proudly. "Six hundred thousand U.S. dollars for a villa! Houses are so cheap in the U.S.! We'll probably move there when she has her baby. I like playing golf when I visit. Golf is so cheap in America. Public courses are only thirty-five U.S. dollars!"

David shuddered, imagining his landlord in California, standing in a suburban driveway in a pair of golf shorts and sunglasses, smoking, shouting on the phone at some business contact in Mandarin. There were whole neighborhoods of Chinese nouveau riche in the United States now, David knew. They swallowed whole communities.

"I guess you'll have to practice your English."

The landlord shrugged. "Beijing's air quality is terrible. It's much better in America."

"It's better in most places."

David accepted the cigarette his landlord offered, and they stood in the living room smoking. The man looked around the room for a moment. Had the landlord ever even lived here himself, David wondered?

"What will you do with this place after I leave," David asked.

"Renovate," the man said without hesitation.

"Renovate which parts?"

"Everything."

They finished their cigarettes and dropped the butts in a beer bottle in the corner of the room. The landlord handed David a white envelope with a small stack of bills, the entirety of his apartment deposit. David began to count the bills and thought of Panzi. As they walked outside together, they arranged for David to leave the keys beneath the dust-covered cardboard box in the hallway.

Out on the black-slush street, David followed the tire tracks down Dongzhimennei Avenue. The restaurants along Ghost Street — bright and raucous at night — were nearly deserted this early in the morning. Bags of garbage were strewn along the curb, staining the snow orange. Large gas umbrella heaters stood near the entrances, chained together like prisoners. Bits of crayfish shell. A pile of frozen vomit. Even in the cold, the street still smelled dumpster-sour, as it did every morning before the garbage trucks arrived to haul away the bags, before the slop and oil were whisked into the cracks of the pavement and began to seep into the earth beneath.

The year David arrived in China, Ghost Street still had red lanterns strung up everywhere — dangling from the gaunt trees and wires above the sidewalk — thousands of swaying red lights illuminating the night sky, beckoning. A few years ago, the city had swept through and taken down most of them. Fire hazards, they claimed. But their removal didn't seem to change much. Every night, Ghost Street was as bustling and traffic-choked as ever. The neon signs still burned bright.

The street was still loud and gaudy — a mirror image of the clientele it attracted. People like his landlord. People like Dai. They abandoned their gleaming cars along the side of the road and shouted at the greeters, the hostesses, the waitresses — swaggering up and demanding tables. The restaurants begged to be trashed, stained, burned by cigarettes — cheap restaurants with expensive prices.

Staff were already milling inside some of them, David could see. They dragged colorless rags over the table-tops and hauled buckets of slop to the curb that faintly steamed in the cold air. Getting ready for another night. In twenty-four hours, David's plane would be landing in St. Louis, and they would still be here, shoveling wet garbage. It would go on forever, this endless cycle of wreckage and repair.

David suddenly pictured Rachel's disgusted face from the previous night at Square Bar. What was it he had said during his speech? China not having anything to respect. Did he really believe that? He was pleased with the concept, at least. Yet the bleakness of that vision felt at odds with this quiet, snowy street. The city didn't seem all that bad when you had a chance to breathe. A little space, a little peace. Or maybe he was relaxed because at five o'clock this afternoon he was leaving China forever.

The snow had all but stopped by the time he reached the western end of Ghost Street. David turned right, heading north toward the Lama Temple, cycling through the phrases he'd been rehearsing for his re-entry to the U.S. job market. Mandarin fluency. TV and film acting credits. Script consulting work with exciting young Chinese documentarians. Deep knowledge of the Chinese media landscape.

He was probably overthinking it, anyway. Once he was settled back in the U.S., would anyone even care about his time China? It had always surprised him whenever he visited home just how few people there were interested in life in China. His years in Beijing would fade eventually, David was sure of it. Well, no, he would stay in touch with Trish; she was his best friend here, after all. And Phil, probably. And there were his language skills. All that couldn't go away completely, right?

David's mood began to blacken as he passed the shops selling cheap golden Buddha statues and incense. Recordings of Tibetan chanting played on repeat: *Om mani padme hum, om mani padme hum....* A group of tourists stopped in front of him on the sidewalk and he had to shoulder his way through. There must be other people in Beijing who would notice when he was gone; it wasn't as if he were just disappearing from the city after six years, without a trace.

When David stopped to pat down himself down for his phone, he felt his landlord's envelope in his front pocket. His deposit! Shit, what was he going to do with three thousand kuai? Why waste it exchanging it into dollars at the airport? David checked the time on his phone: ten a.m. He still had a few hours to kill. David thought for a moment and then dialed Cindy's cell phone. She answered after four long rings.

"Hi Cindy! It's David!" he enthused. "Hello?"

"I'm here." Cindy's voice sounded completely neutral.

"So, how have you been? Long time." He spoke to her in English.

"Uh, I'm fine. Pretty busy. How are you?"

"Yeah, so, I'm leaving Beijing. Today, actually. Ha ha. Listen, how about getting lunch and catching up in a few hours? We should go somewhere nice. My treat. Or, I can come to you."

David waited, imagining Cindy's apartment — its hardwood floors and striped pillows. He imagined her sitting in her living room, chewing her lip, weighing his offer.

"Oh, you're leaving?" she said finally. "Where are you going?"

They talked through the details of his move; David's energy began to flag. "So, how about lunch?" he pressed.

"No, sorry, I can't. I'm in Shanghai. Good luck with everything though. It sounds like you're doing well."

"Yep, I am!" David looked up and saw that he was standing in front of a convenience store.

When they hung up, he walked inside and bought a bottle of cheap *baijiu*. It was an odd choice; he hated the stuff, hadn't touched it in years. But fuck it; it's not like he'd be able to drink it back in the States. He opened the bottle and took a shuddering gulp, realizing halfway that it still tasted sickeningly of overripe pineapple. He walked a little further into the hutong and took another gulp, that one slightly better.

If the dog-walkers and delivery-cart drivers thought anything about a foreigner wandering down Qinglong Hutong with a bottle of Niulanshan on a Tuesday morning, they kept it to themselves. Still, it was easier for David just to avoid the eyes of those he passed altogether. As he walked, he concentrated on the roofs, where the pure white snow had settled in the dark grooves of the scalloped tiles. He peered inside each shop he passed — quick-fry restaurants, hairdressers, convenience stores

— and was pleased each time when he saw there was nothing he couldn't buy with three thousand yuan.

David stopped to bum a cigarette from a fat man standing in his pajamas, who lit it for him and then stepped back into his house. David passed a shopkeeper standing outside in his long underwear, whisking cold water from the steps with a straw broom, the primitive kind made of a bundle of twigs lashed to a bamboo pole. At the mouth of the alleyway, David could see cars rushing by — motion and noise and people. A foul *baijiu* belch rose up, and he turned back in the direction he'd come from, deeper into the hutongs.

He meandered down another side alley too narrow even for motorbikes. He stopped at a narrow shop opening with a large, pixelated photograph of a man's head — skull cap, wispy beard, serious eyes. "Master Xu — Naming Chamber — Thirty-Year-Old Beijing Brand." David scanned the menu — yellow characters printed on vermillion: "Fengshui," "Personal and Company Naming," "Mobile Phone Numbers," "Marriage," "Palm Reading."

David took another swig from the bottle and knocked on the glass. A woman appeared, pushing aside the heavy blanket hanging in the doorway.

"Is Master Xu in?" asked David brightly. His head was buzzing nicely. "I wanted to ask him about reading my fortune."

The woman, easily in her seventies, eyed him for a moment. David could smell something cooking from inside the room.

"Do you have an appointment?"

"No, I was just walking by. Is Master Xu in?"

It took some convincing, but she finally let him inside

before disappearing out the front door, presumably to go fetch the master. The naming chamber was cramped and warmed by a pot of chicken stock bubbling on a hot plate in the corner. The walls were covered with mass-printed posters and diagrams that David vaguely recognized — an open palm peppered with technical terms, a giant octagon with a yin-yang symbol at the center. There were Buddhas and Taoist goddesses and also cartoon bags of money, for good measure.

The glass door slid open again and a man who did not look like Master Xu maneuvered around David and sat down across from the counter. He looked to be only ten years older than David and wore a black North Face coat. No beard, no cap.

"Uh, where's Master Xu?"

"*Wa!* Your Chinese is really great!"

"Master Xu from the picture outside?" David tried.

"That's my father. But I'm also Master Xu."

David caught the man glancing at the bottle of *baijiu* sticking out from his coat pocket. Sneaky bastard was already gathering clues.

"Well, I heard that Old Xu is a very famous for-tune-teller," David lied. "I was hoping to speak with him."

"I have learned everything I know from him. What do you need advice on? Business?" The man smiled.

"I was really hoping to talk to Old Xu."

"He's not here."

"Well, where is he?"

"He's dead."

David closed one eye and studied a diagram on the wall of a broad, cartoonish Chinese face covered in dark-blue dots. His stomach growled, and he realized he hadn't eaten anything all morning. He should leave, go grab lunch.

"Your mind is preoccupied," the younger Master Xu ventured. "You are facing problems."

David snorted but sat back down and crossed his arms.

Xu asked David for his hand.

"How much?"

"We have one hundred, three hundred, and eight hundred options. The last one is most comprehensive."

David placed the back of his hand on the table, and Master Xu began to rub his palm as if trying to smooth the lines. The man himself had delicate fingers with perfect cuticles. David stared at the chicken broth for a few minutes, trying to remember the last time he'd felt skin-on-skin contact. The master released David's hand and consulted a battered book with a frayed red cover while David finished off the last of the *baijiu*. He was starving.

"You must take better care of your health." Master Xu closed the book and looked up.

"And?"

"That's all I can say for certain."

David began to laugh. "So, nothing about 'great changes' coming to my life soon?"

"Hmm, no, nothing that I can see. Your life looks steady."

"Oh yeah?" David shouted, amused. "I think you need to check the stars a little closer, Master Xu! You may be missing something!"

Xu seemed almost apologetic for the non-future he had proffered. David began ranting about the changes he was facing — the move away from China, the daunting job search, the dread of facing his family and friends back home — he didn't know why. He was drunk and it seemed vital that Master Xu understand how wrong he was.

Master Xu smiled and told him he wouldn't accept any money, a point that David didn't fight him on. They both stepped back outside, and David held the blanket to the side while the master carried the steaming pot of soup next door. David almost expected the man to invite him inside for lunch, but Master Xu just said goodbye and wished him luck in the future.

David touched his front pocket and felt the pleasing bulge of the bills. He still had three thousand kuai to spend. He couldn't seem to get rid of it.

22

Little Goddess of Mercy

Conditions at the Stars Hotel had improved in the six months since Yanmei had last visited. The shelter's large open room — then a free-for-all of mattresses and cardboard boxes — was now divided into private quarters by thin plywood boards that stopped just short of the ceiling. Each new cubicle had a stenciled number next to a pale-blue curtain hung as a door.

Guang Fei propelled his cart forward across the smooth concrete floor until they reached Room 8. He yanked aside the curtain.

"Not bad!" Yanmei exclaimed.

Two low twin beds were separated by a wooden nightstand and a large pink plastic thermos of hot water. Guang Fei told her to sit on the bed and busied himself pouring hot water into small paper cups. On the far wall were the room's only decorations: a portrait of

Mao Zedong and a wall calendar from an electronics shopping mall hung side by side.

Guang Fei blew into his paper cup. "They charge me rent, but it's subsidized. I pay only a hundred yuan per month."

The steam from the hot water seemed to be warming the room, or so Yanmei felt. As she listened to Guang Fei talk about life in the Stars Hotel — his roommate, the meals, the steady improvements — a wave of tenderness came over her. Room 8 was freezing cold but Guang Fei looked modestly healthy. He seemed modestly safe, stable, maybe even modestly happy here. This was a modest nest, but enough. And he was taking good care of it.

"What's the matter?"

"Nothing," she said, wiping away a few escaped tears. "It's good to see you, Uncle."

Suddenly, a man on the other side of the divide erupted into shouting. "Cabbage! There's no cabbage!"

Guang Fei laughed at Yanmei, who was startled by the outburst.

"That's Old Tang. Ever since the beginning of November, he's been yelling about cabbage. I went out and bought him some, just to shut him up, but someone stole it."

Her phone rang; Yanmei knew who it was without answering. "Uncle, I'll be right back. He's here."

Yanmei made her way back toward the shelter's entrance, taking deep, steadying breaths along the way. In the hallway, she paused at a window to check her reflection. It had been months since she'd last seen Panzi — the morning he'd ambushed her at the *Evening News* office with that bizarre foreigner in tow — and she somehow expected him to look completely different. He certainly *sounded* different. They had spoken a handful of times on the phone, and each time his voice was oddly serene. Even as he recounted his run-in with Xiao Song's killer — some absurd fistfight on a basketball court? — his voice had never quickened beyond a calm, steady cadence. It had put Yanmei on edge. Where was that familiar yelp? Had discovering the truth about Xiao Song scrambled his brain somehow?

He was waiting for her in the sunshine just outside the door.

"Your hair!" she said, hoping her voice sounded playful. "Did you try to cut it yourself or something?"

Panzi smiled and sheepishly ran his fingers over the back of his head. His short bangs jutted straight out, casting little shadows on the upper reaches of his forehead. He looked healthy, perhaps a few pounds heavier. Everyone was getting healthier.

"Sorry, what I mean is you should grow it out. It suits you," she added.

"It covers my ears, you mean."

Yanmei laughed and resisted the impulse to batter him with questions. Perhaps it was getting choked up with Guang Fei just now, but seeing Panzi like this, standing close to him and inspecting the details of his face again, brought back a flood of warmth that she wasn't prepared for. Yanmei shoved her hands deeper in her coat pockets.

"So, he's inside?" Panzi said finally. She nodded.

"So, how do you want to do this?"

"I guess I'll go first," she said.

"Don't worry. He'll be fine."

"I know. He seems ... I don't know ... like he's doing really well. I just don't want to, you know —"

"He'll be fine," Panzi repeated. "It's going to be okay."

That eerie calm voice again, Yanmei thought. It was a voice that didn't belong to the Panzi she had known. Again, she fought down an urge to ask him who this new person was. Instead, she led them back into the Stars Hotel and down the hall to Room 8.

Guang Fei greeted them anew and poured fresh cups of hot water. Panzi and Yanmei sat next to each other on the bed in their heavy coats, watching the steam rise from their cups. Panzi and Guang Fei made small talk for a few minutes before Yanmei spoke up.

"Listen, Uncle. There's something I need to tell you. I'm changing jobs soon, which means I'm leaving Beijing."

Yanmei studied Guang Fei's face for a reaction, but he remained looking at Panzi, oddly. "I'm moving all the way down to Guangzhou," she went on. "So, I won't be able to come visit you anymore."

"Are you going with her?" Guang Fei asked Panzi.

"Me?" Panzi said. "No, I'm staying here."

"Then when are you two getting married?" Guang Fei teased.

Yanmei's eyes went wide. Panzi blushed violently.

"What? No! *Uncle!*"

"Well, you'd better bring me some wedding candy before you elope!" Guang Fei was grinning now.

"Cabbage!" came another outburst. "They're going to be sold out!" It was Panzi's turn to flinch at Old Tang's outburst.

"Who said anything about cabbage?" Guang Fei yelled back.

Yanmei cast her eyes around the room, desperate to change the topic of conversation. Her gaze settled on a neat stack of newsprint inside the open cupboard and recognized a familiar *Evening News* layout. She walked over to it, just to move her body, took one copy off the top of the stack, and unfolded it on the bed. "Searching for Song Gang."

"I still don't know why you asked me for ten copies if you're just going to keep them locked up," she said. "Why don't you stick one of them to the wall?"

Guang Fei leaned forward and studied the photograph of the Idiot for a moment, as if considering her suggestion.

"That ugly face? Why would I want to hang it up and have to look at *him* every day?" Guang Fei was still cracking jokes; wasn't he hurt at all by the news of her departure?

"Have you seen him recently?" Panzi asked.

Guang Fei looked away from the Idiot's face on the newsprint. His eyes weren't laughing anymore.

"No," he said softly. "And I haven't seen the girl either."

The little room was very quiet. Panzi glanced at Yanmei, who nodded back.

"Listen, Uncle. There's something else you need to know," Panzi began.

Even now, telling Guang Fei about Xiao Song's death, Panzi exuded that new calm Yanmei had noticed over the phone. His hands barely moved; his eyes were hooded, almost as if drunk. She looked at Guang Fei, who seemed transfixed by the same serene spell. *She's gone*, Panzi said, and Guang Fei only nodded. Panzi moved from the bed to sit on the cold ground next to Guang Fei. *She's gone*, he repeated.

Yanmei watched them — two of the closest people she had in her own small, sad Beijing life — huddled together on the ground, like reunited believers of a lost faith. Yanmei sat alone on the bed, an invisible body burning with a single thought: No, she was not gone; Xiao Song was still everywhere.

Yanmei rose from the creaking bed and walked out of the room without a word, flipping the curtain aside. As she made her way down the corridor of plywood walls, she brought her fingers to her cheeks but couldn't tell if her face was burning or her fingers were cold. Little Goddess of Mercy, she thought bitterly. *Goddess of Mercy*. As if the girl were some kind of saint, some bodhisattva.

Down one of the hallways, a line of men and women in padded coats and cloth shoes shuffled toward lunch.

"My son says I need to buy cabbage!"

Old Tang, the shouter from earlier, was bent forward at the head of the line, jabbing a pair of chopsticks into the chest of one of the cooks. Tang was shockingly small, Yanmei could see now; it seemed impossible that such a loud voice belonged to that slight frame. Each time he roared, a thick vein popped out of his neck.

"Where is it?!" he demanded. "Where's the cabbage?"

"What do you think you're doing?" the cook hissed, snatching the offending chopsticks.

"My son says —"

"What son? Go sit and eat!" yelled the man waiting behind him.

Old Tang turned and paused, uncertain of which direction to direct his ire. The cook placed a white bun atop the oily vegetables piled high in Tang's bowl and handed back the chopsticks.

Yanmei watched him as he joined the others in the dark hall. They all had the look of the countryside: dark, leathered skin and camouflage pants. A handful of them squatted against the wall, hunched over iron bowls of stir-fry and tearing off pieces of the buns with their teeth.

They had been abandoned here, Yanmei suddenly realized. There were no sons, no daughters, no families to care for any of them. Perhaps some of them had wandered to the Stars Hotel on their own volition, like Guang Fei, and had never been sought out again. She imagined Xiao Song in this hallway, squatting alongside them. This is where she would have been one year ago, after all — feeding the Idiot lunch, moving slices of potato from her bowl to his, making sure he had enough to eat.

Xiao Song. Song Gang. Were they related? Could that have been why she cared so much for the Idiot? Was that why she came to the Stars Hotel in the first place?

Ever since she'd met Panzi, Yanmei had always imagined Xiao Song as some perfect, selfless spirit — the Little Goddess of Mercy. But perhaps it was more complicated. Perhaps Xiao Song had come to the Stars Hotel to look after her own family, which, yes, made her a good, decent person, but not a saint. Why had she never mentioned the Stars Hotel to Panzi at all? Why had she never told Guang Fei her name? Why all the secrecy? Was she hiding something? Was she ashamed?

There were only more questions — endless, spiraling questions. And as Yanmei watched Old Tang chew his food, pondering them, it occurred to her that Panzi and Guang Fei wouldn't care about any of them. They didn't care who Xiao Song really was or how she had come into their lives. They were not back in Room 8 mourning a person, they were mourning something else — the kindness, compassion, and mercy they read into her. They were starving for a connection, for a goddess to believe in.

When Yanmei returned to Room 8, she saw they had barely moved. She reached down and touched the shoulder of Guang Fei's army coat, which smelled like stale cigarette smoke.

"Talk, Uncle," she said finally. "Tell me what you're thinking."

Guang Fei stared vacantly at the wall, arms crossed tight across his chest.

"Uncle...."

"It's nothing," Guang Fei said. The three of them sat in silence for a few more moments. "I was just.... I was just thinking of something she told me right before she left. She told me the Idiot's birthday was coming. She wanted to take us to Meizhou Braised Pork Restaurant.

"The Idiot got really excited when he heard us talking about braised pork. You should have heard him!" Guang Fei laughed and then started to tear up again. "I told her it was too expensive. Forty-eight kuai for one serving! You can eat for two weeks at the Stars Hotel for that much money! But Xiao Song wouldn't hear it. She said we were going to Meizhou Braised Pork Restaurant. It was a special occasion."

"Let's go now!" Panzi blurted out. "C'mon, the three of us can go now. We'll take you there!"

"No," Guang Fei said. "That's not right. I'm supposed to eat it with the Idiot. It was supposed to be his birthday."

He looked down at his wooden cart. "When I find him, we'll go eat braised pork, but I need to find him first. If Xiao Song is really gone, somebody has to take care of him."

Guang Fei led Yanmei and Panzi to the entrance of the Stars Hotel, rolling his cart around the piles of clothing and splintered furniture. His two guests stepped over the raised doorway onto the alley and turned back a final time. The brass buttons of Guang Fei's army coat caught a few rays of afternoon sunlight. Yanmei stepped back and bent down to hug him.

"I'm really going to miss you, Uncle."

Yanmei waited for Guang Fei a moment, on the chance that he might say something more. But all he said was goodbye.

* * *

Neither of them was ready to return home. There were still a few hours of sunlight left, Panzi pointed out. Why not go to Jingshan Park since Yanmei had never been and wouldn't have another chance? She shrugged; as long as it wasn't a restaurant.

Inside the park, they wended their way along the stone paths — past the retirees singing patriotic songs and the waltzing grandmothers and a man kicking a shuttlecock by himself and a girl in a pink tutu holding a pinwheel — aimless, engrossed in conversation. Panzi updated her on his life over the last few months. He was still living inside Duanqiruifu, at the professor's old room. He'd gone back to studying at Silicon Valley English but had a new teacher, a young woman from Australia.

They began climbing the stone stairs of Prospect Hill. She told him the details of her plans to leave for Guangzhou the following week, and he asked her all the questions she'd hoped for. Words flowed between them easier than she'd expected, and the noise and bustle of the park filled the lulls in their conversation.

At the top of the hill, vendors hawked yellow Qing dynasty garb for tourists to dress up in. A pair of boys fought each other with plastic swords. Couples and families sat along the bannister below the highest pavilion, taking selfies with the afternoon sun hanging in the frame.

Panzi and Yanmei found a spot near an outcropping of white stone and looked out over the orderly sprawl of the Forbidden City, the former center of the universe, the way one did. The city's haze squatted low across the roofs of the complex below.

"Are you going to stay long in Duanqiruifu?" she asked.

Panzi shook his head. "They're moving everyone out soon. The government says it's for historic preservation."

"It's so strange that you ended up back there."

"It's even stranger that it kind of *feels* the same," he said, still surveying the structures below. "I thought it would, I don't know, be different now. I still feel like I'm just waiting around...."

Yanmei looked out in the direction of his gaze. The sky was orange.

"Waiting for her," she said.

Panzi wasn't calm, Yanmei realized; he was numb. She knew she was supposed to say something encouraging, touch him on the shoulder, and urge him to get out of Duanqiruifu, but she couldn't bring herself to do it. She waited for the familiar tug, that maternal instinct, to well up and was surprised when it didn't come. The sun waited dimly a few inches from the horizon.

"I've been talking to my grandpa a lot about my dad," Panzi said softly. "He gets really confused sometimes and thinks my dad is still alive."

"What does he say?"

"He tries to cheer him up, tells him not to feel so lonely."

"I see."

"I don't think my dad had anyone to talk to," Panzi said. "From the way Grandpa talks, I think my dad was off isolated in his own world for a long time. He had these feelings he wanted to express but didn't have anyone to express them to. That's all he wanted."

"I never really wanted anything either, you know?" Panzi let out a little laugh, suddenly self-conscious. "I didn't care about studying or basketball or girls or music. I couldn't figure out what was wrong with me. I wasn't useful for anything, you know? And she was the first person to tell me that was okay, that there was nothing wrong with being useless."

"Panzi, you know you're not useless," Yanmei said softly. He had begun to tear up.

"No, it's okay. My dad didn't have anyone, but I *did* have someone. I had *her*. She was the person who made me feel less alone. When she vanished, I was so afraid I was going to forget her. I wasn't sure if any of it was real. Mother went back to selling apartments; Grandpa went back to his pigeons. The red gate got repaired. Nothing changed."

"Panzi, listen to yourself. You haven't forgotten her, not for a second!"

The words must have come out harshly, because Panzi turned toward her in the fading sunlight and asked if she was all right. Yanmei fixed her gaze to a glass high-rise in the distance. What a waste, she thought, to be bitter and jealous in their last moments together. No, she wasn't jealous of Xiao Song anymore, just saddened by the realization that she would never be the one to convince him of how special he was. He needed to hear it from Xiao Song.

"I'm fine," she muttered. "I should probably be getting back."

The sun had disappeared behind the buildings, and the tourists on all sides began jostling for position at the top of the stone stairs. Panzi and Yanmei walked all the way to the park's gate in silence, and only after they were out on the sidewalk did Panzi speak.

"It was funny what Guang Fei said about us two getting married."

"He's got a crazy imagination."

They walked together toward the stoplight. Had she really thought she might have been in love with this boy once? The thought seemed preposterous now. That wasn't love, Yanmei thought; maybe she'd just been as starved for kindness as Panzi had been. Maybe that was why she had latched on to him; he was the only person in Beijing who made her feel a little less alone. That, too, was modest, but enough.

A taxi stopped in front of them. She hugged him and climbed into the back seat of the car. He motioned for her to roll the window down. When she did, he passed her the blue USB drive.

"I'm done with this," he said. "Maybe you can do something with it."

Yanmei said she would try.

"You said up there that nothing's changed, but you've changed; you must see that," she said. "You met me and now I'm changed too. Guang Fei too. And it's all because of her. She's not back there in the past; she's still here now with you, in the present. You're keeping her alive, not by hanging around some old buildings, but in the people around you."

Panzi smiled his goofy smile.

"Maybe I'll visit you in Guangzhou," he said.

Yanmei smiled back. The offer surprised her.

23

The Empty Space

THE Boss had half-expected a giant metal chest with a padlock on the front — something like the ballot boxes he'd seen from news coverage of foreign countries. Instead, the scene inside the Duanqiruifu community center when he arrived on voting day looked like an insurance office. Three of City Planning's flunkies sat smiling behind a wooden table, arms crossed over stacks of papers. Whenever a resident approached, the cadres consulted their lists, ticked accordingly, and slid a paper across the surface.

The page was a less a ballot than a one-page contract stating that residents agreed to relinquish their seventy-year lease on their properties. In exchange, they were to receive the best relocation package in the history of the city; they would be compensated one hundred thousand yuan per square meter and receive a large modern apartment unit outside of the North Fifth Ring Road.

Still, some of the older residents stood at the table a long time, bent over, carefully reviewing every character of the agreement. A few rubberneckers standing in the wings urged them to hurry up. What was so difficult to understand, they demanded? We're all signing the same thing! When each signee had finished his review, he handed it back across the table. Then, someone from City Planning ticked another box and slipped the paper in a briefcase. The ballots never left the table.

There was no hidden drama, no suspense in it, which suited the Boss just fine. City Planning already had the funds available for disbursement; there would be no waiting around for years in limbo. Once everyone was in agreement, the relocation process would start in a matter of weeks, an unprecedented timeframe. They would be able to move so fast because everyone was on the same page. That was the power of giving the people a say.

Sure, there had been a few holdouts, but only one who posed a real threat to the project's perfect harmony. There was nothing surprising about Granny Niu — sturdy build, coarse gray hair, cloudy eyes. She had lived in Duanqiruifu most of her life. While her neighbors were busy moving out furniture, she locked herself inside her room, Room 40, and stayed there with a bedpan for a week, refusing to answer the door. The Boss himself had paid her a visit, explaining through the locked door that she stood to be compensated more money than she had made in her entire lifetime.

The Boss talked and talked, but Granny Niu didn't seem to understand democracy. Such a waste of time and energy. In the end, the Boss had to dispatch Fat Liang and his roughneck friends to break into her room and invite her to stay at a hotel on the outskirts of the city, at least until the vote was settled. Granny Niu struggled with them a bit and almost got herself hurt.

The Boss crossed the room and stood next to the voting table.

"How many more are left?"

"Sir, please come around this way!" a young voice responded, not looking up.

"I'm not voting," the Boss said in a low growl.

"I see." The idiotic kid from City Planning looked up at him and offered a wide, exaggerated smile. "Well, we're kindly requesting that every resident —"

"I'm not a resident," the Boss snarled. "I'm the project developer. How many more names are still outstanding?" The Boss waited for the boy to recognize him, but the vacant grin remained plastered on his face. He must be, what, twenty-two, twenty-three?

"Shouldn't be too much longer!"

The Boss stared at him for another beat, rage panting from his chest. He was about to lose his temper when he spotted Qinyan watching him near the sidewall. The little shit turned away from him to help a middle-aged man with a pen. *Don't make a scene*, her gaze said.

When the Boss had first met Qinyan, months ago in this very room during the consultation meeting, he knew she was different by the way she smelled. What was it? Sandalwood? Something expensive, at least. That fall morning he had been standing outside alone, smoking, listening to the muffled shouting from inside. The door swung open, and a woman emerged and walked directly toward him. She was dressed like nearly all the other retired academics — puffy down coat, knee-high boots. She wore no jewelry; her handbag was unremarkable. Yet when she arrived in front of him, the air smelled different.

Qinyan slipped the Boss her business card that morning — a stiff, fibrous thing you could cut your finger on — and in the following months, as he and Zhenhua finalized their plans to hold a residents' vote on the project, the Boss checked in with Qinyan occasionally for updates. She had heard about the Duanqiruifu Luxury Restoration project from her network months before the Boss had, he'd learned, and already scooped up properties. Impressive. Qinyan was the one who had told him about the problem with Granny Niu.

Here, surrounded by the proles on voting day, Qinyan dressed the part — bulky coat and shapeless wool pants — auntie camouflage. It was best if people didn't see the two of them together, the Boss decided. He turned and left the room alone.

Long, gauzy threads of afternoon sunlight angled down through the trees, but they weren't enough to warm the Boss. He stalked between the peeling old buildings, letting cigarette smoke roll up his cheeks and into his eyes. He stopped and scraped a small mound of snow with his shoe; its surface was rough and hard as stone. He scratched it harder, digging his toe in, sending little chips of ice under the bushes. It was white all the way down, clean.

The Boss lit another cigarette and jammed his hands

back in his pockets, balling up Granny Niu's ballot in his right palm. He saw her as she'd appeared days ago, installed in her hotel room on the edge of the city against her will. When he had entered the room, she was sitting hunched on the edge of the bed. She began cursing him immediately.

That afternoon at her hotel, the Boss waited near the window, gazing between the rusted metal bars, letting Granny Niu's insults wash over him. She called him greedy, selfish, despicable, a traitor to China; but the Boss didn't respond. He knew you had to remain perfectly calm with these old-timers. There was little to look at in the room — two twin beds with wool blankets, a boxy silver television with a piece of paper wedged beneath it, a wall-mounted lamp, a basket of pay-for condoms, a disconnected phone on the nightstand. A two-star hotel.

When Granny Niu seemed to exhaust herself, the Boss spoke to her in a low, even tone. He spoke of the need for change, the unhealthy attachment to old things — old ways of thinking, old habits, old buildings. She was facing a big opportunity for the future. With this much compensation money, Granny Niu could provide for her family well into the future. She had to think beyond herself.

"Compensation!" Granny Niu spat back. "What do I need compensation for?"

"Well, you can do whatever you like with it," the Boss said brightly.

"I'm going to leave this world soon! What the hell am I going to do with compensation?"

"Well, your family —"

"Family! What do they need money for? They're just

greedy. It's my home, not theirs. They can sell it when I'm gone, but I'm not leaving."

"No, Madam Niu, this is a one-time offer. This project is going forward, and if you don't vote, you'll get nothing. I'm trying to help you."

Granny Niu glared at him with the brighter of her two eyes.

"Now," the Boss continued, "if you don't vote, I'll vote for you. And then I can't guarantee that you'll get anything. I'm giving you a chance to sign for yourself."

The Boss looked over at the unsigned contract wedged beneath the TV. He was doing her a favor; she would be thankful once she made it back into the city, would realize how fruitless it was to vote against the development.

"You should be ashamed!" she said. "You're nothing but a selfish son of a bitch!"

"*I'm* selfish?" the Boss shouted back. "What are you then? You're willing to fight this project alone, to ruin this opportunity for every one of your neighbors, take away money for their children's education, take away a new home they've been dreaming about for years. That's not selfish?"

"Twist it however you want," she muttered, suddenly weary. "I'm too old to argue. I don't care about anybody else. The only thing left I care about is where I'm going to die."

* * *

The Boss stubbed out another cigarette on the snowy armrest of a bench at the center of the Duanqiruifu grounds. He had to hand it to the old crone, Granny

Niu was stubborn all the way until the end. She was still at that godforsaken hotel, waiting. He would have to leave her out there for another month, at least until all the paperwork cleared and he had somewhere else to take her, a new apartment in her name. She would appreciate those modern comforts in time, especially on days as cold as today.

What was he still doing out here, shivering, chain-smoking Zhongnanhais one after the other? He should go back inside, drop Granny Niu's ballot in the briefcase, and go warm up someplace. It wasn't doing him any good lingering around the grounds like this. It wouldn't be safe to talk with Qinyan until later anyway.

The Boss took a deep breath and gazed through the branches once more. It was peaceful right here in the center of the city. His aching fingers scratched around in the cigarette box once more. No harm in walking the grounds just a little bit more.

After all, Duanqiruifu wouldn't be like this much longer. As he walked along the path, the Boss imagined it bustling with tourists, bellhops, and cleaning ladies once the buildings had been gutted and turned into luxury hotel rooms. The Duanqiruifu Luxury Restoration Project would be lavish and exclusive and profitable; but it would not be tranquil, not like this. There were no places in Beijing like this anymore, places big enough to be left alone in peace.

The Boss followed the path a bit farther around a stone pillar and noticed a figure sitting alone on the steps outside the compound's main building. A flicker of irritation. A trespasser on his grounds. As he approached, the Boss thought he recognized the boy's face, but it wasn't until he made it to the stone steps that he realized it was Qinyan's boy. She had shown him family pictures.

"Smoke?" the Boss asked. He shook his open box of cigarettes toward Panzi. "It's too cold out here otherwise."

Panzi looked up. "Oh, no thanks."

The Boss lit up by himself and sat down.

"I know your mother," the Boss explained.

Panzi nodded. "You're the project developer, right?"

The Boss nodded back.

"She told me you've been staying out here since November. Looks like it's grown on you."

"You could say that," Panzi replied.

Panzi kept his gaze trained toward Duanqiruifu's red gate, which allowed the Boss to take a closer look at him. The boy seemed calm and centered, which wasn't how Qinyan had described her son. Though the Boss had met with her only a handful of times, mainly to discuss business, Qinyan always found a way to mention Panzi, how worried she was about him. He was troubled and moody, she had told the Boss. Uninterested in the family business. Uninterested in anything, really.

"She's a clever woman, your mother," the Boss said. "I imagine you two get along well."

"You're more like your father."

Panzi turned toward the Boss for the first time, suddenly interested in what he had to say.

"What?"

"She said you were more like your father," the Boss explained. Panzi seemed unable to respond, so the Boss struck a philosophical tone. "People are different. It's natural to be closer to one parent than the other."

Panzi thought about this for a moment.

"What did she say about my dad?"

The Boss wondered if Panzi was jealous that he had grown too close to Qinyan in the past months. There was nothing between him and Qinyan, but why *shouldn't* the Boss still be considered a threat?

"It just came up," the Boss said.

"What did she say?"

The Boss exhaled a plume of smoke. Why were they even talking about this?

"She just said that she sees a lot of him in you. You help her remember him. That's it."

"She said that?"

The Boss could tell something he'd said had struck a nerve, but he wasn't sure why. In the awkward silence that followed, the Boss followed Panzi's gaze down the slope until it met Duanqiruifu's main entrance.

As he stared, the Boss imagined a procession of gleaming luxury cars entering through the red gate, swarming the grounds. Then a blur of white inside the opening caught his eye. It looked incongruous at the very center of the red door, red walls, and red pillars. It took the Boss a moment to realize that it was the long, blank spirit wall, standing across the street.

"I've never looked at the gate from the inside," the Boss said, trying to change the subject. "That spirit wall, for instance."

"If you left it to my mom, she would fill every inch of it," Panzi laughed. He did an impression of his mother. "There's nothing there! What a waste of space!"

It was true. The empty space seemed to await advertisements, political banners, graffiti — something. Most spirit walls were decorated with elaborate engravings or wistful landscape paintings, but Duanqiruifu's was completely blank, expectant. Would it also belong to him once he took over the grounds? the Boss wondered. There were so many things he could do with it.

"This place will look a lot better after it's renovated," the Boss put in. "Heated floors, rooftop terraces, a spa."

"Sure," Panzi said vacantly. He wasn't impressed.

"You weren't cold staying here these months? The conditions aren't good at all."

"No, I didn't mind."

Panzi's mind was clearly elsewhere again. What was he so pleased about all of the sudden? The Boss felt an urge to bring him back down to reality.

"They're just a bunch of old buildings anyway," he said. "The new ones will be better."

The pair sat together in silence for a few beats, each lost in his own thoughts. The Boss stubbed out his cigarette with a sense of finality and almost stood to leave. Then Panzi spoke.

"Old buildings are good for some things, even when they're ugly and run-down and impractical. They're still not useless. They can still connect you to people."

The Boss frowned. "You can't go around clinging to old buildings just because they have a bit of history. You have to move forward."

"I think you're right," Panzi said. "As long as you have people around you, the buildings don't matter much one way or another. You only cling to old buildings when you don't have anyone else to cling to."

The Boss broke eye contact and turned to examine the spirit wall once more, occupying himself with thoughts of new signage or a guard station, but after some time, these plans and possibilities drifted away. The vision of expensive cars and hordes of tourists vanished too. The longer the Boss stared at it, the wall appeared less like a blank canvas. Its white seemed final somehow, a void that couldn't be changed.

Some part of his brain knew that spirit walls had been originally designed to block out evil spirits — ghost stories he'd heard about as a young boy. Perhaps this was why the Boss found himself suddenly adrift in childhood memories as he peered into the white. He summoned his uncle, long deceased, taking him by the hand, walking him through the neighborhood wet market — past the wriggling eels and twine-wrapped crabs. He saw his mother, also gone, adding a honeycomb briquette of coal to the stove to heat his family's cramped, shared room....

"What about the gate?" Panzi said finally.

The Boss's mind snapped back to the present with a shiver. How clear the details of the memories had been! He hadn't thought about his mother or uncle in years, yet their faces had appeared as if projected on the white wall itself. The images were sharper than anything he could remember from the past year. Too much had changed.

The Boss angrily rubbed his eyes and reached for his pack of cigarettes — empty. He looked back to the spirit wall to see if it offered any guidance, but it was no longer a portal; it was simply a blank surface again.

"What?" the Boss replied, still dazed.

"Are you going to renovate that too?"

* * *

Weeks later, when the last of the families had been paid and moved to the city's outskirts, the abandoned buildings looked older. Black grease stains crawled up the walls. Withered bits of leaves and garlic skins. A cracked wardrobe. Piles of soggy cardboard. Bits of splintered wood. A gray T-shirt jammed in a corner. Faded red tissue paper plastered to a doorframe — couplets written for wealth and longevity — half-ripped away. A thick layer of dust.

The Boss walked down the littered hallway, squinting at the small red numbers painted above each door. The building was nearly dark; it was evening and the electricity to the Duanqiruifu complex had been shut off. He passed a ghostly clean spot on the tile wall — where a cooking stove had stood unmoved for decades — and once again marveled at the terrific silence. His ears buzzed. 36 … 38 … 40. He pulled a key out of his pocket and unlocked the door.

Room 40 looked eerie in the dim light. Granny Niu's solitary life — her neatly made twin bed, her uncapped hot water thermos — was frozen in time from the moment Fat Liang and the others had taken her away last month. A few articles of clothing were strewn about at the foot of the bed — the remains of what they couldn't jam in a suitcase for her. Two of the old woman's sweaters were hung on a clothesline between the closet and a curtain rod.

The Boss sat down at the desk and lit a cigarette. His cell phone rang, but he ignored it.

The Boss had been wandering around the abandoned

grounds of Duanqiruifu for over an hour, so it felt good to sit. The first few nights he'd roamed from room to room but never entered Room 40. He would never have admitted it to anyone, but a small part of him feared opening the door and finding Granny Niu herself inside, sitting on the bed. Or was it hope? Yet when he did finally go inside, the Boss found her room empty and oddly comfortable. Perhaps it was being surrounded by all the rotting vegetables and forsaken furniture outside, but Granny Niu's tidy, unchanged room soothed him.

Sitting at her desk in the dark helped push down a mounting sense of dread — meetings planned with contractors and architects and investors and conservation experts. In the weeks since voting day, the prospect of restoring Duanqiruifu — more noise and money and guile and effort — began to feel crushing. He was tired and wanted quiet. He occasionally thought back to Panzi's tranquil face from weeks ago and had to admit the boy might be right — *old buildings are good for some things.*

The Boss pushed Granny Niu's bedpan under the bed with his foot, where he couldn't see it. His cell phone began to ring again, and this time he answered it.

"You don't need to check in with me like this," the Boss said.

"I think I do," Zhenhua replied. "Whenever President Qian and the others can't find you, they call me."

The Boss carefully twirled the lighter on the desk.

"Well?" Zhenhua said. He had called the Boss every day over the past week, twice yesterday and today.

"Well, what?"

"Are you going to contact them? Everyone is waiting for your approval to start."

"We still have plenty of time," the Boss said. "The hard work is finished now. We can afford to be a little patient. There still may be some adjustments to be made."

"Adjustments?" There was a rustling on the other end of the line. "What are you planning on doing?"

Nothing, at least for the moment, the Boss thought. The idea of delaying construction had seemed so fanciful when he'd first had it, here, in Granny Niu's room a week ago — do nothing. Of course, the sooner the project started, the sooner he would make his millions. But, for the time being, he wasn't ready to give it up. The Duanqiruifu grounds belonged to him, not City Planning, not investors. It was up to him. He could sit undisturbed for hours here if he wished. He could start construction whenever he wished too. He pictured Granny Niu and thought, *I don't have to do a goddamn thing if I don't want to.* He'd earned the right to rest awhile.

"We still have time," the Boss said.

"Listen," Zhenhua went on, "is it the floor plans? Like I said, we're still discussing...."

Poor kid, the Boss thought as he listened to Zhenhua chatter on. He stood and left Room 40, stepping around a dark stain outside the door.

"... you know the promises I've made. You know what I have riding on this project."

"I understand," the Boss said gently.

"No, I don't think you understand what —"

"Listen —"

"No," Zhenhua's voice hardened. "I don't think you know what you're doing —"

The Boss cut him off again. The patronizing note in the young man's voice rankled. So, this was going to happen now.

"I understand *exactly* what I'm doing," said the Boss in a low, simmering voice. "What business of that is yours?"

"What business of it is mine? We just paid out eighty percent of City Planning's annual budget! We relocated forty-four families! We have to start work!"

"You did your job! And *I'm* the developer! I'll proceed as I see fit. It's *my* business."

"It's not *your* business! You owe me Duanqiruifu!" Stress and exhaustion poured through the tiny speaker.

"I don't owe you anything!" the Boss roared back. "*You* came to *me* with this opportunity, as I recall. I helped you; you helped me. It's a transaction."

The violence in the Boss's voice seemed to startle Zhenhua for a moment. The line was silent.

"Baiheng was right about you; you're a snake," Zhenhua said. "That's why you screwed them all over, isn't it? They all knew who you really were."

"You watch your mouth."

"I know what you did —"

"I'm the only reason you are where you are!" the Boss shouted. "Without me, you'd be nothing! You got what you wanted, didn't you? You're director of City Planning. You're in a position to help the people, just like you wanted."

"As soon as I —"

"Look around! Who do you think you have left to support you?!"

"You think you —"

"You're alone!" the Boss yelled. "You've got no one! Understand? Don't you dare threaten me!"

The line was silent. The Boss realized he was standing outside, panting. His entire body felt hot. He looked up through the bare branches and saw that a few stars were out.

"No, that's not right," said the voice on the other end. Zhenhua's voice was calm again, as if he'd just remembered something. "I do have someone."

Then a single beep. Then nothing.

The Boss pocketed his phone, lit yet another cigarette, and looked around at the silent buildings once more. The only sound was the faint sizzle of burning tobacco. It was too fucking quiet here anyway. Not even a little goddamn wind blowing. He needed to get out, go home, get some rest.

He walked toward his BMW, which was parked in front of a faded, fraying banner that had been left out in the elements for months: Innovative, Green, Lawful, Harmonious. He unlocked the door, paused, then locked it again. He should walk awhile. He could leave the car here overnight. Of course he could leave his car here if he wanted to! His legs were trembling a bit when he walked through the red gate.

The streetlights and traffic on Zhangzizhong Road calmed him somewhat. The Boss made his way down the wide street, walking west. Another cold, clear night. Cars raced past him.

As he waited for the light to change at the intersection, the Boss noticed a figure making his way down the opposite sidewalk. Crossing in front of the bright storefronts, the silhouette looked familiar — a limping, staggering gait. In an instant, the Boss recognized him — the neat bowl haircut and padded army coat. It was the idiot that Fat Liang had abused that summer night on Nanluogu Xiang. The Boss crossed the street and saw that the Idiot was grinning.

He was also not alone. A crippled man on a little wooden cart with little wheels was clattering alongside him. He wore an identical army coat and propelled himself forward with ratty tennis shoes he wore on his hands. The Boss paused on the sidewalk and watched them approach, transfixed by the peculiar sight.

The pair steadily made their way closer and closer to the Boss, not once looking up or noticing him. As they brushed past him, the Boss was forced to take a step to the side, down onto the packed dirt next to a tree trunk. He watched them swing open the door of a restaurant below a large red sign: Meizhou Braised Pork.

The Boss approached the restaurant's slightly steamed window and peered inside, curious to see how the strange duo would be received. He stood for a moment in the cold, but it was no use. He couldn't make them out, only his own reflection.

Acknowledgements

I began working on *The Soul of Beijing* in 2011 and, through fits and starts, finished a draft in the fall of 2016, as I prepared to leave the city for good. Beijing never stood still in those years (and still does not, I'm sure), so trying to capture it with any kind of fidelity is necessarily a work of collage.

One of the great joys of writing this book was that it rekindled my love and level of engagement with the city. It was the perfect excuse to set out into new neighborhoods and comb the back pages of local newspapers. More than anything, it was a constant reminder of the openness, humor, and dynamism of Beijingers that made the city such a rich place to live and explore.

Ben Carlson and Alec Ash gave much-needed encouragement over whiskeys at Amilal (RIP) as I limped toward the finish line. Ben, Alec and Te-Ping Chen were three of my earliest readers and gave thoughtful comments and helped me navigate the publishing waters. Big thanks also to Alex Eble for setting me on my China path, holding down summers in the city with me, and taking the terrific photo for this book's cover. Yanhong Xu, Rebecca Wang, Caroline Kan, Jon Rechtman, Susan

Barker, and Paul French all graciously made time to read the manuscript and gave support.

Michael Cannings, Mark Swofford, and John Ross at Camphor Press were a pleasure to work with. They helped fine-tune language and caught countless errors and discrepancies.

Thank you to my family for the love and encouragement to pursue my passions, even when they took me far from home.

And finally, Magdalena – my best friend and first reader. Your brilliant suggestions and hard questions helped shape this book into what it is. Writing can be a lonely process, but your patience, support and insight never made me feel like I was doing it alone. I love you so much.